*To Patty
much Love,
Sally*

of FRIENDS *and* FOLLOWERS

of FRIENDS *and* FOLLOWERS

S.A. Jewell

AMBASSADOR INTERNATIONAL
GREENVILLE, SOUTH CAROLINA & BELFAST, NORTHERN IRELAND
www.ambassador-international.com

Of Friends and Followers

ISBN: 978-1-62020-954-7

eISBN: 978-1-62020-966-0

Cover Design and Page Layout by Hannah Nichols
eBook Conversion by Anna Riebe Raats
Edited by Daphne Self

AMBASSADOR INTERNATIONAL
Emerald House
411 University Ridge, Suite B14
Greenville, SC 29601, USA
www.ambassador-international.com

AMBASSADOR BOOKS
The Mount
2 Woodstock Link
Belfast, BT6 8DD, Northern Ireland, UK
www.ambassadormedia.co.uk

The colophon is a trademark of Ambassador

To Steve, my husband
and
New Beginnings.

CHAPTER ONE

MIRIAM WAS EXHAUSTED. HER THIRST and hunger were taking over what little strength she had left. Walking for hours along this dusty, rutted road hoping to find at least a small village to beg for some food and water was her total focus, but she didn't come across any sign of human life. She was warned not to take this road because it was unsafe. Few travelers and many wild animals. For hours she hadn't seen a thing. Just dirt, rocks, and thirsty brush.

Yes, she was traveling alone, since she was recently deserted by similarly destitute travelers—two widows and a child. They decided they could go on no further. The child was ill, and their water was low, and the other two women simply had enough and decided to turn back to where they last camped while they still had the strength.

Wearily they argued with Miriam. "We have no idea how far away Capernaum is and we're nearly out of water."

"And food," the other woman whispered as she barely held onto the child on her hip.

Miriam spread out her hands in supplication. "How can we give up now?"

"From where we are now, Miriam, it's only a day's walk to bring us back to where we were, and we know there's water there and a hill full of fig trees we can glean."

The woman with the child set him gently on the ground. "And we've got to get nourishment for Josiah. I can't continue to carry him." The little boy sat listlessly, ignoring the adults and holding a smooth rock in his little brown hand.

"I can't go back," Miriam sighed, shaking her head. "I understand the situation and I'm so sorry." She indicated the child. "Please forgive me for not going back with you, but there's little future for me back where we were. I must get to the city." Miriam was saddened to move on alone but was determined to get to Capernaum.

"Miriam, you'll die out here. There's no water, food, and you have no idea how far you have to walk to get to the city. If lack of water won't kill you, it'll be some wild beast or bandit. Please come back with us."

"No, no. I can't. I must move on." The women shook their heads and coaxed the little, ill boy to stand, and each grabbed a hand. She kissed them goodbye "I pray for God's traveling mercies!"

"We will pray for you as well. We all need God's protection." They left her.

Miriam, like them, a homeless widow, had no idea how far she was from Capernaum, but the city was her only hope for survival. There she would have a chance to beg by the synagogue; she would have food, water, and with God's help, maybe she could find a man to take pity on her and take her on as a servant for his family.

She never realized how difficult traveling alone was, particularly not knowing how long it was going to take to get to the city. She had now been walking for hours and realized soon, she would have to stop and rest, but with little food or water, how long would she be able to continue without finding some help? Maybe the women were right.

As she trudged along, it was getting more challenging to put one foot in front of the other. Hours ago, she drank some of her water and now, so weary and thirsty, she wondered if she should stop and take a sip of water with a bite of bread.

"Should I keep walking?" She said aloud as she looked down at her dusty, blistered feet. Her mouth was dry, and her lips burned. She longed to take off her sandals, dip her feet in a cool stream, splash water on her face, and take a deep drink. Oh, to just close her eyes under the shade of a cool tree. Sleepily, she closed her eyes and slowed her steps.

Rocks bounced down an earthy slope. Her eyes snapped open. From behind a thicket of weeds and rocks, a man, filthy in flesh and clothing, popped out in front of her, grinning toothlessly, dancing toward her with his arms open wide.

She screamed, "No! no!"

Adrenaline surged through her body and she twirled to run, only to find another man, equally filthy and deranged creeping up from behind. Mustering her strength, she charged pass the man until a boney fist struck her cheek. She staggered back, then lurched forward and grabbed his beard, wheeling around trying to maintain her balance.

He cursed pulling back, "You witch!"

But she held onto to his beard bringing them face to face. He shrieked as he batted her hand away, but she clawed his face sluicing gobs of skin under her nails.

The other man grabbed her cloak, turned her around as she let go of the first man's beard, who punched her squarely in her stomach. She dropped to her knees, painfully gasping for air. At that moment, they were both on her cursing, spitting, and hitting. A kick to the thighs. An open slap to the face. A kick to her knee. Helplessly she struggled. A blow to the ribs and one to the head. Mercifully, the air went black.

The one she harmed leaned over her body swearing and blaspheming, grabbing her satchel and pulling at her robe. "I'll teach you, you sow!"

"Don't rip clothes!" his companion screamed.

"Did you see what she did to me?" the man screeched back. "The witch gouged my face and tore out my beard!" Gingerly, his hand went to the bleeding naked spot on his chin.

The older ignored the younger one's rant, dropped to his knees, and started tugging at Miriam's clothing.

The younger angrily went through the satchel muttering and cursing. "There's no money in here, just stupid stuff, a bowl and . . . " The bowl went flying to the ground and both hands flew to his head. He screamed in pain and surprise.

"What? Now what?" The man stopped and looked up at his partner howling in confusion and pain and pawing at the sticky blood oozing out the top of his head and flowing into his eye. Miriam looked dumbly at him and in seconds, a stream of blood sprouted from his own forehead.

Dazed, he fumbled to protect his head, lurched up, only to get caught up in Miriam's robe at his feet. Toppling over, he fell to the ground onto his hip as another wound exploded on top of his head.

Blood ran freely through his matted hair onto the side of his face and splattered his tunic as he rolled over in fright dragging himself toward Miriam. "I will beat you to death!"

The younger, shrieked, "Leave her be!" and ran to help the elder, roughly pulling him to his feet while several dark cloaked and hooded figures in stained rags, hobbled slowly toward them from a rocky slope across the road.

"Unclean! Unclean!" they hoarsely chanted. With their hands wrapped in soiled and blood-stained cloth, the dark-clad figures lobbed another volley of stones at them, hitting them in their lower bodies.

"Run, Phinehas, run! They're lepers!"

Stumbling in their haste and terror, the two men ran toward Capernaum, grasping Miriam's satchel. They never looked back.

CHAPTER TWO

THE WOMAN LAY MOTIONLESS ON the side of the road. Blood trickled from her nose and her left eye was swollen. The tallest of the cloaked figures raised his hand. "Don't get near her. Stay away."

The group fell back. Perplexed, they conferred about what to do.

"We can't just leave her there with her tunic up around her waist!" one said.

"If other robbers don't attack her, then wild animals surely will!" another reasoned.

The man shook his head. "We cannot touch her. We are unclean. We must get back before anyone should see us near this woman. They might think we attacked her. This is a dangerous situation for us."

A small figure emerged from the back of the group and haltingly walked over to her beaten body. "I said, don't touch her!" the tall man warned.

Draped in rags, with much of its face hidden, it merely turned and looked at the man. The group shifted about and went uncomfortably silent. Shaking his head, the man did not rebuke again, but signaled for the rest of the group to be on their way. It slowly knelt beside the woman's crumpled and exposed body.

Turning back to the small figure, the tall man gently said, "Cover her. Help her up and get her off the road into the protection of rocks and trees but follow us quickly. Do not linger. It is too dangerous."

The group shuffled away while the ragged creature gently pulled down Miriam's tunic to cover her nakedness. With a clean, but covered hand, it gently shook her shoulder causing her to groggily awaken. Disoriented and confused, Miriam strained to see the partially covered face hovering in front of her. Terrified, she made a keening noise whether in grief for herself or for the vision in front of her, it didn't matter. The sound embodied her fear, pain, and the tragedy of her rescuer's face.

The creature drew back from the woman cowering in the dust. Miriam breathed in deeply to calm herself and looked around seeing no one but the small figure in front of her. Slowly the little one leaned forward again and stretched out it's hand. Miriam realized that it was there to help, not harm her. She couldn't discern gender, or age, but she knew then her only hope was crouching before her extending its hand in peace.

With surprising strength, it helped a pain-wracked Miriam to a kneeling then stooping position. Weak and faint, she desperately looked around for her satchel crying raspingly for her possessions. "They've taken all I had! What am I to do? Oh, where is my bowl? I need my bowl! I can't eat, drink, or beg without it!"

The small figure steadied her, then half supported, half-dragged Miriam to a tree-lined, but level terrain not too far from the road. The creature had her sit in a small clearing, bordered by two boulders, surrounded by several dense bushes, where she couldn't be seen from the road.

Once seated, Miriam wiped blood from her nose with her sleeve as she wailed, "Please, oh please, help me. Where is my husband? Where are my children?" She paused in fear. "Where am I? I need a drink of water . . . " She closed her eyes and knew no more.

Feeling a gentle prod with a stick, Miriam opened her good eye and focused on the bowl held before her. Her bowl! Filled with water! The bowl came deftly to her bruised lips and she drank deeply. She savored the water filling her dry mouth and sliding down her parched throat.

"Please, a little more." Again, she felt the bowl at her lips. She took another drink and tried to focus on the being holding the bowl with hands totally wrapped in clean linen.

"Who are you?" Miriam softly asked.

A little cloaked creature peered back, closely examining her. Putting the bowl down, it quickly pulled out a few small pieces of cloth. Gently, with protected hands still wrapped in clean cloth, it used its water-skin to wash her wounds and cleanse around her sore eye. Next, from a tiny decanter, it poured oil on the exposed gashes. Seemingly satisfied, it pulled from another pocket a large folded leaf. Carefully opening it, there centered, was a piece of unleavened bread with a huge dollop of honey. Too weak to move, like a child, Miriam opened her mouth. The little creature fed her.

Eating the last of the bread and honey, Miriam barely whispered, "What is your name?" No answer. "How did you come to help me?" The little cloaked figure turned and busied itself with its satchel. *Perhaps it is deaf and dumb.* "You are kind to help me." Again, there was no response.

She drifted in and out of consciousness but fully awaken as the night descended with a swift blackness, as skittering, dark clouds covered the crescent moon. Disoriented, she attempted to sit up, but pain shot throughout her body stilling her movements. Slowly, she forced herself to a sitting position. Leaning against a smooth rock, she remembered her beating. She remembered the horror of the attack and fear shot through her soul. Slowly her hand went to a stinging sensation on her head. Her fingers came away with a sticky dampness. The side of her cheek throbbed, and she could see out of only one eye. Gingerly she touched her nose. She didn't think it was broken, but it hurt, and she had a terrible sharp pain in her side and knee. She stilled her body and sat motionless in the dark. She must stay awake to get through this night.

The denseness of the dark was terrifying. She was alone, in dreadful pain and thirsty again. Thoughts skittered through her mind.

She patted the ground for her bowl hoping there might be some water left. It was not by her side. "The little creature took my bowl!"

What was she to do? *Pray.* Huddling in her robe, she moaned, "Please, God, oh please. Protect me through this night."

CHAPTER THREE

A RUSTLE AND SCRAPING SOUND pricked her ears and stirred her from sleep. Straining with her one good eye, she squinted into the dark, but it was difficult to see anything beyond the immediate trees and brush nearby. Beyond that, it was impossible to make out shapes or movement in the darkness. Another sound. Twigs snapping and small rocks rolling. *A wild animal!* Stiffening, her agony increased, and her heart thudded loudly against her chest. *Surely, the beast will hear my heart and tear me to pieces!*

As the sound of the beast scraped and crunched closer, it stopped. Miriam held her breath. Unexpectedly, there was a flame in the dense gloom. *An evil spirt!* Miriam covered her mouth to prevent a scream from escaping. Bobbing up and down in the air, a tiny light came closer and closer, and shortly a little covered hand was exposed extending a bowl full of water.

"Thank God the Father it's you!" With shaking hands, Miriam took the bowl and drank while the little creature started a small fire from the flame of the lamp. Satisfied with its fire, it extinguished the wick of the lamp. It dug into its satchel and pulled out a few pieces of flat bread and soft raisins.

Miriam popped them in her mouth and sighed, "I appreciate your help."

Gratefully, but carefully she chewed. As she slowly ate, it lay at her feet and settled down to sleep. It was dark, her thirst was quenched, she had food in her belly, and with her little friend, and a small fire, she slept.

For three days, her friend would spend the night, help her up in the morning to relieve herself then set off to get her food and water. During the day Miriam was alone, but her helper would come back at dusk with provisions and spend the night. Miriam tried to coax out conversation, but the cloaked figure would never speak.

"Please tell me your name." But the little one would only shake its head. This person was suffering from leprosy and she was well aware its horrors. Tongues could be devoured by the disease. "Are you in pain?" Miriam simply asked.

A response was a shake of the head, and a pointed mitt toward Miriam, who responded, "Yes, I'm still in pain and I know it will take a while before I can really move around, but I'll get better, with God's help."

No one in their right mind would be around anyone with leprosy, but this situation was her only hope for immediate survival. There was no direct contact of its skin with her skin and it was careful to cover the lower half of its face. What happened to her later, well, she would worry about it when and if it happened. She never would have survived if this little one did not have the courage to stay and help her.

With time on her hands, she couldn't help but go over and over about what happened to her. She recalled her widow friends and the sick child going back from where they came and that she had decided to forge ahead to Capernaum. Should she have gone back with them? *No!*

But her decision trapped her. Overcome with exhaustion, hunger, and thirst she relived her attack recalling the names of the men who assaulted her: Phinehas and Hophni. What would ever have become of her had not this little leprous creature not sustained her with food and water?

On about the fourth day and feeling stronger she asked, "Can you show me where water is?" The small figure turned and pointed across yonder. *Well, it can hear.*

Getting up slowly, she followed the little cloaked one through the bush. Taking several short breaths to steady herself and manage the pain in her side, she continued a short distance until she had to rest.

Finding a shady spot, she sat down and said, "I don't think I can walk any further. Let's stay here for the night." Looking around she continued, "It's protected. You can take me to the water tomorrow." The small figure nodded, took her bowl, and left.

She wiped sweat from her face with a stained sleeve and gave thought to her location. Lepers lived in colonies, and this little one surely came from somewhere where there were more lepers. They were ostracized from the public and always lived outside of the city. This meant that she couldn't be too far from Capernaum because their family members or friends would bring them food and other needed items. Certainly, anyone bringing them supplies from within the city would return the same day. No one would stay the night out in the wilderness and not in the colony. So, the good news, was that she was a half a day's walk, maybe less, to Capernaum.

In the meanwhile, the day was not to be wasted. She had to rebuild stamina. Hefting herself up again, she walked a bit more hoping to see where a path might lead to water. Pushing past the discomfort, she wandered a short distance and spied a deer run. *That must be the path. It slopes downward. To a riverbed?* Turning, she needed to rest, and feeling more in control of her life, she went back to wait for her helper to return.

That evening it came back with a double helping of food, water, and a wineskin with a mouthful of wine in it. "Are we celebrating my walk today?" Miriam asked playfully and gratefully filled her mouth with sweet mixed wine. "I walked a bit more after you left. I think I saw a path that leads to the river. We'll go there tomorrow, okay?" The tiny creature nodded and settled in at her feet.

"I know you won't speak to me, but are we near Capernaum?"

The little one stretched out its arm toward the path that led to the river.

CHAPTER FOUR

THE NEXT MORNING, SHE AWOKE alone.

She turned her head to listen for any movement in the bushes, but only heard a raven cawing in the distance and the whisper of wind high in the trees. "Are you out there, my little friend?" she called. *I really wish I knew your name!* She called aloud again. No answer.

Getting up, and taking careful steps, she made her way into the bush. After managing a simple task on her won, she returned to her place. She waited idly, as she watched the sun move across the sky in its appointed route. Time went by. No sign of her friend. Worry and anxiety filled her heart. *What was going on? Was it hurt or sick or have I been abandoned?*

The only thing to do was wait the day out. There was still enough water along with leftover bread and dried fish from the night before. The wine skin was empty. She would hold off eating until the evening but would sip the water when needed. Hopefully, her friend would return with provisions, soon.

It didn't.

Carefully chewing and taking tiny sips of water she listened for any sound that might indicate her helper was returning, or if an animal was prowling about. Earlier she collected a small stash of rocks that she kept by her side in the event of an unwelcomed furry visitor. As darkness settled in, she lit the lamp but seeing that the oil was low, she used the sputtering flame to start a small fire to get her through the night. Crying softly, she wondered what happened to the little person who was so kind and attentive.

The dawn quietly and dependably brightened as she waited for her helper, the sun was promising to be hot. She needed water. She couldn't wait any longer; it was time to go, to move on. She gathered her bowl, mantle, and wineskin and looked around one more time.

"I've got go, my friend." Only the wind heard her words. "I will miss you and always love you. You saved my life!" She shouted. Her eyes welled with tears hoping for some response.

Nothing.

She cautiously picked her way through the brush to find the deer run. Miriam followed it downward, carefully picking her way through the rough, narrow path until she found a small, protected beach displaying only the hoof prints of early morning wild goats and deer. She was alone with the water and overjoyed! It was time to drink and wash!

Though it was late in the morning, she dared take most of her clothes off, placing her robe and belt on the shore, but leaving her inner tunic on. Edging into the shallows and cupping her hands to scoop water, she washed herself, then rubbed her outer tunic, cleaning away the dirt and blood, and hung it on a low-lying branch to dry. She couldn't resist going deeper in the attempt to wash out her hair.

While waiting for her tunic to dry, she continued to splash about the water keeping an eye on her surroundings. Gazing toward the small hill rising from the shore, she suddenly spied a figure appearing on its crest. She took a deep breath, then went deathly still, calculating how quickly she could get to her clothes and escape, but to where? How fast could she possible move out of the water and onto the shore? Before she could make a move, a woman bellowed, "Woman, you are asking for some serious trouble!" Miriam squinted to see a young full-figured woman dressed in clean pale blue and white robes, laboring toward the shoreline, pointing to her dingy gray clothes hanging on the branches. "Are you crazy? If anyone comes by, he'll steal your clothes, rape you, and likely murder you! Now get out of the water now!" In fear and anger, the woman put down her water jug, and craned her neck up and down the riverbank.

Frightened into obedience, Miriam slogged quickly to the shore, awkwardly covering the wet tunic clinging to her breasts with her hands.

The woman narrowed her eyes examining Miriam's near-nakedness. "What on earth happened to you? What are those bruises? Were you raped already?" She threw Miriam her cloak who hastily put it around her body.

"No, I was beaten and robbed," Miriam answered defensively tying her belt.

"Well what are you doing out here alone, in the river?" The woman pursed her lips and furrowed her thick brows. "Just swimming around without a care in the world while those ugly clothes dry? How did you get beaten? Where is your husband?" Not waiting for an answer, the woman put her hands on her ample hips. "Ah, I know. You don't have a husband, or maybe you have many husbands," she snickered good-naturedly. "Believe me, I know about many husbands."

Miriam looked silently at her. She was attractive in a hard way, that is, lots of fine powder dusted on her face and kohl outlined her eyes. Her honey-colored hair peeked out from under her veil.

Looking away, Miriam explained, "Not many husbands. I have no husband. I'm a widow." She reached for her clothes.

"Don't you dare put those clothes back on! They are an embarrassment to women. Here, put on your robe, tightened your belt, and follow me. Throw this shawl over your head. Luckily, I was just given this as a gift this morning." The woman smiled, although Miriam didn't know if it was in regret or sadness.

Adjusting the robe and veil, she plucked the damp tunics from the low-lying branches and rolled them in a ball. Taking along her bowl and wineskin, Miriam said in defiance, "I'm taking these clothes. I don't have money for new garments. And where are we going?"

The woman turned with pity in her eyes. "My tent's not too far from here and I don't normally take in poor widows, but seeing you like a child playing in the river, made me worry for you. How naive can a person be?"

Vexed, she pointed up the hill. "There's a leper colony not too far from here, and up river, the caravans stop to water their camels. All it would take is for some foreigner or leper to wander down here and see you—then, I guarantee it would be your end." Stopping for a breath, the woman tucked her long hair behind her ears and adjusted her own veil. "I'll come back later for water. Now, we need to get dry, clean clothes on you. Come along."

Miriam followed. There didn't seem to be settlements along the river, at least among the path she followed.

Pushing ahead again, the woman asked, "What's your name? I'm called Tamar, like Tamar of ancient days. Except Tamar of our ancestors had a little more success than me."

Miriam blinked. She guessed what kind of woman this was.

CHAPTER FIVE

MIRIAM'S KNEE AND SIDE THROBBED, but to her relief, they soon came to an open clearing where she could see a cluster of dwellings. Tamar explained her perceived parallel between herself and the long-ago Tamar.

"See, I was married to a man who died, then I was given to the next brother in line, to bring forth an heir for the first brother, but alas, the second brother died too. I had no children from either man. I was sent back to my father's house who despised me because I was a widow without income. Desperate to have a child and have some kind of security, I seduced a man with the intent of getting pregnant. My plan was that he would be forced to marry me to prevent scandal to his family. Well, my plan failed. That rotten man denied me! Said he had nothing to do with me! And what could I prove? To escape stoning, I ran from Jerusalem."

"What about the baby?" Miriam asked cautiously.

"She died at childbirth. God's will I guess," she answered solemnly. "I worked my way as a prostitute to Capernaum and put Jerusalem far behind me." She said waving her hand. "You haven't told me your name."

"I'm Miriam."

Tamar laughed. "Like Moses' sister. She was a prophet and jealous of her brother." She turned to Miriam adding to the story, "And because of her jealousy for Moses' leadership, and it seems his Cushite wife too, the Almighty God punished her with leprosy!"

"Yes," Miriam nodded, "but she was healed after seven days." There was a parallel of sorts to her and the ancient Miriam as well: Leprosy. The bittersweet memory of her leprous, little cloaked caretaker tugged at Miriam's heart. *Was it a girl, boy, man or woman? Was he or she alive? God took pity on Moses' sister Miriam and healed her. Could her little friend be healed too?*

They entered a settlement with several tents, make-shift shelters, naked children running and playing, goats nibbling weeds, and chickens aimlessly pecking in the dirt.

Tamar waved at two well-dressed women crossing their path. Tamar smiled.

Miriam watched their retreating backs and concluded, that for them, it was better than begging. She couldn't stoop to that though. No. She would beg first.

"Come over here, Miriam." They approached a small, colorless tent, pitched sturdily on level, cleared ground. Tamar dramatically opened the flap for Miriam to enter. "This is home."

Inside a colorful rug lay on a swept dirt floor, a single pallet with rolled blankets and two pillows were arranged, a stool with a lamp was beside the pallet, and cooking items and utensils filled a basket set beside a small trunk.

Tamar set down her empty water jug. "I don't bring men here. There are children." She swept her hand towards the outside where little ones were laughing and shouting. "We have our standards. We do our work elsewhere." Bending over the trunk, she lifted the lid and pulled out clothing. "Here. You are much thinner than I am but in time you'll put on some meat." She grinned and handed Miriam an inner and outer tunic, lovely and clean.

Miriam slid Tamar's veil from her head, draped it over her shoulders and held the clothing up in open admiration; she had never seen such fine items.

After a few moments, she sighed, "Tamar, I'm not going to prostitute myself. I'm going to beg." Tamar opened her mouth to argue. "No, don't, Tamar. I won't." Miriam shook her head and handed the clothing back. "I'll wear my old clothes. How far are the gates of the city from here? I plan to sit near the synagogue."

"You and half the other beggars. They sit there or at the market, but if you insist on not using your body, you're still welcome to stay here. Trust me; you'll never survive out there alone without shelter or friends. But," she wagged her finger, "you'll have to pay rent. I'm charged for this tent and with two people, I'll be charged more."

Miriam agreed. "I'd be happy to contribute." She couldn't believe her blessing. A friend, and a safe place to live! She unrolled and shook out her wrinkled garments and walked outside and lay them to dry on some low rocks just outside Tamar's tent.

When she came back in, Tamar had prepared pieces of bread in curded goat's milk. She handed Miriam a bowl. "Sit, eat, then tell me about yourself."

Miriam sat on the rug with Tamar, dipping the soft fresh bread into the tart goat curds savoring each morsel. She smiled at her new friend. *God is good.* He had blessed her with improbable helpers. First a leper and now a prostitute. What an unlikely occurrence!

Wiping her bowl clean, she began. "My husband and I were happy even though I was barren. We lived in a one- room building on the property his older brother had inherited from his father. His brother, their mother, the brother's wife, and four boys lived in a home on the same piece of land as well. They were always keeping an eye on my belly and because it remained flat, they constantly made mean and degrading remarks. They ridiculed my husband for having a childless, useless wife. Can you imagine a family so cruel?"

"Yes, I can," Tamar replied. "A woman's main purpose is to have children. Without children you are nothing."

"My husband's brother's wife was always talking about her boys, boasting how bright, handsome, and clever they were. Then she would glare at me and ask me when I would bring a child into this world. His mother was worse. She berated us day and night." Miriam stopped for a moment.

Continuing, she said, "We couldn't have a family meal without one of the adults complaining of my childlessness. The stress of trying to conceive was indescribable. And worse, our humiliation was forever discussed not only with us, but also with our neighbors," she sighed in contempt.

"We had just about given up and accepted my inability to conceive, when I found myself pregnant. We rejoiced in the Lord! I was to have a child! Finally, my in-laws shut up and the women at the well and market stopped their mean remarks and whispers of pity. I was elated! And what do you know? God blessed us with twin girls! Imagine! Two babies! I named them Rebekkah and Rachel.

"Yet my in-laws were far from satisfied. Girls? It was a heartbreak to them! They were so overwhelming disappointed and let us know it. Why, one boy was worth more than two girls they exclaimed. 'Why couldn't you have had a boy? You must have sinned against God!'

they scolded. Even the women of the village pitied me for my babies, and my sister-in-law told me not to look to her boys for husbands." Miriam shuddered. "I would never even consider that.

"And then, then . . . " Miriam gathered herself for a few moments, took a deep breath, and continued. "In less than a year, my husband and twin babies took sick with a fever. They suffered terribly and there wasn't anything I could do for them. In one week all three died." *The pain of a broken heart is far worse than broken and bruised bone. Flesh will heal. The spirit? Don't know if ever . . .*

Taking a deep breath, she sadly shook her head. "At the same time other people in the village came down with the fever too. There was no hope; they all died. The decree in the village was that anyone who housed a person who died from the fever must burn his house as a sacrifice. To cleanse it of pestilence and sin. My in-laws were furious; they said because of my sinfulness the family was ruined and now they must burn down the house. My in-laws told me to get out or they would burn me along with it."

"Who knows where fevers come from?" Tamar responded despondently. "Some claim demons, some claim sin, but who really knows? But the men make the rules, and the women follow and agree." She helped herself to more bread and curds and offered some to Miriam who held out her bowl.

"Yes, I agree. There was no sympathy from my sister-in-law or mother-in-law. They went along with everyone else. My in-laws gave me enough rations for a few days and showed me out. I had no place to go . . . but many others were forced to leave too."

"Did you travel alone?" Tamar asked.

"No, I set off with two widows who lost their husbands and a child who was orphaned with no relatives willing to care for him. My plan was to get to us Capernaum. I thought we might have more opportunity near a large synagogue. My hope was that our people there would have mercy on us and feed us. I just didn't realize how far away the city was from where we lived. We walked for several days, finding food and water along the way, but as time went on, we slowed down—the widows were older and frail, and the child was cranky and tired all the time.

"We were forever asking strangers the way to Capernaum." Miriam sighed then continued. "One person told us this, another told us that and it was now clear none of us knew how far away the city was. Finally, my friends gave up. The child had taken sick and they were exhausted." She took a last piece of bread and curds. "They turned back. I went on alone. I was attacked, but I was cared for or I would have surely died."

Immediately she regretted her last statement as an alarm sounded in her head. She couldn't tell anyone about being cared for by a leper, even if it did take precaution not to touch her.

CHAPTER SIX

"WHO TOOK CARE OF YOU?" Intrigued, Tamar leaned toward Miriam waiting for an answer. Miriam stalled, thinking of a truthful response. "How long were you hurt that you needed someone to take care of you?" Tamar demanded. Miriam started to sweat. What answer could she give? "Listen to me," Tamar hissed, "and don't be throwing camel dung at me. No one takes care of a widow, leper, or whore, except a widow, leper, or whore. Which is it?"

"Why is this so important?" She hid her trembling hands under her cloak. "I'm well now and I can help with the rent and get provisions by begging."

Tamar placed the last piece of bread in her mouth and put her bowl on the floor. "I know who took care of you. Yes, woman, I do. I know this area far too well to see that your options of someone caring for you outside the city gates are limited. I know it wasn't anyone from the city nor anyone from this camp or other settlements that are dotted around the city from that direction. No. You would never have been down by the river alone. Therefore, it wasn't a group of widows who took pity on you, or even a prostitute. Am I right?"

Miriam sat silently bowing her head in shame and fear, trying to figure out how to tell Tamar who helped her. The little one never touched her skin to skin or breathed on her, but before she could lift her head to speak, she was cut off.

Tamar hissed, "I'll tell you who took care of you. Lepers!" Hastily, Tamar stood and reached for a veil to put over her head. "You have exposed me to that hideous disease!" Miriam looked up to explain. "I don't want to hear it," Tamar whispered. "You have got to leave. Now." Tamar was trembling and holding back angry tears.

Distressed and desperate, Miriam stood and opened her cloak exposing her bruised body. "I'm battered, Tamar, but I'm clean. Look!"

Tamar refused to look. "It doesn't matter. You have no idea how fast or slow it spreads."

"I was never touched or breathed upon by a leper! And there was only one who help me, and it was always protected!"

"It, Miriam?" Tamar shrank back in horror. "You couldn't even tell if it was male or female?"

"Tamar, we never touched, and I never touched you!"

"Go, Miriam."

Miriam's heart broke once again. "Can I just get my clothes from outside and change in here?"

Tamar stomped back to her pallet, picked up the clothing she had given to Miriam, and threw the two lovely tunics at her and the veil. "You've touched these. They are unclean now. I can't wear them so take them, get your clothes, and go."

Miriam wept.

Tamar threw three coins at her, "You'll need some money!" She stormed out of the tent toward the river to wash herself thoroughly. "I'll take my chances with bandits and camel drivers, but not leprosy."

Desperate, Miriam picked up the coins. Tamar gave her enough money for food, but as a lone woman, where would she find safe shelter? Safety was found in numbers, and possibly she would find begging widows who would let her stay with them, but now she had to leave. She put on her old damp clothes, folded Tamar's fine clothing including the shawl, and tucked the bundle under her belt, in the back of her tunic under her cloak. If she was going to beg by synagogue, or market, she couldn't be dressed in prostitute's finery, lest they think she was one.

Outside in the bright sunlight she looked at her hands. They were still clean. How long would it take to catch leprosy from someone once exposed? Either she would get it or not, but she fervently prayed nothing happened to Tamar because of her own carelessness, because in truth, who could blame Tamar's reaction? Anyone would have been horrified and devastated to learn they were involuntarily exposed to leprosy, but still, she argued to herself, she had never touched the little leper's skin and it always had a cloth over its mouth and nose.

Yet even as she thought about it, the right thing to do would have been to warn Tamar off by explaining her exposure, but she didn't give a thought to her own possible contamination. Now her moments of comfort and peace had been shattered.

Looking around, she saw a child playing in the dirt. "Which way is the city?"

The child, confused, shook his head and shrugged his shoulders, continuing play with a broken piece of pottery.

"Capernaum?" Miriam insisted. "Capernaum. Which direction?"

Hearing the city name, he looked and pointed to a path leading outside the settlement.

Putting the episode with Tamar behind her, she hurried on and came across a chatty groups of travelers except for the men walking with satchels on their backs or donkeys laden with goods. She tagged behind a motley group of two men, two women, and a handful of noisy, complaining children who were pushing and shoving each other while their mothers and fathers scolded. In less than an hour, the increased traffic, signaled by clouds of dust, fresh animal dung, and humans shouting and calling lay ahead.

As she approached the city gates, small shelters were scattered about serving as home and market stalls for vendors who were excitedly hawking fruits, vegetables, salt, flour, and more. The larger shelters housed animals: goats, sheep, and doves used for sacrifice at the temple as well as for food. Other shelters and tents were selling cloth, sandals, premade tunics, cloaks, wineskins, and satchels. The intensity of confusion of people milling about the stalls combined with the cacophony of vendors shouting, beggars wailing, and animals bellowing was overwhelming.

Yet the chaos of hurried people, animals, carts, and donkeys was welcomed to her current state of loneliness and isolation. It seemed impossible that not long ago she was happily married with a family. Her heart nearly burst when she pictured her little ones taking turns at her breasts. She willed herself to step away from the memories, for they would crush her like a foot on a dried morsel of bread. Before it was too late to retreat from the anguish, building in her heart, she willed herself to stop or she would go crazy. She concentrated on the scene spread out before her.

Lame, blind, and deformed beggars, swatting flies, shaking cups, and holding out their hands shouting for mercy, sat in the dust and glaring sunlight. In strategic spots where shoppers and travelers passed, they told pitiful stories as they plead for alms. They were of all ages. Men, women, and children all vying for a stranger's toss of a coin or a piece of rotten fruit. Miriam kept her eyes averted and walked through the gates holding her robe close to her body, as young children pulled at her crying for food or begging for a coin.

Inside was more of the same, but the buildings and alley ways of the city took precedence over the teeming commotion of people coming and going. Fascinated by the strength and beauty of the structures, the cobbled roads, and the expansive archways, Miriam looked up and around in awe, colliding with a Pharisee praying loudly on a street corner.

He abruptly stopped chanting and sharply elbowed her away, exclaiming, "Woman! Watch where you are going! Go beg somewhere else!" With disgust, he gathered his cloak around him to avoid contamination, and moved to the adjacent corner and continued to pray even more loudly, shooting disapproving glances at her.

CHAPTER SEVEN

A SLENDER BUT REASONABLY NOURISHED street urchin, wearing a colorless tunic and selling palm brooms watched Miriam with open amusement. Laughing loudly, he waved a broom in the air. "Don't feel bad. They're all the same," he called so the Pharisee could hear and see him from across the busy street. "So holy, so dignified! But they're really just loudmouths and mean as hungry dogs!"

Miriam looked behind her and nearly bumped into the boy. Not wanting to cause trouble with a holy man, Miriam diverted the urchin's attention away from further confrontation. "Can you tell me where the synagogue is? I need help, I'm alone, and . . . "

"And you have no money, no food, no place to stay. I know. I've seen it all, heard it all. You found the right guide here. I'm Caleb." He pointed at his thin chest and scrutinized her with the eye of a merchant buying an ewe. "Are you sure you haven't any money? You could buy one of these brooms and sell your cleaning services."

Desperate to find the synagogue, she dug in her satchel and pulled out a coin from the money that Tamar had given her. It was more than enough for a broom and directions. The young boy raised his eyebrows, whistled, and snatched it out of her hand. She took a broom.

You never know. I might need it.

"Follow me, woman. By the way, what's your name?"

"Miriam."

So as not to lose him in the crowds, she followed closely while he laughed and joked along the way, giving her small tidbits of his life. He was an orphan, sold palm brooms for a vendor, and for that, he slept in the vendor's stall and kept it clean for one meal a day.

"Not much of a meal, but at least it's more than a morsel and I beg when I can, which is often. All in all, I'm pretty well off for a scrounger."

As they wound their way through the streets, he called out greetings to fellow beggars and merchants, keeping a wide berth from the stone-faced guards that marched through the streets and the righteous temple guards that roamed the alleys.

Approaching stone steps, her guide pointed upwards to an expansive plaza. "From the plaza you'll see the temple. A word of advice. Don't sit alone. Sit with the other women. You'll find them in groups. But sit a butt's-width apart from them." He laughed and spread his hands wide. "A fat ladies' butt size."

"Except beggar ladies' butts tend to be a little thin," Miriam murmured, looking around.

Caleb, laughed. "Maybe so but listen to my advice. I've been around. You sit with a group, but a little apart. That way you'll be safe, and you'll have a better chance of catching someone's eye and won't get lost with the other women blubbering for attention. Because you're pretty, you should do okay. But nothing is a sure bet when you ask people to part with their money for no return," the young boy nodded sagely. "I've got to get back to my spot before someone takes it."

"Thank you for the advice, Caleb." He left her gawking at the synagogue and its grounds ahead, the mass of people streaming in and out of the gates, the money changers at their tables, the sick, lame, and blind beggars, and the vendors in movable stalls selling goats, sheep, and doves.

In some areas, teachers of the Jewish law were instructing small groups of men and women, and in other places holy men walked about in pompous piety with robes flowing, long tassels swishing, and phylacteries, the small leather boxes containing bits of Scripture that the Pharisees prominently displayed strapped to their foreheads. The bigger the better.

Getting down to business, and skirting the building and its immediate courts, she looked for a spot that would work. Twice she tried to sit down near groups of women but both times, either their children chased her away or their heated shouts insisted she leave. The choice spots were taken this late in the morning.

Finally, spying an area that had some traffic and shade, she sat near a crippled man and a hunched woman, who sat on the hard stones with only a thin blanket they shared. In front of the blanket, they set a small bowl for alms. Sorry as their lives where, they smiled and talked with one another like a happy old married couple. As she approached, they nodded to her as she sat down. Miriam felt tears of gratefulness spring in her eyes and yearned in that moment for her husband. *No! Pull the memory from your mind!*

Quietly, she said, "Thank you." She sat down with all she had on this earth—a broom, a wineskin with water, a bowl, two coins, and a change of prostitute's clothing.

She set the bowl in front of her. She thought about selling the broom but held onto it. The day was long, and the bowl remained empty. Although she had water, the only food she had was in the morning at Tamar's tent and she was hungry now. She could wander and buy food, but she wasn't sure where she could stay the night. A few coins had been thrown to the old married couple, but all she got were propositions from men of all ages: Sneers, lewd gestures, and threatening remarks of God's wrath. She was discouraged. The couple hadn't spoken to her all day.

She scooted close to the old woman and said, "Where do you sleep at night?" She hoped the woman understood Aramaic.

"Here." The old woman looked intently at her for the first time. "You are welcome to share the blanket with us. We move under that small archway." She pointed to an overhang on an elevated walkway that wouldn't provide much protection, but it was better than being in the open. The old woman pulled two coins from her bowl. "And if you will get us all some food and water, you will be blessed for your kindness. Here, take the money."

"I have some money still, and I'll get us refreshment."

"Let me tell you where to go. The food is good, cheap, and not spoiled."

CHAPTER EIGHT

MIRIAM SPENT MONTHS WITH THE old couple. She discovered where a public well was, where to go for cheap food, and where to take care of her bodily functions with some privacy. She also visited her young friend Caleb who always had a piece of fresh fruit and a comical story to tell her. Usually the story was about the Pharisee who made a show of praying loudly on the street corner for all the community to see. The holy man never flipped a coin or offered a prayer for anyone, but he enjoyed the attention his piousness brought. Although the people would bow to him, they would smirk behind his back and some even cursed him.

"I have a story that's really different. I've heard of a man in Cana, Galilee that can turn water into wine!" Caleb came bounding up to Miriam who was sitting under the overhang in the shade.

"What? Caleb, that's impossible!" Miriam crinkled her brow. The old couple sitting beside her listened keenly.

"Seriously, listen, this is what I was told," insisted Caleb. "An engaged couple had their wedding ceremony at Cana in Galilee. The man who performed the miracle was with his mother and some of his friends. When the wine was gone, this man's mother said to him, 'They have no more wine.'

"Then the man says, 'Woman why do you involve me? My hour has not yet come'"

"What does that mean?" asked Miriam.

The older couple chimed in, "Indeed, that's a strange remark."

Caleb shrugged his shoulders. "I don't know, but his mother told the servants at the wedding to 'Do whatever he tells you.' Nearby stood six stone water jars, you know, the kind used by the Jews for ceremonial washing?"

"Yes, they hold anywhere from twenty to thirty gallons," the old man said.

"Well, he told them to fill the jars with water and they did—to the brim!"

"Then what?" asked Miriam, now intrigued.

"He asked them to draw some of the water out and give it to the master of the banquet to taste. They did, and the master was surprised! He said to the bridegroom, 'Everyone brings out the choice wine first and then the cheaper wine after the guests have had too much to drink; but you have saved the best till now.'" Caleb handed a piece of dried fruit to each of his three friends.

"Do you believe it?" Miriam gratefully nibbled the fruit.

"I'm not easily fooled—but I have heard this story from many people coming in and out of the city."

"Did you catch his name, Caleb?" asked the old man.

"No, I didn't."

CHAPTER NINE

IN TIME, MIRIAM LEARNED THE finer points of begging, turned a deaf ear to the constant propositions and coarseness, and between the three of them, they survived along with Caleb's help. She also sold the broom. One morning before dawn, Miriam awoke to find the two huddled together unusually motionless. Fearing the worst, she touched her old friend's sweet lined face, then his. Stone cold.

Oh, No! Moaning, she stayed on her knees softly lamenting and patting them on their bone-thin arms. *Another loss!*

Pulling herself together, she stopped. It was still dark, no one was stirring, and there was nothing to do but leave. She must find Caleb to tell him. She gathered her few belongings and hurried across the plaza. Miriam paused and looked back at the couple in the milky gray light. *How curious they died together, but God truly blessed them. Their poverty was behind them now.*

She grew to love them; they were like family. Lydia and Thomas.

Numbly she walked away, through streets to search out Caleb, but he wasn't in his usual spot. She prowled around the vendor's stalls but couldn't find him. She searched well until sun-up, but he was not to be found; time was running short. She must get out of the city for fear she would be accused of robbing the old couple and killing them, particularly since they both were dead, and she was known to beg with them.

People were stirring. Livestock were bleating to be milked, early morning vendors were setting up their wares, and the odd woman was already on her way to the city well. She had to leave without talking to Caleb. Outside the city she walked toward the Sea of Galilee, also called Kinneret, Lake of Gennesaret, or Lake Tiberius; the freshwater lake in Israel. There, she would take her chance of bathing, wash her old clothes but put them aside, and then put on Tamar's finery including shawl. She wasn't sure what her next move would be but getting out of beggars' clothes would help disguise her should anyone come looking for her. Not that anyone would waste their time on beggars, but one never knew.

Dotted on the water were many fishing boats and on certain parts of the shore there were more boats grounded, nets being mended, and fishermen sorting fish into large baskets from their night catch. The shore was rocky in places, open and hilly in others, little coves afforded privacy, and she found just what she was looking for.

Miriam walked down a gentle slope, ducked through a stand of small skinny trees, and carefully hopped over rounded, smooth rocks. She surveyed a deserted area protected from paths and prying eyes. Deftly she pulled off her clothing that was threadbare and fragile, with seams pulled and holes throughout. Once washed, the flimsy linen fabric would be more damaged and not possible to wear, but she could use the pieces for something. Dipping her rank body in the water, she closed her eyes in peace and luxury. The water was cold, but it revived her senses and freshened her body as she scrubbed herself with fine sand. Ducking underwater, she rubbed sand in her long, tangled hair, and scalp. Rinsing and rinsing, grubbiness and dirt floated off into the water and was pushed away by the gentle wind. Swishing her old clothing around in the water, she laughed that she would soon be wearing true finery. *Bless Tamar!*

Renewed and clean, Miriam sat on a rock with ever an eye out for intruders while the mild wind did its job of drying her off as she ran her fingers through her hair to get out the tangles. Satisfied, she put on her friend's clothing, and covered her wet head with the shawl. *How exhilarating it was to be washed clean! And to be wearing fine clothes!* Her mind and body rejoiced in her cleanliness.

"If got leprosy, I would be showing signs by now," she said aloud, looking over her arms, hands, legs, and feet. She was still clean. "Praise God!"

She stood and found a path towards a beach. In the distance, fishermen busying themselves with their catch. *Would they sell me a fish?* She spied a fire cooking fish ahead of her. Her mouth watered with the thought of broiled fish. *I'm like a prostitute, so maybe they'll have no qualms about selling me anything.*

She just had to be careful. Walking on the shore, she approached the fishmongers.

Gathering her courage, she pointed to a fish. "How much?"

A wizened man in torn patched linen leered at her. "I'll give you the fish for free and maybe more, if you give your beautiful self to me in such a way to make me smile."

"No. I just want to buy one fish."

"Not until I feel what's under that robe."

"Look, all I want is . . . "

The man hopped over his basket of fish and roughly grabbed her shoulders "And all I want is a piece of you!" Miriam squirmed from his grip.

"Tamar, Tamar!" A voice called from behind her. "Is that rat bothering you?" A hand lightly touched her shoulder. "You do look mighty good, but, oh, woman, you are skinny and boney! You've lost some of your curves since I last saw you," he said in concern as she desperately pushed the man in front of her away. Turning in fear to the man behind her, she stumbled away from both men, but the second man gaped at her in surprise.

He stepped back in surprise. "You're not Tamar. What are you doing with the shawl I gave her?" Pointing at the man, he shouted, "Sheba, back off. Leave her alone!"

Sulking and mumbling the man went back to his fish. "I'm not selling that whore nothing!"

"You'd turn down a sale, you old snake? Here." The fisherman flipped him a coin. "I want that one." He pointed to a fresh, gleaming, fat fish with sparkle still in its eyes.

The vendor, angry, wrapped the fish in palm leaves and handed it to the fisherman, who then handed it to Miriam, still trembling in fear.

He took her arm and guided her along the beach. Obediently, Miriam allowed him to walk with her. "At least you had the good sense not to run from me. If you did, you would have missed out on a free meal. Coming down to beach alone is not a good idea. I'm Jacob. But wait," he stopped and looked her over. "I gave that veil to Tamar as payment for her services. How come you have it?"

Miriam regained her sensibilities. "First of all, yes, she's fine, and about the veil, it's a sorry story. Secondly, I didn't run away because

I wanted the fish. I'll pay for it. I don't need anything free from you!" She pulled a coin from her robe pocket.

"I didn't mean to insult you. It's my pleasure to buy this fish for you." He comically bowed. "Now, tell me about Tamar and the veil."

Miriam was hungry. She wanted to eat, and she didn't want to talk to this man, but she was cornered. "As I said, it's a sorry story."

CHAPTER TEN

"LET'S TALK OVER FOOD." JACOB pointed up the rocky shore to a man broiling. "My treat."

He took the fish from her and went up to the fire. She hesitated before following him.

"I know a good Jewish boy should never be alone with a good Jewish girl, but you look like a prostitute, so this crowd certainly doesn't care," He said over his shoulder and nodded with his head toward the fishermen working on the shore, mending, selling, cursing, laughing. "You are a prostitute, right?" He looked her over with hope in his eyes.

"I'm not a prostitute!" Miriam stopped mid-stride and bristled. "And I am a good Jewish girl! My name is Miriam." She had to straighten this man out. "Let me explain myself, please!"

"I'm all ears."

Miriam looked closely at his head. He was indeed all ears, but she dared not snicker. Built like a hardworking man, he was strong, lean, and in work clothes that hadn't been repaired in a while. She hung back and watched him discuss with the cook how he wanted it prepared. He came back to her and took her by the elbow and directed her to a smooth boulder to sit. She did.

"Any wine in that wineskin, I hope?" He pointed to the wineskin flopping over her knees.

"No. Just water."

"Guess that'll have to do." He took it from her lap and took a deep drink, nearly choking. "Did you get this from here?" He pointed to the water in front of them. "It tastes like fish guts! Don't use water from here—get it from the city well!"

She retorted, "When you're thirsty, you do not care from where it comes!" She grabbed it back from him, taking a long drink herself, but after she swallowed, she agreed she'd tasted better water.

They sat in awkward silence until the cook yelled at him to get his fillets. He rose and then returned with a portion for her and a much larger one for himself. She eyed his portion.

"I'm a hard-working man and you're . . . small," he explained ignoring her look. "Tell me your story about Tamar." He plucked a piece of fish laying on a leaf, howled a moment because it was hot, then popped it in his mouth.

"Do you mind if I eat first? I'm starving." He shrugged, watching her devour her food. When finished, she wiped her mouth and took a drink of water and offered him a sip. He declined.

"I have to begin at the beginning; otherwise you'll have questions as to how Tamar and I came to even know each other." She began without emotion holding down the desperation threatening to break through her story. She wanted so badly to skip over the part of a small leper helping her, but she couldn't lie, and besides, if Tamar ever met up with Jacob again, the story would be out.

"I'd say you dodged the rock on getting leprosy." Jacob scrutinized her face and hands, and his eyes went to her poorly sandaled feet, the only parts of her body fully visible. "But it might take a while for it to show. No one really knows about the disease; some religious people say it's caused by sinning." He paused for a moment then shrugged his shoulders. "I'm not so sure about that, and anyway, I'm not worried about it, especially if your little friend never touched you. Being in that close contact for that amount of time, your caregiver must have known what he or she was doing because it doesn't sound like it would put you in the position of contracting the disease. ou say it's been a few months since you it helped you?"

Miriam nodded.

"Then I'd say Tamar didn't get it either, so praise God. Now we've got to think how you are going to be cared for. Particularly since your friends are dead. The authorities might question you about their deaths. But then again, they probably won't care. Two less beggars to look at."

Miriam stared at him stonily. "They were my dear friends . . . "

"Sorry. I've insulted you again. I usually don't do that to attractive women."

"Only to the ugly?"

Jacob sighed. "I'm sorry again. I mean no harm." He spread his hands wide in supplication.

She straightened her back and followed his glance as he gazed out onto the water. A low riding boat was coming in with three fishermen readying it to bring into shallow water.

"They got a good catch last night," He pointed thankful to change the subject. "Look how low the boat is in the water. I know those guys. I was supposed to go, but didn't . . . Now, I can't share in the profits."

"Why did you not go out with them?"

He looked at her and smiled mischievously. "I had an engagement and couldn't make it. Ah, well. Now, I suffer the consequences! But it was worth it. Come."

They tossed the remnants of their meal to the gulls hovering about and walked to the shoreline. Two burly fishermen and an old man jumped off the gunnels pushing the boat into thigh-deep water as day laborers ran from the beach to greet them.

CHAPTER ELEVEN

"SOME HAUL, TIMOTHY!" JACOB WAVED to a man splashing in the shallows, grounding the shallow keeled boat in the gravely sand. Miriam trailed behind him, pulling her veil tight, all the while wondering what she was going to do now that she had some food in her belly.

"Where were you last night, you monger? We could have used your help. Look at the catch! One of our best nights!" Timothy shot back. One of the crew, an old man named Jonas, began hauling the full net to shore along with the third fisherman. Hangers-on hoping to be hired to help sort the catch for a fish or two stood in the ankle-deep water.

Timothy slogged toward Jacob. He nodded at Miriam and pointed to Jacob. "Man, you need to be more responsible! We waited for you and when you didn't show up, we asked Jonas to help." He nodded toward the old man who was dragging the net; a man still strong and willing. "Thank our God he did, because we needed another set of hands on-board."

"Cousin, I can explain . . . "

"I'm sure you can, but I don't want to hear it. Who's your friend?" He tilted his toward Miriam who stood away from the men and out of the water.

Standing uncomfortably with the men looking at her she again wondered what the next move was going to be. Should she stay or leave?

"Just met her, but I know she's a widow, with no family, she's been begging near the synagogue." They both continued to stare at her.

"She doesn't look like a widow. Pretty fancy veil," Timothy raised his eyes to Jacob. "Are you sure she was begging?"

"Cousin, she's a respectable Jewess. Not from around here."

Timothy dismissed the conversation. "I need some help with these fish now. Do something for a change. Earn a day's wage. Help us sort so I can get them sold before they rot!"

"What about her, Timothy? I just can't leave her here."

Timothy looked around, thinking. "We can take her to Uncle Jerome's wife, Ann. She's pregnant and maybe could use her. She'd get food and shelter at least, but we can't take her now. Tell her to take off that fancy veil and cover herself with, I don't know . . . "

He jogged back to the boat and leaned over the rails and scooped up a dark wrap. Returning with a stained, fish-smelling man-shawl he tossed it to Jacob. "Let her to cover herself with this and she can help us sort fish."

"You're going to pay her?" Jacob asked incredulously.

"Well of course I will. She's working, isn't she?"

"But . . . but . . . what if . . . "

"Will you just shut up and do some work? Let me worry if a Pharisee comes wandering down on the beach and sees her working." He stormed off muttering, "As if a holy man would show up with the working class."

Several hours later, along with many drinks of water, another broiled fish consumed, Miriam finished sorting the last of the catch with the men, who only paid attention to her when she held up a sea creature she wasn't sure about.

"What about this one?" She asked. "Toss it," someone would reply, or "That's a keeper." So, she separated the good from the bad and the baskets were either taken up by the day labors to the vendors on the beach or the vendors going to the markets dotting the roadsides and inside the city walls.

Timothy approached her. "Your wages." He handed her a few coins. "Just keep it to yourself that you worked for me." Exasperated, he looked around the beach. "And where is my slacker cousin now?"

"Over by the bread stand. He has a bottomless stomach."

"And brain. We must get you over to Ann's house and see if she can use you. I could use you to help me sort fish. You work faster than any of my crew or day laborers."

"Thank you for allowing me to help and paying me . . . and I appreciate being fed." Timothy just grunted. Gingerly, she took off her fish-smelling shawl, washed her hands and splashed water on her face, and put Tamar's nice veil back on.

She followed Jacob and Timothy up the beach. Her clothing was much too fine to be walking along with two sweaty and grimy fishermen, and no doubt people thought she was bought for the night, but as people glared at her when they passed by, she didn't care. Let them think what they will. She needed a place to stay in safety.

The men talked as they walked, ignoring her. She hoped this was going to work out. They seemed kind enough, but she learned in all her days of begging never take people for who you thought them to be. Like the time a young aristocrat dropped several coins in her bowl. She thanked him profusely, only to have two of his body guards roughly haul her to her feet and drag her to the man's chariot. Her screaming put a stop to her abduction when Caleb came upon the scene and rallied the beggars against the men. A terrible fight ensued and was broken up by the Roman guard. The man in the chariot was a rich foreigner and the Romans had no use for him. He and his body guards had been arrested.

Or the time when a seemingly kindly woman dropped coins in her bowl and hurried off, with two temple guards chasing her and one temple guard stopping and scooping her bowl from the ground, dropping all the money she had collected for the day in a sack, claiming the woman had stolen the money from a money changer. He took the old couple's money too, just for spite.

CHAPTER TWELVE

TURNING INTO A NARROW ALLEY, Jacob and Timothy with Miriam trailing behind, came to small, two-room house, with a manger for goats and a roosting coop for chickens in the back of the small property.

A pregnant woman sat outside cleaning vegetables and the men called to her. "Aunt! We have a proposition for you!"

Children, thrilled to see them, ran fast and collided into them. Delirious with joy they begged, "Pick us up, pick us up!"

"You're too big to be picked up!" both men jokingly complained. "You'll break our backs!" The children milled and chattered around them, then focused on Miriam, shyly touching her hands and clothes with big, trusting smiles and giggles.

"Miriam, go play with the children while we talk to Ann," Jacob instructed.

The children delighted with a newcomer, took Miriam's hands. "Come see our baby goats!" They squealed, and Miriam trotted after them, keeping an eye on the group of adults discussing her immediate future.

She couldn't hear what they were saying but it was evident the discussion was serious because Ann darted a worried look at her while Jacob paced, and Timothy waved his hands. She hoped this was not going to be problematic because the reality of her homelessness tore her deeply. Looking at Ann's children brought memories of own children and great loss. She had nothing. If Ann didn't take her, where would she go? "Miriam, come!"

Jacob called. She left the children and walked quickly back to the men keeping her eyes on a concerned looking Ann.

The woman, although younger than Miriam, was thin and worn. Miriam stood in front of her and the younger woman sighed. "I can only give you food and a small shelter. But money? We have little to spare."

"I have nowhere to go and I would be blessed to help you with the household for food and shelter. Believe me, I would be so grateful." *Please make this work!*

Ann turned to Jacob and Timothy. "Still, nephews, I must talk to Jerome first."

"Ann, we don't know when he's coming back. In the meantime, where will she go?" Jacob threw up his hands.

"I can't bring her home," Timothy argued. "We have less space than you!"

"And I can't take her home. I don't think my parents would be happy . . . It wouldn't look right." Jacob looked down at the ground.

Miriam squirmed with embarrassment. *Maybe this wasn't meant to be.* "Please, don't worry about me. I'm used to finding a place to shelter. I, I have my bowl for alms, and I can go back to the village square. You do have a village square?"

"No!" Jacob responded. "I mean yes, we have a village square, but no, you'll not go back to begging!"

Ann and Timothy exchanged surprised looks, raising their eyebrows. "Unless Jacob wanted to get engaged," teased Ann, slyly. "Miriam's quite pretty and young."

"Yes, you so need to get married!" Timothy scolded, wagging his head. "Get respectable!"

"She's a widow!" Jacob protested.

Miriam narrowed her eyes. Were they all crazy? And they were talking about her as if she wasn't even standing in the middle of them. If Ann didn't want her, she'd go on her way.

Ann pointed a finger at Jacob. "What difference does that make? You certainly can't marry a prostitute!"

Jacob opened his mouth in shock but before he could protest, his aunt continued. "I might be at home most of the day, but I do get out to market and when I do, I hear plenty of gossip about my nephew's sinful philandering! And we all know with what types of women you play with, so please don't give me that innocent look."

Miriam shot Jacob a look, but he quickly looked away. A rooster ran between the adults, with children the trying to catch it. Ann indicated they all get out of the way of the chaos and showed them seats. Miriam sat, and her robe opened to the very nice, expensive outer tunic.

"Those aren't widow's garments," Ann remarked, eyeing the high quality linen.

"It's a long story," Jacob said before Miriam could explain. "She's not a prostitute, Ann settle your mind!"

Embarrassed, Ann sputtered to protest, but Timothy broke in. "Ann? Can Miriam stay?"

"Oh, all right," Ann sighed. "But you both must speak to Jerome." She cast a meaningful look at Miriam. "Jerome is to come home today, at the very latest, he said."

"Where is he?" Jacob stole another look at Miriam. "Meeting another goat herder in the wilderness someplace?"

"Yes, he's loaning out Ziph; you know that animal sires the most beautiful kids and has made quite a reputation for himself with the herders. They all want Ziph's progeny." Her look of pride turned to uneasiness. "But I worry so when they are gone so long. This time they took a boat across the Sea of Galilee, then down to the Jordan. God is with him, I keep telling myself and continually pray to the Almighty to protect him and our family." Shuddering, she extended her hand to Miriam. "This is going to work out."

Miriam certainly hoped so, but worried about Jerome. What would he say? Her thoughts were interrupted by Jacob and Timothy who were leaving to go back to the boat for supplies to build the shelter for her. Watching them go, she prayed this would indeed work out, but if not, she was prepared to go back to begging. She had no choice.

CHAPTER THIRTEEN

WALKING ALONG THE SANDY AND rocky path to get the supplies, Timothy plucked at his chin, pulled out a piece of dried sea grass from his beard and observed, "Jerome has been traveling with goats since before he married Ann. You think she would take it in stride."

"You can't help but worry when someone is gone so long," responded Jacob. "Especially with him out in the wilderness someplace along the River Jordan where anything can happen and her being pregnant and having two little ones to care for. There's nothing worse for a woman to be widowed. But at least she has us as family should anything happen to Jerome."

Timothy laughed. "Since when did you become so empathetic?"

"Good word, my cousin. I do know what it means. And for your information, I do have a heart." He punched his cousin's arm not too lightly.

Arriving at the boat, Timothy shouted to Jonas who was packing up for the day. "Jonas, tell my wife I'm going to be late for supper, but hold it for me. I have some work to do over at Ann and Jerome's house."

"I will, Timothy." Jonas waved, gathering up some of the fish in a sack and walked away as the men gathered the needed supplies.

"Why am I caught up with your escapades?" Timothy asked as he tossed an old sail from below decks to Jacob standing on the beach. "You're always getting tangled up with drunks, tax collectors, and prostitutes. Now it's a widow no less! Poor, without family, or home."

"I feel responsible for her, Timothy. She's a clever woman and a good worker as you saw," Jacob answered causing his cousin to slow down a moment and stare at him in amazement. "I do feel like we need to take care of her," Jacob insisted folding up the sail. "She has quite a story." He looked up at Timothy standing in the boat, with hands on hips smirking at him. Jacob smiled back. "And you'll never guess who she made friends with, that is, until she lost the friendship."

Timothy shrugged his shoulders, half- interested as he pulled up a hatch in the deck to look for his tool bag containing nails and a hammer. "What friend did she lose?"

Jacob paused for dramatic effect, and then blurted, "Tamar!"

"Tamar?" Timothy pulled his head from the hatch and laughed aloud. "Oh, this is going to be good. So, tell me on our way back." He threw the cushions at his cousin along with extra line.

"Okay, but as Miriam says, I have to start at the beginning," Jacob said. Walking back to Ann's house, Jacob started with Miriam losing her husband, children, and being cast away from the only family she had. He spoke of her attack, the little leper who cared for her, the friendship of a young man named Caleb, and her brief friendship with Tamar.

"It's miraculous she never got the disease, but she never was in the leper's colony, and wasn't physically touched by leprous skin," Timothy said thoughtfully. "You know that Jerome's father got the disease? Jerome would go daily to their colony to bring food and sup-plies. The old man died last year."

"What colony was it?" Jacob asked, vaguely remembering his old relative.

"The one outside the city by the river."

"That's the same one that Miriam's little helper was from. Too bad the old man is dead. We could have had Jerome ask about the little fellow. He or she remains a mystery."

"I think Jerome and Ann are glad he doesn't have to bring supplies there anymore. The farther away from sickness, the better," Timothy stated. "But I think Miriam should tell Ann her situation of possible exposure."

Jacob agreed. "Can you imagine she met up with Tamar? Of all people?"

"That is a surprise, but losing Tamar's friendship, well, that's probably for the best," Timothy added thoughtfully. "She doesn't need the temptation of easy money." He stopped and rubbed his head. "Yes, and I know Caleb too. He's quite a character. Very savvy. He's like the royalty of street urchins."

Jacob laughed. "She said Caleb was very good to her. Often gave her food and always had some news from travelers and foreigners." As they walked along the path he added, "I might never have had met her if we didn't show up at the beach at the same time."

Timothy turned again to his cousin, grinning. "Or that you fi-nally showed up to work. But late is better than not." He hesitated, squinting his eyes and said, "I think you like this woman."

Jacob didn't answer for a while. They walked in silence for a few minutes, then said, "I think I do too. But for now, it's too early to think about anything. Besides, can you imagine the reaction of my mother and father?"

"Yes, I can. They already had you set up not once, but twice with women you wanted no part of — and both were nice women from good Jewish families. A little old, maybe, but still in childbearing age. You need an heir and you, cousin, aren't getting younger. You better think about getting married soon." Timothy advised.

"I know. That's what I'm doing. Thinking."

The men returned to Ann's back yard carrying a folded sail, three cushions, a hammer, nails, and line to construct the shelter.

Miriam touched Jacob's sleeve as he put the cushions down. "I can't thank you enough, Jacob, for taking me under your wing. Ann is wonderful, and I love her children. I hope that Jerome will be okay with all of this. But I think I need to tell her and Jerome about the little one who helped me when I was beaten."

"Jerome is an amazing man, Miriam. Full of wisdom, generosity, and fun. His father died of leprosy. While it could be a problem with others, I don't think it will be with Ann and Jerome."

"I pray so," Miriam said looking soulfully at Jacob.

"Cousin!" Jacob turned to Timothy's shout, his heart beating just a little faster than he would like. "Get yourself over here. I can't do this myself." Timothy waved a hammer in the air.

CHAPTER FOURTEEN

IT WAS NEAR SUPPERTIME AND the two cousins were finishing the shelter when Jerome and Ziph the goat, weary from their travels, trudging up the path from the Sea of Galilee, entered the small yard. Man and beast were loaded with backpacks stuffed with supplies. Crying aloud in relief, Ann jumped up and hugged her husband while the children crowded around pulling at his dusty clothing and patting the ornery Ziph all the while shouting they missed their papa and wanted presents.

Surprised and happy Jerome asked, "What're you two scoundrels doing?" He squinted at a new addition to his back yard: the lean-to tent. "Making a new room for our Prince Ziph or the baby?" He laughed, until he saw Miriam standing near the fire. A concern shadowed his face for a moment, and then Ann, Jacob, and Timothy started talking at once. "Whoa, one at a time. I'm being ambushed." He stepped back and took off his pack and told the children to unload Ziph's packs. "Gently! Be careful!" he hollered at them.

"I can explain." Ann grabbed his hand once he set his bundles down. Quickly, she explained the situation.

"Mmmm," was all he said and went quiet. Jerome, a rangy, tall man without a bit of loose flesh on him looked older than his years.

He took off his cloak, exposing tanned arms and gave the garment to his wife.

Miriam held her breath. *Please don't drive me away,* she prayed. She stole a glance at Jacob, who was smiling and nodding at her.

Jerome crossed his arms over his chest and stated, "Of course she can stay; we can use the help. Now, I'm starving. Let's all have supper. I've brought some provisions." He bent down and untied several bundles and handed dozens of small wrapped parcels to the two women. "And I have an amazing story to tell you all."

"Pappa! Look! We got all the stuff off Ziph!"

"Good children. Now take his princeling to his stall, water, and feed him. And don't tease him. He's a little short tempered since he had to leave his many admirers."

"Before you start husband, sit, let me get you some water for your feet and a cup of goat milk for your thirst, then you can tell us your story." Ann took his arm and settled him on a stool.

Miriam touched Ann's shoulder. "Let me help you."

The two women hurried away.

Ann came alongside Miriam smiling. "Jacob is quite agreeable and amusing, Miriam. He also has a job fishing with Timothy. His parents have a large home suitable for additional family," Ann blushed at her own boldness. "I'm not trying to be a matchmaker, but he would make a good husband," Ann blurted out reaching for a cup.

Miriam smiled too and looked at the men gathered around the fire, laughing and joking with one another. Yes, Jacob was appealing. She knew she needed to be married but she had nothing to offer a potential husband except the possibility of children, God willing, which would give her value to her husband and future in-laws.

She turned to her much-needed friend. "Ann, only time will tell if it should come about, but in the meantime, there is something I must tell you."

After Miriam finished, Ann seemed torn.

Gently taking Miriam's hand she tapped her palm. "It's been many months now and you are fresh and clean. You said you were not in the colony and that neither of you ever touched skin to skin nor that your little helper even breathed on you because its mouth and nose were covered. I'm not afraid and I want you here. I know my husband will be agreeable. Perhaps God brought you here not only for us, but for Jacob too. Come, let's get back to the men." She let go of her hand.

Timothy stood up. "I really need to get home to Elizabeth and the children. Jerome, can we hear your story tomorrow?"

"No worry, my husband," a delicate, tiny woman said approaching from the side of the house. With her were Jonas pulling a large covered clay pot in a small wagon and two children lagging behind. "If Jerome was back, I knew you'd be gone for hours hearing the latest gossip, and I know how much you love lamb, so I brought supper to you all! Lamb stew!"

They cheered and applauded, but Timothy complained, "That means only a cupful a piece!"

"Timothy, my endearing nephew. We have plenty of food—at least tonight. I have dried meats, fruits, vegetables, cheese—and I won't mention dried fish— along with other tasty and unusual items. Ann, Miriam, Elizabeth, prepare our meal." He clapped his hands delighted with himself. "It's wonderful you're all here because, as I said, I have some exciting stories to share. And I won't have to repeat them!"

A short time later, the group sat on the ground on cushions in the back yard, around the open fire and enjoyed a feast of lamb, boiled and raw vegetables, fresh unleavened bread, a variety of olives, dried figs, hard cheese, and mixed wine. It was a sumptuous meal by even a noble's standards. Sweet crisps with honey finished the meal.

Miriam couldn't believe her good fortune. How amazing! *Here I am a beggar in the morning, to a well-appreciated servant by night. This is truly a blessing!* She was overwhelmed with gratefulness to Jacob even if he was a little rough on the edges. He saved her life. She believed strongly in a God of blessings. Now, two families surrounded her with children and all accepted her.

"Tell, us about your trip, Jerome," his wife urged.

"First. I missed you." He leaned in and kissed her cheek. "It was a successful trip, in more ways than one. Ziph performed admirably, I was paid well, and I got to enjoy the kinship of fellow herders and hear news from Judea." He shook his head and poked at the fire. "Do you remember the prophet Isiah saying, 'A voice of one calling: In the wilderness prepare the way for the LORD; make straight in the desert a highway for our God'?"

"Yes," Timothy responded. "It's often read in the synagogue by a Pharisee or Sadducee."

"I never got what it really meant," admitted Jacob. "It sounds like its meant to clear obstacles for God, but I don't think he needs anyone clearing obstacles for him."

Jonas nodded his head in agreement. "'Make straight in the desert a highway' is like repairing roads for royal travel."

"The teachers in the synagogue refer to the passage as the prophet's reference to the return of the ancient Jews from captivity in Babylon," Jerome clarified, "but there is a present way of looking at the verse too."

Jerome threw another piece of wood on the fire. "Bear with me. There's a man, not too old, maybe earlier thirties, not married. He's a prophet. Lives in the wilderness. He dresses in camel's hair with a leather belt and exists on wild locusts and honey."

"Sweet and crunchy," Jacob approved. "Good combination."

Jerome ignored the comment, although Miriam smiled. Continuing Jerome said, "He's been wandering in the wilderness up and down the Jordan preaching for repentance, you know, telling people to turn from their sins—to anyone who will listen. And, those who publicly repent, he baptizes in the River Jordan."

"What's that all about?" Jacob furrowed his eyebrows.

"Baptizing, that is getting dunked in water, and displays a symbolic washing away of sin." Jerome replied. "Now, what's important to this story and Isaiah's Scripture of a 'voice calling in the wilderness', is that this is the man, 'the voice'!"

"Go on," said Miriam whispered, intrigued.

"It was reported that this man said to the people that came to see him, something like, 'I baptize you with water, but he who is mightier than I is coming and will baptize you with the Holy Spirit.'"

He looked at them expectantly. "Do you see what he meant?" They looked at one another.

Jacob tossed a hand up. "No."

Miriam was brought back to Caleb's story of a miracle worker in Cana. "I think I understand," They looked her way for an explanation, but before she could reply, Ann squeaked out a pitiful, sharp cry.

CHAPTER FIFTEEN

ALL EYES TURNED FROM MIRIAM to Ann's hands clutching her swollen and distended belly. Her face was pale, and her eyes wide in surprise and pain. Everyone waited.

Jerome jumped up and put his arms around her. "Can you get to the pallet?"

Beads of sweat were dotting her brow, and this time she screamed. The two cousins jumped to her and between the three men, they carried her to her room prepared for childbirth. Miriam and Elizabeth following in haste, directing all children to go to bed. Now. Jonas sat by the fire, drinking wine.

"It's coming early." Jerome and the men gently laid Ann on the pallet. Miriam and Elizabeth got to work as the men exited the room. Staring back at his wife in the dim room he said softly, "We thought it would come in at least another week. Oh, I praise the Lord I came home when I did. I just felt I needed to come home. There was one more stop I was going to make, but I decided that Ziph and I had enough fun for one trip. Thank God, Elizabeth and Miriam are with her. What would have become of her if she was alone?" he lamented looking at his two friends with tears of worry in his eyes.

"That's not to think about. She's in good hands. Both women have had children, so they know what to do. Come. Let's wait with Jonas.

Have some wine. The children are in bed. All is well," comforted Timothy and steered him outside to the fire.

Jacob hung by the doorway and turned back to the birthing room. "Miriam! Miriam!" he whispered in fear. She hurried to him as he looked over her shoulder. "Is everything going to be all right?"

"It's too early to tell, Jacob, but I think so. Go outside. Sit. She's in labor and since this will be their third child, it should go quickly. Just pray."

And quickly the baby came.

Miriam came out of the house with a swaddled mewling infant in her arms and a huge smile on her face. "You are papa once again, Jerome. A boy. You now have two boys and a girl. A perfect family!"

Crying with delight, Jerome took his tiny son in his arms and cooed at him as the other three men looked on, in awe.

"Well, done Jerome!" They shouted and patted him on the back, each taking a turn to peek at the red-faced little boy with tightly shut eyes and tiny pursing lips.

"Well done, Jerome? What about poor Ann? She's the one who did all the work. Jerome was the one to enjoy!" Miriam chided with a smile.

"Well, we hope Ann enjoyed too," Jacob chuckled.

Miriam took the baby from Jerome's arms and went into the house and later, came out walking toward the men.

"The miracle of birth never gets dull." Miriam wiped her hands on a towel wrapped around her waist and sat down by the fire. They were all exhausted, but grateful that the birth went smoothly. "Even though women can have many children, there was always the possibility of something going wrong, and it takes only one, but Ann is blessed with a healthy child and she's doing well." The men grunted in acknowledgment.

Jerome turned to Miriam. "My story, earlier. You said you got what I was trying to say. What do you think?"

Miriam became pensive. The three men looked at her expectantly.

"What's his name?" Miriam put her hand to her chin.

"I'm told it's John. They call him John the Baptist. I wasn't far enough south along the River Jordan to personally hear him speak because he was in Judea, somewhere near Bethany-across-the Jordan. But word was spreading fast about—Wait. Let me stop. Before I go further, please answer my question about what I was trying to say."

"The Kingdom of God is near," Miriam said pensively. "This John the Baptist is the voice calling out in the wilderness prophesied by Isaiah. He is calling people to turn from their sins and prepare themselves to be ready for the great one who is soon to come."

She and her old beggar friends were always speculating when a leader would come to free the Jews from the tyranny of Rome and the corruption of the Jewish religious leaders. "It's the beginning of the good news for the Jews." She kept the story of the miracle worker in Cana in her heart. It was too strange to repeat.

"That's what I think too, Miriam," Jerome responded gently running a hand down his beard.

"Could he be preparing us for the conqueror we've been waiting for who'll free us from Roman rule?" Timothy leaned toward in excitement.

"He sounds more like Elijah the prophet—a hairy man, with a leather belt around his waist," Jonas sipped more wine.

"I don't know, but there's more. Throngs of people from Jerusalem and throughout Judea are going out to the wilderness to hear him speak and be baptized by him. People are confessing and repenting of their sins! It's astonishing."

"This must be a very persuasive prophet," Miriam added.

"You said he's called John the Baptist, but who is he really?" Jacob looked around the group.

Jerome said, "You aren't the only one with that question. Because all Jerusalem has been talking about him, word got to the Sadducees and Pharisees and it even traveled to Herod. They all want to know the same thing, *who is this man?*

"So, the Jews sent the priests and other Levites to find John and ask him who was. They trekked out to the wilderness along the River Jordan, following the crowds that were looking for him too. When they found him, they got frightened and threatened because the crowds were filled with expectation and hope wondering if John was really the Christ!"

"Christ?" Miriam stared at him. "The Messiah? The anointed one?"

"Listen. He said he was not the Christ. Then they asked him if he was Elijah—"

Jonas interrupted, "See, I told you he looked like Elijah, hairy and grizzly—"

"Shush, Jonas," Jacob held up a hand. "Go on."

"John responded no, he wasn't Elijah. They asked if he was the Prophet; again he said no. And again, they demanded who he was. He answered, *'I am the voice of one crying out in the wilderness. "Make straight" the way of the Lord, as the prophet Isaiah said.' Then the priests and Levites asked, 'Why then do you baptize if you are not the Messiah, nor Elijah, nor the Prophet?' and John said, 'I baptize with water, but* among you stands one you do not know He is the one who comes after me, the straps of whose sandals I am not worthy to untie.'"

Miriam, and the four men, remained silent but excitement rose in her heart. The Messiah is coming? Soon? But Miriam wondered if he was already here. *Who was the man that in Caleb's story who turned water into wine? Only a person with spiritual power could do that.*

"Wait until you hear what else he said to the Pharisees and Sadducees." Jerome pulled a worn piece of scroll from his tunic pocket and unraveled it. "I had to write this down, so I wouldn't forget it." With a huge smile on his face, he read, "John said to the priests and Levites, 'You brood of vipers!'"

Jacob howled in laughter. "You have got to be kidding me! He called the Pharisees and Sadducees a brood of vipers?"

Jerome grinned broadly. "Wait, it gets better. Next John said, 'Who warned you to flee from the coming wrath? Produce fruit in keeping with repentance. And do not think you can say to yourselves, 'We have Abraham as our father.' I tell you that out of these stones God can raise up children for Abraham.'"

Miriam put her hands to her mouth. No one in their right mind would ever speak to teachers of the law like that. She looked over to Jacob who was laughing for joy along with Timothy and Jonas who were shaking their heads in incredulity, laughing loudly too. Caleb would have loved to hear this!

Jerome became serious and held up his palm. "But listen to what else he said. 'The ax is already at the root of the trees, and every tree that does not produce good fruit will be cut down and thrown into the fire.'"

"Do you see what this means?" Miriam asked cautiously. "John the Baptist is preparing the way for the arrival of the Lord and is warning people to prepare. Turn to the Lord, confess sins, and repent. The teachers of the law are not willing to prepare themselves by confessing any sin, much less turning from their sinful ways."

"That would be profitable ways," Jonas stated flatly. "They would take the last mite from a poor widow."

"And any tree that doesn't produce good fruit will be burned," Miriam added in wonder.

Timothy looked questioningly at Miriam. "Did you see any mercy or kindness from the Pharisees to the beggars around the plaza or synagogue?" She shook her head. "So, no good fruit from those trees."

Jerome rolled up his scroll and said, "I'm going to check on Ann," leaving Miriam and the three men sitting around the fire lost in their own deep thoughts about the coming of a messiah for the Jewish people. This could mean an upending of Roman rule.

Miriam snapped out of her reverie. "I must go too and help Elizabeth with Ann."

Coming up behind Jerome, she caught his sleeve. "Is there more to your story?"

Jerome stopped in the main room. He looked tiredly at her. "No. I felt the need to get back home, so I was unable to question anymore people, but Miriam, this is radical. For a man without so-called authority to challenge the teachers of the law, to be speaking openly about confessing sins and turning from evil ways, is astounding. I heard that he counseled even tax collectors and soldiers who asked what they should do live an honest life. It's extraordinary and so exciting that there is someone who is greater than John the Baptist and he is on the way to save us Jews."

CHAPTER SIXTEEN

THE DAYS TURNED INTO WEEKS. Miriam cared for Ann, the children and baby, cooked, cleaned, shopped, and mended clothing. Jacob fished with Timothy and Jonas, and Jerome went on other trips, limiting them to north of Capernaum closer to Chroazin and Bethsaida. This territory would be profitable for Ziph's possibilities and to his delight, it was paying off.

"I'm only happy that you and Ziph are working closer to home," Ann sighed in relief while holding her infant to her breast and staring at Jerome. "You traveling in the wilderness along the Jordan is scares me. The threat of robbers and murderers is real."

Working the routes closer to home, Jerome visited more often with his nephews on the beach, having to use the road that ran along the shore to get home. It worked out well because he would tether Ziph in brush, gossip about his travels with the men and lend a hand to help the men unload their boat in trade for fish.

After one such day, packing several fish in his sack, he called out, "I'm going home." Jacob broke away from the crew and went after Jerome. "I need to talk to you. Can you sit for a moment?"

The men walked across the beach and settled each on two large, smooth boulders. Jerome could see that Jacob was nervous, so he bided his time until the younger man collected himself to speak.

"I want Miriam for my wife, Jerome. She's unlike any of the women I've known. My parents tried to marry me off to women I had no interest in, and you know I've had my share of females, but Miriam is different. I've fallen in love with her and I want to be married soon. I've talked it over with my parents, and though they've not met her—yet, they believe she must be worthy if she's living in your household."

"Usually, Jacob, the father of the groom meets the father of the bride to arrange a contract and agree to a dowry, but this of course, is different."

"I've told them a little about her; some details they don't need to know about. They do know she's a widow, had children, and is without family, and that you and Ann took her in to help with the household. Personally, I think they want to marry me off and gain a woman to help my mother with the house."

"You don't want her to become a house slave, Jacob. You see the wonderful marriage that Timothy and Elizabeth have. My marriage is wonderful too, and although both sets of parents chose our wives, we grew to love them as they grew to love us. You have the advantage that you and Miriam have been attracted to each other from the start. I could tell from the day I met her she had eyes for you. Don't neglect that first love.

"I'll tell Miriam your intentions. Extend my agreement of your betrothal to your parents. I'll offer a pair of goats to them, and we can make arrangements for a ceremony that works for both families." Jerome was truly delighted for both of them. He knew Ann would be sad to lose Miriam, but she would be gaining a niece. Miriam would go to live with Jacob in his father's house, but both although Jacob's parents were good natured, long suffering, they were now quite elderly. The addition of Miriam to the family would be a blessing.

When Jerome and Ann told her the news, Miriam nodded her head and softly said that she was agreeable to the match.

Ann cried in sorrow but also in happiness.

The ceremony wasn't extravagant, but the guests were well-fed, and there was plenty of wine, especially for Jonas. As for Miriam's wedding finery and jewelry, all the women, including Jacob's mother, contributed.

"Finally, Jacob is married! And what a lovely bride! I hear she is a widow who lost two babies as well. Such a blessing they both found each other, I hope dear Ann won't be too lonely; she does have three rambunctious children. Oh, the new couple will be living close by: they will see each other often. I hope they have children soon. Did you hear how delighted Jacob's mother is? Usually the mother-in-law complains immediately about the new bride . . . this food is delicious!" and on, and on went the comments from the women.

The men gossiped too. "She's quite pretty and young. Did you hear about the other women Jacob's parents tried to marry him to? He was wise to wait. She's a prize. Ah, but she's a widow without property or possessions. She didn't bring anything to the marriage. Oh, I heard Jerome gave Jacob's parents a pair of goats, one being the progeny of Ziph. Oh, that's good news! They will have quite a nice herd before long. Ah! You think that Jacob will quit fishing to become a herder!"

"Where's Caleb?" Miriam looked over Jacob's shoulder.

"He's over there pocketing sweets! Some things never change."

"I'm so happy you found him, Jacob. I was so distressed to leave him when I discovered my old friends dead and thought I'd never see him again! Caleb was a much-needed friend during my days on the streets." She touched her husband's sleeve. "Jacob? I have an idea. The goats that Jerome gave your father?"

"Miriam, I am not becoming a goat herder. Never!"

"I know, but what if we got Caleb to care for them? He's so clever, he can do anything. He could tend to your father's goats, increase and sell, and benefit the family. There's plenty of room in the manger and its better than sleeping in a vendor's stall. What do you think?"

Jacob smiled at his bride. "It's a great idea. Let me talk to my father."

CHAPTER SEVENTEEN

JACOB AND MIRIAM OFTEN VISITED Jerome and Ann, along with Timothy's family. The men would bring fish, the women bread and other provisions, and they would cook up a hearty meal for a communal supper. Caleb and Jonas always tagged along too. Months went by, and on one evening, they gathered for not only supper but anticipated news from Jerome who had just returned from villages near Bethsaida.

"Tell us the news," Jacob implored, grabbing another slab of buttered bread.

Jerome visibly brightened. He enjoyed telling everyone the latest news. "Now, mind you this is just what I heard. I didn't see or hear it for myself because this happened in the River Jordan, but several months ago, a man came from Galilee to find John and be baptized by him. When the man came up to him and told John to baptize him, John was surprised, and said to the man, 'I need to be baptized by you, so why are you coming to me?'"

"John the Baptist thought himself unworthy to baptize this man," Miriam said barely audible.

"I don't get it," complained Jacob.

Jerome said, "When John questioned the need for the man to be baptized, the man said something like, 'It must be done because we must do everything that's right.'"

"I still don't understand what he meant." Jacob shook his head.

"Nor do I, friends," Jerome admitted.

Miriam became breathless. Her heart raced. "Wait, everyone! This must be the man John was talking about to begin with. 'Make way for the Lord'!"

They all jabbered excitedly. Could it be so soon they would be freed from Roman tyranny and turncoat Jews? Could this be the Messiah they had been waiting for? Was there going to be a revolution?

"This is the part that's truly astounding," Jerome continued breaking into their digression. "John baptized him and when he came up out of the water, a dove fluttered down. Those who witnessed this, reported that a voice actually spoke from the heavens and said, 'This is my son whom I love.'"

His listeners were dumbfounded. How could this be? Who was the voice from heaven? God? What did the voice mean, 'my son'? Were they really living in a time where they and their children would see change, hope, and peace for the Jewish people?

"The man that John baptized has been in Nazareth, to Bethany-across-the Jordan, to the Judean desert, to Bethsaida, to villages and towns of Galilee. In all those towns, he's been teaching, preaching, and performing miracles and now I hear he is on his way to Capernaum!" Jerome said excitedly.

"Miracles?" Jacob looked around at the others. "Miracles?"

But Miriam was thinking, *he's coming here?*

Jerome couldn't add any more detail to the miracles, just generalities. "This is hearsay, but he's been healing sick people, casting out demons, and even giving sight back to the blind!"

"Sight back to the blind! That's impossible!" argued Jacob. "I can see people faking being sick, or faking having a demon, and a charlatan in on the scam comes along and performs a miracle, but you can't fake receiving sight if you are blind."

Jacob sunk back against the cushions confused and questioning, but Timothy shouted out in enthusiasm. "You are right, Miriam! That man has to be the one John was speaking about when he preached to people to make way for the Lord!"

"Do you know anything more about this man?" Jacob demanded.

"I don't know where the man was born, but he comes from a very humble background, I was told." Jerome nodded. "He's a carpenter by trade, and has a mother, some brothers and sisters. He hangs around with fishermen too. He's friendly with what we would call low-life.

"Fishermen aren't low life!" retorted Timothy, indignant. Jerome held up a hand. "I mean, you know, tax collectors, prostitutes, those kinds he's friendly with. His close friends are fishermen."

"Then how can he be a miracle worker with friends like that? And he's a carpenter? Come on. This is all crazy talk!" Jacob stomped away to get more food. Over his shoulder he called, "I was hoping for royalty, or a warrior, or someone with some authority and might!"

Miriam trembled. She didn't quite understand the baptism thing either, but her focus was the voice from heaven that said, 'This is my son whom I love'. Was God referring to the man as *son*?

"Did anyone tell you his name?" Miriam asked.

"They said his name is Jesus."

CHAPTER EIGHTEEN

JACOB WASN'T TO BE DISTRACTED over the talk about this man named Jesus, so he avoided the eager conversations about him from Miriam. It was difficult, because she was so enthralled with a man they truly knew little about, other than from gossip. There were other things she should be concentrating on and it didn't help him that his other friends were just as intent upon the discussion. He had other things to be excited about.

Jacob kissed Miriam. "I'll see when I get back, not sure yet."

Miriam smiled and watched him pick up his food and gear to walk the well-worn path towards the beach. He carried a skin of water over his shoulder, a loaf of bread, and dried meat in a sack.

At the top of the hill he met up with a sleepy-eyed Timothy. "Timothy," Jacob called. "I've got great news," he puffed, running up the sandy slope. "Miriam's pregnant, praise God!"

Timothy stopped and waited for his cousin. "Congratulations, Jacob. That didn't take long, I bet your parents are relieved . . . I mean delighted."

"Delighted? They're ecstatic! I've done two things they are proud about, well maybe three. One, I earn a living fishing. Two, I married Miriam, and three, they are going to be grandparents. Finally!"

"Now you're going to have to work harder. You'll have another mouth to feed including Caleb who might as well be your son than servant," chuckled Timothy.

Descending the rise to the beach, both men surveyed the lineup of boats, taking in the busy work of the fishermen preparing to shove off, as they arranged their nets, coiled their lines, and hoisted up mainsails. Curiously, they saw only Zebedee sitting in his boat midships, alone, without his sons, mending nets.

Both men walked across the beach to the shallows where the boat was anchored, facing into the wind. Timothy called, "Zebedee! Where are John and James?"

Looking up from his net, he flicked a hand towards Capernaum. "They went off with a man who wanted to speak with them; they met him awhile back near Bethany-across-the-Jordan. I thought they might be coming back, but they said they would speak with me later. They seemed very excited. I let them take the day off. They worked a long day yesterday and had a great haul. Tore some nets, so I'm repairing them. The boys needed a break."

"We all need breaks, Zebedee, but can't afford to take them no matter how good the haul the day before. It must be something you're very agreeable with," Timothy retorted suspiciously.

Before the man could respond, Jacob interrupted. "Simon and Andrew are gone too?" He pointed to their empty boat in the shallows. Simon and Andrew were from the city of Bethsaida, across the lake but not far from Capernaum. They worked all sides of the sea and sometimes dropped anchor here.

"Yep," the old man nodded.

He turned to Timothy, "That's strange. They wouldn't miss a day of fishing. Where would they go?"

Zebedee answered, "With the same man. Name of Jesus. They all met him at Bethany-across-the-Jordan when they were fishing there. You've heard of him, haven't you?" He stopped his darning and looked closely at both men.

Jacob answered, "Yes, we have. We've heard he's a carpenter, but someone of possible importance. You know of John the Baptist?"

"Indeed. He baptized this man Jesus. I heard that John saw Jesus coming toward him and said something like, 'Look, the Lamb of God, who takes away the sin of the world!' I'm not sure what this means, but this Jesus? I want my sons to find out more about him."

"We think Jesus is the man John the Baptist was talking about, when he said 'prepare the way for the Lord.'"

Zebedee put down his darning needle, crawled over the stern, and jumped in the water. Sloshing closer to Jacob and Timothy he said, "I think so too. I've heard stories about the miracles he's been performing in Judea and Galilee. My boys have told me about his teaching. It's amazing." Nearly whispering he stated, "I think he's the Messiah! The Sabbath is tomorrow. I suggest you go to the synagogue and see for yourselves. Jesus will be there."

They left Zebedee climbing back over the gunnels of his boat and they continued to the far end of the beach. Throwing his gear on board, Timothy said, "This is our opportunity to see this man Jesus for ourselves."

Jacob looked out over the sea with mixed emotions. He couldn't quite understand his own reticence over Jesus. Miriam couldn't stop talking about him and conjecturing all sorts of wild ideas.

"This must be the Messiah!" she argued. "Who else could possibly do all the things people are saying he's doing? He's come to liberate us!"

Jacob would respond, "You know how people exaggerate! And if he's just a carpenter, how can he possibly lead people in rebellion against the Romans and the Jewish leaders? He'll be slaughtered by either group. Does he even have a following other than the poor, ignorant people that claim he can perform miracles? Does he have an army?"

Miriam would grow quiet and not reply, but he knew her well enough his arguments didn't sway her belief that this man was of God and certainly, the one she's been looking for.

CHAPTER NINETEEN

MIRIAM, OVERJOYED AT THE PROSPECT of seeing and hearing Jesus, followed Jacob along the cobbled street with Ann and Jerome, Timothy and Elizabeth, and Jonas, who were talking and arguing about Jesus. Caleb tagged behind. All the children were with Jacob's parents although elderly, they still enjoyed little ones, but a walk to the synagogue was too much for them.

Miriam fell back to Caleb who was walking alone. "What are you thinking, Caleb?"

Caleb shrugged his shoulders and wagged his head. "My heart is telling me that this man could be the one, but my brain is telling, how can this be? He's no better than any us. He's just a carpenter!" He picked up a broken cup, looked at it, and seeing that it was of no use, he threw it in the weeds.

"But, Caleb—he performs miracles. He can't possibly be any ordinary man!"

"Miriam, I don't know. Let's just see what happens. I think of the man who turned water into wine awhile back. I believed the stories because too many people repeated it. So could this be the same man?"

"Yes, I'm thinking he could have been the one we're going to see . . ." The grounds of the synagogue were crowded, and the plaza brought back some happy yet some disturbing memories for Miriam as she surveyed the area she once called home.

Caleb nudged her as the party passed the spot where she and her old friends begged and the archway where they died. "Our lives have certainly, changed, eh, Miriam?"

"They certainly have. I'd never have dreamed I'd be a visitor to the same area, walking with a husband and friends. And to be pregnant!"

She took in the chaos around them. Beggars, the sick, crippled, healthy, wealthy, and poor and all ages were eager to see this man named Jesus. The crowd surged, ebbed, and flowed like a human tide.

From where they were, she could see the entryway to the court of prayer for men. On the other side of the complex was the court for the women, but in one court, men and women could be together to hear teaching and preaching. This was where Jesus was going to be, reaching out to men and women together.

Miriam took hold of Caleb's sleeve. "Don't let the rest of them know that this is where I used to beg. It's so . . . so . . . "

"Depressing," Caleb finished for her. "Don't worry. I don't want to remember the street corner I used to sell brooms on either!" They quickly left the area and hustled up to where her husband and friends stopped, who were taking in the sights, sounds, smells, and the incessant talk about Jesus.

Miriam spoke aloud what everyone was thinking. "All these people milling around, and they're all talking about Jesus! I've never heard such excitement and hope."

"It's amazing to me, too, that so many people want hear a man who isn't a rabbi or teacher of the law," With a tilt of his head, Jerome indicated the masses of people, enthusiastically talking.

Jacob agreed. "How can a man who hasn't been trained by the teachers of the law command so much attention? I've never seen so many sick people milling around. Miriam, keep a distance from them. You don't want to catch anything."

One man walked by their group arguing with the people he was with. "I've seen it with my own eyes! He's healed the sick and given sight to the blind! I was there and I'm not lying! He even touches lepers!"

The response from one in his group countered, "Well, we'll see this for ourselves, if this is true or just blather. Who in their right mind would touch a leper?"

It was beyond so many people's comprehension that a human being could perform these wonders but touch a leper? That was unheard of.

"He has no problem reaching out to the sickest of the sick and the poorest of the poor," Caleb said to Miriam, hearing the man talk. He, too, was astonished at the level of Jesus' compassion.

"A Pharisee or priest would never touch a leper," Miriam added. "Never. The leaders and elders of the church are strict with ritual, ceremonies, and the law."

"I can appreciate that," Jacob was defensive. "They have to work within Moses' law. They can't have unclean people pawing at them, defiling them, looking for help."

"Forget the law," Caleb scoffed. "Our religious leaders care little for the poor and sick. They teach and believe their diseases and deformities are brought on by sin, even sin as far back as their grandparents!"

Miriam gazed at her husband. "The teachers of the law and the priests are more intent on emphasizing their elevated learned positions than giving thoughtful instruction or even help. They thrive on their power of intimidation and self-righteousness."

Jerome could only agree. "I believe they show little mercy to those who really need it because they don't understand the poor and needy."

"Because their main concern, aside from their reputation and social status, are tithes, sacrifices, and making sure all of us Jews follow The Law regardless of the circumstance!" Caleb complained.

"I think we should keep our voices down," Jacob advised noting some people were casting them disapproving glances.

Quieting down, they followed the crowd to the communal courtyard, and when they got there, it was already populated with scores of people. Many sat on the ground, some on top of the walls, but the Pharisees and Sadducees sat on stools and benches in the best spots to hear the one they were already prepared to condemn.

Caleb nudged Miriam. "Look at those men whispering to one another. They're too frightened to speak out loud."

"They have the sense to keep their mouths shut or be attacked by the mob." She acknowledged. People stood or sat with hurt or sick companions and the lame and blind, all hoping to catch the attention of Jesus were lying or sitting on the periphery of the crowd. Altogether they were waiting impatiently for Jesus to enter the courtyard and climb the steps to the archway to teach and to heal.

And it was so that the healthy and wealthy were looking for entertainment that they might see him perform a miracle or two and the Pharisees, leaders, and teachers of the law wanted to know what they were up against. This man Jesus was stirring the crowd in a most dangerous way, threatening their authority, position, and possibly creating concern and anger from their Roman rulers, if they, the Jewish leaders could not keep their people in control.

An excited murmur passed through the crowds as people craned their necks to see a small contingency of men entering the courtyard. "Jesus is coming, Jesus is coming!"

CHAPTER TWENTY

IF IT SEEMED POSSIBLE, SEVERAL moments of absolute stillness and quiet enveloped the unruly crowd. A medium-statured man, neither handsome nor ugly, fat nor thin, entered the courtyard with an equally unremarkable small group of men. His robes were shabby and non-descript, his beard cropped in Jewish tradition, and his dark hair was on the unkempt side. On his feet were well-worn sandals repaired with bits of string. He stopped at the edge of the courtyard and calmly looked around. Every eye was on him and all emotion was quelled until he moved. Then the crowd went wild, calling and crying, praising and beseeching.

Jesus held up his hands and moved with difficulty through the tightly packed people as the poor and desperate called out to him trying to touch him. Hands reached up to grasp his robe or touch the hem of his cloak.

Many wept, many shouted, "Jesus! Jesus! Please help me!" The cacophony of pleas melded into a roar of "Jesus, my son is sick! I can't walk! My husband is crippled! My child has a demon!" The sound was deafening.

As he walked, he lightly rested his hand on the tops of people's heads or lightly touched their shoulders. Quietly he acknowledged them with compassion and blessings. The men following him, formed a tight barrier protecting him, because the people tried to get up and close in on him.

"Stand back! Stand back! Let the teacher pass!" his men shouted and the crowd, unbelievably obeyed.

The Pharisees and religious leaders eyed the crowd with squinted eyes and pursed lips. Occasionally one would lean into another and make a remark resulting in a waspish response, or sarcastic laughter. Their behavior was not lost on the crowd, or Jesus' followers.

Miriam poked Jacob. "Do you see how those grown men are behaving? They're acting like spoiled jealous children!"

Jacob kept quiet until he recognized the men surrounding Jesus. "Look," he pointed. "That's Simon, Andrew, James, and John." They all watched the tight procession of men wind their way toward the platform under the archway.

"They must be joining Jesus in his mission," Jonas stated. "It's got to be pretty serious for them to leave fishing."

"Who said they did?" argued Jacob. "Zebedee never said his sons were leaving fishing."

"I might be jumping to conclusions, but if they don't return to their boats tomorrow it's a fair bet they are following the man. And if they do, this is something to take note of. They wouldn't leave their livelihoods on a whim."

"I wonder what their father would think if they left fishing . . . " Jacob looked to Jonas who merely shrugged his shoulders.

Weaving his way around people sitting on the ground, Jesus ascended the steps and raised his hands in greeting to the Pharisees and to the crowd. A respectful hush fell over the eager listeners.

Jesus lifted his voice loudly, "The kingdom of God has come near."

All were soon amazed at his teaching because he taught with an unusual insightful and powerful authority, nothing like the teachers of the law and unlike the teachers of the law; Jesus held the rapt attention of listeners.

Miriam spied the Pharisees and Sadducees continually whispering and angrily gesturing among themselves while shooting hateful looks at Jesus, who kept on speaking; his audience enamored with each word that fell from his lips.

"Hey! Watch what you're doing!"

A commotion came from behind Miriam, and before a woman was thrown against Miriam, Jacob grabbed the woman by her robe and pushed her back into the path of an agitated man shouldering his way through the crowd. She angrily yelped, but the man plowed against her, stepping and climbing over people on the ground and squeezing and pushing people standing. Many times he was indignantly shoved and pushed, but he still kept on his feet steadfastly moving forward.

Jesus' men reacted too slowly to protect him.

The man crouched down like a dog in attack mode confronting Jesus shouting, "What do you want with us, Jesus of Nazareth? Have you come to destroy us? I know who you are—the Holy One of God!"

Jesus held his hands up to his men to back off. Frightened, the crowd buzzed, "That man is demon possessed. He called Jesus the Holy One of God! What will Jesus do?"

"Come out of him!" Jesus demanded. The man jerked violently, screamed, then fell to the ground convulsing. The crowd, not prepared for the rapid drama that just played out before them, murmured in astonishment. A communal gasp filled the air and the bewildered man staggered to his feet, dazed. The Pharisees and Sadducees jumped up in fury.

A baffled scribe stared at Jesus then at his colleagues. "What is this? He can command demons?"

"A demon calls him the Holy One of God? It's blasphemous!"

A Pharisee pointed a shaking finger at Jesus. "What do you think you are doing?"

Another bellowed, "Who gave you the authority?"

Everyone was babbling and mumbling with each other about the power of Jesus banishing a demon, the teachers of the law were sputtering disbelief, and the man who had been demon possessed stood crying unintelligibly in a stunned state of confusion.

Miriam clapped her hand over her mouth equally incredulous. "Jacob! Did you see that?

Jesus expelled a demon from a man before all of these a witnesses including the teachers and leaders of the Jews!"

Jacob looked on the confused scene. "Hush up! Don't draw attention to yourself! Of course, I saw it! But why aren't our leaders doing anything? Why aren't they awe-struck too? Why aren't they praising him?"

"Surely they saw what happened!" Caleb hissed. "Jesus is far more powerful than any of those men sitting in their so-called high places."

"See how angry they are!"

"He has authority over demons!" People kept repeating as they looked to one another with enthusiasm and exhilaration. Over and over it was repeated. Many looked onto the scene still dumfounded, others looked to Jesus, who stood quietly, and still others watched and internalized the reactions of the religious leaders. Clearly, their leaders were not impressed. In fact, they were openly antagonistic.

Unexpectedly, Miriam felt a sense of urgency rippling through the crowd: a possible riot of people wanting to touch, plead, or cry to Jesus.

"Please, heal me! Please make my son well! I want to see! I can't walk!" Repeatedly the people, desperate, begged Jesus to help them.

The crowd surged forward with the sick and lame while indignant anger and fright animated the faces of the teachers of the law. Speaking rapidly with each other and making sweeping motions with their hands and staffs they stood to push the people back.

"Will they call the temple guards, Jacob?" Miriam held her husband's arm seeing that this could get ugly.

"It would certainly put an end to people trying to get to Jesus!" He watched as men and women stood up, elbowing their way closer to get a better look at the man Jesus healed.

Someone grabbed the man's arm and quickly led him away in a dumfounded, yet grateful daze. The man's docile behavior only served to create more commotion as more people sought to reach Jesus.

The four men and Jesus were now on the move from the archway. Clearing their way through the throng, they hastened through the courtyard and disappeared into the swell of people in the plaza.

"Where did he go?" the people asked one another and began pushing and shoving to find and follow him.

Jesus was gone.

CHAPTER TWENTY-ONE

WORMING THEIR WAY THROUGH MASS of men and women, Miriam clutched Jacob's hand. "I believe he could be the Messiah! You heard how he spoke. He's come from nowhere—a carpenter teaching about the kingdom of God! We've heard rumors of his miracles and now we've seen with our own eyes his power. Commanding a demon to be gone!

"And think about this: Look how big this courtyard is," she swept her arm toward the back of the expanse. "Yet everyone could hear him clearly. He was not shouting or speaking loudly as speakers often do. How remarkable that in this multitude everyone heard each word!"

Now that Jesus was gone, the people began clearing out of the square. Miriam and her friends cautiously moved to leave, watching and listening to the those who were milling about or hastily passing to find out where Jesus had gone to.

Caleb tilted his head. "The Pharisees and Sadducees are pretty heated. Look at them glowering and grumbling. They hear the people praising Jesus and wondering aloud if he's the Messiah."

Miriam kept her eyes on the Pharisees. "How could they not wonder along with everyone else? They saw the miracle for themselves, and they heard every word that came out of his mouth. He's far more knowledgeable and gracious than any of them."

Outside on the grounds of the synagogue, away from the teachers of the law, the question intensified by all who witnessed the miracle of the banished demon. "Could he really be the Messiah?" was on everyone's lips.

"Jesus touched me! Look, my sores are gone!" A woman shouted. Jacob took hold of Miriam's arm and pointed as a woman fell to her knees amid the crowd and held her hands up high, crying, "He touched me! I'm clean!" Her robe fell away from her arms showing clean, healthy skin.

At the same moment, a man tossed a walking stick in the air and caught it. "Look! I walk!" He pranced a few steps and twirled as several folks stopped and gaped at him, praising Jesus loudly.

Many were witnessing to anyone within earshot about their healing from the light touches of Jesus on their heads, or on their shoulders as he walked by them.

Miriam and friends were astonished by another story: "I was deaf and dumb! He put his fingers in my ears and on my lips, and I now I can hear and speak," one toothless beggar shouted as his friend said, "Yes, this is true!"

People desperately looked for where Jesus might have gone. A word went through the crowd that Jesus was going to the home of one of his disciples, but it wasn't known who this man was or where his home might be. Regardless, some in the crowd were encouraged.

"He's not leaving. Come, let's find him," two lame beggars said to one another and stumbled after a group of people who thought they knew where Jesus had gone.

Miriam wanted to follow them. Sometimes she wished she was not married, but free to come and go like when she was a beggar herself. Hastily she put that thought out of her mind. She was blessed! Guarding her heart, she quietly followed Jacob and their friends, listening attentively to snippets of conversation from passersby hoping to hear where Jesus might have gone.

Jerome, Caleb, and Jonas were paying attention to Timothy who was holding up a finger making a point. "I now understand why Zebedee let his boys go with Jesus and why Simon and Andrew followed him too."

"I can guess, but let's hear your words." Jerome lightly patted Timothy's shoulder.

"Well, just recently, Jacob and I had been talking with the rest of the fishermen down on the beach about the political situation in Galilee and Judea. Zebedee's boys and Simon and Andrew? They talked the loudest about the conditions of the poor and how the teachers of the law are doing little to help any of them or any of us for that matter."

Jerome stroked his beard. "I can't argue that. The teachers of the law lay heavy burdens on the Jewish people and do little to help them. They have many concerns, sure, but those concerns are for themselves and the synagogues. Tithes, donations, offerings, are all so willingly accepted, but they do little to ease the burden of the people."

"They are blind guides," piped up Caleb, giving a nod to Miriam.

"Like all of us, Zebedee's boys are looking for a leader. Someone who'll get us out from under Roman rule and to tame our Jewish leaders. With all this talk about John the Baptist and this man Jesus coming on the scene, everyone believes that maybe this man is the one. Maybe this man is from God to free us from tyranny . . ."

A motley group of men hurried alongside the friends. Miriam recognized one of the men who used to beg near Caleb's corner when he was selling palm brooms. The man was a hustler, but in fairness, he had some sort of disease that caused his stomach to distend and his legs, ankles, and feet to swell up. He could get about, but he was slow moving. He and Caleb had become friends sharing what little they could glean from the travelers jostling about Capernaum. Today, however, he was moving quickly and boldly squeezing through the crowds.

"Zach, Zach!" called Caleb and fell in step with the man. "Where are you going?"

The man stopped, took in some deep breaths, and wiped his brow with a soiled cloth. "I heard Jesus is going to some small village outside of Capernaum."

Miriam came up alongside of Caleb and Zach. "Do you know where?"

"Not sure, but Jesus and his men came out to this intersection and I was hoping to catch up to those who seemed to know where he was going."

"I don't think he went in this direction. The next village is ours, and I don't know of anyone who is one of his disciples that live there," Caleb said with sureness.

"I'll take your word for it. I'll try this way then." The man tapped his staff. "Why don't you come with me, Caleb? We can help each other if we get into trouble and if we find Jesus, I'll be healed!" The man's eyes twinkled in hope.

Caleb's eyes lit up. "Jacob!" Caleb called. Jacob fell back with Miriam and Caleb.

"What? What's going on?" He looked critically at Zach.

Caleb grabbed his arm. "Jacob, this is my friend Zach. He's going to find Jesus. We believe he's in some village down the road."

"Do you know how many villages are that way?" Jacob pointing down the road. He looked down at Zach's feet. "And I don't think you'll get very far, my friend, in your condition. It's going to take several hours just to get to the next village."

Miriam asked, "Jacob, can Caleb go look for Jesus with his friend? He can help Zach, if he gets into trouble."

She sorely wanted Caleb to find Jesus. Upon Caleb's return, he would then be able to tell her where Jesus would be or where he was going. She couldn't let this man, their possible Messiah, slip through her hands. She wanted a connection to Jesus. Her very soul was stirred.

"No. I need Caleb to help with the goats tonight. But listen, if you want to combine two trips with one, I'm good with it. I've got to sell off some of our does. The flock is expanding and we're at a point where we can start selling, so if you can get Jonas to cover for you, you can take time off, but not tonight. If you still want to track down Jesus, who will probably be gone somewhere else by then, and sell three of our does, I'm okay with it, but only if Jonas agrees to cover for you."

Miriam was as disappointed as Caleb. She wanted him to go now.

Caleb put his hands on the ragged man's shoulders. "I guess that says it all, my friend. Maybe I'll see you along the way. Get going while you still have some light. I'll keep an eye out for you if I can get away tomorrow. God speed."

Forlorn, Miriam watched Zach hobble away and when she turned back to speak with Caleb, he was already chatting with Jonas.

CHAPTER TWENTY-TWO

ESTHER, PERCHING ON A LARGE rock, looked down upon the scene below and strained to hear what a fellow leper was saying to a man surrounded by a group of burly, strong men. They were on the road from Capernaum.

The man's friends were obviously alarmed about themselves and their friend being so close to a leper, "Jesus, the man has leprosy!" one of the men warned, nearly hysterical with fear. Jesus showed little concern paying no attention to his friends repeated warnings.

The man pleaded with outstretched arms, "If you are willing, you can make me clean." Jesus stepped closer to the trembling bundle of rags.

Esther held her breath. This was exactly what she was hoping for . . . except for herself! But she couldn't begrudge another leper's healing. The disease was tortuous and terminal.

Jesus reached out his hand and touched the man. He fingers drifted across leprous skin. The men who had already stepped back from Jesus and the leper, shrank back in horror.

"I am willing," he said.

"Be clean!"

Immediately the leprosy left the man and he was cleansed. Jesus' followers gasped in shock, their hands flying to their mouths.

Esther stealthy scrambled closer toward the group as the leper on the road cried out in elation, looking at his hands, feeling his face, "I'm clean!"

In awe he looked down and wriggled his renewed toes. He whipped of his hood and cloak and twirled around, "Clean! clean!"

Esther fell back on her haunches. It was true. The rumors were right. This man could perform miracles! He could cure leprosy!

"See that you don't tell this to anyone. But go, show yourself to the priest and offer the sacrifices that Moses commanded for your cleansing, as a testimony to them," Jesus admonished the deliriously happy man.

In awe, her eyes on the scene below, she watched as the man skipped away. *This is a miracle of colossal proportions, but why didn't Jesus want the man to tell anyone about it? Why? More importantly, how can I present myself to Jesus? I'm so weak, now. I can barely walk without stopping for rest.*

She surveyed the narrow deer run winding its way down to the road from where she was hidden. *Can I make my way down this hill in time to catch him before he walks away? I've got to try.*

Carefully, Esther moved forward toward the rocky, dangerous slope. *I can do this.*

She had been waiting to find the man and beg for cleanliness, but she only had one way of doing this. It meant she would have to take her chances in finding Jesus by waiting daily along the road to Capernaum, hiding in the bushes high above travelers who would have only fear and hatred for a leper. Her plan was to reach out to Jesus as he traveled either to or from the city. After all her planning, she was usurped by another leper with the same intent who also had been hiding and waiting too, only closer to the road, but she wasn't giving up.

Only a few days ago, a kind and generous man who regularly brought food to the leper colony excitedly told the people of a man named Jesus who performed miracles in Galilee and in Capernaum. Miracles to the degree of even commanding a demon out of a possessed man!

"Maybe he can cure leprosy?" one of the lepers asked listlessly, not believing anyone could cure the disease. Some in the colony thought about it, others did not. In the end, they were too afraid, or sick to leave.

"Besides," someone asked. "How would we ever find him?"

Now, her heart nearly burst with joy in her diseased and sunken chest after witnessing this miracle. *It was true! This was the man of miracles!*

Slowly, awkwardly, Esther slid downward. Before she could make it to the road, the men had hastened Jesus away. Her diseased mouth couldn't form the words to shout his name! *No!*

Tears leaked from damaged tear ducts, dripping down wasted cheeks. *I'm not giving up!*

Getting down to the road, she followed at such a slow pace that she fell far behind but saw Jesus and his friends enter a small village yet dared not enter. Looking for a place to hide, but still able to see the road, Esther spotted a good clump of dense brush.

Several hours later, she finished constructing a small shelter within sight of the road that meandered through the settlement. She didn't know which house Jesus went into, but if Jesus were to leave, he would likely leave the way he came, since there was only one major way in.

At least I think so. I hope so! If I can see him leaving, I have a chance to be healed. Digging into her satchel, Esther pulled out a piece of crust. Hugging bread to her chest, and water skin over her shoulder, she was prepared to wait.

She woke the following morning hearing crowds of people walking along the road, looking for Jesus. Some were sick, carried in litters by friends or family. Lame men, women, and children hobbled along as well as the blind who held the hands of compassionate relatives.

Esther stood well off the road watching the ratty procession of wearied humanity. In great disappointment, she knew that she couldn't mingle with the hopeful looking for a touch from Jesus. Even they would chase her away.

"They're looking everywhere for Jesus." A voice came from behind. Startled, Esther turned to see a young man smelling strongly of goats standing close saying, "One of your friends, a fellow leper has been telling everybody in the city and in the synagogue about Jesus who healed him. Now the sick masses are out to find him."

Esther tried to speak as the young man stepped closer. She desperately needed to share her deep disappointment, even though her tongue was damaged. All she could utter was, "me . . . too."

The young man stepped closer to her, looking into her eyes as if to determine if she was male or female, but she quickly held up her hand in warning not to come any closer.

"It's okay," the young man said taking a step back. "I just want to know who you are. Maybe I can help you get close to Jesus because I do too. I'm Caleb."

He invited her to squat down on the ground and sit near him. He pulled a chunk of soft goat cheese out of his tunic and passed it to Esther, who took it eagerly, making sure she didn't touch Caleb's outstretched hand.

She pointed to her chest, "Esther."

"Are you from a leper colony?"

Esther nodded.

Caleb was silent for a moment then asked, "Is it the one outside Capernaum?"

Again, she nodded.

A sense of excitement seemed to course through him. "Do you know a woman named Miriam who had been attacked, then cared for by a leper?"

Caleb stared at Esther as she sat across from him, nearly holding his breath as he waited for her response.

Slowly, she nodded her head and pointed to her thin chest. "Yes. Me."

CHAPTER TWENTY-THREE

CALEB WAS BURSTING WITH DELIGHT. He couldn't wait to tell Miriam and see her reaction, but ultimately, the question was, how could he help this young woman? His personal plan to see Jesus had changed. It was more important now to get this young woman healed.

Jacob and Miriam would know what to do. They could devise a plan to get Esther before Jesus. He healed one leper, he certainly could heal another.

"Esther, look. You can take your chances on the side of the road and hope to get before Jesus, but with all these crowds coming after him it's likely he might have to hide or get away from the mobs for a while. Let's do this. Go back to your community. Miriam knows where it is, and she and I will come get you. Let's make it three days from now, late morning, and we'll look for you outside of your camp. Is there a place we can meet? A land mark? We'll figure out a way to get you to see Jesus."

Esther nodded, but her damaged tongue garbled her words. Stopping, she held up her hand for time, then whispered, "Colony marked with sign. 'Beware. Unclean.' Near sign big rock with bushes. I'll hide . . . there." She pointed to her chest. "Wait for you."

Smiling, he reached out for her, but pulled back remembering her disease. "We will be back, I promise." He hustled away in excitement and great anticipation.

After he left, Esther sat quietly, dumbfounded. What were the chances that she would meet a servant of the woman she cared for, so long ago? *And that he was willing to help me!*

She barely breathed. Finally, she made her way back up the hill, through the brush and home to her colony to seek out the man who was like a father to her. When she arrived, her excitement dampened. She could see he was very ill and unable to speak. The caretakers made room for her by his pallet and left them alone.

"Seth, can you hear me?" The only sound from his blistered lips was the sound of air laboring to escape his damaged lungs. "Please hear me. Do you remember . . . " Esther told her story. Hoping for a reaction, there was none. He was in and out of consciousness and was unable to respond. Finally, the caretakers came back in and shooed her out.

Crying softly, she sought out a woman who was like an elder sister to. She told her story.

The woman drew back, horrified. "You can't go out of the colony like that! If anyone sees you, they'll stone you to death! They might even come after us for not keeping you under control!"

"Sister, listen! Jesus healed a leper! I saw it! . . . he could heal all! A chance of being made whole again! I come back . . . get you bring you to Jesus! Or here!"

"Speak no more of it!" the woman threatened and stood up pointing her ragged paw at her. "You are dreaming. No leper has ever been healed! You are desperate! Insane! The disease has eaten your brain! If you leave, our leaders will never let you come back here again for the danger you are putting everyone in."

Esther slunk away to her corner of the cave.

One man confronted her in front of the others. "You are crazy, a liar, or both! You are a danger to us. It was only by the tolerance of our Jewish leaders that we're allowed to stay here to begin with! If they found out a leper left this colony, it's possible they'd banish us even further from the city and then what would we do?"

Another crept towards here and whined, "Now our suppliers are able to get provision to us within a half-day's walk. If we move further away from the city, we would lose those people that are helping us! We would starve!"

Someone else in the gloom rattled, "We have water here. We can never leave this place. We would die of thirst. If you try to leave, we'll stop you!"

"Yes, indeed we will. We will not allow you to endanger us and the only place we can call home!"

Why were they so hostile. Here was an opportunity to be made well. She witnessed the miracle! She so wished her mentor was well enough to speak. He would guide her and convince the others that there is still hope!

She huddled in her dirty shawl and crept to the fire for a portion of supper, desperately thinking of when to escape. The women ignored her, and no one offered her even a tiny morsel. Saddened, she sat away from the group hoping someone would leave just a piece of bread. No one moved. Hurt, she painfully got up, took her bowl and hobbled to the spring that ran through the community grounds. Stooping, she filled it, took a sip of the cool water and felt it trickle down to her empty stomach. Could she live on water for the next days until Caleb and Miriam would come and get her?

Walking back by the dying fire, she saw they left her two pieces of bread. Carefully and gratefully, she chewed a corner with her loose teeth. Finding her spot in the dismal cave, she sat amid the others trying to sleep in their pain and discomfort. She thought about Jesus, his power, his compassion, and fearlessness.

She wanted badly to her go to the man that was like a father to her, he but was in the men's portion of the cave and she couldn't go there at night. *Are you dying dear friend? Will I ever get the chance to speak with you again? I need your advice. Would you say to me, "Go, find Jesus! And if you can, bring him back to us."*

Settling on her pallet, she made up her mind. She was going to meet Caleb and Miriam. If they were willing to take the risk, she would. The worst that could happen is that she would get stoned to death—by either her friends from the inside, or people from the outside. And she had to die sometime. She drifted off to a troubled sleep.

CHAPTER TWENTY-FOUR

CALEB TROTTED NEARLY ALL THE way back home, anticipating Miriam's delighted reaction when she heard about his discovery. Boundless happiness expanded with each step. The hours flew by and he only stopped for water and to stuff his mouth with bread and honey. With a burst of energy, he plowed into the back yard where he surprised Miriam preparing supper.

"Caleb, you're home and in time for supper. I expected you to be gone much longer." She wiped her hands on the towel around her waist and hugged him as he trotted over to her. "You're home so soon. Did you find Jesus?" She looked at him closely.

Jacob popped his head from the backdoor grinning, "If it's food, Caleb can smell it all the way in Capernaum!" He walked over to his young friend and hugged him too. "How did the sale of our goats go?"

"Good. Sold them all to the same man. He wants more when we have our next set of kids and they want Ziph's services too. I'll let Jerome know." He dug into his satchel and pulled out a pretty bowl he bought for Miriam, who squealed in delight.

Jacob joked, "I hope you got some money left!"

Caleb went back in his bag, "I do and cheese. The best in Capernaum." Along with the money, Caleb handed Jacob a wrapped-up hunk of well-aged cheese. Unable to contain himself, Caleb dragged over two stools. "Sit, down, sit down. I have something urgent to tell you."

"What? Something's wrong?" Jacob sat furrowing his brow and gave the cheese to Miriam after taking a bite. He pocketed the money. Miriam stopped stirring the pot over the fire, sat down, and indicated Caleb to begin.

His voice was trembling with excitement. He looked directly at Miriam. "I found your little leper."

Miriam's hand flew to her heart. "You did?"

"Her name is Esther!"

"My helper is a girl? How did you find her?" With great detail, he told them how he came about to meet her. Thrilled, she took her husband's hands. "We must get her to Jesus!" Jacob weakly protested. "But you're pregnant!

"So? I'm strong and able to travel."

"I don't know where we'll find Jesus," Jacob worried. "If throngs from the city are out to track him down, he's probably long gone from that village he went to and is likely out in the Galilean wilderness by now. And if people see us with a leper, they'll stone us!"

Miriam ignored his argument. "Jacob, send Caleb to Capernaum tomorrow to find out the gossip about Jesus and where people think he is, or Caleb, go back to that village he was last seen in and find out. Gossip travels fast."

"Gossip travels fast, but Caleb doesn't travel that fast. He said we'd meet Esther in three days."

"Friends," Caleb said. "We can get to the leper colony in one to two-days' time, depending on Miriam's condition. We can even camp out the night before if we get there early. We'll pack up provisions and load up a goat cart. Jesus can't be that far away in a handful of days, can he? I heard in Capernaum that he might even show up at the synagogue again."

"But what about Timothy? I can't just leave him to fish alone," Jacob continued to worry. "And what about us all being exposed to a leper? Who knows how you can catch the disease— and Miriam's pregnant! I don't want to risk it!"

Miriam put her hand out to Jacob. "Explain to Timothy how important this is. He can find others to help, and we'll ask Jonas to care for our goats and keep an eye on Mother and Father. We'll also let Jerome and Ann know that we are going to find Jesus for Esther. They'll pitch in to help."

"I heard my name!" It was Jerome, rounding the corner of the yard.

"What are you doing back?" Jacob asked getting up to greet him.

"I'm just passing by on my way home, to stop for some water for Ziph. We had a very successful trip."

Miriam rose and stuttered, "Jerome, we have news!"

Jerome sat in amazed silence taking in Caleb's astonishing story. "Listen, you don't have to go out into the wilderness to look for him. I just heard he's on his way back to Capernaum. I'm sure he'll be going to the synagogue."

"How do you know?" Jacob asked.

If anyone knew, Jerome would. He knew of all the coming and goings of things happening in Capernaum, the villages, as well as in the wilderness and as far as the Sea of Galilee.

"That's the word on the streets and I think it's fairly accurate. He should be there in a day or so and plans to stay awhile. He'll be teaching in the synagogue and other places no doubt throughout the city."

Caleb touched Jerome's sleeve. "I've got another session for Ziph," Caleb smiled, but before Jerome could ask for the details, the men were interrupted by Miriam.

"But how will we get Esther into the city, past the crowds, to see Jesus? They'll stone her before they let her in!"

Jerome sat quietly for a time, thinking. "I don't know what the answer is, Miriam. I truly don't, but at least you needn't go out to the wilderness looking for him." They sat around the fire for a while discussing possible plans.

After he left, Miriam prepared dinner for the men. They were all preoccupied with a way to get Esther into the city to see Jesus. Caleb had faith he could and would heal her, but getting her before him, through the crowds would be the problem.

Supper was a quiet affair

"Gossip is often wrong as it is right," Jacob said. "So where will he really be? Agreed, it's a relief we don't have to set out on a long journey into the wilderness somewhere, but we still must be at the right place at the right time—assuming he'll really be in Capernaum. Now, then, this is just as hard: how are we going to get through the masses of people with her?"

"We can't get her onto the synagogue grounds, that's sure. The teachers of the law and the people will stone us if we're with a leper." Caleb tore off a piece of bread and chewed it vigorously. "We better figure it out. She's counting on us!"

Miriam was quiet as she cleaned up after the evening meal. She tapped a pot with a spoon in frustration. "We must come up with an idea of how we can do this!"

Jacob shifted on his stool and ran a hand through his hair. "I have no ideas. This is impossible Miriam, like Caleb said, if we're discovered bringing a leper into the city, we are really looking for serious trouble." He threw a stick into the fire. "I don't know if I can go along with this. Hiding her, finding him, presenting her, hoping he'll heal her! It's all guesswork!"

Caleb shook his head. "I can't let Esther down. I told her we'd be there to get her to see Jesus . . . "

"As ingenious as you think you are, Caleb, even you don't have a clue about how this is all going to work!" Jacob complained. "Miriam, we have to think this through." Turning back to Caleb he placed a hand on his knee. "I know Caleb you don't want to let her down, but you don't want to get us all killed either!"

CHAPTER TWENTY-FIVE

NOT WILLING TO GIVE UP, Miriam grabbed Jacob's hand. "I have an idea. Caleb, listen to this." Caleb sat back down. "Esther's tiny. What if we put her in our goat cart and covered her over? No one will know she's in there. We can easily bring her into the city under the covers."

"Then what?" Jacob was doubtful. "I'm not sure how close we can get with a cart to see Jesus with all those people milling around also waiting and looking for him. He's got more than four disciples surrounding him and they're very protective. And if we did get close enough and she popped up, what if he didn't heal her? We'd all be killed!"

"Jacob," Miriam gently scolded. "Where is your faith? If he healed one, he'll heal more. That's what he's come to do. To help the poor, sick, and needy. The kingdom of God is near!"

Jacob raised his eyebrows in doubt, but Caleb smiled encouragingly and said. "Miriam's right, Jacob. He's done miracles. This is a great idea. Jesus is waiting for us, I just know!"

"You know I'm with you every step of the way, so I'll go along with this," Jacob answered with a trace of misgiving. "I'll let Timothy know what's going on and that I won't be fishing for a few days." He took a deep breath and let it out. "Ok. Let's do this. We'll get Esther, keep our ears to the ground to see where Jesus is, then plan from there."

That next day Miriam worked from the storeroom loading provisions, a mat, a blanket, and a canvass cover for the cart. Caleb got Jonas to care for the goats. Miriam prayed to God that all would be safe, and Esther would be healed, and wished that their other friends could join them, but this was best done with few people in the event their plan went wrong. They all could be killed.

The three left before daybreak the following day with Caleb's favorite strong white goat pulling the near empty cart along the road circling the city. Along the way, they stopped and rested with many other travelers who had wonderful stories about Jesus and were told he was probably going back to Capernaum to a home where he had been staying and he would be teaching on the Sabbath at the synagogue. The camped out that night and before the sun came up, they continued their journey.

Before midday the small party came to the area Esther said she would be waiting. It was on a scrubby knoll not too far from the leper colony, south of the city. The party stopped and pulled to the side of the road to allow the goat to nibble weeds and get a drink, watching travelers going toward Capernaum in small groups.

"See that sign?" Caleb pointed, Miriam and Jacob nodded and waited as he scanned the small, rocky hill. "Look! there! That must be the rock and bushes she said she would be hiding waiting for us."

A small figure emerged from behind a clump of low, dense bushes and hiked down the small hill as best she could without tripping, while the road was empty of travelers. Hesitantly, she lifted a hand in greeting to the group waiting for her.

Jacob held Miriam back from running to the girl; she wanted so desperately to hug her. Esther, fully covered except for her eyes, walked haltingly toward them, raised a shy hand again in greeting.

Miriam cried out, "Esther! Esther! I can't believe Caleb found you and that we're here together again! You've been deep in my heart and in my prayers. Have faith! We *will* see Jesus!"

Caleb indicated Esther step off the road and into the bushes where they hid the cart and goat. Esther tried to speak as they showed her where the cart was.

Esther listened as Miriam quickly explained, "We won't keep you cooped up long if we can't find him, but you must lie inside the cart and we'll cover you over. We're going to the city."

"Capernaum?" Esther was frightened.

"Yes, don't worry." Yet Miriam as well as Caleb and Jacob did worried, but the commitment to Esther was made. "See here, I have cushions for you. But first, take and eat some bread and drink some water. Caleb knows hiding places in the city where we can give you a break from the cart and keep you away from people and from being discovered."

Esther obeyed without speaking. She nodded, nibbled some bread, and took a small sip. Once in the cart, she obediently lay down. Caleb covered her.

"We still have a good part of the day left. Let's hurry."

When Esther was comfortable, Caleb hitched up his goat and the small party got on the road to back to Capernaum.

Another group of travelers were coming up behind the small party. Jacob asked a chatty stranger who bragged that he had spent time with Jesus in and around the city and villages, if he knew where Jesus was staying.

"I'll tell you how to get there." The man gave him directions but said, "Be prepared for the droves. Jesus can't go anywhere anymore without hordes of people swarming around him begging to be healed."

Jacob thanked the man who hurried off to join his fellow travelers. "Let's prepare for the worst. A huge crowd, then." Jacob placed an arm around Miriam and squeezed.

"Don't worry, friends," Caleb assured them. "This is going to work. I just know it."

They walked only for a short time until other travelers going into Capernaum began streaming by. The closer they got to the city, the more crowded the road became. People who had been in the villages outside of the city, or those who camped in the hillside were all making their way to see Jesus, or, some were vendors with goods on the backs of their donkeys, some were buyers with empty baskets and satchels, but most were people intent on not only hearing Jesus but being healed by him.

They came in all conditions, most were poor, and all were excited and hopeful. Gossip abounded about the many miracles that Jesus had been performing in the countryside. Word was spreading rapidly throughout Judea.

Miriam looked around before speaking and waited for more travelers and their animals to pass then said just above a whisper, "Esther, I truly believe that Jesus will heal you. I hope you can keep still for a while. The road is rough, but it will be worth the discomfort. Just let us know if you need to stop. Knock on the side of the cart. I'll be beside you the whole way."

Caleb walked ahead leading the goat and Jacob left Miriam's side to walk along the other side of the cart. Caleb turned around to around and assured them, "We're going to find him, and Esther is going to be healed."

Jacob sighed to Miriam and Caleb. "At least you two are confident."

CHAPTER TWENTY-SIX

ENTERING CAPERNAUM WAS EASY. THEY blended in with all the other travelers and visitors at the city gate looking to buy and sell a vast array of products and animals as well as many who had come to hear Jesus who would be teaching either at his friend's house or in the synagogue, on the upcoming Sabbath.

Entering the gates, Jacob scratched his head and looked around for one of the many residential areas of the sprawling city, that the stranger said that Jesus could be. In the covered wagon, Esther lay uncomfortably, but quietly. Caleb led the goat, and Miriam and Jacob followed behind in worry and prayer.

"Caleb, up ahead, take a right," Jacob instructed, seeing the crowds maneuver this way and that through the streets. "I think this is the street we need to go down."

"Along with everybody else," Caleb mumbled in uneasiness, as people jostled and pushed through the crowds, donkeys laden with goods, and sheep and goats headed for market or sacrifice at the synagogue. The streets were a mess.

"Caleb, here take another right. I think this is the street where that man said is the house Jesus is supposed in."

Dutifully, Caleb led the cart down a narrow side street to a surprisingly wide cleared area and stopped. Ahead, a tight group of

people talking excitedly stood in the front yard of a house. The walkway and doorway were crowded and the windows were full of people
peering in as some were reporting back to the people about what was
going on inside.

"How will we ever get close? There are so many, many people!"
Miriam groaned.

"Everyone wants to get close to him, and the house is already
packed with people and scribes who want to hear him teach," A
woman said to Miriam. "I brought my daughter who has terrible sei-
zures and I only wish I could have him just but touch her, but he's
inside and there are so many people wanting to just touch his cloak!"
The little girl was thin, dirty, and tired. Dully, she chewed on a piece
of dried fish, leaning against her mother's thigh.

Leaving the woman and child, they moved as close as they could,
but the cart was in the way of people who complained it was taking
up valuable space. Some even wanted to climb on it to get a better
look into the house, but Caleb shooed them away.

"It's unlikely we're going to get an audience with Jesus and it's
dangerous to have a leper hidden in middle of this throng," Jacob
whispered to Miriam and Caleb. "Escape will be slow, decidedly
unsuccessful, and probably terminal!"

"Maybe we should leave now, while we can," Jacob pressed.

How could they possibly get an audience with Jesus under these
conditions? Just as they decided that they should leave, four men
were pushing and bullying their way through the crowd lugging a
man lying on a pallet. Fascinated with the men dragging the man to
the house, Caleb stayed rooted to his place.

"Caleb, come on. Now's the time to leave!" Jacob got hold of the goat's lead while everyone's eyes were on the men.

"I don't think so," answered Caleb. "Look around."

Miriam stood on tip-toes to survey the way out which was blocked by many people.

Unable to get to the front door, two of the men climbed up the side of the house to the roof. As people on the ground watched intently, the men proceeded to pull the tiles off until they had a hole big enough to get a man through the roof. The men shouted to the other two on the ground and all four proceed to haul the man up, who looked to be paralyzed.

Once the pallet was on the roof, two jumped through the hole and two stayed on the roof and carefully lowered their friend through the opening to the main room of the dwelling. The crowd applauded and cheered as the ones on the roof, joined their friends inside. Soon, the throng settled down to see what was going to happen with a full house of disciples, Jesus, the paralytic, his friends, and Pharisees and Sadducees.

"Esther, you're not going to believe this," Caleb quietly described the scene enough for Esther to know why they weren't moving on. "We can't budge. People are packed in here so thick and have no intentions of getting out of the way and making way for a goat cart. We're stuck. Hold tight."

A man at a window motioned everyone to be quiet and began telling them what was going on. "His friends just put him in front of Jesus now," he shouted back to the eager crowd.

"What's he saying?" someone yelled. Other voices rose, creating a din.

"Shut up will you! I can't hear with all your babble. Jesus is saying something to the man." Everyone quieted. "He's saying, 'Son, your sins are forgiven.'"

A questioning murmur arose. "He can forgive sins?"

The man at the window said, "Oooh. I don't think the teachers of the law like what Jesus just said. They're squirming." The crowd laughed. He held up a hand for quiet. "Wait." The man cackled. "Jesus just asked them: Why are you thinking these things? Which is easier: to say to this paralyzed man, 'Your sins are forgiven,' or to say, 'Get up, take your mat and walk?'"

The man at the window held his hand up again for quiet. Hold on." He listened intently. Jesus just said, 'But I want you to know that the Son of Man has authority on earth to forgive sins.'"

The people broke out in noisy discussion. Again, the question rumbling through the crowd was, "He can forgive sins?"

"Who is this Son of Man, Jesus?"

The man turned to the people and hollered above the racket, "Jesus just told the paralyzed man to take his mat and go home!"

Just as he finished the sentence, the man with his pallet under his arm, burst through the packed doorway, scattering the bystanders like dried twigs. His four friends trailed behind, praising God, laughing and crying all at once.

All the people agreed nearly in unison, "We've never seen anything like this!" and pushed one another to get a better look at the healed man walking.

Jacob cupped Miriam's shoulder. "Let's go. This is getting rough. We can't risk this. Someone's going to stand on the cart or fight us because we're in their way. Come, let's go, now while we can. This is getting out of hand."

Caleb agreed, and shortened up the goat's lead, scanning for a break in the density of bodies surging around them.

"Just move, Caleb. Go! They'll get out of the way," Jacob commanded. "Force your way through!"

The cart moved with a sudden jerk. Caleb led the goat around, who was frightened and barely manageable through the angry, cursing men and women. Jacob protected the rear, and Miriam stayed close to the side of the cart, keeping it steady.

Men and women, some with children, were pushing and shoving now, trying to get closer to the house. They wanted their turn with Jesus. Sick people were wailing, women were crying, and men were pleading. The goat was close to bolting and took all Caleb's strength to keep him steady.

Clearing their way to a passable street Caleb looked at Jacob. "I know a safe place where we can stop, get her out of the cart for a bit."

CHAPTER TWENTY-SEVEN

CALEB TOOK THEM ON A circuitous route away from Jesus' volatile throngs and hastily guided them through narrow streets, passing by marching centurions flexing their muscles, spying temple guards looking for improprieties, thieves hoping to pick a pocket, and prostitutes looking demure. They eventually came upon to a deserted narrow alley, littered with trash, dung, and fetid pools of water.

"No one comes down here," Caleb assured them and stopped the goat. He held up a hand and ran to the other end of the alley, checking out both ways just to be sure. "Clear," he called and jogged back to the cart and goat, eager to free Esther from her cramped hiding place.

Miriam looked around. "I realize this will have to do, but Caleb, this is nasty." She side stepped human dung, along with animal droppings.

"Hopefully, no one will wander down here," Jacob grimaced and watched where he was stepping too.

Caleb plucked a small bowl hanging on the side of the cart and filled it with water from a skin for the goat, while Miriam leaned over to pull the cover from Esther, but the sound of thudding sandaled feet on packed dirt and the splash of a foot in a shallow pool followed by a curse whipped Miriam's head around and Caleb sloshed the goat's water to the ground. Miriam dropped the cart cover. Caleb dropped the bowl.

Two ragged thugs jogged at a fast pace down the alleyway, coming to an abrupt halt before the cart. Without a place of retreat, Miriam shrunk behind Jacob who stood defensively with Caleb in front of the cart. The men arrogantly looked them over while lightly bouncing clubs in the palms of their hands.

"You're in quite a hurry, friend," one of the men grinned menacingly at Caleb, pointing his club at him.

Jacob stepped forward. "What do you want?"

The shorter of the two tilted his chin at Jacob. "We've followed you quite a distance, and saw that you were in a big hurry, so we're thinking you must have something pretty valuable in that wagon."

Caleb shrugged innocently. "We have some provisions."

Jacob shook his head, "Friend. We have nothing of value."

"Don't call me friend, you swine. I'm not your friend!" the man hissed.

Suddenly the man shouted at his partner. "This is unbelievable, Phinehas! Look! Do you know who that is?"

The man pointed with his club to Miriam cowering against the muddied wall of the alley. The name Phinehas sounded all too familiar to her. She knew exactly who they were and the dreaded the day of meeting up with them had arrived. She trembled uncontrollably.

The second man was thunderstruck. "It can't be! We left her for dead! Even the lepers wouldn't touch her!" Both men ogled her with renewed hatred and lust.

Neither Jacob nor Caleb had any weapons. No question they were outmanned. They could fight and only hope they would overtake them, but if they didn't, the two thugs would rape and kill her and club Esther to death.

Hoping to diffuse the situation and buy time as Jacob implored the men, "We don't have anything but some food and water. We'll give you that, just let us go!"

The other man now took out a small sword. "No, you're not going anywhere. We want her," he pointed his sword at Miriam, "and we want the cart and goat."

"Hophni, we've no time to waste. Let's kill the men, take and kill her, and be off with the goods. My chin still smarts from her pulling my beard last time."

"I think Phinehas, that's one of your better ideas. But I want to see our spoil." He tore off the cover of the cart, to see a small form covered with a blanket. "Take off that blanket!" he demanded and grabbed it off, instantly recoiled in horror. "A leper!" Esther grabbed the blanket back, and pulled it back over her head, shrinking.

"Kill her, Hophni! Now!" shouted Phinehas. "Stab her! She's a filthy leper!"

Esther, terrified, curled tightly into a ball waiting for the fatal blow.

Caleb lunged at the man with the knife.

At the same moment, Jacob went for the other, catching him by surprise and wrestling for the club. Miriam looked around for a weapon, but there were only scraps of rotted food, dung, and broken pieces of pottery strewn across the alley. Jacob deflected a whack to the head, but the bludgeon landed with a dull thud on his arm; he grunted, fell to his knees. Miriam turned to see Caleb with blood leaking from the side of his shoulder still fighting the crazed man with the knife.

Howling in fierce anger, Miriam lunged at Phinehas, scratching his face and ripping his beard, like she did the first time he attacked her. Screaming in rage and surprise, he turned from Jacob.

Miriam went wild, thrashing about, not letting go of his beard and hair Miriam could hear running, slapping footsteps and saw two men running toward the fight.

More footsteps and shouts filled the alley as two centurions ran from the head of the alleyway and two more came from the other end running, sealing them all off. The two attackers, Phinehas and Hophni stopped fighting instantly and dropped their hands to their sides.

Jacob, sharp pain radiating through his arm, struggled his way up from the ground while Caleb staggered to his feet, putting a hand over his bleeding shoulder. Miriam slumped to the fetid dirt, sobbing.

Jacob was the first to speak. "They attacked us, trying to steal our wagon and goat! They were going to . . . "

"Shut up, Jew," the leader of the foursome said looking over at a crying Miriam and terrified Caleb who was still holding a hand to his wound. Blood seeped freely through his fingers.

"Tell us what happened," the Centurion said to Phinehas pointing a spear at him. "But first tell me what you are."

"I'm not sure what I am, but I'm not a Jew. My name is Phinehas."

The soldiers laughed. The commander shrugged. "Didn't think you were a Jew. You're far too filthy to be one. What happened here?"

The other man, Hophni started to explain. The centurion turned on the man as quick as a viper. "Did I ask you to speak?" He wacked a length of his spear across Hophni's windpipe; the thug choked, went down on one knee, holding his neck and gasping for oxygen.

"We don't have all day. What happened?" he demanded of Phinehas, now holding his spear against his mid-section.

"Sir, we thought the wagon had smuggled goods in it, or at the very least, stolen merchandises from vendors. We, who are also vendors, demanded to see what they were hiding because they were going through the streets in great haste."

He smirked and shook his head. "You two are vendors. What do you sell?"

"Whatever we can, sir."

"I bet. Go on." One of the soldiers walked over to the cart, ready to lift up the cover.

"Don't do that!" begged Hophni. "Stand back! There's a leper in there. These people have been moving about the city bringing in the unclean to contaminate the clean!"

The centurions commanding arrogance was eclipsed by angry fear. The latter being far more dangerous.

The commander turned to Jacob, "We will kill you right now and have these two dogs—" indicating the two men, with a toss of the head, "haul you all off to the waste heap outside of the city and burn you." He demanded of his subordinate, "Confirm what this dog is saying. Lift the cover off the cart. Do it with the tip of your spear!"

The soldier stretched out his hand with the spear. "Everyone, stand back," he ordered.

Deftly the long-armed soldier put the end of his spear under the cart's cover and slowly lifted it up. Miriam's heart broke; they and their unborn baby would soon die a gruesome death.

Silently she prayed, *Lord only you can save us!* Jacob and Caleb stood stoically. What could they possible do?

CHAPTER TWENTY-EIGHT

DELICATELY, THE OFFICER DRAGGED THE cover off with the hook of his spear; the thugs and the soldiers pulled in a breath and instinctively stepped back. Miriam place crossed hands over her heart and the men clenched their fists in rage. Soon, they would all die. Exposed, Esther went from a lying curling position, to kneeling, fully shielded with her blanket, like a gray ghost.

"Take it off!" the officer snarled.

Slowly she pulled it off her head. The centurions gaped. The thugs' eyes flew open wide and unbelieving. Esther, still kneeling beamed a clean, brilliant smile. She picked up the blanket and modestly draped it over her gleaming dark hair. Her eyes were bright and sparkled clear. Her nose and mouth were perfect.

Firmly and indignantly she spoke. "Those men attacked my friends! I was weary and sleeping in the cart. You can see that we have nothing of value in this cart. Just some water and little bread." She held up her hands, "And I'm not a leper!"

Her beauty mesmerized the men. Shyly she outstretched her clean, unblemished hands towards Caleb who stumbled towards her to help her from the cart. Her uncontaminated sandaled feet stepped over the wagon rails onto the grimy, dirty street. She looked down at her toes in amazement, wriggle them, and tip-toed around the trash and broken pottery.

The centurion, furious, spat out to Phinehas and Hophini, "Liars!"

He smote Phinehas across the face with his hand and kicked Hophini to his knees. "Get these men in chains now and throw them in prison with the other vermin!"

Roughly the soldiers put the two men in chains and using ropes they led them away, staggering and pleading for mercy they whined, "Please, please! Have pity on us. We didn't know—we really thought she was a leper. She was covered like one!"

The centurions shoved them forward forcefully, causing them to fall into each other. Landing on their hands and knees they slid into a pile of human excrement.

"Get up you pigs!" screamed the officer and ordered his men drag them along the ground until they stood.

Ignoring the chaos of the alley, Miriam stepped forward and lightly touched Esther's perfect face. Jacob and Caleb were dumbfounded.

"You're healed!" she whispered. In the foul-smelling alleyway, the friends not paying attention to the shouts of the soldiers and the cries of the arrested men, were unable to take their eyes off the sweetness and wholeness of Esther. Her deep olive skin was smooth and fresh, her brown eyes clear and her dark hair, poking out from under the blanket shone in the sun. They watched her as she repeatedly, in her own amazement, looked at the front and backs of her hands, smiling and laughing.

"This is miraculous!" breathed Miriam. "When did you feel the healing begin?"

"I didn't." Esther stared at her hands, still thunderstruck. "I was feeling more alert, but I thought this was because I was so afraid you were all going to die on account of me! If I died, who would care? I'm a leper destined to die, but you? No! It was so unfair. You were trying to help me. I was so devastated! I began to cry, as quietly as I could. When I wiped my cheeks, they felt different, smooth, and round. And then my nose started running and I wiped it with the back of my hand. Then I realized. My nose! I have a nose! That's when I knew I was whole again, and I wasn't afraid."

Miriam hugged Esther's thin little body. "It was Jesus! He healed you and didn't even have to touch or see you!"

Caleb stared mutely at the incredible beauty of Esther.

Jacob was equally stupefied "P-praise God!" he stuttered, "This is our own miracle!" He hugged Caleb who was rendered speechless. Jacob snapped him out of his trance and lightly pulled his arm. "Caleb, women, come; let's get out of here before the centurions change their minds."

Up ahead, the men were being dragged off and struck repeatedly by the officer's hands and rods.

"First, we need to bandage Caleb's shoulder and look at your arm," Miriam tore off a piece of her torn veil, washed Caleb's wound with the water they had left, and wrapped the cloth around his shoulder. Jacob's arm wasn't broken. He could barely move it. Gently she fixed a sling to take pressure of the arm.

They each took a drink of lukewarm water and gave the poor, confused goat water too. Caleb patted his pet's head, took the lead, and the four of them quickly escaped the wretched alley, entering the main road, passing streams of people going the opposite way, looking for Jesus in the city.

"Where can he be?" they asked.

"At the synagogue!" came a reply.

"No, no. He's at some friend's house," another answered.

"This is pandemonium!" mumbled Caleb as he led his goat around clumps of people grabbing arms of strangers asking the main question on everyone's lips: "Do you know where Jesus might be?"

Outside the city proper, Miriam relaxed a bit, but was still on edge knowing they had nearly lost their lives including the life of her baby. Breathing deeply and holding Esther's hand she mused over the miracle of Esther casting a side-long glance to her. Clean and beautiful! Only Jesus could have healed her. Surely, he was the one they were looking for! And he certainly healed the paralyzed man too.

She called to Caleb. "Remember the story you told me so long ago of the man that turned water into wine?"

Caleb turned around and walked backwards alongside his goat, eyes growing big, staring at Miriam as the memory came rushing back. Grinning he said, "Of course! It must have been Jesus!"

"Caleb, tell Jacob and Esther the story of Jesus turning water into wine at the wedding in Cana." After he finished, Esther and Jacob marveled and agreed it must have been one of Jesus' first demonstrations of power.

Then Caleb sighed. "Friends, I'm so sorry about what happened back in town. I thought for sure we'd be safe in that alleyway. It's so filthy and smelly, people try to avoid it. I just didn't think . . . "

"Please, Caleb. Don't fret." Esther spoke clearly with healed tongue. "How were you to know what was to happen? Besides, look, I am healed!" With delight, she held up her hands and waved them high. "And we're safe!"

"Those two men saw us before we went into the alley, anyway, Caleb." Miriam looked back over her shoulder at the gates of the city. "God has shown us he's in control. Never forget that. He works in the most difficult of circumstances for his glory and our good. And as Esther said, she was healed!"

"And our attackers were caught, and we were let go without any major injuries." Jacob gently touched his hurt arm.

"Praise our God," murmured Esther.

Miriam squeezed Esther's hand. "Those two men have been a reoccurring nightmare to me."

"They won't be bothering anybody for a long time now," Esther said Letting go of Miriam's hand she went to Caleb, who lost in thought, was automatically guiding his goat along the cobblestones avoiding holes and debris.

Gently she pet the goat's head and said hoarsely, "How can I thank you all for taking such an enormous risk for me? Caleb, thank you for coming back for me and even Miriam being pregnant! I'm blessed. By Jesus and my friends!"

Miriam came beside her and reached for her hand again. "You are coming home with us to stay . . . or do you have family you want to go home to?"

She shook her head. "Not anymore. When I was younger my mother died leaving me alone with my father, who was a vendor outside Capernaum."

"Oh?" Caleb's interest was piqued. "What did he do?"

"He sold anything. I'd follow him with our donkey as he went into the villages to buy whatever they had to sell, and then bring back the goods to resell at his stall," she recalled affectionately. "His passion was small clay pots and bowls, and when he came across one, he inevitably bought it. He was known for having that unusual piece a housewife or servant would prize. His business was solid, he built an honest reputation, and we always had food on the table."

"He must have been before my time."

CHAPTER TWENTY-NINE

ESTHER BLINKED AND SLIGHTLY TILTED her head. Memories came flooding back. She remembered saying, "Father. Hold still."

Esther stared at a red, dusty spot above his eye and put out her fingertips to wipe it away. It didn't go away, and she rubbed it again, harder, thinking it red clay from one of his potter friends. Looking at her finger tips, she saw it wasn't clay dust, but skin.

"What is it?" He coughed, and wiped mouth. "Clay from the pots?"

"No. It's skin." She held up her fingers.

At the same moment she spoke, he touched her then drew back his hand as if his fingertips brushed a burning coal.

The silence was deafening, but for the blood pounding in her ears and her heart thudding against her thin chest as her father stared at her fingertips and uttered, "Leprosy."

Neither spoke for many moments. Too many awful thoughts were running through their minds. "Daughter, this disease is highly contagious. I ... I'm heartbroken ... for you. Surely you have contracted it too. I must have caught in our travels." Too late to mourn, he simply said, "We must get our house in order."

Esther came out of her past for the moment and looked to Caleb who was unable to stop staring at her. Continuing she said, "He probably died before your time on the streets. My father got leprosy. We didn't know it until it was too late for me. We sold everything we had and made arrangements with some kindhearted people to supply us with food, water, and clothing. We knew it would be a matter of time before we died from the disease and who knew who would go first? We just hoped that the money would last until we took our last breaths . . .

"And true to what he said, after the disease made its appearance on my father, it soon showed up on me. For him, it came on with a vengeance but by that time we were in a leper colony and he died shortly thereafter. For me, it's been a long process."

She swallowed hard. The images continually floated in her mind of once having healthy skin, fingers, and toes to seeing reddish-gray skin, mangled digits and weeping sores, and boils. It was a horrifyingly slow way to die.

"When we came into the colony, the leaders told us what to expect. Over time, we would lose our fingers and toes. Our face would become misshapen and our nose would become badly deformed and sunken. We'd have a hard time breathing and likely lose eyebrows— as if that mattered, but maybe sight too, and our hands would turn into claws."

She continued, "My father eventually died, our money ran out, and I depended on the kindness of the others. And they were kind. They respected me, and in some ways, loved me even though they had their own problems." She smiled. "The leader practically adopted me as his daughter and was forever sharing his food and always giving advice. He had lost his own daughter to the disease. It had run rampant through his family and only he was alive . . . and barely at that."

Caleb slowed beside her. "What does it look like in a leper colony? Is everybody sick and miserable all the time?"

Jacob shot him a look. Some things were best not discussed or re-membered as far as he was concerned, but Esther willingly answered.

"Those are good questions. The Jewish leaders banned us from any visitors or family, which we wouldn't have anyway. We're impure and would cause grievous defilement to anyone who would ever venture in to help . . . unless they were Gentiles. And there's always the fear of spreading the disease. We were—and now they are pretty miserable all the time."

The three couldn't keep their eyes off her as she spoke. "Our colony has two connecting caves that were large enough for men and women to have separate sleep areas. It is a little cramped for families who have to set up tents, or shelters made of branches. We commu-nally cook at the mouth of the women's cave."

She paused in her mind's eye, seeing those pitiful, hopeless people trying to maintain some kind of normalcy. How could you be normal when so often, a woman would pick up a boiling hot pot, or hot rock not feeling the fiery burn causing more damage to her skin?

"An ongoing problem is that after a while, you lose your sense of touch, so you don't know if you've hurt yourself or not. There's little pain except for your insides and your mind. I can't tell you how many lost a toe of finger to a chewing rat because they didn't feel it while they were sleeping."

Caleb looked away and caught up with Jacob who wandered ahead after hearing about rats eating fingers.

Esther kept up and overheard Caleb as he took the goat's lead from Jacob asking, "How do you feel about Esther living with us?"

Jacob turned a smile toward Caleb and looked over his shoulder to Esther who pretended not to listen, but she heard him say, "I think it's great. She can help with the new baby, and she can help you with the goats. It's a winning situation. Why?"

Esther didn't want to be overt in her eavesdropping, but she clearly heard Caleb answer, "You know we're both about the same age . . . and I was thinking . . . "

Just then Miriam came along side of Esther and she could only hear the last of Jacob's remarks to Caleb. " . . . follow strict Jewish rules concerning prenuptials."

Miriam heard him too and raised an eyebrow at Esther. Esther smiled.

Miriam and Esther caught up with the men. "What are you talking about?"

"Just things, Miriam. Not to worry. All is well and just couldn't be better!" He slapped Caleb on the back and laughed.

Esther guessed that Miriam knew. Both women smiled.

Esther, eager to be back to civilization, was in awe of this new beginning. One that she never would have had, if not for this man Jesus. Who was he? A man who performed miracles, who wasn't afraid of defilement by willingly touching a leper, and a man some said was the Messiah. Was he really? They all walked in silence to Jacob and Miriam's home, each with their own thoughts.

Before they arrived, Esther touched Miriam's elbow. "I have to go back to the leper colony to speak with the man who took good care of me. I must let them know about Jesus. It could be their only hope."

"Esther, listen to me." Miriam stopped and took Esther's hands. "Going back to the colony would be dangerous, not only to you, but to this family. I'm pregnant. If you came back to us, I wouldn't want to risk exposure. I was blessed once. Now, you've been healed and don't forget—you made the effort to be healed. You sought out Jesus to be made whole again."

Esther interrupted. "You sought out Jesus for me!"

"But you looked for him first and it was a combination of Caleb, Jacob, and me willing to get you to Jesus. It wouldn't have happened if you hadn't already made the effort to reach out to him."

"But my friends . . . they might be healed . . . "

"Esther, each one of them had the opportunity to be along that road to seek his help too. You had the courage to do so. They still have an opportunity to find him. I'm not saying you can't go back, I just don't want you to be exposed again, because if that happens, you can't stay with us." They walked on.

She couldn't put her new family in jeopardy, but her heart ached for those left behind. Perhaps there was a way to let them know she had been healed, without going to the colony herself? Up ahead she watched Caleb, joking with Jacob. Her healing had given all of them a sense of joyous renewal. She had a new home.

CHAPTER THIRTY

TIMOTHY, WITH HIS WIFE ELIZABETH helping, was down on the beach working separating fish from the recent catch for the market. Esther, Caleb, Jacob and Miriam showed up to help.

"Did you hear the latest about Jesus?" Timothy asked looking up.

"We heard he went to Jerusalem for the Second Passover, but I'm hearing a lot of things most days, but what is it?" Jacob shrugged as he sat down and began to sort.

"In Jerusalem he went to the Sheep Gate where there's a pool called Bethesda."

"Yes, I know what you're talking about," Miriam responded. "It has five roofed colonnades and that's where all the sick and lame sadly waste away while waiting to get in the pool when it gets stirred. Once in, they hope to be healed. People from my village often made pilgrimages there."

"Well wait until you hear this. One of the fish vendors was here this morning and told me the story about a man who had been lying there for thirty-five years! Can you imagine, thirty-five years? He told me about Jesus and this man."

"What did Jesus do?" asked Jacob.

Timothy threw a fish in the basket designated for good fish, then looked up. "Jesus asked him, 'Do you want to get well?' 'Sir,' the invalid replied, 'I have no one to help me into the pool when the water is stirred. While I am trying to get in, someone else goes down ahead of me.' Then Jesus said to him, 'Get up! Pick up your mat and walk.' At once the man was cured; he picked up his mat and walked!"

"Another amazing miracle!" Miriam cried. "This man *must* be the Messiah! We have seen our own miracle close and personal in Esther." They all looked to Esther who blushed but beamed.

The friends had discussed many times about following Jesus, but because of families and work, it was impossible, particularly for Miriam, pregnant and married.

She looked over at her husband who was sitting thoughtfully. *Could we both follow Jesus? Could they all follow Jesus?* She shook her head. *No, it wasn't practical, not with a husband, a child on the way, and chores of running a household . . . but when he was close by, we could indeed, follow him.*

Timothy laughed pointing at Jacob. "Hear this; the healing of this man, this miracle, took place on the Sabbath!"

Within minutes of Timothy's story, Jerome came running down the beach. Nearly out of breath he bent over and rested his hands on his knees. "Did you hear the latest about Jesus? About healing an invalid who had been crippled for thirty-five years?"

"Yes, Timothy was just telling us," Jacob gestured with slippery wet hands toward Timothy. "Sit down. Help us with the fish and talk."

"Did you hear what the Pharisees said to the man that was healed?" Jerome probed sitting down beside a pile of fish that needed sorting.

"No." Timothy looked up in interest from handling an eel.

"The Jewish leaders said to the man who had been healed that he couldn't carry his mat because such an act is considered forbidden on the Sabbath.

"Ha! See! I told you so," smirked Timothy. "How idiotic is that?"

"Oh, that is so typical of the Pharisees," stated Caleb glancing over at Esther. "They don't care about anyone but themselves. Healing on a Sabbath? Forget about it. It's all about their tradition, rules, and regulations. What did the man say back to the Pharisees?"

"He just said, 'The man who made me well said to me, 'Pick up your mat and walk.' Then they asked who was it that told him to pick up his mat and walk and the man answered that he had no idea who healed him, because Jesus disappeared back into the crowd."

Caleb interjected again. "Oooh! The Pharisees must have been fuming."

"They were furious. They later found out who healed the man and when they caught up with Jesus, they confronted him about working on the Sabbath! He responded, 'My Father is always at his work to this very day, and I too am working.'"

"What? That must have put them over the edge! Do you understand what that means, everyone?" asked Miriam. "He is making God his father, making himself equal with God!" Her mind flited back to when John the Baptist baptized Jesus and the voice that came down from heaven said, 'this is my son, whom I love.'

"Oh, you're so right, Miriam," Jerome nodded. "When they heard this, they were beside themselves that this Jesus would equate himself as the Son of God! Word has it that they are out to get him!"

Miriam dropped a fish and frowned, "Out to get a godly man. What are they thinking?"

"They're jealous of Jesus!" Caleb tossed a fish in the basket. "I know how dangerous the teachers of the law can be. The Pharisees and Sadducees can be along with the high priest. Living on the streets, if I didn't see it, I heard about it. There's no room in their hearts for competition, even from God. It would disrupt their corrupt way of life."

Miriam agreed, picking up another fish and tossing it into a basket. "I too, have seen and heard a lot out on the streets. They have a lot to lose if they recognize Jesus as Messiah. All their power, influence, and money will evaporate. Yet, there is so much evidence that points to him being the Son of God! Still they don't believe him!"

"But there's more to it," Jerome added. "How are the Romans going to react?" Everyone quietened.

They continued to sort fish, throwing the bad ones to the side, and the good ones in overflowing baskets. Miriam was certain now, that Jesus was the Messiah. As each heart and mind were trying to understand the impact of this revelation, Ann came striding down the beach, with the baby on her hip, picking her way around the small rocks with her children running and stumbling ahead of her.

"Don't leave me out of this, Jerome!" Ann, Jerome's wife scolded, putting the baby in Esther's willing outstretched arms. "After you left to find Timothy, I went by Miriam's to speak with her about your story but was told all of you were at the beach! This is important to all of us."

Jerome went to stroke her hand, but his hands were slimy with fish scales. "Ann, Ann. I didn't mean to leave you out. I'm sorry if I hurt you. I didn't know everyone was here helping Timothy. He had a huge haul today that's why everyone is here to help. Believe me, we are all in this together, all of us."

Esther shyly piped up, "It's good to hear you say that we are all in this together, because in truth, we are. There is no separation of person type to God and having said that and although we all have our responsibilities," she shot a glance at Miriam, "we must follow Jesus to hear and see more of what he has to say while we can, while he's here in Galilee and Capernaum. Do you agree Caleb?"

The group raised their eyebrows. This was a match made in heaven for sure: Caleb and Esther.

Caleb flushed. "I do agree."

Jacob broke the moment. "You're pregnant, Miriam. I worry that all that walking, being with rowdy crowds, the pushing and shoving . . . I don't know if we should follow."

Miriam patted her belly. "Jacob. I'm not going to deliver tomorrow."

Timothy spoke to Elizabeth about his own concern about the children. Elizabeth interrupted. "I'm going too. This is Jesus we're talking about, not some entertainer or sorcerer . . . I have a deep feeling in my spirit about him. We've heard about his miracles, his standing up to the teachers of the law, his compassion for all types of people. The very fact that he refers to his Father as God! This is powerful!"

"But what about the children?" Timothy asked.

Miriam held up a mediator's hand. "Men, if Jesus is close by, we will make the effort to seek him out to hear him preach. If we can't, then we can't, but at least we need to make the effort. We will work it out, so let's just stop worrying about it."

Esther walked back to the house with Miriam, carrying a small basket of fish. "I know I was outspoken in wanting to follow Jesus and including Caleb, but Miriam, the miracle he performed on me is truly unforgettable. I'm grateful beyond words. I so want to see him, hear him, touch him and thank him. If I get my work done, may I go too?"

Miriam stopped. "Esther, you are not a slave. You're a part of our household."

CHAPTER THIRTY-ONE

WORD WAS SPREADING FAST ABOUT Jesus throughout the region of Galilee, the cities in the area called the Decropolis, and from Jerusalem, Judea, and even beyond the Jordan. His miraculous deeds were exciting the people but raising the alarm of the Pharisees. Astoundingly, Jesus was healing the sick, lame, diseased, and even those possessed by demons. By his miracles, he revealed power over all types of sickness and evil. People were traveling from faraway places to wherever Jesus was, hoping to be healed by him. Many believed if they just touched his clothing, they would be made whole again.

He preached that the kingdom of God was for all who confessed their sins, repented, and believed in him through his words and works. All were welcome into the kingdom he said, even the poorest of poor.

His words resonated among the people, particularly when he instructed them to love God with their whole heart, soul, strength, and mind and said, "in everything, do to others what you would have them do to you, for this sums up the Law and the Prophets."

Jesus was to be at the synagogue on the Sabbath the friends set out to the city. On the way to the synagogue, they cut through fields of grain and spied Jesus, some of his followers, and a handful of Pharisees up ahead.

Drawing closer to Jesus, Miriam couldn't take her eyes off him. He looked like any other Jewish man in his early thirties. He could blend into a crowd and no one would have been impressed or even been able to describe him. If she had to guess, she would know he was a tradesman because his hands were large and rough, and his arms, though lean, were strong. He wore what appeared to be a seamless tunic. On his feet were basic sandals. Overall, a regular looking Jew.

"He looks normal." Esther was surprised.

"He looks like he's hard worker," but to Caleb almost every Jew in Israel worked hard if they wanted to survive.

"He does looks like he could have been a carpenter," Jerome pointed out looking at his hands.

"Come, let's get closer." Miriam walked a little faster.

The party inched their way through the small group of people to get behind the Pharisees who walked along side of Jesus. Esther could hear the conversation as Jesus' followers picked at the wheat, eating the kernels because they were hungry.

The Pharisees were indignant. "Why are they doing what is not lawful on the Sabbath?" They demanded.

He answered, "Have you never read what David did when he and his companions were hungry and in need? In the days of Abiathar the high priest, he entered the house of God and ate the consecrated bread, which is lawful only for priests to eat. And he also gave some to his companions." Then he said to them, "The Sabbath was made for man, not man for the Sabbath. So the Son of Man is Lord even of the Sabbath."

One of the Pharisees, jabbed his companion hard in the ribs. "How dare he? He's calling himself Lord of the Sabbath!"

"Who is this 'Son of Man'?" demanded the other. "Does he think he's the Son of God?"

"We must put an end to this soon!" declared the outraged Pharisee and the two began whispering so no one could hear but Miriam, who was horrified.

Esther tugged at her sleeve. "What does Jesus mean about David?"

Jerome answered, "Our ancient King David, who was not yet king, was on the run from King Saul who was out to kill him. Exhausted and hungry, he and his companions came to the priests and he asked for bread for his men. The priest said they had no common bread, only holy bread made for God. Yet the priests understood the need and gave the bread to the hungry men."

"Meaning that rules were made to serve and help humans, not humans to serve rules," Miriam clarified.

"Those dogs," Caleb said under his breath. "They truly don't want to hear the word of God. Just their own words."

As the crowd neared the synagogue, the Pharisees broke off to join the other teachers of the law and congregated together whispering and watching Jesus closely to see what he would do on the Sabbath. As Jesus entered the temple, a man with a withered hand was there and Jesus asked the man to come close. Everyone crowded around to see what he was going to do.

Jesus turned to the Pharisees and speaking loudly enough for all to hear he said to the man with the shriveled hand, "Stand up in front of everyone."

Then Jesus asked them, "Which is lawful on the Sabbath: to do good or to do evil, to save life or to kill?" But they remained silent. He looked around at them in anger and, deeply distressed at their stubborn hearts, said to the man, "Stretch out your hand." He stretched it out, and his hand was completely restored.

A loud reaction came from those witnessing the miracle. The friends gaped at the healing of the man's hand. It was extraordinary, but more so was Jesus question to the Pharisees and teachers of the law who wouldn't respond to his question. How could they be so blind to not to understand that their laws didn't help the poor and sick?

Then Jesus began to teach. "The Father judges no one, but has entrusted all judgment to the Son, that all may honor the Son just as they honor the Father. Whoever does not honor the Son does not honor the Father, who sent him. Very truly I tell you, whoever hears my word and believes him who sent me has eternal life and will not be judged but has crossed over from death to life."

Miriam leaned into Esther. "The Father is God and the Son is Jesus, I'm convinced. Do you understand what he is saying?"

Esther nodded. "Yes. For those who don't honor Jesus as the Son, they do not honor God the father."

Jesus said much more, and the listeners were astonished at his instruction. After Jesus finished speaking, he left the synagogue with his disciples leaving the friends wondering aloud where this was all going.

Caleb was the first to speak. "You can be assured that the teachers of the law are without doubt, out to get Jesus— and I mean kill Jesus."

Outside the synagogue, on the way home, the group was distressed. How could their savior be put to death because the teachers of the law believed their status and power were threatened and they were more important?

Caleb clenched his fists in anger. "I overheard one say they should go to the Herodians, you know, the Jewish sect who support Herod the Great's rule with Rome? They want to figure a way to destroy Jesus!"

"But I thought he Herodians were in direct conflict with the Pharisees because they support Roman rule and the Pharisees don't!" Jacob spread out hands in question.

Jerome stepped forward and held up a finger. "Yes, they willingly go along with Herod and Roman rule for convenience, and yes, the Pharisees want Jewish independence, but neither group will get what they want if the people see Jesus as their Messiah. All political groups will be thrown into chaos."

CHAPTER THIRTY-TWO

ESTHER WAS HELPING A VERY pregnant Miriam at the market, giving Jacob the opportunity to wander off and look at fishing gear at one of the booths. Esther watched as a strange woman came up behind him. She was attractive, not young, and dressed like a typical Jewish matron. She saw the woman tap his shoulder. He turned around in happy surprise. Esther, concerned for her mistress, wandered near the fishing gear booth to listen.

"Tamar! It's been a long time since I've seen you. How's business?"

Tamar? Esther cocked her head. The name was familiar. She edged closer to the conversation.

"Jacob, believe it or not, my life has changed. I don't do that sort of work anymore," the woman looked up at him with a hint of embarrassment in her eyes.

Jacob stepped back and made a show of looking her over. "That's a surprise. How are you surviving?" He asked bluntly.

"I spend time here at the market selling whatever I can along with some scarves that I've sewn. When I have enough to pay for rent and food, I take time off for a very special person."

"Oh, are you betrothed? That would be wonderful, providing he's okay with the way you've lived your life . . . " he drifted off.

Esther hurried back to Miriam and pointed to Jacob and the woman. Miriam, surprised, took in a quick breath, and walked towards them.

"No, I'm not betrothed, let me explain..." Seeing Miriam approach, Tamar was distracted from Jacob for the moment. "Miriam?" Tamar clutched her head covering with one hand and pointed at her with the other.

Miriam waddled quickly to Jacob and Tamar. Esther could see that there was with a hint of concern in her eyes, no doubt wondering what was he doing talking with Tamar?

"Tamar," Miriam finally spoke and stepped closer to her. "How are you? May I hug you?" She stretched out her arms.

Esther realized that Miriam's request wasn't lost on any of them; they all knew the Tamar and Miriam story. Tamar stared at her. "You escaped the disease," she marveled and leaned in to hug Miriam who responded with sincerity. Stepping back to look her over, Tamar smiled. "And I see you're very soon to deliver! My, you've been doubly blessed. Where is your husband?"

"Right here. With you," Miriam grinned, putting a protective hand on her husband.

Tamar put a hand to her heart staring at Jacob. "Jacob?" Her jaw fell open. "You're married to Miriam? I can't believe it!"

Esther stood by quietly, but Miriam tugged at her sleeve. "And guess who this is?" Tamar shook her head. "This is my dearest little leper who saved my life!"

Tamar's eyes flew open wide. "This little beauty? A leper?" She stumbled for words.

Miriam started to laugh, breaking the tension. "Come, let's get something to drink and talk." Miriam led them to a stall that provided beverages, snacks, and seating. Once settled, Jacob explained to Tamar how he and Miriam met, with Miriam giving background of her life on the streets and how her life had changed so radically. Esther knew all this history including Tamar demanding Miriam leave when they first met.

"But, Tamar, what about you? You've changed too." Miriam exclaimed.

Esther couldn't help but see that Tamar looked like any ordinary Jewish woman. She would never think she was a prostitute.

Before Tamar could answer Miriam, Jacob interrupted. "What's this about a special man?"

"I have to start at the beginning. This is an amazing story. You know Levi, the tax collector?"

"Who doesn't?" complained Jacob. "Although I haven't see him around much."

"Well, I was invited to a dinner at his house awhile back along with other sinners. Levi always used to spend time with us," she smiled at the memory.

"Anyway, a group of men came in as well, and one in particular stood out as the leader. They all reclined with us at the table and as we were eating, drinking, and laughing, he talked to us in such a way that it was mesmerizing. He spoke of God and told us that the kingdom of heaven was near. That we needed to repent of our sins while there was still time. We all stopped our foolish talk and listened intently.

"At first, some of us thought him foolish, but soon his words carried us to a place of forgiveness and acceptance we had never been to before. His words were like honey to our famished, miserable souls! He gave us hope that we could change our shameful lifestyles and we could find true life!"

"It was Jesus!" Esther and Miriam exclaimed at the same time.

"It was!" exclaimed Tamar. "The Pharisees, who were hovering around the courtyard, asked his disciples, 'Why does he eat with tax collectors and sinners?'"

"Do the Pharisees not sin?" Miriam exclaimed in exasperation. "Who do they think they are? Everyone sins!"

"He had a great answer for those so-called virtuous men. Jesus said to them, 'It is not the healthy who need a doctor, but the sick. I have not come to call the righteous, but sinners.'"

Esther licked her lips nervously. "Where is this going to lead? He's making enemies of the Jewish leaders."

"If he's the Messiah, he has it all under control," Jacob said with a hint of sarcasm.

"I know what you're thinking," Tamar said quietly staring into his eyes.

"What are you talking about?" Jacob barked. Esther and Miriam blinked in surprise at Jacob's hot retort.

Tamar answered. "Here is a man, from out of nowhere, performing miracles that no one has ever done and even commands *demons*! You're thinking about what the Pharisees believe: That Jesus is possessed by Beelzebub. Let me assure you, it is not true. Jesus responded to their taunts and charges when they accused him of casting out demons by the help of the prince of demons. He said, 'How can Satan drive out Satan? If a kingdom is divided against itself, that kingdom cannot stand. If a house is divided against itself, that house cannot stand. And if Satan opposes himself and is divided, he cannot stand; his end has come.'

"Then Jesus said, 'In fact, no one can enter a strong man's house without first tying him up. Then he can plunder the strong man's house. Truly I tell you, people can be forgiven all their sins and every slander they utter, but whoever blasphemes against the Holy Spirit will never be forgiven; they are guilty of an eternal sin.'"

CHAPTER THIRTY-THREE

JACOB WAS VISIBLY UNEASY WITH Tamar's discussion. Gently
Miriam explained, "Jesus is the stronger man who can enter Satan's
dominion, bind him up, and plunder his domain, free the captive.
This applies to all of us sinners. Jesus can free us of Satan's grip. We
all sin, and will continue to sin, but Jesus can save us from this doom."

"I get it!" but clearly Jacob wasn't convinced. Miriam guessed that
Jacob believed if the Pharisees didn't endorse him, why should he?

Tamar placed her hands on her knees and leaned forward. "I'm
not a disciple of money and sex anymore. I'm a disciple of Jesus, who
loves me for who I am now, not who I was before. Jesus has saved me.
I've changed!"

Jacob wiped his mouth. "I need some more food," troubled, he
walked away from the women.

Tamar hugged Miriam and laughed at the strange events
that brought them all together. "But tell me how you were able to
reconnect with Esther and . . . and . . . " again she was lost for words.

"Please let me explain." Miriam looked to Esther who nodded.
And she did. She recounted events from start to finish.

Tamar was shaken. She touched Miriam's arm. "Forgive me for
treating you so poorly when I thought you might have given me leprosy. I worried for months! I am so sorry. And now this miracle!"

"Tamar, I'm sorry too for being so careless in putting you in possible danger. I wasn't thinking and I, too, worried for months. We're sisters, now, along with Esther, my "little helper". Look! Clean and beautiful. Without Jesus even touching her! And those terrifying men that attacked me? They are in chains, in prison, surely to die there."

The three women looked at the approaching Jacob eating sweet bread. Tamar lifted her brows and looked to Miriam who only smiled. "It's in the past, Tamar . . . all in the past." Tamar kissed Miriam, hugged Esther, waved to Jacob, and left.

Days later, Esther, Caleb, Miriam, and Jacob waited for the rest of their friends on the outskirts of town to go to a place that Jesus was going to be. Excitement filled the air as early travelers passed them on the way to hear his teaching, knowing that they might possibly see miracles as well.

"I wonder if they hope Jesus will heal their souls, their bodies, or to just see a magic show?" Miriam asked seriously. People jostled by, laughing and joking, some serious and crying. All looking for Jesus.

"Some of each, I suspect," Jacob responded. Miriam guessed even Jacob was not sure what he wanted from Jesus.

When the rest of their group arrived, they speculated where Jesus' ministry was going giving Jerome an opportunity for his opinion, saying who opined, "As Jews, we're hoping for a messiah to free us from Roman rule. As for me, I'm hoping he'll free us from the hypocrisy of the Jewish leaders, as well as the Romans. We're all looking for a descendent of King David, a warrior, a king promised by God to be on the throne forever."

"Meaning a man defeating our oppressors, the Romans and corrupt Jewish leaders," Caleb said emphatically.

"Or," added Timothy, "We're thinking of someone like Moses, who, with the Lord's power, freed the people from Egyptian slavery and established them as a nation. That's what we want. To be a nation."

Caleb clapped his hands. "Don't forget what John the Baptist said, 'His winnowing fork is in his hand to clear his threshing floor and to gather the wheat into his barn, but he will burn up the chaff with unquenchable fire.' That sounds to me like someone who will be waging war and issuing judgement."

Miriam cupped her elbow and put a thoughtful hand to her chin. "I think what we're seeing and hearing is not a political Messiah, but a spiritual Messiah. He's offering forgiveness of sins, not judgement, and he's offering the kingdom of God to sinners, not to self-proclaimed righteous people. While he has the power to heal people physically, he also has the power to heal and forgive peoples' sins."

"Like the paralytic," Esther concluded. "Jesus told him his sins were forgiven."

"Yes, exactly. Remember what he said to the Pharisees who were so affronted and claimed that only God could forgive sins?" Miriam asked. They all nodded. "Jesus asked, 'Which is easier: to say to this paralyzed man, 'Your sins are forgiven,' or to say, 'Get up, take your mat and walk'? Jesus then said, 'I tell you get up, take your mat and go home.' And the man did!"

They fell silent, each in their own thoughts until they came to the area where Jesus was teaching, surrounded by his disciples. Groups of people were spread out on the grass, some were picnicking, others were talking among themselves. Children ran around. All were abuzz waiting for this strange and humble man who was sitting in front of the large gathering on the slope of a hill, visible to all lounging on the grass to speak.

Winding their way closer to Jesus, they found a spot where they could all sit down as Timothy nudged Jacob and pointed. "Look. There's James and John, and see Simon and Andrew? Looks like about twelve men around him."

Timothy waved, catching their eye and the four men waved back with big smiles, delighted to see Timothy, Jacob, and Jonas, their fellow fishermen.

"Looks like Zebedee's boys and Simon and Andrew have made a commitment in following Jesus," Jonas said to Timothy. "They haven't been fishing for a long time."

"Shhh. Everyone. Jesus is getting ready to speak," someone from the crowd admonished.

Jesus stood up and the crowd settled down, and the children quieted. He began to speak.

"Blessed are the poor in spirit, for theirs is the kingdom of heaven. Blessed are those who mourn, for they will be comforted. Blessed are the meek, for they will inherit the earth. "Blessed are those who hunger and thirst for righteousness, for they will be filled. Blessed are the merciful, for they will be shown mercy. Blessed are the pure in heart, for they will see God.

"Blessed are the peacemakers, for they will be called children of God. Blessed are those who are persecuted because of righteousness, for theirs is the kingdom of heaven. "Blessed are you when people insult you, persecute you and falsely say all kinds of evil against you because of me. Rejoice and be glad, because great is your reward in heaven, for in the same way they persecuted the prophets who were before you."

As Jesus paused, many people were wiping their eyes with sleeves, or hands. Many were whispering, "Is he our Messiah?", and others were responding, "If he's our Messiah, he's not the type we expected."

Many agreed. "He speaks with compassion. Hardly a warrior-type, or politician, or even a teacher of the law. Who is this man really?"

Miriam knew and explained it to her friends. "This is a different Messiah. He's not going to raise an army, overthrow the Romans, or fight the Herodians. He's fulfilling the words of the prophets like Isiah who said he would be called a wonderful counselor, a prince of peace, and of his government there would be no end reigning on David's throne."

Esther knew too. "Jesus is bringing the kingdom of God to all types of people, not just the rich and powerful."

Jesus then began again to speak on anger, lust, divorce, oaths, and retaliation--all typical human frailties and sinfulness.

He admonished those with vanity of spirit, and in a surprising turn from Jewish teaching, he taught, "But to you who are listening I say: Love your enemies, do good to those who hate you, bless those who curse you, pray for those who mistreat you. If someone slaps you on one cheek, turn to them the other also. If someone takes your coat, do not withhold your shirt from them. Give to everyone who asks you, and if anyone takes what belongs to you, do not demand it back. Do to others as you would have them do to you." Jesus paused to let his listeners internalize his words.

Miriam grabbed Jacob's arm and spoke to them all. "Remember a while back we were told he said, 'in everything, do to others what you would have them do to you, for this sums up the Law and the Prophets?' Do you see, Jacob, friends?" she asked as she looked around her group. "He's not here to counter Roman rule. He's here to establish the kingdom of God through love, forgiveness, and righteousness."

Jesus continued. "Do not judge, and you will not be judged. Do not condemn, and you will not be condemned. Forgive, and you will be forgiven. Give, and it will be given to you. A good measure, pressed down, shaken together and running over, will be poured into your lap. For with the measure you use, it will be measured to you."

"His teaching is just amazing," Esther sighed. "So counter to the way we live."

"Can you imagine the Pharisees understanding this?" Caleb asked with a wondrous smile.

"No," responded Esther. "They have hardened hearts, but some of us have too. We need to turn from our own twofaced ways."

CHAPTER THIRTY-FOUR

MIRIAM REACHED FOR JACOB. INTUITIVELY, she believed that Jacob, while hearing Jesus' words and seeing his miracles, was still questioning in his heart. Perhaps the teachers of the law have muddied the waters for him in not supporting the work and words of Jesus. Perhaps because of their lack of acceptance, Jacob was having difficulty accepting it all too. While the rest of their group eagerly listened and digested Jesus' words, Jacob was expressionless looking for diversion and scanning the vast sea of people.

Jesus taught for a little while longer. He told them a parable. "Can the blind lead the blind? Will they not both fall into a pit? The student is not above the teacher, but everyone who is fully trained will be like their teacher."

The crowd murmured thinking these over. Then Jesus continued, "Why do you look at the speck of sawdust in your brother's eye and pay no attention to the plank in your own eye? How can you say to your brother, 'Brother, let me take the speck out of your eye, when you yourself fail to see the plank in your own eye? You hypocrite, first take the plank out of your eye, and then you will see clearly to remove the speck from your brother's eye."

The group sitting on the ground looked around at each other. "Powerful," said Jerome. One needs to listen carefully to keep up with his points."

"Agreed," nodded Caleb and Esther.

Miriam winced as a sharp pain stabbed her lower belly. Instinctively she cupped her lower belly and grimaced.

"Miriam, what is it?" Jacob's voice echoed fear.

"I don't know. A pain." She held her belly and grimaced.

"It seems too early," Esther exclaimed. "What should we do?"

"Don't worry, I'll be right back!" Jerome jumped up to get a donkey from one of the bystanders, who, after hearing Jesus speak, was happy to oblige the use of his beast for Miriam's comfort. The man, along with the party left immediately while Jesus continued his teaching and so were unencumbered with traffic as they made their way out of the grassy area, along the road to Jacob and Miriam's home.

Uncomfortably sitting on the donkey, her pains were coming in ever shortening waves. Esther and Jacob held her steady and the man who owned the animal led it carefully with the others following closely, their minds fleeting between the words of Jesus and Miriam's gasps of pain.

Finally home, Jacob and Timothy half-carried Miriam to their sleeping room. The women attended her while Jacob sat with Jerome, Timothy, Caleb, and Jonas. By now it was early evening and the days were mild and the evenings cooler, so a small fire was started in the garden more for diversion than warmth. Timothy's mother brought out a meal they all shared as they chatted quietly, waiting for the baby, pondering Jesus' words, and wondering who really was this Jesus who had such depth and power in teaching.

An hour later, Esther came dancing out of the house. "It's a boy!"

Jacob hurried to Miriam's side. Tired and weak, she looked up at him with the baby in her arms.

"Mother and child are healthy!" exclaimed his mother as she took the baby from Miriam's arms and handed the baby to her son.

Miriam watched as Jacob, overcome with joy, held his baby close. Tears squeezed out the corner of his eyes as he laughed and cried at the same time.

Miriam sighed. "Have you told our friends the baby's name yet?"

"No, I will." He took the baby outside, and Miriam leaned up from the pallet to peer out the window. She saw the men crowding around congratulating him on his heir as Jerome grinned, "You must name this baby. Have you come up with one yet?"

"We have. It will be Joseph!"

"Ah, like our ancient father Jacob's eleventh son. A confident boy, with God-given visions, who went through terrible trials, to ultimately help his family from starvation by bringing them to his home in Egypt with Pharaoh's blessing." Jerome said putting a positive spin on the Israelites history.

"Of course, Pharaoh died, everyone forgot Joseph's legacy and the Hebrew generations ultimately ended up as slaves in Egypt," Timothy pointed out.

"But God appointed Moses to work His will in freeing them . . . " Jerome countered while Caleb and Jonas smiled at one another. Jerome the historian.

"Truthfully, I chose the name Joseph because I liked it," Jacob interrupted. "And yes, there's interesting history to his name, but let's celebrate!"

Softly laughing, Miriam fell back against the cushions waiting for Jacob to bring back tiny Joseph.

CHAPTER THIRTY-FIVE

DAYS LATER, JACOB, TIMOTHY, AND crew came in from fishing for the night, in good spirits. It was a good haul, but when they dropped anchor, they were surprised to see so few laborers milling about the shoreline looking for day work in separating fish, darning nets, or repairing sails and other odd jobs. Even the fish buyers were gone.

Timothy groaned. "Not again! We need more workers and buyers. Where is everyone?" bellowed Timothy to a young man splashing through the water.

"So many are off to follow or look for Jesus in Capernaum," the young man replied taking the line out to drop anchor in the shallows.

"If Miriam wasn't with an infant she'd be gone too," mumbled Jacob.

"We all want to follow Jesus, but we all have to eat. I don't mind going when I can, but I have a family to care for," Timothy huffed wondering how he was going to sell all this fish before it went bad.

"Let's use this to our advantage," Jonas suggested. "I might be old, but with old age comes wisdom," he cackled. "There are lots of people in Capernaum wanting to see Jesus because he's back in the city. This is a good opportunity to sell the fish in the market place without the middleman. I've got a cart and donkey. Let's load up the cart and go to the city! What we can't get on the cart, we carry in baskets."

Jacob protested, "We haven't had any sleep! And what about the trash fish? Are we going to take it all together with the good?"

"Of course! People will buy anything and besides, look for yourself; we have few customers here." He swept his arm across the shore. "C'mon let's get going." He turned to the young man. "We'll pay you a good wage if you help us unload and go to the city with us."

Timothy raised his eyebrows to protest but relented. "Okay, let's do this."

It proved to be a very good idea to bring the fish into the city. People had traveled from many areas around Capernaum, as far south in Judea to north from Syria to see and hear Jesus. Whatever their motives were in seeking him out, they all had two things in common: They were hungry and thirsty and the vendors in the market place, along the streets, and roads were doing well.

Arriving near the gate of the city in record time, they scouted out an area with good customer access. Even while setting up their spot, people were clamoring for fish. Jonas set up a fire for those who wanted to eat immediately. Fresh fish was a treat and the people lined up, eager in their hunger.

As people milled about, ordering fish cooked or uncooked, Jacob spied Tamar, sitting on the ground on a colorful mat, selling lengths of twine, satchels, and scarves.

"You're asking for trouble," Timothy warned when he saw Jacob spot Tamar who quickly waved but went back to doing a brisk business.

"I just want to go over and say hello. We have history, you know."

"Yes, I know. That's why I say, stay away." Jacob didn't listen. He wiped his hands on a cloth and ducked around the cart, stepping into the parade of people and animals. "Hey! We have customers!" Timothy yelled. Jacob heard him but didn't care.

He ached to talk to Tamar about old times, life, and maybe even . . . ? No, he couldn't do that, but he could revisit their time together. Shutting out Timothy's words, he trotted over to Tamar with a flirting grin patting his dark mane.

Adjusting his tunic, he squatted on the ground close to her hip and touched a piece of cloth and gazed into her eyes. "You are looking beautiful, Tamar, even without all that make-up and finery! Can you take a break?"

Tamar volleyed a hard look at him. "Why? What do you want? Where's Miriam?"

"She's at home. She just had my baby. A boy. Joseph. He's handsome like me," he smiled charmingly and casually pulled the neck of his tunic down to lightly scratch his chest.

"You should be home with her, or if you're here to sell fish, sell fish. It looks like your men are busy and you're interrupting my sales," she snapped and turned her attention to a customer.

Insulted, Jacob popped up. "Who are you to tell me what to do? I remember not too long ago I was telling you what to do! I know what you do and how you do it, so please, don't get all righteous on me."

She looked up at him, standing in shadow with the sun on his back. "I told you. I'm not that person anymore. I know what real love and truth is. Haven't you been listening to a word Jesus has been saying? I know you've heard him and have seen him perform miracles. Are you deaf and blind? Don't define me by what I was. I am a new person and not interested in flirting with you or in anything else you might have in mind."

Jacob, mind slapped by Tamar, never expected that reaction from her. They had history! He turned on his heel and stormed away fuming. There was a time when Tamar delighted in him—looked forward to seeing him! She was always wanting presents and money he lavished on her. Now she's saying she's changed? He didn't believe people could just change because of a few words from some man. He certainly hadn't changed. He was his own man, making his own decisions.

"Didn't go well, huh?" Timothy asked sarcastically, wrapping up a plump fish for a waiting customer.

"She says she's changed."

"She follows Jesus?" Timothy guessed.

"What do you think?" Scorn dripped from Jacob's lips.

"I would say, yes, she does. Jacob, I've heard testimony from all sorts of people saying that after hearing Jesus preach and teach, they've turned from their sins, committed themselves to him, and have really changed. Look at all these people milling about. They've all come to hear Jesus, not listen to the Pharisees. And just so you know, what little I've heard from the man, even I've changed my way of thinking."

CHAPTER THIRTY-SIX

POINTING TO A FISH HE wanted, the next customer in line man asked Jacob, "Did you hear the latest about Jesus? About the centurion's servant?"

Jacob growled, "No," and was about to say he wasn't interested when Timothy tilted his head and asked the customer, "What about him?"

"I was there," continued the man, "so it's not hearsay." By now, the customers in line to buy fish were waiting to hear the story too. "We were in the courtyard just beyond this market place listening to Jesus teach," he pointed, "when a centurion sent elders from the Jews in his town to ask Jesus for help on his behalf. The elders said the centurion loved the Jewish nation and even built them a synagogue, 'so please,' they implored Jesus, 'consider helping him'. Jesus wanted to know what the centurion wanted. And the elders said he had a servant who was sick and close to death and the centurion, who heard of Jesus, wanted him to come heal his servant."

"What happened?" someone from the back asked.

"Jesus took off with the elders, and some of us followed. When he wasn't far from the house, the centurion sent friends to meet him saying, 'Lord, don't trouble yourself, for I do not deserve to have you come under my roof. That is why I did not even consider myself worthy to come to you. But say the word, and my servant will be healed.'"

The group of people around the speaker grew still for a moment until someone said, "A centurion said that? Called him Lord? To a Jew?" for they all knew Jesus was Jewish and the Romans and Jews were like oil and water. A surprised murmur rose from the listeners.

Holding up his hand for quiet, the speaker continued. "The centurion explained, 'For I myself am a man under authority, with soldiers under me. I tell this one, 'Go,' and he goes; and that one, 'Come,' and he comes. I say to my servant, 'Do this,' and he does it.' Jesus was amazed at the centurion's words. He turned to us and he said, 'I tell you, I have not found such great faith even in Israel.'"

"What happened to the servant?" someone asked.

The man replied, "When the men returned to the house, they found the servant healthy!"

Excitement rose from the bystanders. Conversations, questions, and praise rang through the huddled group by the fish cart.

"What do you think of that, Jacob?" Timothy passed a fish to an extended hand and gathered coins.

"I don't know what to think. I'm confused. If only the leaders of the synagogue would endorse him, I'd feel a lot better."

Jonas, picking fish for a customer, looked at Jacob in disappointment. "Since when have you had respect or admiration for those vipers, as John the Baptist would say? You saw the paralytic man being lowered through the roof on a pallet. Then he walked out the door, because he had faith Jesus could heal him. You personally have seen the miracle of Esther's cleansing from leprosy and Jesus wasn't even near her, but even you had faith Jesus could heal her— that's why you went along with Miriam and Caleb in the first place. You even saw Jesus cast out a demon who called him the 'Holy One of God'!"

Jonas shook his head in surprise and poked him on the arm, saying, "And you've heard and seen other miracles Jesus did . . . he's shown you power over flesh and over the spiritual realm and yet you still doubt?"

A customer, overhearing the conversation interjected. "And what about his preaching? He asks us to confess and turn away from our sinful ways and says that we will be forgiven! We don't need endless sacrifices, year after year, to cover our sins."

Jonas poised a question. "What have the Pharisees ever done for anyone other than take their money, give them burdens under laws— which, by the way they created, and require animal or food sacrifices?"

Jacob went quiet, unsettled. Thankfully, because the cart had drawn listeners, it was busier than ever so the men stopped their talk and went back to the business of selling, wrapping, and making change. Yet Jacob was in spiritual and mental turmoil. He couldn't help but keep a secret eye on Tamar and wondering how she could have changed from successful prostitute to a disciple of Jesus. Even though he loved Miriam, he still desired Tamar even though she clearly rebuffed him.

What is wrong with me? Why can't I forget the curves of her body? Jesus would consider my lustful thoughts sinful. Adulterous. Is this true? Most men think this way when looking at a beautiful woman! And why am I having a hard time in accepting Jesus for who he said he is?

"Jacob! Snap out of it. There're three people in front of you waiting to buy!"

Dismissing his conflicting thoughts, he sought out the next customer. "Next!"

Near the late afternoon, Timothy and his men had sold most of the fish. What started out as a disastrous morning, turned into a success story, here in the market place. Although they were exhausted from fishing all night, then selling all day, they were happy with the sales. Before the day ended, they heard many more stories from customers about Jesus and the miracles he performed, leaving Timothy and Jonas even more convinced about the power of Jesus.

The big question on everyone's lips, was, "Is this man the Messiah?"

Miriam, greeting him at the door, said, "I was so worried you didn't come home earlier, but Caleb told me you and the others had to go to the market because everyone was in town looking for Jesus and no one was at the beach to help or buy. You must be so tired. Did you sell all the fish?"

"Yes. The place was crawling with people from around the country looking for Jesus to hear him speak and no doubt watch him perform miracles, so we had a lot of hungry customers and they bought it all. Trash and good. Goes to show you'll eat anything if you're hungry enough."

"Did you see Tamar? She must have been selling too."

"I saw her, but she was busy too. She was doing a good business with twine and cloth."

His wife became quiet. He knew she had much more to ask, but he was not in the mood for talk. Finishing his meal, he kissed her and went to bed saying little more because his mind was in a jumble. Jesus, Tamar, Miriam, . . . he felt like his mind was burning up and oh, how he wished for simpler times when he had no conscience!

CHAPTER THIRTY-SEVEN

JACOB GOT UP EARLY AND headed to the beach. They weren't going to fish until later that night and he would catch a nap in the afternoon, but for now, there was some work to be done on the boat and nets.

He was surprised when he went down the path and saw to his far left a crowd gathering on the open expanse of beach. They were milling about, some sitting, some standing, and all were excitedly talking.

"It can only mean one thing," Jacob complained aloud putting his hands on his hips. "Jesus is there, or on his way . . . again!" He trudged down the path.

Timothy met him by the shoreline, excited. "We can wait on the repairs. There's not much to do anyway, thanks to Jonas keeping things in shape. I sent him off with his donkey to tell everyone that Jesus will be speaking here soon."

"Miriam too?"

"Of course, Jacob. I told him to get everyone."

Jacob opened his mouth to complain that Timothy had no right in disrupting his household's routine but thought better of it. Caleb and Esther, who would soon become engaged, would be unhappy if left out and of course Miriam would come with the baby.

"Come, let's get a spot by the shore. He's not here yet but will be soon and I want to get a space for all of us." Timothy walked through the milling people with Jacob in the rear and found an area large enough to hold the all of them. They marked it off with boat lines and stakes, much to the annoyance of others who complained it wasn't fair, and they shooed anyone away who tried to sit down.

"I hope they all get here soon, or we'll be run over," complained Jacob eyeing the pathway where lines of people were walking.

In a short time, Jerome with his wife Ann crested the hill along with Timothy's wife Elizabeth, then Jonas, Miriam with baby, Esther and Caleb. The women, with the exception of Miriam who had Joseph on her hip were carrying baskets of food and the men had water over their shoulders expecting to stay awhile. Jacob and Timothy waved and caught their eye.

When the party settled, Jerome said, "I heard that not only Simon, Philip, and Zebedee's sons have been made Jesus' apostles, but there are eight others that are his core apostles. He has scores of other disciples that follow him too. I can tell you, from what I hear, the Pharisees and Sadducees are becoming more alarmed as time goes on, especially in Jerusalem."

"Do they have the Romans and the Tetrarchs on their side?"

Jerome shrugged. "I don't know how much the rulers know of Jesus. Obviously, they know of John the Baptist, but as for Jesus, I believe they think he's the Jew's problem at the moment, not theirs. But that won't last long even though he's not talking of overthrowing any government. Once they hear about crowds of people from all over Galilee and Judea gathering, they might change their minds. Right now, they're thinking to let the Jews deal with their own jealousy."

Excitement rippled through the people as Jesus made his way to the shoreline so he could address the people. Upon seeing so many, he instructed one of his disciples to get a boat so he could get in it and speak from the water to those assembled on the beach and beyond. Miraculously, everyone could hear each word as he began to teach.

"Listen! A farmer went out to sow his seed. As he was scattering the seed, some fell along the path, and the birds came and ate it up. Some fell on rocky places, where it did not have much soil. It sprang up quickly, because the soil was shallow. But when the sun came up, the plants were scorched, and they withered because they had no root. Other seed fell among thorns, which grew up and choked the plants, so that they did not bear grain. Still other seed fell on good soil. It came up, grew and produced a crop, some multiplying thirty, some sixty, some a hundred times." Then Jesus said, "Whoever has ears to hear, let them hear."

Many of the people didn't know what he was talking about and questioned among themselves, "What does he mean? Why is he talking about a farmer?"

"This is what I'm talking about, Miriam," Jacob rubbed his bearded chin in exasperation. "Who can understand him when talks like this?"

"It's a parable, Jacob. What Jesus is saying is that he is like the farmer who is sowing the word of God and news about the kingdom of heaven. The people who listen, are like seeds. Some are like the seed sown along a path, but as soon as they hear God's word, Satan, like a bird, flies away with it. Other people are like the seed sown on poor, rocky soil. They hear the word, but it doesn't take root and the word withers under conflict. And other people are like seed sown among thorns. They, too, hear the word but life gets in the way, takes precedence and soon the word is choked off. But others, are like seed sown on good soil, hear the word, accept it, and produce a crop of good thoughts, words, deeds, and actions."

"Well, said," a person sitting close exclaimed. "In truth, I didn't get what he was saying either, but now it makes sense."

Jesus continued to speak in parables. Some understood, others didn't. Some grumbled, others tried to explain.

Jesus warned, "Why do you call me, 'Lord, Lord,' and do not do what I say? As for everyone who comes to me and hears my words and puts them into practice, I will show you what they are like. They are like a man building a house, who dug down deep and laid the foundation on rock. When a flood came, the torrent struck that house but could not shake it, because it was well built. But the one who hears my words and does not put them into practice is like a man who built a house on the ground without a foundation. The moment the torrent struck that house, it collapsed and its destruction was complete."

Jesus spoke more parables and told them what the kingdom of heaven was like. " . . . the kingdom of heaven is like a net that was let down into the lake and caught all kinds of fish. When it was full, the fishermen pulled it up on the shore. Then they sat down and collected the good fish in baskets, but threw the bad away. This is how it will be at the end of the age. The angels will come and separate the wicked from the righteous and throw them into the blazing furnace, where there will be weeping and gnashing of teeth."

Jacob tapped Miriam on the hand and said, "That I get."

CHAPTER THIRTY-EIGHT

THE FRIENDS HAD GATHERED AT Timothy and Miriam's home to celebrate the child's circumcision. Jerome and his goat Ziph had been traveling a few days prior but he made sure was back for Joseph's ceremony. Everyone looked forward to seeing Jerome after he had been traveling because he came with news from so many different areas in Galilee, Judea, and sometimes Jerusalem.

While Esther was helping Miriam with the meal, and Caleb and Jacob were pouring out wine, Caleb told them he heard that after Jesus spoke on the beach, he went on to Nazareth, his home town, to teach in the synagogue, but was criticized there.

"More opposition from the Pharisees?" Miriam asked over her shoulder as she peeled unleavened bread from glowing hot rocks.

"As well as from the town's people," Caleb replied handing Jacob another jar of wine.

"What happened?" asked Jacob.

Caleb quickly told the story because the guests were beginning to recline at the table. "They disapproved of him. Couldn't believe he could speak with such authority because he was just a carpenter and they knew his family. In other words, he was nothing special."

Miriam watched Jacob follow Caleb into the meal. Maybe that was a part of his problem with Jesus. Jesus was just a fellow Jew. There were no armies under him, no religious leaders hailing him, and if anyone was supporting him, it seemed like the dregs of humanity.

After the meal, Miriam prompted Jerome. "Let's hear your stories."

"Yes, we're all eager to hear the latest!" Caleb agreed.

Jerome sat silently for a moment

"Husband, what's wrong?" Ann studied Jerome with concern. "Are you ill, or tired? Is Ziph all right? We can hear your stories later." He was usually bubbling with news and boasts about Ziph, but this time he was subdued.

"No, no. I'm fine. It's just that I have a lot to tell you."

Miriam sensing anxiety, brushed a stray lock behind her ear, she asked, "Is it about Jesus and what went on in his home town of Nazareth?"

Jerome softly answered, "No. It's about John the Baptist. John criticized Herod for taking his brother Philip's wife, Herodias, and all the other evil that Herod's been doing."

"We hear a lot of what Herod does from the fisherman who travel the different ports and from traveling salesmen in the market place," Timothy said. "He's an evil man."

"You should hear the tales spread about him in Capernaum," Caleb added. "There's no shortage of stories that's for sure. The man is murderous."

Jonas looked at Caleb and whispered tapping his temple, "He's not right in the head."

"Herod threw John in prison," Jerome continued. The listeners moaned.

"No good will come of that," Jacob sighed.

"The story is that while John was in jail, Herod threw a birthday party for himself and invited a lot of people. They were all drinking, eating, and carrying on. Then Herodias' daughter danced for Herod. I guess she danced so well that he said he would give her anything she wanted, up to half his kingdom!"

"He must have been drunk!" Miriam objected.

"Well of course he was," Jacob responded. "I've heard what those parties are like. Even I wouldn't go to one of them."

"So his wife prompted her daughter to ask for," he stopped for a moment and gathered his emotions together. "For . . . John the Baptist's head on a platter, to be delivered to her at the party in front of everyone!" His listeners involuntarily put their hands to their mouths, horrified and sickened.

"Did he?" demanded Miriam.

"Yes."

Shocked and angered, the company sat quietly around the fire. Miriam hugged herself in sorrow. She so wanted to spare her baby boy the hard reality of living in these murderous, contemptable times.

People were living in darkness without spiritual comfort and light. Even the majority of Pharisees and Sadducees only cared about their own comfort and power, and poorly ministered to their flock, their own people. All of them wondered about Jesus. How would he take the death of John the Baptist? John had baptized him.

CHAPTER THIRTY-NINE

AFTER THE FRIENDS LEFT, MIRIAM sat rocking her baby to sleep while Jacob watched the fire. She heaved a sigh. "We need a man like Jesus to lead us and heal us, Jacob. I know you're struggling with who he is. You're not the only one, because many thought that Jesus would be a conqueror and commander like King David, but that's not who he is."

"Miriam, how can we need a man like him? He wasn't even welcomed in his home town of Nazareth! Did you not hear Caleb telling us earlier? That Jesus went into the synagogue to teach and the people were surprised and asked where he got this wisdom and how was he able to perform these wonders?"

"Yes, I heard. They asked, 'Wasn't he the carpenter's son, and wasn't his mother Mary'?"

"And they also said that his brothers and sisters were also from the town and so they wanted to know where all this—meaning his knowledge and power come from?"

"But you heard what Jesus response was didn't you? Jesus said, 'A prophet is not without honor except in his own town and in his own home'." That's why he didn't do many miracles there-- because of their lack of faith."

Jacob was still uncomfortable about the role Jesus was playing: was he real, or acting? "I know that most of the Pharisees and

Sadducees are out for themselves and won't acknowledge Jesus. I get that. They see him as a threat to their lifestyle and position, but there are some righteous teachers of the law in our synagogues. What bothers me is that *they* haven't come out in open to support Jesus either," Jacob said stubbornly.

"Like who for instance?"

"Like Nicodemus. He's a Pharisee and a Sanhedrin. A judge even!"

"Perhaps he's afraid."

"I think he is," Jerome said as he came up behind them in the dark, startling both Miriam and Jacob. "Sorry. Ann left her cloak and I had to come back and get it. It's the only one she has."

"Here, have a cup of water with us before you go back." Jacob poured a cup and Jerome sat down.

"I couldn't help but hear a part of your conversation, I know of Nicodemus and of all the Pharisees and Sanhedrin, he is a righteous man."

"See, I told you Miriam," Jacob argued. "If he can't speak out on Jesus' behalf, then I'm not sure what to think either."

Jerome sat quietly looking from Jacob to Miriam. "We can't change a person's beliefs. We might be able to influence, but you Jacob, must make your own decision, not based on other's opinions. Even for those of us who believe he is the Messiah, we don't know what's going to happen. He's made it clear to us that we must confess and repent our sin, believe in him, and take his teachings to heart, but there are more questions than answers at the moment. And as for Nicodemus, well, he's searching for answers too."

"But do you see my point, Jerome? Not one Pharisee, Sadducee, or the high priest has come out in favor of Jesus' works or teachings!" Jacob poked the fire in agitation.

Miriam shot her husband a look, but Jerome not fazed, merely replied, "I have it on good authority that Nicodemus came to Jesus under the cover of darkness to ask some questions. Now I don't know if he went on his own, or under the auspices of the Sanhedrin, but it was unusual because he visited Jesus at night. Maybe he didn't want anyone to see him? Anyway, Jesus immediately told him that unless one was 'born again', that person could not enter the kingdom of heaven."

"Born again?" Sarcasm jumped from Jacob's mouth. "If Jesus isn't talking in parables, then he talks nonsense at times! How can a person be born again?!"

"Hold, on listen," Jerome said. "Nicodemus reacted the same way and asked, I'm sure with the same measure of incredulity, 'How can he enter a second time in his mother's womb and be born?' But Jesus said to him that unless one was *born* of water and Spirit, that person can't enter the kingdom of heaven."

"Water and Spirit? Jacob was exasperated. "What does that even mean?"

"Jacob. Perhaps Jesus was saying that in order to enter the kingdom of heaven one must have a rebirth of the heart, soul, and mind? And water, used by John the Baptist symbolizes repentance of sin, and then the Spirit, God's Spirit, renews that person. We become new people, putting away our old ways of thinking and behaving," Miriam said, kissing the top of Joseph's sleeping head, praying Jacob would understand.

Jacob abruptly stood up. "I don't know. Why can't this Jesus just speak plainly and not in riddles? I need to check on the goats." He left the fire.

Jacob looked back at Jerome and Miriam and heard her say, "My heart aches that he doesn't seem open to letting Jesus word's sink into his heart. Jacob is a good man, but he seems to be closing his mind to Jesus."

Jacob was stung she didn't understand his feelings about Jesus. Even Jerome's own wife had withdrawn from following the man around. She told them all that she had too much work watching the children, running the household, and making sure the animals were cared for when Jerome was traveling. Sulking, he moved a few clumps of hay around the shelter, musing that even the scribes doubted that the prophesies pointed to this lowly man Jesus. What was he, uneducated as he was to think?

Jerome stood up to go. Jacob strained to hear what Jerome was saying, but his friend called out to him. "The other thing Jesus said to Nicodemus was that the wind blows where it wants, and while we might hear its sound, we don't know where it comes from or where it goes . . . and so it is with anyone who is born of the Spirit of God."

Jacob turned his back on them and tossed a clump of hay in the manger. *What was he talking about now? Too many riddles!*

He barely heard Miriam say, "God goes where he will . . . "

Jacob walked back to his wife. "Where's Jerome?"

"Gone."

CHAPTER FORTY

THAT MORNING, JACOB WENT DOWN to the beach to start his workday. He was subdued, wrestling with his thoughts about Jesus, still not believing Tamar could change so radically, and wondering why he didn't have the confidence in Jesus that his other friends had, including his wife. He met up with Timothy who was arguing with a shipwright repairing the hull near the shallow keel of his boat.

"We've got to get out today. I've missed enough fishing. When can you get it done?"

The man looked at Timothy and scowled. "You're not going anywhere. You've pretty much torn a hole in the bottom running aground as many times as you have. I'm doing the best I can to patch her up."

Timothy bit his lip and walked away with Jonas and Jacob who was deciding whether or not to go home. Trudging along the sand towards the road the three men saw groups of people hustling along the shoreline going north.

"What's going on?" Timothy squinted his eyes in question.

Jacob shrugged his shoulders. "It's got to be Jesus again. He must be somewhere close."

A man passed beside them. "Yes, it's Jesus. He's someplace not too far from Bethsaida."

"Let's go! We can't fish!" Timothy started to follow the people.

"Bethsaida?" Jacob complained. "We don't know where he'll be! He could be anywhere!

Jonas agreed. "Let's follow. We'll find him. We have a free day."

"We don't have any food or . . . ," Jacob began, but his friends were already on the move. *This is crazy,* thought Jacob but joined his friends as they hurried back down along the shores of the Sea of Galilee.

A few miles later, they came to a wide desolate spot with a small hill half encircled by a shallow cove. Thousands of people had shown up and were settling in groups, eagerly waiting for Jesus to arrive.

Timothy and Jonas exchanged surprised looks. "This, I never expected!" Timothy wiped his brow with a corner of his turban taking in the sight of thousands of people.

"Look, there he is!" a series of cries went up from the multitude. A small boat approached dropping its sails and coming in on oars. Jesus was at the bow and a few of his apostles were rowing in. Near the shallows, one man jumped in with an anchor and line in his hands and lodged it in the sand on the beach.

Jesus climbed over the gunnels, splashed down in a foot or so of water and made his way to the beach. People surged toward him, but his apostles kept them at bay as he and his followers inched their way toward a small rise where Jesus chose to speak from.

Scanning the crowds, Jacob choked when he saw Tamar and Miriam, without the baby in the crowd near where Jesus had sat down. Desperately he waved at them, but they were too focused on the man who was about to speak to see him. "Look, there's Tamar and my wife! How did they know Jesus would be here?" he asked more to himself than to anybody.

"All they needed to see were the hordes of people walking by your house, Jacob," Jonas nodded taking the mass of people in. "You'd have to be deaf and blind not to know Jesus was somewhere to be heard and seen."

"Yes, but how did they both meet up?"

Jonas gave Jacob a look. "How would I know?"

"Let's see if we can get up close to where they are." Timothy interjected and set out squeezing through the crowds.

The women were happily surprised to see the men who pressed in beside them. "This is a miracle in and of itself, you seeing us here!" Miriam exclaimed. "There must be thousands of people here and look how close we are to Jesus!"

"Where's Joseph?" Jacob demanded, ignoring her comments.

Miriam gave him a withering look. "With mother. She was delighted to watch him. I'm surprised you're here and not fishing."

"The boat is being repaired and so we thought we'd see what's going on," Jacob shrugged, ignoring Tamar.

"Good. I'm really glad you're here," Miriam beamed and reached for her husband. Tamar got up, kissed Miriam goodbye, and pushed onward to the small group of men and women sitting beside Jesus who made room for her.

"How did you two happen to be here?" Jacob wanted to know.

"Tamar was on her way to be with the rest of the disciples and passed our house. She saw me outside, and suggested I go with her. I did," Miriam explained.

Jacob opened his mouth to argue, but Timothy held up a hand to quite them. "Shhh. Let's hear what Jesus has to say."

Jesus began, and he taught until evening.

Hours into Jesus' teaching and during a break, Miriam overheard a couple of Jesus apostles speaking, "This is a remote place," they said, "and it's already very late. Send the people away so that they can go to the surrounding countryside and villages and buy themselves something to eat."

She heard Jesus respond, "You give them something to eat."

They said to him, "That would take more than half a year's wages! Are we to go and spend that much on bread and give it to them to eat?"

"How many loaves do you have?" he asked. "Go and see."

She watched them go to someone who held a satchel of provisions. They came back to Jesus and said, "Five—and two fish."

Then Jesus directed them to have all the people sit down in groups on the green grass. So they sat down in groups of hundreds and fifties. Taking the five loaves and the two fish and looking up to heaven, he gave thanks and broke the loaves. Then he gave them to his disciples to distribute to the people. He also divided the two fish among them all.

She was astounded that they all had enough to eat with left-overs so that the disciples picked up twelve basketfuls of broken pieces of bread and fish when everyone was finished.

Timothy nudged Jacob watching this feeding project unfold. "Do you know how many people are here? It's incredible!"

Jonas calculated, "There must be over five thousand and he fed us all with just five loaves and two fishes!"

Miriam looked squarely at Jacob. "How would the Pharisees explain that?"

Jacob shrugged his shoulders.

CHAPTER FORTY-ONE

MIRIAM BREATHED IN THE SCENT of her baby and smiled. "How extraordinary Jesus was able to feed more than five thousand yesterday— because don't forget, there were women and children there too, Jacob. All he had was a little bread and two fish! You can't deny any of the miracles you've seen with your own two eyes. How you can you explain it, if he's not the Messiah?"

Tying twine around a post and rail, he responded, "I can't explain it and there are other things I can't explain either, like the 'kingdom of God is near'."

"I think it means Jesus, if he's our Messiah and I think he is, has brought the kingdom to us because sinners who repent, including the poor and sick are welcome into the spiritual realm of the kingdom now."

"So this implies that the Roman Empire, the supreme military dictatorship that caters to the powerful and wealthy is merely an earthly power and limited at that?"

"Yes, I would say so. The kingdom of God doesn't necessarily *not* welcome the powerful and rich, but all are welcome with conditions and Jesus has brought it to us. It's revolutionary teaching!"

"He also claimed God was his Father, equating himself to God. This puts him in direct conflict with the Jewish leaders." Jacob wondered how the Roman rulers would view his claim because there was no lack of gods and goddesses in the Roman Empire.

"Remember the parable of the seed growing, Jacob? Jesus said, 'This is what the kingdom of God is like. A man scatters seed on the ground. Night and day, whether he sleeps or gets up, the seed sprouts and grows, though he does not know how. All by itself the soil produces grain—first the stalk, then the head, then the full kernel in the head. As soon as the grain is ripe, he puts the sickle to it, because the harvest has come.'"

"Yes, and I remember the one about the mustard seed when he said the kingdom of God is like a mustard seed, 'which is the smallest of all seeds on earth. Yet when planted, it grows and becomes the largest of all garden plants, with such big branches that the birds can perch in its shade.' Why is he always talking in parables?"

"I don't know. Tamar tells me that Jesus is going onward to Gennesaret" Miriam held the baby on her hip and handed Jacob a bowl of water. Jacob, working on the goat's pens, reached for the cup and downed it in one long gulp before speaking.

Wiping his mouth with his sleeve, he asked suspiciously, "By the way, how long have you and Tamar been talking with each other?"

"Since we caught up with each other at the market place."

"You know what type of woman Tamar is!"

"I do know what type of woman she *was* and what she is now. She's changed, Jacob. Believe it."

"But the question is, how come you're spending time with her?"

"I'm not really. She stops by now and then, and I might see her at the market if she's not off with Jesus and his disciples. She and some other women are helping him and the apostles— the twelve they're called sometimes— as they travel. As I told you earlier, that's why I happened to be there yesterday to listen to Jesus. She's told me some marvelous and astonishing stories."

"More than we already know?"

Miriam nodded. "There's so much more we don't know about. If we're fortunate, we hear what is going on in and around Capernaum, but so often, by the time we hear of it, Jesus has already moved on to a different place and when he travels from the region, we might or might not know what he's taught or what miracles he's performed."

"So tell me."

She took the bowl from him and holding the baby with one arm on her hip said. "He raised a young man from the dead."

"What?" Jacob could only utter one word.

"This happened in the town of Nain. Tamar said, 'Jesus and his disciples and a large crowd went along with him. As he approached the town gate, a dead person was being carried out—the only son of his mother, and she was a widow. And a large crowd from the town was with her. When the Lord saw her, his heart went out to her and he said, 'Don't cry.'

"'Then he went up and touched the bier they were carrying him on, and the bearers stood still. He said, 'Young man, I say to you, get up!' The dead man sat up and began to talk, and Jesus gave him back to his mother.'

CHAPTER FORTY-TWO

JACOB, KNOWING THAT JESUS WOULD be in the country of the Gergesenes, wasn't surprised when Miriam pleaded him, "Please ask Timothy if he'll take us all in his boat to see Jesus. It's the only practical way to get to the other side of the Sea of Galilee and I so want to see him! Please?"

Jacob, not really wanting to go himself, but wanting to please Miriam asked his friend as they were getting ready to go out for the day.

"Surely, I will! That's great news. We can make the trip no problem. It might be close quarters because I know that Jerome, Jonas, Esther, and Caleb will want to make the trip too. But I'm good with that if they are."

Jacob asked him about Ann. "Will she come along too?"

"Knowing my wife, she'll want to stay home with all the children. I'd like her to come, but . . . it's her decision."

The following day, they loaded up the boat and Miriam took Jerome aside. "Does Ann not want to hear Jesus?"

Jerome fiddled with a line and pulled it hard. "I don't always understand her. One moment she's enthusiastic about Jesus and the next moment, she's all wrapped up in the children or seeing to the care of the baby goats. I'm disappointed I can't have meaningful discussions about Jesus and all that's happening with her, but it's just the way it is. I can't force interest on someone who really doesn't have interest."

Miriam nodded. "Well, I'm grateful she's taking care of all of our children, but I'm sorry she will miss the experience."

Once underway, Miriam immediately told them the story Tamar repeated of Jesus raising a widow's son from the dead in the village of Nain.

At the conclusion of the story they were speechless until Jacob offered grudgingly, "One thing I can say for Tamar is, she doesn't lie, so even I'm confident this isn't a tale."

Jerome looked out over the water deep in thought. He turned back to everyone who were trying to digest this latest incredulous miracle. "Do you see what is unfolding here? In our generation, for whatever reason, we are being exposed to God himself. If Jesus *is* the Son of God . . . then he's God incarnate. How else could anyone possibly explain raising one from the *dead?* Tell me, how much more does anyone need to recognize who he is?"

Jacob busied himself with a line, keeping his head down. He knew Jerome was talking about him.

The winds were moderate, and the boat was making good time. Where they were headed wasn't that far and if the wind stayed consistent, they'd get to their destination in a handful of hours. There was plenty of time for stories and discussions about the inexplicable character of Jesus.

Caleb, who recently spent time in Capernaum selling and buying Jacob's goats, said, "I tell you this: Spending as much time as I have at the market place, I've heard the rumors that the Pharisees are getting desperate. Their jealousy has blinded them. They are out to get him, miracles or not, by tricking him into blasphemy so they can arrest him."

"I admit," Jerome leaned back on a cushion, his hand light on the tiller. "I was hoping for a conqueror, one who would straighten out the Jewish leaders, put them in their place, and overthrow the Roman government, but after hearing the miracle of Jesus raising the dead, I've come to the conclusion that political upheaval is not a part of Jesus' plan. It's got to be spiritual upheaval."

Miriam gazed at her husband who was still busying himself straightening out the lines to avoid participation in the conversation.

Caleb, Esther, and Jonas were quiet, until Esther spoke up. "How could I not think that Jesus is the Son of God? He healed me!"

Over the last couple of hours, other boats under sail followed them and were also plied with people. "Looks like we aren't the only ones tracking down Jesus," Caleb said watching the boats sluicing through the light chop.

"We're all going in the same direction. Timothy pointed. "That looks like Simon's boat up ahead."

Jonas stepped up on the bow and squinted with his hand over his eyes. "Yes, it's his boat alright. I can see the repair on his starboard side from here." Jonas whistled to another boat that was following them and as it came alongside, Jonas pointed, and the fisherman nodded.

Close in, they dropped sail, took to the oars, while Caleb took the soundings so as not to run aground. They finally moored in water deep enough for the keel, but shallow enough for them to get off the boat.

An incredible sense of peace descended upon Miriam when Esther turned with excitement to Miriam nearly shouting, "From the moment he healed me, I believed!"

Miriam grabbed both of her hands. "All that I have seen: miracles no one has ever done, listening to his teachings, and seeing his sincere love for the poor, needy, and sick—I believed."

"His ways are so radical from the Roman rule that bullies with might, coerces with threats, and demands alliance for nothing in return but harsh dictatorship!" Jerome helped the women off the boat.

On the beach, both women yearned to speak to him, but as always, he was surrounded by his disciples and others who just wanted to touch him, to be healed, to be comforted.

Esther held Miriam's hand. "I want to thank him. I want to tell him I love him!

Miriam squeezed back. "I do to, Esther, but there're always crowds around him and it's so hard to push through to him."

Moving her attention from Esther, she watched her husband tying the off the anchor line knowing he still wrestled with the opinion synagogue leaders, his own personal thoughts, and all the miracles that Jesus had performed. Her Jacob was a puzzle. She never knew him to be in awe of the law or leaders, so she didn't understand why he resisted turning his mind and heart over to what he was actually seeing and hearing, instead of getting hung up on tradition and human opinion.

Jesus' disciples began the climb up a rocky hill dotted with scrub brush and weeds, eagerly following their master. Miriam's party quickly sloshed through the shallow water and went across the beach in the footsteps of Jesus and his disciples.

Esther asked Miriam, "Is Tamar going to be here?"

"She said she was, but I don't see her. She's usually close by the apostles, but there are few women here today."

Standing at the base of a hill one could see several tombs imbedded on the scrabbled incline and further to the crest. Ahead of them, Jesus walked up a narrow footpath, followed by the disciples, when suddenly, a filthy man, naked, bruised, and bloodied appeared. His skin was mottled brown and damaged, his hair matted and twisted far past his shoulders and his wrists and ankles were bloodied and torn. Jacob extended his arm to stop Miriam from moving upward. Everyone, but Jesus, cautiously stepped back.

Miriam could see the man must have been shackled at one time, because of the deep marks and crusted blood on his wrists and ankles. He was lurching about, speaking and jabbering incoherently.

A man from the village came beside Miriam and Jacob, startling them. "No one can bind him anymore because he breaks his shackles and chains, wrenching them apart. He's amazingly strong and out of his mind."

"But why is he here?" Miriam asked.

"He lives among the tombs and no one has the strength to subdue him, so he wanders day and night crying and screaming and cutting himself with stones."

The man stopped abruptly staring at the crowd then bolted toward Jesus. Before his disciples could stop the attack, the crazed man fell to his knees before Jesus. The disciples went deathly still, but in alert mode to jump and subdue the man if need be.

But Jesus said commandingly, "Come out of this man you impure spirit!"

The man cried out with a loud voice, "What do you want with me, Jesus, Son of the Most High God? In God's name don't torture me!"

Then Jesus asked him, "What is your name?"

"My name is Legion," he replied, "for we are many." And he begged Jesus again and again not to send them out of the area.

A large herd of pigs was feeding on the nearby hillside. The demons begged Jesus, "Send us among the pigs; allow us to go into them." He gave them permission, and the impure spirits came out and went into the pigs. The herd, about two thousand in number, rushed down the steep bank into the lake and were drowned.

Miriam and all who were with her were speechless. Horrified. Never anticipated the reaction of the pigs and the men who were tending the animals ran away in terror. Through all this action, the man who was uncontrollable, calmly rose to his feet and walked to a tomb, disappeared inside.

By now, many townspeople showed up and begged Jesus to leave. Miriam was confused. "Why would they want Jesus to leave?" Looking around she was surrounded by fearful, vocal strangers.

Jerome cocked his head listening. "Not sure. Maybe they recognize that this is no ordinary prophet and are afraid of his power and don't want to welcome it?"

The man who was naked, came out of the tomb, and walked down the slope, fully clothed. The disconcerted people parted, making way for him to pass staring at him in absolute shock.

Jesus descend the hill and as he was getting into the boat, the man who had been demon-possessed begged to go with him. Jesus did not let him, but said, "Go home to your own people and tell them how much the Lord has done for you, and how he has had mercy on you."

"Jesus wants him to stay. It's his way of spreading the good news," Miriam said in wonder but looked in confusion and fear at the dead pigs bobbing in the water. "But why did the pigs run to their deaths?"

Jerome wagged his head. "It's likely even they didn't want to be possessed by evil spirits."

Miriam had hoped to speak to Jesus, but he was ferried away by his apostles. Her husband, her friends, stood on the beach shaken, watching the man on the shore who had been possessed praising Jesus as Lord as sane as they were.

Caleb tilted his head to Esther, "Well. That was definitely worth the trip!"

CHAPTER FORTY-THREE

MANY DAYS LATER, MIRIAM SPOKE with friends gathered at her home for supper. "Tamar, as

you know, wasn't at the great pig event because she was seeing to an ill friend, but I saw her at the market today. And I have a story for you."

"Usually, I'm the one everyone wants to hear from," Jerome joked. "You've taken some of the pressure off me, with our news source in Tamar!" They all laughed.

"Now that Tamar has committed to following Jesus, I asked her if she would not only let me know what's going on, but where he might be so we can all go and see him if he's in our area. Just recently, there's been another extraordinary miracle! You all know Jairus?" Miriam asked.

"Yes," Esther answered. "We heard at the market that his little daughter is quite ill."

"Well, he came to Jesus and fell at his feet, begging him to heal is daughter. He said, 'My little daughter is dying. Please come and put your hands on her so that she will be healed and live.' Then some men came from Jairus' house and told him not to bother, his daughter was already dead. Yet Jesus said to Jairus, 'Don't be afraid; just believe.' He didn't let anyone follow him to Jairus' house except Peter and the sons of Zebedee," Miriam explained.

"Who's Peter?" Jacob asked.

"I should have let you know. Tamar told me that Jesus changed Simon's name to Peter."

Jacob crossed his arms over his chest. "That's Simon for sure. Hard-headed!"

Miriam continued. "When they came to the home of Jarius, Jesus saw a commotion, with people crying and wailing loudly. He went in and said to them, 'Why all this commotion and wailing? The child is not dead but asleep.' But they laughed at him.' Tamar said that he put them all out of the house, then he took the child's father and mother and the disciples who were with him, and went in where the child was. He took her by the hand and said to her, 'Talitha koum!'

"The little girl, who was about twelve years old, rose. Jesus told them to get her something to eat, then he left."

Jacob uncrossed his arms and set his hands on his thighs, index finger tapping. "What is wrong with these Pharisees? They've been witnessing the man's powers and if they haven't seen his works first hand, then they surely have heard stories like this one! If Jesus calls God his father, they must see he is equal to God. Surely they could ask his favor, for they're in high positions in the synagogue!" Agitated, he grabbed an iron and poked the fire.

"That's the point, Jacob. They're in high positions and Jesus is threatening their status. Don't you see?" Miriam asked softly. She knew he was conflicted. Loyalty to the religious leaders versus loyalty to Jesus. But how much more would Jacob need to open his eyes to truth?

Miriam didn't tell the men the other story Tamar had told her about the woman who squeezed in among the crowds following Jesus on his way to Jairus' house. Instead, she got up, and beckoned the women into the house on the pretense of helping her get more food and drink. Inside she spoke of yet another wonderful miracle.

"Listen to this. There was a woman who followed Jesus on his way to Jairus' house. For twelve years she had constant bleeding, and you know that made her ritually unclean all those years! Anyone or anything she touched would also become unclean. This meant that she was living in exile, away from her family, home, and friends. Desperate, she willingly took the risk of being in among clean people, risking defiling them and even Jesus."

"Oh, my!" Esther put down a jug of water and sat down. "Any person she touched would have to go through a process of ritual cleansing and being alone until the evening and she probably wouldn't have gotten away from the crowd alive, if she was found out!"

Miriam loaded up a platter of bread and goat cheese, hurriedly continuing. "Indeed! But she heard about Jesus' healing powers and just wanted to touch him . . . so she came up behind him and lightly touched his cloak. Immediately, she felt the flow of blood stop! 'Jesus turned and asked, "Who touched my garments?"' and of course the disciples told him with all of these people closing in on him, who knew?"

"Oh, Oh! What happened?" Esther covered her mouth in worry.

Miriam straightened up, holding the platter of bread in both hands. "She fell at his feet, scared and trembling. Jesus said to her, 'Daughter, your faith has healed you. Go in peace and be freed from your suffering.'"

The women just stared at Miriam. Esther dropped her hands and puffed out a breath of air. "Healed! I can't imagine being ostracized for twelve years from my people because of a disease that caused uncleanliness! Even as a leper I at least lived in a community of people like myself . . . and it was unlikely that this woman had anyone willing to live with her, or if they did, she would live in a prison-like room."

Amazed, they went back to the men bringing more food and drink as Jerome, plucking off a piece of bread to dip in his stew, said, "If Jesus is back in town, then let's go see him at the synagogue. I'm eager to not only hear him but see how our religious leaders are reacting to his work."

"Oh, they'll be in a frenzy! Raising two people form the dead will get back to them swift and threatening. If Jairus, one of their owned witnessed such a miracle, surely, the others will admit to Jesus' claim that God is his Father." Timothy helped himself to more stew.

"Either that, or they'll kill him," Caleb said mournfully.

CHAPTER FORTY-FOUR

MIRIAM SAT WITH ESTHER GIGGLING and planning the festivities for Esther's betrothal agreement with Caleb. Within the year, the couple would be married. Although they both lived on Jacob and his father's property, they each had separate quarters and were devout Jews so neither Miriam nor Jacob had any concerns about the couple's daily interaction.

Everyone knew what was to be expected. After the marriage, a room would be prepared for them that was currently under construction on the side of the existing house. Caleb would continue his goat husbandry, and Esther, until she became pregnant, would help Miriam with Joseph and the household duties. Once she had her own child, she would attend to it, but still help with the household.

A light rap on the doorframe caused Miriam to look up. "Tamar! Come in!" Hopping up from her stool, she rushed to Tamar and embraced her. "We haven't seen you for a while! I've missed you. We were just going over plans for the prenuptial agreement for Caleb and Esther."

"I heard the wonderful news in the market place —where else? And stopped by to give Esther a gift and to chat." Tamar held up a length of purple dyed wool and handed it to Esther.

"This is beautiful, Tamar! Thank you so much!" Esther ran her hands along the fine weave and kissed her on the cheek.

"Tamar, you have the best taste!" Miriam laughed as she admired the finely woven cloth Esther held up.

Tamar sat down and accepted a cup of tea from Miriam. "I have news about Jesus. Jesus as you know has been traveling and along with the other disciples, but we're all back together in Capernaum now."

"We didn't know that," Miriam said looking over to Esther who shook her head and shrugged her shoulders. Miriam explained, "Jacob has been fishing with Timothy and Jonas, and Caleb has been out tending the goats. Jerome is somewhere with Ziph, and we women have been at home. I haven't even seen Ann or Elizabeth in a while, so we haven't had much news."

"Well, many, many people are following him." Tamar spread her hands wide.

"I'll wager many are looking for the miracle of bread and fish. Crowds love free food," Miriam nodded.

"So true!" Tamar laughed. "Jesus said the same thing. 'Very truly I tell you, you are looking for me, not because you saw the signs I performed but because you ate the loaves and had your fill. Do not work for food that spoils, but for food that endures to eternal life, which the Son of Man will give you. For on him God the Father has placed his seal of approval.'"

"Son of Man?" Miriam mused. "That's Jesus."

"Yes. But they asked what works of God should they be doing, and he said that they believe in him whom God had sent."

The women sat back. How much more direct could Jesus be?

"Then they asked him for a sign they could see to believe in him!"

Miriam shook her head in dismay. "Didn't they see or hear about him feeding the many thousands? Weren't many of them there that had been fed and so showed up again for more food? Or raising up a dead child? What more of a sign do they want?"

Jacob stepped through the doorway.

"You're home early," Miriam was surprised to see him but got up to kiss him and take his gear. "Didn't go out today?"

"We hit a submerged log. Took a chunk out of the bow. Had to come in bailing all the way with a half load of fish. Timothy has the shipwright fixing it now and we were lucky to sell off the fish . . . so here I am. Mind if I join you?" He sat down heavily glowering at Tamar.

"Tamar was telling us about Jesus and the crowds that are following him." Miriam recapped the story for Jacob.

"So what was the sign they wanted him to show them?" Jacob looked to Tamar.

"Something that could compare in greatness with Moses' work because they bragged that Moses during the Exodus gave them manna to eat. But Jesus said it wasn't Moses who gave them bread from heaven . . . "

"It was God for goodness sake," sighed Esther, finishing Tamar's sentence. "Everyone knows that, don't they?"

"Jesus then confused them. He said it was the Father that gives them the true bread from heaven. Bread that gives life to the world." Tamar took a sip of tea. "So, they asked for that bread and Jesus answered that *he* was the bread . . . of life and that whoever believed in him wouldn't be hungry or thirsty. He told them that he had come down from heaven not to do his will, but the will of the one who sent him. He also said that the will of his Father is that anyone who believes in the son will have eternal life."

"His Father is God." Jacob said. "Meaning, once again he is equating himself with God."

Esther and Miriam exchanged glances.

Tamar nodded. "After more discussion, he said, 'Very truly I tell you, the one who believes has eternal life. I am the bread of life. Your ancestors ate the manna in the wilderness, yet they died. But here is the bread that comes down from heaven, which anyone may eat and not die. I am the living bread that came down from heaven. Whoever eats this bread will live forever. This bread is my flesh, which I will give for the life of the world.'

Jacob smirked at Tamar. "Here we go again. Eating his flesh? How can we eat his flesh?"

She didn't answer him. "He also said, 'Very truly I tell you, unless you eat the flesh of the Son of Man and drink his blood, you have no life in you. For my flesh is real food and my blood is real drink. Whoever eats my flesh and drinks my blood remains in me, and I in them. Just as the living Father sent me and I live because of the Father, so the one who feeds on me will live because of me. This is the bread that came down from heaven. Your ancestors ate manna and died, but whoever feeds on this bread will live forever.'"

"And now drink his blood? Women, this is crazy! How can you believe all this?" Jacob jumped up in dismissal.

"Wait, Jacob, I think I can explain," Miriam said desperately grabbing for his tunic.

"No!" he admonished her. "I've heard enough. Just when I think this Jesus could be understandable, I lose him. I'll leave you women to your gossip." He left the house.

"I admit it is a strange analogy," Miriam conceded watching him walk away, "but I think what he was saying is that we have a shared life in Jesus, an indwelling so to speak. If we seek him as if to eat his flesh and drink his blood, we have eternal life."

Esther remained silent.

Tamar shrugged her shoulders. "I guess so . . . although I think there's more to it that I don't quite understand, but I'll tell you. Many left him after that speech."

CHAPTER FORTY-FIVE

THE FOLLOWING DAY TAMAR RETURNED to Miriam and Jacob's house. "Jesus will be in the courtyard at the synagogue on the Sabbath."

Miriam and Esther were preparing a noon day meal. Miriam indicated she sit and handed her honeyed bread which she gratefully accepted.

In between mouthfuls, she told them when and where Jesus would be. "Get there early, so you can get close to all of us because I'm concerned about the leaders who will be there from Jerusalem."

"Why? What have you heard?" Miriam was worried.

Wiping her mouth on her fingertips, Tamar shrugged her veil off to her shoulders, revealing luxurious dark hair, saying, "Everyone knows that discussion about Jesus' miracles and wonders have spread all through Judea and Galilee, including Samaria. We all know the Pharisees have negotiated an uneasy peace between Rome and the Jews. So the religious leaders are not only concerned that Jesus threatens their security and prestige among the people by doing miracles, they're also afraid that Rome might take notice. They don't want Rome to think there's internal conflict between Jesus' followers and the teachers of the law, considering the Jews' politics and theology are one."

"You mean they're afraid that Rome could come after us because we see Jesus as our Messiah and the Pharisees don't?" Miriam trembled at the thought.

"It's complicated." Tamar had been in the middle of many of these discussions with the disciples. "The leaders of the synagogue have put more weight on oral traditions of men rather than the written law of God. Jesus sees that our leaders have created their own legal righteousness that is in direct conflict with the law of God that he, Jesus, has come to uphold. Because of this, they see that their authority is called into to question when people see Jesus' miracles and hear his words that overturn their rules of the Sabbath, food prohibitions, cleanliness requirements, and even their exclusion of the Gentiles. They see they're losing their hold of leadership over the Jews. It scares them because of how Rome might react."

After Tamar left, Esther added, "Let's face it; the Pharisees keep us all in line and as long as the Jews are under control, Rome's okay with that."

"And I'm sure they expected that their legal righteousness would be embraced and touted by not only John the Baptist, but by Jesus, who says his Father is God. Both men should have been delighted. Instead, John called them vipers and Jesus calls them hypocrites."

"So herein lies the heart of the matter, Miriam. The Pharisees, Sadducee's, Sanhedrin, and scribes, elders, chief priests, want him gone. They don't want Rome to be concerned about the crowds Jesus is drawing, which could be seen as seditious," Esther concluded.

Miriam went to the corner of the room to check on her sleeping baby. "How can Rome see Jesus as a threat when his description of the kingdom of heaven is like a mustard seed? I can't see implied revolution there. Besides, anyone who wants to go that kingdom has to die."

"I agree, with you, but according to Jerome the Pharisees fear loss on several levels to include their status, power over the Jews, and the ability to hold onto that power given to them by the grace of the Roman Empire," Esther said warily. "In order to keep it all under control, Jesus has to be eliminated. He can't be seen as a leader. It's terrifying for them."

It's terrifying for Jacob too. Not that he would want to see Jesus harmed in anyway, but she knew he didn't want to see his life so radically changed. During his lifetime, and that of his father's and his father's father, and so on down the ancestral line, the Pharisees, Sadducees, teachers of the law, the elders, and chief priests have always dictated how the lives of the Jews were to be ruled from worship to everyday living.

Through much hardship and hypocrisy, it has been the way of life for decades. What has Jesus really come to do?

CHAPTER FORTY-SIX

IT WAS EARLY MORNING WHEN Miriam and Jacob, Esther and Caleb, Timothy and Elizabeth, Ann and Jerome, and Jonas reached the courtyard of the synagogue. People were trickling in from many parts of the countryside and cities in Galilee as well as in Judea.

After the group settled in a spot as close as they could get to Jesus, Miriam spied Tamar with a small group of women sitting near Jesus along with his apostles and teachers of the law including the Pharisees, Sadducees, and others.

Laying down a cushion, Jerome surveyed the men crowding around Jesus. "Look over there by the archway. Those are the Jewish leaders from Jerusalem! I recognize two of them that I met at last year's Passover."

"They came all the way from Jerusalem to see Jesus?" Timothy marveled. "They must be really worried!"

Caleb wrinkled his brow. "I told you they are serious about tripping up Jesus. They want to get their hands on him and haul him down to Jerusalem."

"If God is his father, I suspect he knows all about it, right?" Jacob said with a hint of sarcasm.

"Jacob," Miriam scolded. "They might kill him!"

"They don't have the authority to kill him. Only Rome can order death as punishment. But that doesn't mean they can't convince Pilate. He has total power over the Jews and has to answer to the emperor." Jerome, as did the others, knew the authority Pilate had over the Jewish leaders, but also was aware that the Jewish leaders could be convincing.

Miriam's stomach lurched. It was unthinkable. At that moment she felt a deep anger at Jacob's hard heart and the authorities—both Roman and Jews' power.

Loudly, so all could hear, one of the scribes confronted Jesus, "Why do your disciples break the tradition of the elders? They don't wash their hands before they eat!"

Jesus replied, "And why do you break the command of God for the sake of your tradition? For God said, 'Honor your father and mother' and 'Anyone who curses their father or mother is to be put to death.' But you say that if anyone declares that what might have been used to help their father or mother is 'devoted to God,' they are not to 'honor their father or mother' with it. Thus you nullify the word of God for the sake of your tradition. You hypocrites! Isaiah was right when he prophesied about you:

"'These people honor me with their lips,
   but their hearts are far from me.
They worship me in vain;
   their teachings are merely human rules.'"

Miriam leaned into Esther. "Didn't we discuss this only yesterday?" Esther nodded, shocked at Jesus words.

Caleb was wide-eyed. "He called them hypocrites to their faces!"

The teachers of the law sat straighter and scowled deeper, glancing and mumbling angrily to one another while the people spread the remark through the building crowds.

Jesus ignored them. Instead, he called out to the crowd and said, "Listen and understand. What goes into someone's mouth does not defile them, but what comes out of their mouth, that is what defiles them."

Jesus spoke for a while longer, and the leaders, having heard enough insults and offense, stood up in unison and stormed away. "He insults us! He speaks blasphemy against our law!"

Again, Jesus ignored them. When he finished teaching and blessing, some of the crowd drifted away hoping to catch up with the leaders of the law while others loitered hoping for a blessing and a healing. Jesus stopped and spoke many times to those who tarried, but eventually he was ushered away by his disciples back to the house where he was staying, although a small group continued to follow him.

Miriam was close enough to hear someone say to Jesus, "Do you know that the Pharisees were offended when they heard this?"

He replied, "Every plant that my heavenly Father has not planted will be pulled up by the roots. Leave them; they are blind guides. If the blind lead the blind, both will fall into a pit."

Peter said, "Explain the parable to us."

"Are you still so dull?" Jesus asked them. "Don't you see that whatever enters the mouth goes into the stomach and then out of the body? But the things that come out of a person's mouth come from the heart, and these defile them. For out of the heart come evil thoughts—murder, adultery, sexual immorality, theft, false testimony, slander. These are what defile a person; but eating with unwashed hands does not defile them."

Jacob came up from behind her. "Come. We're not following him home."

Miriam trailed behind the others on the walk back, thinking over the words of Jesus, the complaints of the Pharisees and the discussion she and Esther had with Tamar the day before. Jesus had a power that was indescribable. Oh, she knew of past conquerors like Cyrus the Great, who allowed the Jews in Babylonia to return to Jerusalem, and the might of the Caesars, and the tetrarchs . . . particularly Herod Antipas who was directly responsible for John the Baptist's slaughter. Everyone knew men in power could extinguish life on a whim. They all had military might, but none had the power of Jesus, who was poor, homeless, and without an army.

She walked quietly beside Jacob. He put his arm around her shoulders and kept silent.

CHAPTER FORTY-SEVEN

WITH HIS APOSTLES AND SOME followers, Jesus left Galilee and went to teach and heal in the region of Tyre and Sidon. In Tyre, he healed a Gentile woman's child who was possessed by a demon. Because of her faith, when she left Jesus and went home, she found her child lying in bed and the demon gone.

In Sidon, in the region of the Decapolis people brought a deaf man to Jesus who begged him to lay his hands on the man. Jesus took the man aside, put his fingers in his ears, touched his tongue and murmured, "Be open" and the man spoke clearly, but Jesus told him to tell no one. Yet the more Jesus told people to keep quiet about their healing, the more they proclaimed it.

Still in the Decapolis, a region of ten large cities and many towns and villages, Tamar, and some of the other women following Jesus witnessed another amazing miracle similar to the one in the recent past Miriam and her friends witnessed. Masses of people were following Jesus for three days.

When he saw the crowd that had gathered to listen hadn't any food left, Jesus asked his apostles how many loaves of bread they had.

They replied, "Seven, along with a couple of fish."

One disciple complained, "It's not near enough to feed a crowd of four thousand!"

Undaunted, Jesus directed the people to sit down. He blessed the loaves and fish then had the apostles distribute the food.

"Not only does everyone have enough to eat, but there's even baskets full of broken pieces left over!" exclaimed one of the disciples.

From the Decapolis, he went to the district of Dalmanutha, then onto Bethsaida. Tamar sent word with a fisherman on his way to the shore near Capernaum, to let Jacob and Timothy know that Jesus would be in Bethsaida.

The distance from where Timothy moored his boat to the shores of Bethsaida was less than six miles away.

"It will be an easy sail if the winds hold true," Timothy said hoisting himself over the rail. Jonas dipped his hand in the water and held it up high. "I think we'll be in good stead. The wind is gentle and westerly. It should be a steady sail."

Timothy and Jerome followed to the port side of the vessel. Helping Esther and Miriam aboard, Caleb guided them saying, "This following Jesus has changed my life. I'm seeing and hearing things I never dreamed off. Miracles beyond human explanation and words that pierce my heart. Never have the teachers of the law ever explained God's commands like Jesus does."

"And what's more extraordinary, is that he welcomes all of us! If we were sick, lame, blind—you name it, we'd be sitting by the synagogue gates looking for alms and ignored by the leaders. But Jesus welcomes everyone!" Miriam added.

"And me? Look at me. Once decaying with leprosy, now whole." Esther held up her clean hands for all to see. "How can I not zealously seek out Jesus? If only I could get close enough to fall down on my knees before him and thank him!"

The boat came into the shallows, sails down, the men on the oars with Caleb on the bow ensuring they wouldn't run aground. Alighting from the boat, splashing in the water, Tamar who had been waiting for her friends hugged Miriam and Esther pointing them to where Jesus was teaching.

Miriam eager to hear news, pulled Tamar close. "You've been with Jesus for a while, what's been going on?"

She told them about Jesus feeding the four thousand, about opening the ears of a deaf man and a confrontation he had with the Pharisees. "The Pharisees and Sadducees were looking for trouble and started an argument with Jesus. It's obvious to everyone how hot their hatred is for him! They're not hiding an ounce of their hostility. It spills over every time they open their mouths, continually looking to trip him up in having him say something against Caesar or some perceived blasphemy against God."

"What did they say?" Now on the beach, they all edged closer to Tamar.

"They asked him to show them a sign from heaven!"

Caleb snorted. "Haven't they seen enough signs? Like the feeding of thousands, the raising of the dead, the casting out demons and so much more?"

Tamar indicated they move on to where Jesus was. "Oh, he answered them all right." She recounted the discussion. "He said, "When evening comes, you say, 'It will be fair weather, for the sky is red,' and in the morning, 'Today it will be stormy, for the sky is red and overcast.' You know how to interpret the appearance of the sky, but you cannot interpret the signs of the times. A wicked and adulterous generation looks for a sign, but none will be given it except the sign of Jonah." Jesus then left them and went away."

"The sign of Jonah?" Jacob wondered following along behind the group. "Jonah was in the belly of a big fish for three days . . . now what can he mean by that?" No one volunteered an answer.

Jerome looked back at Jacob and shrugged his shoulders. "Don't have a clue what the sign of Jonah would be."

Jesus was in the midst of teaching another large group. Getting near as possible, they maneuvered their way to a spot they could all sit down. They listened raptly to his words for nearly two hours until he was interrupted by men elbowing and stepping over the jammed in people, dragging a blind man along who was tripping and bumping into those in the way.

The men shouted to Jesus begging him, "Please Jesus! Just touch him!"

Jesus got up indicating the man walk with him away from the compression of people. Many people jumped up to follow including Miriam and her friends. Hurrying to get close, Miriam could see he was talking with the man. She saw an unusual movement.

Stopping, Jesus spat on the blind man's eyes and asked him, "Do you see anything?" Miriam edged even closer to the pair.

The man looked up and said, "I see people; they look like trees walking around."

Once more Jesus put his hands on the man's eyes. Then his eyes were opened, his sight was restored, and he saw everything clearly. Jesus sent him home, saying, "Don't even go into the village."

Miriam grabbed ahold of Jacob who was watching in confusion, scratching his head. "Extraordinary! See Jacob? There is nothing that

Jesus can't do. It's astounding to me, that there are still some who are questioning . . . not only the Pharisees and Sadducees but—"

Jacob pursed his lips and went still turning away from her. Miriam was going to say, "you", but Tamar appeared at her side and pulled her out of earshot from Jacob. "Miriam. Listen. The Lord works on us in different ways and in different times. He knows our hearts and our struggles. Jacob believes, I just think he doubts."

People were praising the miracle and the man was stunned at being able to see: this was nothing less than joyous excitement.

Timothy, Jerome, Jonas and Caleb were in a group talking animatedly, "This is so amazing! Surely, anyone who questions Jesus' power has to be deaf and blind themselves!"

Jacob, standing to the side away from them all kept quiet, as the others digested yet another miracle.

Tamar came up to Miriam and kissed her goodbye. "I am so happy you made it here! We're off to the Decapolis again. Not sure how long we'll be gone. When we get back to Galilee, near Capernaum I will come and see you. I promise. And Miriam, please be patient with Jacob."

CHAPTER FORTY-EIGHT

THE SEA WAS CALM, WITH little breeze. Using two sails like a gull's wing, hoping to catch most of the wind, they sailed wing on wing. Slowly they made headway downwind, away from the shores of Bethsaida.

Timothy broke into their astonished silence as each absorbed what they had seen and heard, saying, "In all of this, his teaching and his miracles, his kindness, and honest warnings did you catch the rumors that so many persistent people were spreading the threats the teachers of the law were making against Jesus? I can't believe their dissent and hostility in the face of his knowledge and power."

"I wonder when they're going to make a move against him. They going to arrest him." Jacob seemed sure in his comment.

Jerome, adjusted the lines to let a little more sail out on each side. "They won't do anything to him around here or in front of the crowds who love him. If anything is to be done, I'll wager it will be in Jerusalem and on the sly. And I heard they want to do more than just arrest him.

Jonas adjusted his turban around his tangled hair. "They want to kill him!"

"Yes they do." Jerome let out some line. "The high priest and the Sanhedrin will surely be involved, but then, even they have to bring any charge to Judean governor Pontius Pilot who, as a perfect, has the sole authority to . . . execute a criminal."

"Execute him? For What? Jesus is not a criminal!" Miriam protested. "He's been healing the sick, performing all sorts of miracles, and teaching on a level we've never heard before! He's teaching us about the kingdom of God! How can they kill him for teaching?"

"We know he's not a criminal," Jonas replied patiently. "But the Pharisees will see to it that Rome views him very differently. They aren't playing games, Miriam. They're out for blood. His blood. They get rid of him, then their worries will be over. They get their status back and Rome backs off against any thought of Jewish rebellion. Everything back to normal."

"You know that Jesus isn't going to stop his teaching or miracles, just because the leaders aren't happy," Caleb pointed out, sitting close to Esther. "He's taking a stand against their hypocrisy and everyone knows it, including the Jewish teachers and leaders."

Jonas took the tiller from Jacob and turned to his friends. "The Pharisees, Sadducee's, Sanhedrin, and the scribes believe that because they know Scripture by heart, can recite the longest and most complicated passage, and because they study constantly, they are God's chosen. They hold firm their place with God because of their 'righteousness'. Never mind their deceitful hearts. They stand on their learning! And so my friends, this Jesus? He is the *living* scripture. *That's* what they fear: that Jesus is the living Word. Sharper than any two-edged sword."

Miriam slumped on a cushion in the stern, looking out over the water. This was almost too much for her to process. To no one in particular, she sighed, "One moment I'm full of joy hearing Jesus teach and seeing miracles that no one else could ever perform. I'm seeing a man reaching out to the marginalized with hope, humility and encouragement; healing the hopeless spiritually and physically." Staring at the back of Jacob's head, she asked, "How can we be ruled by people who are so blind?"

CHAPTER FORTY-NINE

JEROME HAD ONLY BEEN HEARING snippets of Jesus' travel and work. So the friends knew that Jesus and his followers were spending time north of Galilee between Trachonitis and Iturea in Caesarea Philippi, as Tamar had said, and north to Mount Hermon. They weren't sure if he was going to Tyre and Sidon in the Syrian Phoenicia area. Either way, he was gone awhile and, in that time,, Joseph was weaned, and Esther and Caleb were married.

"I'm so sorry Tamar didn't make the wedding. She would have so wanted to be here to be a part of the festivities." Miriam looked over to Jacob.

"I think her not being here was good. We didn't need the diversion of constant talk of Jesus. This was Caleb's and Esther's time for attention." Jacob pursed his lips into a thin line.

Tactfully Miriam argued, "I don't think that's fair, because aside from talk about the food and wine, the talk was all about Jesus anyway."

Jacob pursed his lips again. What Miriam was saying was true. If the guests weren't congratulating the happy couple and filling their faces with food, they were wondering when the Pharisees would finally arrest Jesus. "For what?" was the common question. The common answer was, "Jesus is a threat to the Jew's way of life under Roman Rule."

Even for those who didn't follow Jesus, everyone at the wedding knew the Pharisees had been stalking him, trying to trip him up by their questions.

It was widely known that Jesus had been warning his disciples to "Be on your guard against the yeast of the Pharisees and Sadducees." The disciples thought that Jesus was referring to them not bringing bread on one of their trips, because they had in fact, forgot to bring bread.

When Jesus heard them talking about it he asked, "You of little faith, why are you talking among yourselves about having no bread? Do you still not understand? Don't you remember the five loaves for the five thousand, and how many basketfuls you gathered? Or the seven loaves for the four thousand, and how many basketfuls you gathered? How is it you don't understand that I was not talking to you about bread? But be on your guard against the yeast of the Pharisees and Sadducees." Then they understood that he was not telling them to guard against the yeast used in bread, but against the teaching of the Pharisees and Sadducees.

One guest, who spent some time with Jesus said, "Jesus knows what the Pharisees are up to. I heard he told his apostles, 'the Son of Man must suffer many things and be rejected by the elders, the chief priests and the teachers of the law, and that he must be killed and after three days' rise again.'"

"Rise again?" many tittered. "Come back to life? Who is this 'Son of Man' that he can come back to life?"

In the time that Jacob and the rest had been following Jesus, he was aware that Jesus sometimes referred to himself as the Son of Man, which was confusing because he also claimed that God was his Father, making him the Son of God. So Jacob wondered, *Was he human, divine . . . or both?*

Then the speaker, who by now was drawing a small group of guests around him said importantly, "After speaking somewhat privately with his apostles, Jesus called to us who were following at a short distance saying, 'Whoever wants to be my disciple must deny themselves and take up their cross and follow me. For whoever wants to save their life will lose it, but whoever loses their life for me and for the gospel will save it. What good is it for someone to gain the whole world, yet forfeit their soul? Or what can anyone give in exchange for their soul? If anyone is ashamed of me and my words in this adulterous and sinful generation, the Son of Man will be ashamed of them when he comes in his Father's glory with the holy angels.'"

Many of the guests grimaced, particularly about Jesus use of the term cross. All knew what the cross referred to: A shameful death. The Romans would strip a criminal naked, then tie or nail the person to a large wooden cross, where they would hang until they died from their torture or asphyxiation. It was gruesome. Jacob and others walked away from the man who continued his stories. This was a wedding. Not a place for dreadful stories.

Now looking at Miriam, he conceded his remarks. "Yes, you're right. There were many people talking about Jesus. But I'm still glad Tamar wasn't there. Her being your friend makes me uncomfortable."

"Why? Because you paid her to sleep with you or that you gave her food and nice presents in exchange for sex?"

Jacob squirmed and kept quiet. He was embarrassed and ashamed, because he loved Miriam, yet he still looked at Tamar out of the corners of his eyes. He couldn't help but look at her and relive his experiences with her! But he certainly couldn't tell Miriam this struggle. Tamar was a beautiful and sensual woman. At least she used to be.

Miriam broke into his thoughts. "You love me. I know you have history with her. I can't change that, neither can you, so let's just move on. She told us she's changed, and I believe her. If, for some reason you think she's the same person you once lusted after, then ask her yourself. She's going to tell you once again she's changed. She's not who she was, and you shouldn't define her as to who she was. She's a new woman . . . But it's your decision not mine."

"You know I love you and Joseph! I love our family! I would never change that."

"Then act like it. If Tamar poses a problem for you then I'll tell her."

"Let's compromise. You can still be friends with her. I just don't want the three of us to be around together." He didn't his trust eyes.

"That's fair," Miriam agreed.

CHAPTER FIFTY

TAMAR WALKED UP THE DUSTY road to Miriam's house. It had been awhile since she saw her friend and hoped that she would be home. She was burdened and needed someone to talk to, one who was not so closely connected to Jesus and one who wouldn't judge her. Rounding the yard, she found Miriam alone making fig cakes while Joseph played in the dirt with inquisitive chickens.

Miriam looked up at the sound of Joseph yipping like a little puppy and toddling away from his feathered friends.

"It's Tamar!" Miriam wiped her hands on a towel and ran to greet her. "So wonderful to see you! I missed you so!" Miriam insisted she sit and have something to eat. She handed Tamar a piece of fig cake. "You missed Esther and Caleb's wedding! It was wonderful. I believe they are truly blessed. The so love each other! But I wish you were there."

"I knew I would miss it, and I am so pleased that they found each other. I still open my eyes wide in wonder every time I think about or see Esther. To imagine she was once a leper, to now being one of the most beautiful young women I've ever seen. Each miracle Jesus performs is not singular. It affects so many people! What a blessing for everyone!"

"Oh, indeed!"

"Tell me about everyone!" Tamar chewed gratefully on the sweet raisins. It had been some time since she enjoyed a sweet and was grateful to sit and rest. She was so tired.

"Esther is a wonderful help and of course Caleb is doing so well with the goats. Jacob is still fishing with Timothy and Jonas, and Elizabeth is healthy and so are the children. Jerome still travels with his goat, Ziph, who is still so handsome making beautiful babies! And Ann has been busy with her three children. They're getting so big! And see Joseph! As handsome as his papa." She smiled proudly. "Now, tell me about your travels."

"I'm so tired, Miriam. It's been very stressful."

Tamar was still lovely, but the weariness in her eyes and the fine lines running lightly across her face were witness to worry, travel, and the never ending thoughts about Jesus' safety. Little streaks of gray fell through her luxurious tresses and her hands were tanned and calloused, her nails brittle and broken. Her delicate feet were dusty, and her robes smudged with dirt and clay. Yet although worn and weary, she still possessed a radiance of inner beauty that was arresting. Age and weariness could not erase hope.

"We women look after the men and I'm not complaining. They are good and kind to us and even helpful," she sighed. "Jesus is forever smiling and grateful! But I am so tired. We have covered so many miles and have been surrounded by so many people in need of hope! Jesus went about in Galilee teaching and healing, because he knows now that the Pharisees want to kill him, so for the time being he is avoiding Judea." She took a bite of cake followed by a cool drink of water from a clay cup.

Tamar's hand trembled as she offered a piece of sweet fig to Joseph, who was begging. She took a small bite herself. Chewing slowly, she savored and swallowed. "When we were near Mount Tabor, Jesus went alone with Peter, James, and John up the mountain and we all stayed behind. Something happened up there, and I don't know what, but the men were so shaken when they returned, they were unable to speak to us for hours. We women never said anything to them, because it frightened us that they were in a daze and Jesus was so quiet." Miriam remained still watching Tamar and keeping an eye on Joseph.

Tamar finished her snack and wiped her hands on her tunic. "A bit later, Peter, James, and John regained their composure and they and Jesus joined us to meet up with other disciples who were waiting for them a short distance away. We could that the waiting men were arguing and that there was a small crowd of people gathered. Jesus motioned us to come with him and see what was going on." She relayed the story.

"What are you arguing with them about?" Jesus asked.

A man in the crowd answered, "Teacher, I brought you my son, who is possessed by a spirit that has robbed him of speech. Whenever it seizes him, it throws him to the ground. He foams at the mouth, gnashes his teeth and becomes rigid. I asked your disciples to drive out the spirit, but they could not."

"You unbelieving generation," Jesus replied, "how long shall I stay with you? How long shall I put up with you? Bring the boy to me."

So they brought him. When the spirit saw Jesus, it immediately threw the boy into a convulsion. He fell to the ground and rolled around, foaming at the mouth.

Jesus asked the boy's father, "How long has he been like this?"

"From childhood," he answered. "It has often thrown him into fire or water to kill him. But if you can do anything, take pity on us and help us."

"If you can?' said Jesus. "Everything is possible for one who believes."

Immediately the boy's father exclaimed, "I do believe; help me overcome my unbelief!"

When Jesus saw that a crowd was running to the scene, he rebuked the impure spirit. "You deaf and mute spirit," he said, "I command you, come out of him and never enter him again."

The spirit shrieked, convulsed him violently and came out. The boy looked so much like a corpse that many said, "He's dead." But Jesus took him by the hand and lifted him to his feet, and he stood up.

"We all were stunned, including the boy's father. Once we got inside a quiet place, some of his disciples asked, 'Why couldn't we drive it out?' He replied, 'This kind can come out only by prayer.'"

Tamar took a sip of water. "The father's remark reminded me of Jacob's state of mind. He believes, but doubts."

Tamar could see that Miriam didn't want to talk about Jacob. It was too complicated a subject and they both could talk about him for a long time without resolving his issues. He had to come to his own conclusions.

Miriam asked, "But why did he say this kind of demon can come out only by prayer?"

"Maybe the apostles themselves doubted they could do it?" Tamar shrugged her shoulders and lifted her eyebrows.

"Maybe," Miriam agreed, "and possibly there needed to be more prayerful preparation under those awful circumstances."

Tamar puffed air out between her lips and sagged on her stool. "From there we went to Galilee and he said that 'The Son of Man is going to be delivered into the hands of men. They will kill him, and after three days he will rise.'"

"A man at Caleb's and Esther's wedding said he heard the very same thing. He had been traveling with Jesus but left him." Miriam responded.

Tears welling up in Tamar's eyes. "I don't know what he means!" A sob escaped from Tamar. She threw up her hands in defeat. "None of us do!"

Miriam rose to fetch Joseph who was teasing the chickens. Coming back, she asked, "where is Jesus now?"

"He's here in Capernaum, in the house he stays in." She put her empty cup down. "Do you know what those twelve apostles were arguing about amongst themselves just before we got to the house?" Miriam shook her head no. "They were arguing who was the greatest among them!" Tamar shuddered in distress.

"What did Jesus say?"

"He said that if anyone wanted to be first, he must take last place and be servant of all. Then he took a little child that was playing by him and took him in his arms and said that 'Whoever welcomes one of these little children in my name welcomes me; and whoever welcomes me does not welcome me but the one who sent me.'" She wiped her eyes on her sleeve.

"Then John complained that someone was casting out demons in Jesus' name, and told the man to stop because he wasn't one of the disciples!"

"What did Jesus say to that?"

Tamar, now wiped her nose on a piece of cloth from her pocket. "'Do not stop him,' Jesus said. 'For no one who does a miracle in my name can in the next moment say anything bad about me, for whoever is not against us is for us.'"

Miriam gazed at Tamar, who confessed, "Sometimes, Miriam, I'm happy and at peace. Other times I'm so worried and tired. I love him so much, but I can't help him. All I can do is follow." She heaved a heavy sigh, then smiled. "But I do have a story that is sort of funny. The tax collectors confronted Peter and asked if Jesus wasn't paying his two-drachma tax."

"Oh, no! Tax collectors. What happened?"

She told the story.

When Jesus came into the house, Jesus spoke first, "What do you think, Simon?" he asked. "From whom do the kings of the earth collect duty and taxes—from their own children or from others?"

"From others," Peter answered.

"Then the children are exempt," Jesus said to him. "But so that we may not cause offense, go to the lake and throw out your line. Take the first fish you catch; open its mouth and you will find a four-drachma coin. Take it and give it to them for my tax and yours."

Miriam giggled. "Oh, that's wonderful! Simon Peter the successful fisherman—with the help of Jesus!"

"Yes! Because Peter did catch a fish and did pay the tax!"

Both women grew quiet. "Oh, Miriam, I'm still sick with worry. Jesus plans to stay here for a while, but I know he'll be going to Judea and beyond the Jordan. In my heart, I know he'll go to Jerusalem."

"If goes to Jerusalem," Miriam lamented, "the Pharisees certainly arrest him. We've been hearing about their plans for over a year now!"

"I won't leave him, Miriam." She slowly got up to go.

Miriam walked her to the road and with Joseph on her hip. She waved goodbye.

CHAPTER FIFTY-ONE

NOW THE FEAST OF BOOTHS, *Sukkot* was at hand. Beginning five days after the Day of Atonement, it was one of the three annual feasts where Jewish males were expected to attend the festival in Jerusalem. Because the feast fell sometime between late September and mid-October, the fall harvest was over. This was a time for celebration remembering God's provision to the Israelites during their time of wandering forty years in the wilderness, and God's current provision in the completed harvest.

The many thousands who attended the feast constructed temporary shelters, or "booths" made of branches to recall the temporary shelters their ancestors built during the Exodus. Throughout the eight-day period, the people gave tithes, offerings, and sacrifices.

Tamar was wondering if Jesus, along with the disciples and apostles were going to go to the feast.

His brothers told Jesus, "Leave Galilee and go to Judea, so that your disciples there may see the works you do. No one who wants to become a public figure acts in secret. Since you are doing these things, show yourself to the world."

But Tamar heard Jesus say to his brothers, "My time is not yet here; for you any time will do. The world cannot hate you, but it hates me because I testify that its works are evil. You go to the festival. I am not going up to this festival, because my time has not yet fully come."

Tamar thought back to Jacob who would no doubt say, "What does he mean, 'my time has not yet fully come'"? She turned to one of her women friends. "Even Jesus' own brothers don't believe in him."

"That's not a surprise. How many family members choose what they want to believe regardless of testimony from one of their own relatives? One thing I've learned, is that no matter how close you are to a person, that person has to make their own decisions about their own beliefs . . . even if it means believing in a block of wood!"

Tamar let out a sigh of relief. "At least he's not planning on going to go to Jerusalem! I don't know what will happen with the Pharisees if they know he's there."

Her friend turned to her and asked, "But what does he mean his 'time has not yet fully come'?"

Tamar had to admit, "I don't know, I was just wondering that myself, but it makes me uneasy because it sounds like there is a set time for something to happen."

To the surprise of Tamar and her friend, Jesus did go to the feast, along with the twelve, others, and some of the women, including Tamar who worried along with her women friends about the fate of Jesus. The apostles and other disciples were concerned too, but if Jesus said "Go", they were going regardless of outcome.

On their way to the feast, between Samaria and Jerusalem, a group of ten lepers called out to Jesus loudly. "Jesus, Master, have pity on us!"

Tamar stopped with the rest of the group who stood beside Jesus who he looked upon them with love and pity. Tamar held her breath.

She remembered the other lepers Jesus healed, including, dear little Esther. Her mind flashed back to the entire story of Miriam, Esther, and her miraculous cleansing, without Jesus even touching her!

Tamar's friend tugged at her sleeve. "What will he do? There's ten of them!"

Tamar smiled. "Believe it. Jesus can do anything! Watch."

Jesus said, "Go, show yourselves to the priests."

"Nothing happened," her friend squinted in the direction of the lepers who were making haste to see the priest.

"Something will," Tamar assured her and they continued on their way with the others including the Jesus' own disciples who wondered if the lepers were in fact, healed.

The group trudged along the road, talking and musing with one another over the fate of the lepers when a short while later, a man came running toward them and Jesus shouting, "Praise, the Lord! Praise the Lord! Thank you, Jesus!"

When he reached Jesus, he fell face down at his feet in the dust. All those traveling with Jesus stopped in their tracks, shocked into silence. This was one of the ten lepers who called out to Jesus and they could tell by his dress he was a Samaritan no less! Samaritans were despised because of their pagan ancestry and the disciples weren't sure if they should be horrified to be so close to this man or overwhelmed by the miracle of his healing.

Jesus looked about. "Were not all ten cleansed? Where are the other nine? Has no one returned to give praise to God except this foreigner?" Then he said to him, "Rise and go; your faith has made you well."

The man, still crying and praising Jesus got to his feet, wiped his nose with the back of his hand, and blubbered many thank-you's and praise the Lord's as he loped away. But as he made his way off, he continued to look back at Jesus waving and praising him. Tamar and her friend could watch the running retreating man in astonishment. The other disciples sheepishly hung their heads, avoiding eye-contact with Jesus. Jesus had mercy even on a Samaritan!

They arrived a small village and that day and night Jesus continued to teach. As the evening closed in, he went off to a quiet place to be by himself.

Tamar's friend said to her, "What do you think of Jesus saying that if one of us sins, we should tell him so, and if he repents and asks for forgiveness, we should forgive him, not only once, but if he sins against us seven times, we should forgive seven times!" The woman shook her head in confusion.

"I agree, it is a hard teaching, but I think he means we need to be compassionate and even generous. Because let's face it, we all sin. All the time. If we look for forgiveness, then we should be forgiving others."

"I guess I need to increase my faith for this kind of forgiveness."

Tamar smiled. "Me too. Remember Jesus saying that 'if you had faith like a grain of a mustard seed, you could say to a mulberry tree, 'Be uprooted and planted by the sea' and it would obey you!'"

"That is some kind of faith considering the size of a mustard seed!"

When they arrived in the Jerusalem, it was a mass of humanity. Tamar wondered if Miriam and her husband were here or any of the others. It was a long trip, from where her friends lived, but they were Jews and although the trip would be long, the festival lasted eight days. She craned her neck to peer through the throngs. There were so many people; she doubted she would ever see her friends.

As Tamar wandered through the crowds, she heard many ask, "Where is he?" referring to Jesus because his works and words were spreading through the people like a fire through dried grass. The people had never been spiritually watered or tended to by their religious leaders and Jesus was an entirely new experience for them. Here was someone taking the initiative to speak to the common man and woman, whether poor, sick, or even demon-possessed! All were welcome to his teaching. "Whoever has ears let them hear . . . " was one of Jesus' favorite sayings.

The buzz of the crowds was about Jesus, his teachings, and his miracles and that included many conversations—some for and some heated against Jesus. Yet, nothing was said to any of the authorities concerning the people's desire for Jesus because those people knew that the Pharisees were out to arrest him. No one wanted to be on the bad side of the leaders who would put them out of the synagogue, banishing them from their people.

Mid-week, Jesus made his appearance at the synagogue to teach and the people were not disappointed. In fact, they marveled and were impressed because of his sharp learning regardless of his lack of study with the teachers of the law.

They questioned among themselves and repeated what the Pharisees asked, "How did this newcomer come to know and understand Scripture so well, and how is he in the position of expanding upon it and criticizing the teachers of the law?"

"It is astounding— the courage!" was the common response.

Yet some complained, "The nerve of such a man who is not a teacher of the law interpreting Scripture!"

Jesus answered, "My teaching is not my own. It comes from the one who sent me. Anyone who chooses to do the will of God will find out whether my teaching comes from God or whether I speak on my own. Whoever speaks on their own does so to gain personal glory, but he who seeks the glory of the one who sent him is a man of truth; there is nothing false about him. Has not Moses given you the law? Yet not one of you keeps the law. Why are you trying to kill me?"

"You are demon-possessed," the crowd answered. "Who is trying to kill you?"

Jesus said to them, "I did one miracle, and you are all amazed. Yet, because Moses gave you circumcision (though actually it did not come from Moses, but from the patriarchs), you circumcise a boy on the Sabbath. Now if a boy can be circumcised on the Sabbath so that the law of Moses may not be broken, why are you angry with me for healing a man's whole body on the Sabbath? Stop judging by mere appearances, but instead judge correctly."

Tamar overheard two men speaking in surprise. One said, "This is the man the Pharisees and teachers of the law want to kill, and here he is in the open, teaching!"

The other, put his arms across his chest. "Maybe they believe in him? That he is the Christ? The anointed one, the Messiah?"

"Does the Christ come from Galilee?" someone sneered. "Why don't they arrest him!"

"For what?" another responded defensively. "What has he done other than . . . "

"He's disrespected the Pharisees and chief priests!"

"The Christ is supposed to come from the lineage of David," another insisted. "This Jesus is from Galilee! Not from David's place of birth, Bethlehem." And the debates continued.

CHAPTER FIFTY-TWO

ON THE LAST DAY OF the festival, a great procession of priests left the temple to walk to the Pool of Siloam, a pool cut out of rock in the original site of the City of David.

There, they drew water in great ceremony and recited, "With joy you will draw water from the wells of salvation," quoting from the scroll of Isaiah, the prophet. Going back to the temple, they poured the water out as a drink offering at the altar to symbolize the water that God provided for them in the wilderness during their exodus from Egypt into the Promised Land.

Jesus, in contrast to the symbolic ceremony gathered the people to him and called out, "Whoever believes in me, as Scripture has said, rivers of living water will flow from within them."

Tamar stood watching and listening. Surely one could see that the pouring out of water by the priest was a show of ritual, finite in its meaning, whereas Jesus' words of 'belief' went beyond rituals and letters of the law but offered a spiritual and infinite meaning to true salvation. She had learned so much from him!

Many hearing Jesus' words of 'living water' were saying, "Truly, this is the Prophet!" referring perhaps to Moses who prophesied that after him another prophet would come. He would be a fellow Israelite, like them, common, but who would lead them in a new Exodus away from their captors.

"Could it be that this Jesus will free us from the Romans?" Excitement bubbled through the people who said, "He is the Christ, the Messiah!" Yet, there were those who were skeptical.

The debate continued. "Christ comes from the line of King David, out of the town Bethlehem. He comes from Galilee! He can't be the Messiah!" For they all believed that Jesus was from Galilee.

Because the two officers foiled their plan for arresting Jesus, the Pharisees and others continued to plot against Jesus because he was persistent in teaching and speaking throughout the festival gaining what they had feared: even more followers.

"We must turn the people's allegiances against him. Prove to the people that he's really a traitor or he doesn't know what he's talking about. We need to follow him and trip him up in front of the crowds," a smug Sadducee intoned.

Another Pharisee approved the strategy. "Yes. The key to Jesus' demise will be to turn the crowds against him!"

During the festival Jesus was speaking with Jews who believed in him. He said, "If you hold to my teaching, you are really my disciples. Then you will know the truth, and the truth will set you free."

Tamar nodded. Committing to listen and learn from Jesus would lead into a deeper understanding of faith because the freedom Jesus was speaking of was freedom of sin and its consequences. Nevertheless, there were those in the crowd working on behalf of the leaders of the Jews to confront and disprove Jesus' words. In disgust they argued, "We are not slaves! Why would you think we are not free? We are children of Abraham!"

Jesus said, "Very truly I tell you, everyone who sins is a slave to sin." He went on, "Now a slave has no permanent place in the family, but a son belongs to it forever. So if the Son sets you free, you will be free indeed."

They scoffed and jeered, looking around for support. "How is he going to set us free? We've never been enslaved to anyone!"

"They're thinking of political freedom, not spiritual freedom!" Tamar whispered to her friend who was clearly frightened at their growing anger.

"Didn't you hear?" someone shouted to Jesus. "We are of Abraham!"

"I know that you are Abraham's descendants. Yet you are looking for a way to kill me, because you have no room for my word."

Tamar froze in fear. Men pushed against the people elbowing their way towards Jesus with palpable hostility. But Jesus said, "Very truly I tell you, the Son can do nothing by himself; he can do only what he sees his Father doing, because whatever the Father does the Son also does. For the Father loves the Son and shows him all he does. Yes, and he will show him even greater works than these, so that you will be amazed."

"Our father is Abraham!" they angrily insisted.

Jesus said, "If you were Abraham's children, then you would be doing the works Abraham did, but now you seek to kill me, a man who has told you the truth that I heard from God." Unlike Abraham, they didn't want to hear any message from God. Thus, their so-called relationship to Abraham was spiritually null. He continued. "Whoever belongs to God hears what God says. The reason you do not hear is that you do not belong to God."

They howled in anger. "Are we not right saying that you are a Samaritan and have a demon?"

"I do not have a demon, but I honor my Father and you dishonor me." Jesus continued to speak as they hurled insults at him, but what came to near assault was when Jesus said, "Your father Abraham rejoiced that he would see my day. He saw it and was glad."

The Jews went wild. "You are not fifty yet years old and have you seen Abraham?" Now Abraham had been dead for centuries.

Jesus said simply, "Truly, truly, I say to you, before Abraham was, I am"

Terrified, Tamar grabbed her friend to escape with the disciples who circled around Jesus to hustle him out of the temple as the Jews picked up stones to throw at him.

CHAPTER FIFTY-THREE

"I'm really looking forward to being in Martha and Mary's house." Tamar's friend wiped sweat from her forehead as they plodded along behind Jesus and his apostles as they made their way to the temple; it was the Sabbath.

"Yes, and they live in Bethany. I don't think I can walk much more! It's not very far from Jerusalem." She looked down at her sandals, which were worn, but not overly so. They had survived months and months of walking. She was surprised they had lasted so long and it appeared she would get more use out of them yet.

"We'll leave tomorrow. I wonder if their brother Lazarus will be there?" her friend asked.

"I hope so. He's fun to be around, and he loves being with us and Jesus. He asks such wonderful questions. The three have been good friends to Jesus and all of us as well."

"Yes. They don't seem to mind when our crowd shows up!" her friend laughed, looking forward to a home-cooked meal. "Martha is the best cook!"

They walked on in silence, behind the men and at a little distance from the other women who were chatting excitedly about seeing Martha and Mary.

Tamar's friend touched her arm. "What's in your heart for Jesus?"

Tamar nearly tripped. She had been mulling this over for some time now; this was such a personal question. She hesitated, wondering how much she should say. She liked this woman, who like her, had been through a lot: married, widowed, destitute, with little chance of remarrying. An outcast. Unlike Tamar, instead of prostitution, her friend sold herself as a slave.

Tamar's choice was far worse. She closed her eyes briefly in shame. What was done was done and Jesus knew all about it and although he forgave her, she couldn't always forgive herself. When her past lifestyle raised its ugly head, she struggled with it even though she knew she was made whole again, but she was only human. It's hard to forget about the past.

When she first met and heard Jesus, she couldn't believe how kind and respectful he was, even knowing she was a prostitute. She was captivated by his attention, concern, and understanding. She never wanted to leave his side, but as time and events progressed, she found her adoration transforming into another kind of love. Sort of a higher or purer kind of love.

She decided to share. "I'll tell you the truth. So many years I dreamed of meeting a man who would love me unconditionally But, curiously, I wasn't attracted to him, maybe because I have a hardened heart."

"I understand what you mean. But tell me, did it change for you?"

The question startled Tamar. "Yes. It has been replaced by a love so deep that it engulfs me. It's hard to explain."

Her friend smiled and nodded in acknowledgement. "I found myself in a place of love that I never knew existed. It's a pure, unadulterated love, if that makes sense?"

"Yes, it does. I think you've described it far better than I could. It's a love beyond explanation."

As Jesus' group made their way through Jerusalem, a man was sitting beside a gate begging for money or food. After some discussion, it was determined that the man had been blind since birth. Tamar pitied the poor man and knowing that Jesus never passed by a wretch without speaking and healing, he stopped.

One of the disciples asked him, "Is he blind because he sinned, or because his parents sinned?" It was commonly thought that ailments were a result of sin and could be passed down from generations.

"Neither this man nor his parents sinned," said Jesus, "but this happened so that the works of God might be displayed in him. As long as it is day, we must do the works of him who sent me. Night is coming, when no one can work. While I am in the world, I am the light of the world."

"The light of the world?" Tamar waited for someone to answer.

The friend replied, "Does he mean that by opening the eyes of the blind, he is like a candle that is lit so one in the dark can see?"

"I think's its more than that," Tamar responded in concentration as she watched Jesus spit on the ground, making a little mud, then he touched the blind man's eyes with it and told him to go wash in the Pool of Siloam. The man, with the help of a friend, hurried away to do so.

"Jesus didn't say he would be healed." The women watched the men hustle the blind man away.

"But see the man's faith," uttered Tamar impressed. "The Pool of Siloam isn't just around the corner. It's a way from here."

The man did recover his eyesight once he washed. Overjoyed, he ran to his family and neighbors dancing, laughing, and rejoicing his sight. The neighbors were amazed and questioned if in fact he was the blind man who used to sit and beg?

Some said, "Yes! It is he!" But others couldn't believe it. It was impossible a man blind from birth could see.

Yet the man himself insisted, "I am the man! I can see!" The people wanted to know who healed him. The man answered, "A man named Jesus. He put mud on my eyes and told me to 'Go to Siloam and wash'. I did and now I can see!"

By now, a small crowd had formed around the man and some insisted he be brought to the Pharisees. This was an unusual miracle. Healing a blind man since birth! When the Pharisees heard the story, they asked the man again what happened. Again, the man repeated what Jesus' had done.

The Pharisees were incensed. Work of any kind was forbidden on the Sabbath! "This man is not from God, for he does not keep the Sabbath."

But others asked, "How can a sinner perform such signs?"

Noticeably, the people were divided. They continued to badger the man, who was losing patience with their incessant questioning. They even dragged his parents in to question and they confirmed that yes, he was blind from birth, but knowing that they had to be careful how they answered the Pharisees, they were evasive about who healed him, because they feared of being put out of the synagogue. They instructed the Pharisees to ask their son directly. The religious leaders asked him again.

The man, weary of arguing over fact, finally said, "I have told you already and you did not listen. Why do you want to hear it again? Do you want to become his disciples too?"

Then they hurled insults at him and said, "You are this fellow's disciple! We are disciples of Moses! We know that God spoke to Moses, but as for this fellow, we don't even know where he comes from."

The man answered, "Now that is remarkable! You don't know where he comes from, yet he opened my eyes. We know that God does not listen to sinners. He listens to the godly person who does his will. Nobody has ever heard of opening the eyes of a man born blind. If this man were not from God, he could do nothing."

Overcome with anger at the man's response, the Pharisees launched insults at him and officially threw him out of the synagogue. This was a serious penalty. He was now ostracized forever from his fellow Jews and even employment!

Jesus came across the man as he was hastily exiting the temple with Pharisees indignantly following and threatening him.

Now Jesus heard that they had thrown him out, and when he found him, he said, "Do you believe in the Son of Man?"

"Who is he, sir?" the man asked. "Tell me so that I may believe in him."

Jesus said, "You have now seen him; in fact, he is the one speaking with you."

Then the man said, "Lord, I believe," and he worshiped him.

Jesus said "For judgment I have come into this world, so that the blind will see and those who see will become blind."

Some Pharisees who were with him heard him say this and asked, "What? Are we blind too?"

Jesus said, "If you were blind, you would not be guilty of sin; but now that you claim you can see, your guilt remains."

Tamar watched the scene play out as the Pharisees, in an arrogant huff, hurried back to the temple. Sharing her thoughts, she said, "Jesus is shining his light on minds and bodies, yet the Pharisees steadfastly refuse to acknowledge who he really is! They know of his miracles and see his power. They see and hear of his compassion on the sick, blind, and lame. How can a healing be rejected simply because it is on the Sabbath?"

Her friend shrugged her shoulders in exasperation. "They think their Law of Moses of 'no work' on the Sabbath overtakes God's mercy!"

"But if one of their sheep should fall in a ditch and needs to get out, they will get it out. But help a fellow human?" Tamar sniffed. "They are two-faced . . ."

"Don't say it," her friend laughingly warned, wagging her finger.

CHAPTER FIFTY-FOUR

LEAVING THE AREA, THEY MADE their way to Bethany to the house of Martha, Mary, and Lazarus. Tamar was overjoyed to see her friends, and all were delighted to be together once again. As the women, directed by Martha set about to prepare food and bedding for all, Mary, followed Jesus around, hanging on his every word. When he sat down to teach, she settled at his feet.

Tamar hovered in the doorway wanting to hear Jesus too, but Martha, being the hostess, bustled about serving and making sure all was well. Tamar, darting glances at Martha could detect that she was getting aggravated with her sister who was not helping but sitting and listening to Jesus.

During a break, Martha took Jesus aside and asked, "Lord, don't you care that my sister has left me to do the work by myself? Tell her to help me!"

"Martha, Martha," the Lord answered, "you are worried and upset about many things, but few things are needed—or indeed only one. Mary has chosen what is better, and it will not be taken away from her."

Martha pouted, looked dejected, but only briefly because Jesus smiled widely at her, giving her a hug, taking away her distress. Tamar covered her own grin. When Jesus smiled, he lit up the whole room!

"Come, Martha. Let's take a break from all of this and join the others with Jesus. If they get hungry or thirsty, they know where the food and wine are," Tamar said. "Listening to the Jesus is more important than setting a table."

And so they spent the several days with the family and later traveled through Judea. Tamar constantly marveled at Jesus' teaching and healing for she watched, listened, learned, and as a result grew in better understanding of Jesus' desire to reach out to people. For example, for all of her past ways, he never looked down on her.

As with his other core disciples, he was always asking her questions, listening to her responses, helping her clarify her thoughts. He never left her or any of the others alone. He cared. Certainly, his twelve apostles were always with him as well as his core disciples, but he favored none. Those he gave a lot of responsibility to, he expected results from. If he rebuked anyone, it was always in kindness and love, but it was nevertheless stern and very clear. He hurt no one.

He even loved the little children. She remembered when they were bringing infants to him to be blessed, some of the disciples tried to keep them away, scolding the parents for bothering Jesus. "Don't bother the teacher!"

But Jesus said, "Let the children come to me, and do not hinder them, for to such belongs the kingdom of God."

Tamar remembered Jesus saying, "Truly I tell you, anyone who will not receive the kingdom of God like a little child will never enter it." Powerful words that put things in perspective for the disciples as well as her.

And she remembered good old Zacchaeus who was a tax collector and richer than rich. When they went into Jericho, Jesus drew crowds and Zacchaeus wanted to see Jesus, but he was a tiny man and because he was so short, he had to climb a sycamore tree to see above the crowd.

When Jesus passed by, he looked up and smiled. "Zacchaeus, come down immediately. I must stay at your house today." Overjoyed, Zacchaeus scrambled down the tree and went to Jesus, bowing and holding out his hands in praise and greeting.

But the people were so affronted! How dare he? "He has gone to be the guest of a sinner." They teachers of the law in particular were indignant. "Eating with a sinner? A tax collector? Is he out of his mind!?

When they got to Zacchaeus home and in his dining area, Zacchaeus stood up and said to the Lord, "Look, Lord! Here and now I give half of my possessions to the poor, and if I have cheated anybody out of anything, I will pay back four times the amount."

Jesus said to him, "Today salvation has come to this house, because this man, too, is a son of Abraham. For the Son of Man came to seek and to save the lost."

Tamar recalled how shocked everyone was that the tax collector would give up his money. "Can you believe that?" her friend asked seeing the surprised look on everyone's face. That sent many tongues wagging. But Tamar was more impressed with Jesus' saying that salvation had come to the tax payers house. An obvious sinner!

Yet they all shared a wonderful meal Zacchaeus provided and she remembered how Jesus laughed, the songs that were sung, the prayers that were prayed, and always, the stimulating and awe-inspiring teaching.

Her traveling with Jesus changed her life. He gave sight to the blind, exorcised demons, healed the lame, deaf, dumb, and even raised the dead.

Through it all he humbled himself by proclaiming, "I am the good shepherd; I know my sheep and my sheep know me— just as the Father knows me and I know the Father—and I lay down my life for the sheep. I have other sheep that are not of this sheep pen. I must bring them also. They too will listen to my voice, and there shall be one flock and one shepherd."

This quickened Tamar's heart because she thought of Miriam's husband Jacob as being one of Jesus' other sheep. How she prayed that Jacob would see the light. But it was an interesting puzzle.

She spoke about it to her friend. "People hear Jesus speak and teach. They see the miracles he performs, but they don't believe in him. How can you hear and see and not believe?"

"For one thing he often talks in parables, so not everyone understands. Another is that he says that God is his father and that he knows him personally. What does that really mean? How do we understand that this Jesus is calling God his *father?* No one, not even the chief priest has ever made that claim! Not Moses, the prophets, or King David!"

"True. What it all means to me is that Jesus is saying that he is the *son* of God! He has power and authority, but sometimes he speaks like he and God are one. It's a concept that is so beyond our expectations."

"Therein lies the confusion, the rejection, or the acceptance."

CHAPTER FIFTY-FIVE

JESUS AND HIS DISCIPLES WERE back in Jerusalem for the Feast of the Dedication.

As he was walking with his disciples in the colonnade of Solomon, a teacher of the law confronted him, pointing, "How long will you keep us in suspense? If you are the Christ tell us plainly."

Jesus' answered, "I told you, and you do not believe." And he added, "The works I do in my Father's name testify about me," provoking the teachers of the law to more anger, but when he said, "My sheep listen to my voice; I know them, and they follow me. I give them eternal life, and they shall never perish; no one will snatch them out of my hand. My Father, who has given them to me, is greater than all; no one can snatch them out of my Father's hand. I and the Father are one."

The leaders went berserk screaming "Blasphemy!" and picked up rocks to stone him for equating himself with God.

Tamar, threatened too, ran for cover along with the others, as Jesus disappeared in the confusion of the plaza. It was getting too dangerous for all of them, but it was Jesus the leaders were looking to kill. They soon left Jerusalem to avoid his arrest and went to across the Jordan.

In their camp, word came to Jesus from messengers sent by Martha and Mary that Lazarus, their brother was dying. Tamar was in a fit. "Jesus, we've got to go to Lazarus!"

Others in their party had mixed emotions. "If we go back to Judea the Pharisees will get all worked up again if they know Jesus is back in their territory! We have firsthand experience of a near stoning!" Another cut in, "The leaders have publicly made up their minds they're going to kill him one way or another. We'll all be in danger!"

Tamar was determined. "Jesus, please . . . we must get to Lazarus!"

One of the disciples who didn't want to go back to Mary and Martha's house said, "It's already been a couple of days since we got word, Tamar. By the time we get back he'll probably already be dead."

Tamar cried.

Jesus comforted her and the others. "Our friend Lazarus has fallen asleep; but I am going there to wake him up."

His disciples replied, "Lord, if he sleeps, he will get better." Jesus had been speaking of his death, but his disciples thought he meant natural sleep.

So then he told them plainly, "Lazarus is dead, and for your sake I am glad I was not there, so that you may believe. But let us go to him."

Then Thomas, one of the apostles said to the rest of the disciples, "Let us also go, that we may die with him."

And so they made their way to back to Bethany which was about two miles outside of Jerusalem. As they got closer to their friend's house, Martha, robes flying around her came running along the path. "Lord, if you had been here, my brother wouldn't have died!"

Tamar didn't know what to think watching Jesus grab her arms. Jesus said he was going to wake him up? But Jesus interrupted her thoughts. "Your brother will rise again," he assured Martha, who wiped her tears with her veil.

She ran back to the house and told Mary "Jesus is on the way!" and Mary left the house with the mourners to find Jesus. Many in the house followed her.

When Mary came to Jesus, she said the same thing Martha said. "If only you had been there for Lazarus!" Jesus gently asked to see the tomb where they laid him.

As they came into the clearing, some of the mourners complained and grumbled. "If he could have opened the eyes of a blind man, he surely could have saved Lazarus!"

Jesus viewed the crowd of mourners, and wiped his own eyes, then he ordered, "Take the stone away." A number of men ran to move the stone with leveraged sticks.

The mourners were aghast.

"Lazarus had been dead now for four days!" Someone said suddenly. "The smell will be overpowering!"

Instinctively, the people backed away and covered their mouths and noses with their veils and shawls as the men moving the stone got in position grunting and pushing. Slowly, the stone rolled, exposing the low, gaping entryway of the tomb.

Tamar, like Mary, trusted Jesus, but what if Lazarus was a bloated, rotting corpse? Everyone would be exposed to the ghastly impurity of it all. Her heart thudded against her chest and her palms went damp, as she clutched her friend's hand.

Jesus prayed loudly, on purpose, to his Father in heaven thanking him for hearing his prayers. He then cried out in a loud voice, "Lazarus come out!"

The mourners and sightseers went silent, holding their collective breath. Suddenly, Lazarus appeared out of the black hole, walking haltingly, his strips of white, soiled linen wrapped about face, hands and feet! Stunned into awe, many believed in Jesus at that moment, but the detractors, mouths agape gasped angrily and within moments of Lazarus' appearance ran to the Pharisees to tell them what Jesus had done.

Tamar watched the group of men hurry away. "This is it," she nudged her friend. "They will tell the Pharisees, who will call a meeting with the Sanhedrin. This miracle will only bring more people to believe in Jesus and they will never let Jesus displace their authority. Never!"

Her friend tightened her veil in worry. "Yes. And the Romans? Once they hear of it, they'll think that Jesus is the Jews' new leader or vying to be the new leader. They'll see his growing support among the people as a rebellion! The Pharisees, Sadducees will convene the Sanhedrin and the high priest. Doesn't Jesus see the threat he is to our rulers?"

"The Pharisees, Sadducees, teachers of the law and the priests will never let Rome even think about rebellion among the Jews. They need to be in control, so they are going to eliminate Jesus." Tamar glanced over at Mary and Martha who were crying and pawing their brother in immense love and relief. The awestruck mourners were crowding around Jesus, the women and Lazarus praising and giving glory to Jesus.

Tamar hurried up to Jesus, as did the other disciples and implored him to watch out. "An angry group of Jews who saw the miracle are now on their way to the leaders of the Jews to report Lazarus came back from the dead by your command!" Tamar stammered.

"Jesus, this is serious!" one of the disciples warned. "The leaders will surely take action against you now. This is not only about your safety, but ours as well. We'll be guilty of treason by association!"

One of the more outspoken apostles stepped in front of the man talking and leaned into the man's face. "Treason? What are you talking about man? There is no treason going on except your own words against Jesus!" He pointed to Jesus who was taking it all in. "Our teacher just raised our friend from the *dead*! And you're afraid of the Pharisees?"

This was a miracle, once spread throughout all of Judea, would surely threaten their power. Shortly thereafter Jesus left for Ephraim, a village north of Jerusalem, on the border of the Judean desert.

CHAPTER FIFTY-SIX

JESUS, STAYING AWAY FROM THE hostility and treachery in Jerusalem, spent time in Ephraim teaching and preaching. Later Tamar, the disciples, apostles, and Jesus crossed the River Jordan, and worked in Perea, a part of the kingdom of the previous Herod the Great on the eastern side of the Jordan River. Here, before yet another large crowd, Jesus was teaching and healing when a Pharisee, hoping to trip Jesus up and maybe even get ammunition for the Jewish leaders asked, "Is it lawful for a man to divorce his wife for any and every reason?"

"Haven't you read," Jesus replied, "that at the beginning the Creator 'made them male and female,' and said, 'For this reason a man will leave his father and mother and be united to his wife, and the two will become one flesh'? So they are no longer two, but one flesh. Therefore, what God has joined together, let no one separate."

"Why then," they asked, "did Moses command that a man give his wife a certificate of divorce and send her away?"

Jesus replied, "Moses permitted you to divorce your wives because your hearts were hard. But it was not this way from the beginning. I tell you that anyone who divorces his wife, except for sexual immorality, and marries another woman commits adultery."

One of the disciples laughed, "I guess it's better not to get married then." Others chuckled with him, but many were married, including Simon Peter.

Jesus replied, "Not everyone can accept this word, but only those to whom it has been given. For there are eunuchs who were born that way, and there are eunuchs who have been made eunuchs by others—and there are those who choose to live like eunuchs for the sake of the kingdom of heaven. The one who can accept this should accept it." His questioner shut up.

Tamar and her women friends appreciated Jesus' words. One said, "Too often, women are divorced for a variety of any and all reasons, including for something as ridiculous as burning a meal!"

Another pointed out, "See, hear now. Jesus is saying that divorce is only acceptable when adultery is committed."

Tamar whispered, "And he's putting women on equal footing with men. So that if a man divorced his wife and married another, he, too, would be committing adultery! My friend Miriam was reduced to begging for being a widow," Tamar shared. "No one to take care of her. Widow or divorced, it's a terrible life if you have no one to take you in."

Speaking of widows, her friend said, "Remember Jesus' raising the widow's son in Nain? The town that is a few miles south of Nazareth? He told the woman, 'Don't cry'? That woman would have been poverty stricken if she lost her son. Without a man in the family she wouldn't survive."

"I didn't think of it then," Miriam nodded. "He touched the boy's coffin risking defilement but didn't care. How wonderful Jesus had compassion not only on the love the widow had for her son, but also her position in our society. He gave her back her son's life and her life."

When Jesus finished speaking about divorce, the Pharisees, unable to put Jesus in a theological dilemma, backed away, but continued to listen to Jesus teach and speak.

Later, a wealthy young man approached Jesus and asked him, "What must I do to acquire eternal life?"

Jesus told him he must obey the commandments, of which he named such as, "Do not murder, Do not commit adultery, Do not steal, Do not bear false witness, Do not defraud, and Honor your mother and father."

The young man assured Jesus, "I have kept these commandments since my youth."

Tamar knew that while the man could have conformed to some of the requirements of the law, what was really in his heart? The young man she was told was very wealthy. Would he follow Jesus?

When Jesus heard the young man's reply, Tamar could see that he truly loved him, and told him there was one thing that he still lacked: "Go, sell all that you have and give it to the poor, and you will have treasure in heaven; and come, follow me".

Tamar looked at the sadness and distress in his face. She knew he wasn't going to give up his wealth, but she could see he was devastated with this requirement he just couldn't do: sell everything that he had to follow Jesus. The young man left.

Now it was commonly thought that the rich were blessed and obviously privileged, but Jesus called his followers together and said, "It is easier for a camel to go through the eye of a needle than for a rich person to enter the kingdom of God."

The question was asked, "Then who can be saved?"

Jesus answered "With man it is impossible, but not with God. For all things are possible with God."

Tamar understood. Salvation is totally the work of God. It had nothing to do with anyone's own individual efforts, success, or abilities.

"We can't do it, only through God's grace is it possible to be saved for eternity," one of the disciples agreed.

"It's like what Jesus was saying the other day," Tamar pointed out to her friends. "About the Pharisee and the tax collector."

Tamar along with a couple of other women were preparing a meal for Jesus, the disciples, and themselves. They had come across fresh bread a woman was selling, along with fish and fruit. It was going to be a good meal tonight.

"Oh, yes, I remember!" One of the women added a bit of soft cheese to the platter of bread. "It was about how some people think they're so righteous and more favored by God because they're leaders in the synagogue, or they've been born wealthy and so they think others who are less learned or poor in utter contempt.

"Indeed! The Pharisee praying in the synagogue thought God favored him more, because he was far better and more righteous than the tax collector who was standing far off also praying.

"Oh, the poor tax collector!" The woman looked up from her work. "He humbled himself and would not even look to heaven as he confessed he was a sinner and asked God to be merciful to him."

"So, who do you think God found favor with?" a disciple broke in and stooped to snatch a piece of bread and cheese.

"Philip! Wait for dinner!" Tamar scolded with a smile.

"I can't, I'm so hungry! But—who do you think God found favor with?"

"The tax collector," Miriam stated simply.

"Jesus said, 'Everyone who exalts himself will be humbled, but the one who humbles himself will be exalted . . . and the tax collector, a pariah was blessed.'" The disciple sat down with the women.

"Don't look for more. We'll be eating shortly." Tamar warned adding fruit to another dish. "I am learning that social outcasts, contrary to what common people think, are willing to change, listen, and above all turn from their ways. Not all, I admit, but those who do, find favor with God. Whereas the pious seem hardened, intent on projecting piety by looking down on the people who struggle. Their state of pre-conceived righteousness is false."

"And the truth is that no one has the ability to enter the king-dom of heaven on their own behalf, Pharisee or not. Only those who admit their sins and turn to God. Some believe that just because they follow the rules and regulations of Jewish life, that the gates of heaven are wide open to them."

"Decidedly not," Tamar's friend said.

CHAPTER FIFTY-SEVEN

WELL AFTER DINNER, AFTER EVERYONE had eaten and Tamar was cleaning up with her friend, a thought came to her. "Another interesting point Jesus made about the kingdom of heaven was in his parable about the labors in the vineyard."

Philip had come back to see if there was any food left, took a piece of bread and joined the conversation. "I remember that story well. The first group of men were hired by the owner about six o'clock in morning to work in his vineyard at an agreed to price, a denarius. At nine o'clock he hired another group and at noon. At five o'clock, he hired yet another group of workers to work in his vineyard. At the end of the day, when evening came, he paid them beginning with the last to the first group."

Tamar's wrapped up the remaining cheese. "When they realized everyone was paid the same, the first group of men complained because they had worked the entire day in the heat!"

Tamar put her a hand on her hip. "The owner said, 'Friend I am doing you no wrong. Did you not agree with me for a denarius?' He told the men to take what was theirs and go. He had the right to pay his last worker what he gave to them. After all, it was his money to do with as he chose."

"At first, the story bothered me," admitted Philip. "I wouldn't have thought that a person who worked only one hour would get the same as a person who worked nearly ten hours, but later, when talking to Jesus, I understood what he was really saying. God gives us the gift of forgiveness in equal measure."

Tamar too, had been perplexed by the story but came to the same realization. "The one who belatedly comes to God still receives God's grace and a place in heaven."

The next morning, they gathered their belongings and set off for Jerusalem by way of Jericho and then to Bethany. It was likely they would be spending nights there because Jerusalem would be packed with people for the Passover festival, which was soon. As they were all walking and talking, they stopped for a break near a steam while the women gathered water and prepared a light lunch for the men and themselves. After eating, Jesus took the twelve apostles to the side, which he did often, and spoke to them. As the men joined the rest of the group, they were disquieted, looking distracted.

"Philip! What's wrong with everyone?" Tamar asked, not sure she wanted to know.

"We don't understand what Jesus told us. He said that in Jerusalem 'everything that is written about the Son of Man by the prophets will be accomplished.'

Tamar frowned. "What else did he say?"

"That the Son of Man will be delivered over to the Gentiles and will be mocked and shamefully treated and spat upon. And after flogging him, they will kill him, and on the third day he will rise."

Jesus' followers didn't know who he was talking about because the meaning was hidden from them. Tamar didn't understand the third person reference and like the others, she was unsettled. What did Jesus mean?

As they approached Jericho, Jesus had already drawn a crowd. Two blind beggars were sitting beside the road and when they heard the commotion, one asked, "What is going on?"

"Jesus of Nazareth is going by."

One of the beggars, Bartimaeus, son of Timaeus jumped to his feet and shouted as loud as he could, "Jesus, son of David, have mercy on us!"

The people in front of him turned, and said, "Shut up. Be quiet!"

Nevertheless, he called out all the louder, "Jesus, son of David, have mercy on us!"

Jesus stopped and asked someone in the crowd to bring them to him. The two men, in rags, thin and desolate, stood trembling in front of Jesus. The crowd was unsure how to react. Jesus asked them what they wanted him to do.

"Lord, let our eyes be opened."

The crowd nudged one another, now talking loudly, and crushed forward to get a better look at what was going to happen. Jesus, reached his hands forward and lightly touched their milky, dulled eyes. "Your faith has made you well." Immediately, they regained vision! Excited and delighted beyond measure, they praised and followed Jesus, along with crowds that were growing as news of the healing spread.

They continued down the road that led from Jericho to Jerusalem which was a Roman military road, about seventeen miles long. It went through Bethany where Jesus and his disciples stopped at the house of Martha, Mary, and Lazarus, who he had raised from the dead. Unruly excitement ran through the village as people camped out, waiting for Jesus appear in town and to continue his journey to Jerusalem for the Passover.

Lazarus and his sisters waited eagerly for Jesus, his apostles, and the women helping the ministry.

"Jesus, you are here!" Martha and Mary hugged and cried. Lazarus, stood by, still in awe of what Jesus had done for him.

"Lazarus!" Jesus smiled and stepped forward. He hugged him fiercely. Martha had servants wash their feet and directed the party to the dining area.

They reclined on couches and leaning on cushions they comfortably reached for food that was placed carefully on the low tables. Tamar watched Mary get up. Thinking she was going to refresh beverages, Tamar looked to help, but saw that Mary had a jar in her hand she had taken from the floor by her couch. She walked towards Jesus. Tamar wondered what in the world was she doing until she saw that the jar was alabaster, and Mary snapped off the top. The scent of pure nard, an incredibly costly spice, filled the room as she gently poured it over Jesus' head. Everyone gasped. Then she poured it over his feet and stooped down low to wipe the excess oil from his feet with her hair!

Jesus remained thoughtful and quiet with his hand on her shoulder.

Once the shock wore off, the disciples were indignant. "Do you know how much that cost?" someone asked. "Yes," came an answer. It's worth at least three hundred denarii!"

"That's a year's pay!" Judas Iscariot, the treasurer of the twelve apostles sat up and demanded, "Why was this not sold and the money given to the poor?" Angrily he scanned all the disciples for an answer. The men, taken by surprise themselves criticized her openly.

Jesus immediately came to Mary's defense. He would have none of their complaining. "Leave her alone. Why do you trouble her? She has done a beautiful thing to me." Not expecting to be scolded and thinking that Jesus would agree with them, particularly with Judas Iscariot, the disciples hushed up as he continued, "For you always will have the poor with you, and whenever you want, you can do good for them. But you will not always have me."

The party became subdued and uncomfortable, as Mary sniffled and hugged Jesus, and Martha, Tamar, and the others quietly cleared the tables. What did Jesus mean by saying he would not always be with them? It was almost as if Mary had anointed his body for burial.

The following day, Tamar came from the village to report to Jesus and the others that she had heard there was a plot to kill Lazarus. "Why?" demanded one of the disciples.

"Word got out to the people in Jerusalem that Jesus is here with Lazarus. So now there are many people in town wanting to see Jesus as well as Lazarus who was raised from the dead!"

"What does this mean?"

Tamar answered again. "There is a plot. The chief priests are planning to kill Lazarus because more people are now believing in Jesus."

All eyes looked to a horror-stricken Martha who ordered, "Find Lazarus. We've got to get him out of here, Mary. We need to hide him." Mary ran out of the house.

Tamar was shaking. This was all too much. How could priests want to kill Lazarus and how could they then now, not believe in

Jesus? It only proved that the raising of Lazarus in front of so many Jews this close to Jerusalem brought the crisis to a head with religious leaders. Those Jews that witnessed the bringing back to life of Lazarus was undeniable proof of Jesus' power.

CHAPTER FIFTY-EIGHT

THAT MORNING OVER BREAKFAST, JESUS sent two of his disciples on the Roman road to Bethphage, which was a town on the southwest side of the Mount of Olives. When the men got to the village, he said they would find a colt tied that no one had ever sat on or rode.

Jesus instructed them to "Untie it and bring it to me. If anyone asks you, 'Why are you untying it?' say this: 'The Lord has need of it.'"

Tamar shifted uncomfortably on her seat. This could only mean one thing. Jesus was going to ride the animal into Jerusalem. Jesus' use of the world "Lord" only solidified his continued revelation that he was Lord and by using a colt, he fulfilled the prophesy of Zechariah. Agitated, she made prayerful preparation in her heart for whatever was about to transpire.

Later in the day, the men returned and said, "Jesus, they asked why we were untying the colt and we said, 'Because the Lord has need of it and they let it go with us. They never objected!'"

Tamar followed along with the other the disciples as they threw their cloaks over the back of the donkey and Jesus, riding the donkey, traveled the Roman military road to Jerusalem. The crowd who was waiting for Jesus to make his way into the city and the festival heard the donkey was just a colt.

Many exclaimed, "Look, see how calm the animal is and it's a colt. Never had anyone on its back!"

"He's not bucking at all!"

"This is amazing."

"Has any unbroken donkey let a man on its back for the first time without a fuss?" The pilgrims from Galilee followed along as excitement ran through the crowd. "Surely, he is the Messiah! Look, he approaches the city like a king! Hosanna!"

~~

Miriam, her husband Jacob, Jerome, without Ann, who again volunteered to stay home with the children, walked in excitement of their own towards Jerusalem. Timothy and Elizabeth, Caleb and Esther, and Jonas were also present.

All were looking forward to seeing and hearing Jesus more than listening and watching the rituals of the priests performing for Passover. They had spent several days traveling to their destination, but always stayed in a village for the night where they ate, rested, and fellowshipped with the other pilgrims making their way to Jerusalem for the festival.

"Luckily we've been able to keep up with some of Jesus' ministry." Jerome adjusted the luggage on Jonas' donkey. "It's still clear that Jesus will be in the city for the Passover. From what some of the townspeople say, the Pharisees are at their breaking point because of Jesus' support among the people."

"Oh, I hope to see Tamar and Jesus," Miriam said breathlessly. "It's been so long since we've seen them." Jacob remained silent.

The previous night, they stayed in a village abuzz with the story of Jesus raising Lazarus from the dead, and the subsequent reaction from the teachers of the law. Many people were eagerly looking forward to the deciding confrontation between Jesus and the Jewish leaders. Not so much Miriam and her group. They couldn't see how Jesus could continue his teaching without being arrested.

They traveled the road with many others, and up ahead, they came to an intersection. Throngs of people were alongside of the road cheering and waving large palm fronds.

"It's got to be Jesus!" Miriam exclaimed and the group hurried to see what was going on.

As they neared the main road, they people were all talking of Jesus arriving soon. Miriam craned her neck up the road to see a tight group of men and women around a man on a donkey. People ran alongside shouting and giving praise to Jesus as Lord!

Jacob touched her shoulder. "There's Tamar with some of the women who follow along with the disciples." He pointed to Tamar walking along speaking animatedly with another woman.

Overjoyed, Miriam waved and called Tamar's name, but in the clamor, her voice was drowned out. Trying to see, she was obstructed by taller people trying to get close to the procession. The crowd reacted spontaneously, spreading their own cloaks on the ground as Jesus passed. Some even put down palm fronds on the ground before him.

So many were chanting, "Hosanna in the highest! Hosanna!"

Because of all the commotion, Miriam was afraid to break away from the protection of her group, so didn't squeeze ahead to reach out to Tamar who looked tired, but beautiful as she passed. The crowds closed in behind Jesus, Miriam, and the other disciples. Miriam and her group followed behind the crowds along with Jonas' well-behaved donkey.

"Jacob! Do you hear the people? They love him! Surely, the leaders will recognize Jesus as the Son of God!" Miriam was overwhelmed with the people's response to Jesus— especially those from Jerusalem.

"That's a very strong statement, Miriam. Be careful where you say such things. There are spies everywhere and we're not above being seen as traitorous to our own leaders," he said flatly. "Keep it down."

Miriam shut her mouth. She didn't want to say anything to him she would regret, but she was dumbfounded he would even think such a thought. *Traitorous?*

Men, women, and children shouted, "Blessed is he who comes in the name of the Lord!"

Conversations bounced from person to person about Jesus taking control of the city and lifting them out of captivity from the Romans and even the Jewish religious leaders. "Hosanna! Blessed is the coming kingdom of our father David! Hosanna in the highest!"

The people were overjoyed, shouting, singing, and waving palms. Jesus slowly came to a stop. They were on the slope of Mount Olivet. The people continued their noisy celebration.

Jesus began to murmur with tears in his eyes, "If you, even you, had only known on this day what would bring you peace—but now it is hidden from your eyes. The days will come upon you when your enemies will build an embankment against you and encircle you and hem you in on every side. They will dash you to the ground, you and the children within your walls. They will not leave one stone on another, because you did not recognize the time of God's coming to you."

"Is this a prophesy of destruction for our great city?" Miriam asked aloud to no one in particular. "It's ironic, isn't it?" She continued gazing toward the city. "Jerusalem means peace, and yet our leaders can't see the peace Jesus is bringing to them."

"Our leaders will have their way, Miriam. They have already rejected him, his teaching and any belief of his messiahship." Jerome looked around at all the many different people, of all ages, from so many different places, pushing and shoving. He spotted Tamar, nudged Miriam, and pointed.

Calling out loudly, she waved, then took a scarf from around her neck and waved it higher. Tamar, who was scanning the crowd, caught the movement and waved back immediately.

While Jesus rested for a moment, Tamar gestured Miriam and the others on.

Miriam jostled Jacob sleeve. "Tamar's waving. Come quickly; let's catch up. We can get close to Jesus while he is stopping."

The small party hurried forward using Jonas' donkey as their gentle, but big, battering ram. The sea parted for them with grumbling. Coming up to Tamar, Miriam flung herself at her friend hugging tightly. Both women laughed and cried. So many questions, so many answers, and now they were all together.

"A blessed reunion in a sea of confusion!" Tamar laughed.

Walking, Tamar wanted to know all about the children and especially Miriam's little one, Joseph. "He is well and thriving and Ann stayed home to take care of him and the children. Jerome is disappointed she didn't come, but we all know there's different levels of dedication toward Jesus." Miriam nodded toward Jacob who was taking in the commotion of noise, singing, and shouting.

At the entrance of the city, the crowd pushed through the gates and filled the streets with more of a subdued joy. Jesus stopped for a moment, spoke briefly with the people, then pushed towards the temple while some of the people drifted away, in fear of the teachers of the law or cautiously followed, eager to see if there would be a confrontation with the Pharisees.

"Are they really dedicated to Jesus or are they looking for entertainment?" Miriam warily asked Tamar who only shrugged.

CHAPTER FIFTY-NINE

JEROME DIRECTED HIS FRIENDS. "CALEB, take Esther and Elizabeth to our lodging. Here are the directions." He drew a map in the dirt of the street.

"But we want to go with you! Miriam's going!" Caleb complained as he watched Jerome scratch in the dust.

"Please. Not now," Jerome ordered. "Take care of the women. Settle in; we'll be back to join you."

Jacob was about to tell Miriam to go with the women, but she had already scooted up ahead with Tamar. He hustled toward the group that was walking beside Jesus. If things got out of hand with Jesus going to the temple grounds, he would have to get Miriam to safety; he couldn't leave her side.

When Jerome and Jonas came abreast of the disciples and other followers, Simon Peter, Philip, and the sons of Zebedee cracked huge smiles seeing their fellow fishermen. "You finally arrived! We weren't sure you would make it." Peter hugged Timothy and clapped Jacob and Jonas on the back.

Jesus dismounted the colt and handed the reins to one of his disciples, instructing him to return it to the owners. As he and the group entered the Court of the Gentiles, the smell of animals, their dung and urine filled the air. Tamar and Miriam crinkled their eyes and covered their mouth and noses with scarves. Even Jerome, a man of animals was repulsed by the filth as he gingerly stepped over puddles and piles of dung.

In addition to the assault on the olfactory senses, the din of moneychangers assaulted the ears. Because of the Festival of Passover, the vendors had set up shop for the convenience of the people in the courtyard to buy animals for sacrifice and for moneylenders to change standard Greek and Roman currency for temple currency.

"I can tell you right now, the wheeling and dealing we're seeing is not in the interest of the customers," Jerome commented to Miriam as he looked around in disgust. "These are the temple grounds. And here they are selling animals for exorbitant prices and changing money at sky-high rates! Listen to the arguments!" He was appalled. The loud bickering of the buyers and sellers filled the already oppressive air.

Jesus was incensed. No one had never seen him like this. In anger, he suddenly overturned the moneychanger's tables, sending coins flying everywhere. He flipped the seats of the dove sellers, who screamed at him furiously while doves escaped flimsy cage doors that popped open. Frightened animals, bucked and kicked. His followers, stunned, became statues. No one dared move.

With a fierceness, Jesus drove out all of those who were selling and buying on the grounds of the temple. "My house shall be called a house of prayer, but you make it a den of robbers!"

Miriam and Tamar got out of the way of the overturned tables, cages, and stools. Frightened animals pulled against their fragile restraints and bolted. Huddling close to Jacob, Timothy, and Jerome, the men put their arms around the women. The rest of Jesus' followers regained their senses and slowly, with extreme caution approached Jesus who was out of breath and subdued, all the while keeping an eye on the now arriving Pharisees and temple guards.

The religious leaders were enraged taking in the carnage. "What do you think you are doing? How dare you!" They threw out wild arms, with robes fluttering and tassels tangling.

"He's challenging our authority in front of everyone!" one of the men said through clenched teeth to his colleague who was agape at what had happened.

The people in the courtyard were shocked. The vendors terrified, fled. Animals ran. Those in the midst of conducting purchases took off in all directions.

When the chaos settled, the area cleared, the people watching pressed forward.. Some were eager to hear his teaching, some avidly sought his words, but in truth, many wanted to see an event like had just occurred. A drama played out between Jesus and the Jewish leaders.

CHAPTER SIXTY

AND SO PEOPLE GATHERED AROUND Jesus shortly after the rabble was dispersed from the temple grounds. The lame and blind came to him regardless of the political tension; he healed them and the on-lookers were continually amazed. Even little children cried out, "Hosanna to the Son of David!"

The Pharisees, infuriated over the attack of the vendors on the temple grounds hissed, "Do you hear what they are saying?"

Jesus, turned to them. "Yes; have you never read, 'From the lips of children and infants you, Lord, have called forth your praise'"

"Jesus is quoting a Psalm," Miriam noted to Jacob. "Look, he's justifying and confirming that he was and is the messiah!"

Jacob nodded. "I remember the Psalm of David well:

Through the praise of children and infants

you have established a stronghold against your enemies,

to silence the foe and the avenger.

When I consider your heavens,

the work of your fingers,

the moon and the stars,

which you have set in place,

what is mankind that you are mindful of them,

human beings that you care for them?"

He took a breath. "But does that mean he's the messiah? Is that what he's saying?"

"I believe so, Jacob." Miriam sighed in frustration. Her husband was not understanding.

Jesus continued to spend time in the temple preaching and teaching. Many settled on the pavement to listen. For Miriam and friends, it had been so long since they heard Jesus' words. When Jesus paused for some water, Miriam and Tamar briefly updated one another.

The big question, *Has Jacob come to believe?* would be on Tamar's mind, Miriam knew.

Miriam was hesitant to speak, but she could confide in Tamar. "When you, the disciples, and Jesus left for Perea, we tried to follow Jesus' ministry as best we could by listening to people passing through town telling us of his words and work, and of course by hearing the latest from Jerome who has been traveling with Ziph an awful lot."

"Ah, Ziph our famous goat is still making beautiful babies?" Tamar laughed.

"Indeed. His fame is far and wide and for that reason, Jerome is gone quite a bit leaving Ann home with the three children and the rest of the herd, but Caleb has been so helpful to Jerome and Ann, as well as to us. But as for Jacob. Honestly, I don't know. He doesn't say much. He rarely asks a question of Jerome or anyone else who has news of Jesus, so I don't push him. He has got to come to his own belief and faith. I'm hoping that us being here for Passover and his chance to listen to Jesus in person might open up his heart."

"What of Ann?" Tamar asked.

Miriam turned to her friend. "As you know, Ann was excited when she first heard Jesus speak and when we followed him as he spoke in Capernaum and Galilee—as long as it was close by, but once he was out of sight, it was like he was out of mind for her. She's caught up in taking care of the family and the herd—she's quite a business woman now—even the men respect her. So, we don't see much of her. She claims she doesn't have time for our fellowship meetings."

"Fellowship meetings?"

"Ah, yes. Some of us decided in order to keep our faith alive we would meet once a week, have supper together, and talk about Jesus's teaching. There are at least ten of us!

"Jacob usually attends, but sometimes he volunteers to work longer hours so Timothy and Jonas can come to the meetings."

"How do you feel about that?" Tamar asked cautiously.

"Tamar, I've said as much as I can say. It's really his decision now. I can't influence him, other than putting forth the effort to live the way Jesus would want me to live and hopefully he can see my joy."

Caleb, Esther, and Elizabeth came from behind. "We've been looking everywhere for you! Were you there when Jesus cleared out the temple grounds?"

"Caleb, it was crazy!" Miriam took a breath. "Jesus overturned tables, money and doves went flying, sheep bolted, and the vendors and customers ran for cover! The Pharisees went crazy as well but the temple guards never did a thing. The people knew exactly why Jesus did what he did. The Pharisees and Sadducees allowed the temple to be defiled! So aside from hollering, they did nothing!"

With Esther close to Miriam's side, Miriam asked Tamar, "When Jesus finishes speaking will you introduce us to Jesus?"

"Introduce you? I thought he already knew you. When we speak he often brings up you and Esther as if you were good friends. He probably knows more about you than I know about you. I thought it was strange, you always hung back from him, considering he knows you so well."

For a moment, Miriam didn't know what to say. She had never spoken to Jesus. She could never get close to him. There were always too many people around him, particularly his apostles, or, he seemingly disappeared when she wanted to speak with him, or Jacob was eager to get home. How could he know her?

"Miriam!" Jesus said suddenly, turning from his men and smiling. "I've been waiting for you to come to me!"

Miriam nearly went to her knees in surprise. Ever since the first words he had spoken, she loved him. She knew who he was, but how did he know so much about her? She never spoke to him. Then her mind flew to Esther. He never touched her, yet he healed her.

Eagerly, she ran to him. Jacob hung back keeping careful attention to the situation. Jesus hugged her and laughed. He asked about Joseph and teased about the beauty of Esther who shyly came forward. He hugged her too.

"You've given us so much hope!" declared Miriam. "You've brought us the kingdom of heaven!" In her heart she pledged her utmost faith for him.

Esther wept. "You healed me. You've given me a second chance!"

The crowds closed in on Jesus, so excited to hear Jesus speak and so aware of the eyes of the Pharisees and temple guards on Jesus and on the crowds.

"Very truly I tell you, unless a kernel of wheat falls to the ground and dies, it remains only a single seed. But if it dies, it produces many seeds. Anyone who loves their life will lose it, while anyone who hates their life in this world will keep it for eternal life. Whoever serves me must follow me; and where I am, my servant also will be. My Father will honor the one who serves me."

"Hates their life?" Jacob question hung in the air with the same utterance of others who had the same question.

"I think Jesus means that he's the priority; his commandments, his teaching, and his requirement that we admit and turn from our sins, and turn to him in faith." Miriam paused for a moment to think then continued. "If we value are lifestyle more and aren't willing to see another way of living, then we'll lose our lives . . . "

"Because with sin comes death, but with confession and faith in Jesus comes eternal life," Jerome cut in.

She turned to him and grabbed his hands. "Jacob, I can't tell you what to believe. But you have heard his words, you have seen his miracles, and you know that there is a better way to live than the way the Pharisees and Sadducees live their lives." She squeezed his hands hard when he opened his mouth to protest, but she didn't relent. "I know what you are going to say, Jacob. Even if you think there are some good religious leaders, teachers and lawyers, they are not good if they're more afraid of their leaders than God. Now I have nothing more to say. You need to make up your mind about Jesus before it's too late."

CHAPTER SIXTY-ONE

IN THE MORNING AS TAMAR and the disciples were walking, Jesus came across a fig tree. Now Bethphage, translated is called "house of unripe figs", was a village known for fig trees that never ripened properly. When Jesus saw the tree, he was hungry and went to see if there were any figs on it.

The tree was in full leaf, but there were no figs at all. And he said to it, "May you never bear fruit again!" Immediately the tree withered. The disciples were stupefied. Right before their eyes the tree withered!

When the disciples saw this, they were amazed. "How did the fig tree wither so quickly?" they asked.

Jesus replied, "Truly I tell you, if you have faith and do not doubt, not only can you do what was done to the fig tree, but also you can say to this mountain, 'Go, throw yourself into the sea,' and it will be done. If you believe, you will receive whatever you ask for in prayer."

Tamar also thought, *there's another side to this: you know a tree by its fruit.* This tree looked lovely; one would expect fruit, even if it wasn't fully ripe. *This tree was like the pretense of the Pharisees. They appeared righteous but were not.*

After a day of teaching and preaching, and before Jesus and his disciples left to go home, word of the religious leaders' anger was escalating. It was well known through-out the city that the Pharisees would soon make a move. Tamar and others concern was growing because Jesus was not worried and continued about his work with focus and singlemindedness.

The following morning, they met with a sense of foreboding and anticipation. Jerome spoke first. "Tamar, we were with others last night at supper and we fear that the hatred of the Jewish leaders has finally come to a head."

"We know that too," Tamar answered simply. "We talked about well into the night. But what are we to do? Jesus will never run away from the Pharisees."

They walked along the streets and the topic of conversation among all was Jesus, particularly his reaction to the rabble buying and selling on the temple grounds and his subsequent cleansing of the Court of the Gentiles. While most were impressed and even delighted with his actions because that kind of activity on God's grounds was blasphemous, others saw it as great sport and drama, pitting the teachers of the law against an essentially unknown man, while others harbored the feelings of the religious leaders and wanted Jesus out of the way.

When Jesus entered the temple, the Pharisees accosted him. Still smarting from the clearing of the courtyard grounds the day before, they demanded, "By what authority are you doing these things, and who gave you this authority?

The disciples stood close to Jesus. Miriam and Tamar stood away with the others. If there was going to be trouble, they could help

Jesus escape, but they shrank back behind the men as Jesus replied, "I will also ask you one question. If you answer me, I will tell you by what authority I am doing these things. John's baptism—where did it come from? Was it from heaven, or of human origin?"

They discussed it among themselves and said, "If we say, 'From heaven,' he will ask, 'Then why didn't you believe him?' But if we say, 'Of human origin'—we are afraid of the people, for they all hold that John was a prophet."

Jesus waited patiently for their response as the disciples talked with one another, keeping an eye for any appearance of the temple guards. The air was thick with tension as the people crowded closer to hear the Pharisees answer.

They answered hotly, "We don't know."

Then Jesus said, "Neither will I tell you by what authority I am doing these things."

The Pharisees backed off, but not before complaining loudly so all would hear, "He won't answer us! He has no respect for *our* authority!"

At the end of the day, walking through the city to the gates, and while Jesus was speaking privately with his apostles, Tamar, Elizabeth, Esther, and Miriam discussed the day's events as they trailed behind the men.

"I'm troubled. When Jesus spoke the parable of the two sons, the parable of the tenants, and the one of the wedding feast, it was obvious he was referring to the Jewish leaders, especially when he asked them, 'What do you think?'". Miriam pulled her shawl tighter around her shoulders.

"The Pharisees are deaf. The parable of the two sons was wonderful. The older son said he wouldn't go work in his father's field and the younger son said he would. But the one who wasn't going to go, changed his mind and went to work for his father, while the other son who said he would go, didn't.

"The first son did the will of his father and can be compared to the likes of us: the prostitutes, thieves, and tax collectors who at first say no to God, but then repent and carry out the Father's will. The leaders of the synagogue are like the younger son who said 'yes' to his father but didn't carry out his commitment . . . just like the hearts of the Pharisees who lead everyone to believe they are carrying out God's will but they are not! Do you think the Pharisees got it?" Tamar wondered.

"I think they did, as well as with the parable of the tenants. The landowner, who is God, tends his vineyard, Israel, with care and protection, then gives it over to tenant farmers, religious leaders, to take care of the vineyard while the owner is away. When the owner sends his servants, the prophets, to collect his fruit, the tenants, beat, stone, and kill them. Finally, the owner says, 'I will send my son. Surely they will respect him.' But the tenants kill the heir too! And that's what scares me," Esther admitted. "Jesus has been sent by his father to save us! And our leaders want nothing to do with him!"

"It's frightening me too about how they know Jesus is talking about them." Tamar shuddered. "And what about the parable of the wedding feast where he compared the kingdom of heaven to a wedding feast a king gave for his son? Everyone was too busy to show up and even attacked and killed some of his servants trying to invite them. Then the king instructed the remaining servants to go out into the streets and invite all the people. Many came to the feast, but one guest who had accepted, didn't dress or prepare appropriately and was thrown out. As Jesus said, 'For many are called, but few are chosen.'"

"You know what is similar in those three parables? The story's build on second chances for those to choose to be in God's will and or not. The endings of the stories are the defining moments of those decisions," Miriam added softly.

The women kissed each other good-bye and went their separate ways until the morning.

CHAPTER SIXTY-TWO

IN THE OUTER COURTS, THE following day, Jesus settled in to teach without concern for his welfare

Tamar nudged her friend and pointed cautiously from under her robe. "Look, over there. Those men are Herodians!" A group of men were importantly entering the courtyard, plowing through the density of the crowd.

"How can you tell?" Miriam looked the men over. There were so many people in Jerusalem in many different costumes and headgear that it was impossible to tell where people came from. But by the way they were belligerently looking around and speaking among themselves, they were obviously showing off their authority.

"By the color of their robes and tunics, and see how animated they are, speaking with the Pharisees and the other leaders. This could only mean trouble!"

The men came sweeping by, forcing people out of the way, stepping on hands, feet, and robes as they barged their way to get in front of Jesus with the Pharisees close behind. Those whose were violated, didn't complain because they were far too excited to witness a confrontation. How would Jesus handle all these learned men who were teachers of the law and of Scripture? They were swooping down on him like vultures, robes flapping in the wind.

"We all know what they are trying to do. They want to trip him up, so they're bringing in all sorts of scholars," Jerome decided as the Herodians flounced to a halt in front of Jesus.

Miriam crossed her arms on her chest. "They will never out do Jesus."

Without a greeting, they turned from Jesus and importantly addressed the crowd as if it was a collective moderator. The lead spread his hands and simpered while shooting him a side-long glance, "Teacher, we know that you are true and teach the way of God truthfully, and you do not care about anyone's opinion, for you are not swayed by appearances . . . tell us, is it lawful to pay taxes to Caesar, or not?"

"Doesn't everybody see what they are trying to do?" whispered Tamar fearfully.

"I certainly do. They're trying to accomplish two things. One, they want to know who Jesus sides with: The Pharisees who pay it, but don't like it, or the Herodians who don't care? Or, they want to expose him as treasonous to Caesar and Rome if he denies the tax," Miriam stated coldly.

Miriam and Tamar took a united deep breath, as did the other disciples as they waited for Jesus to respond. This was clearly a face-off.

"You hypocrites, why are you trying to trap me? Show me the coin used for paying the tax." They brought him a denarius, and he asked them, "Whose image is this? And whose inscription?"

"Caesar's," they replied.

Then he said to them, "So give back to Caesar what is Caesar's, and to God what is God's."

The crowd and disciples breathed out in relief, and at the same time mocked the openly confounded reaction of the religious leaders who clutched their robes about them in embarrassment at being foiled. Yet, reluctantly, the Herodians couldn't help but tilt their heads together in agreed admiration for such a clever answer. The Pharisees on the other hand, held no such thought and painfully aware of the derisive expressions on the faces of the people enjoying the drama, faded back into the crowds with contempt for all: Jesus, the people, and his disciples.

A short while later a group of Sadducees showed up to interrupt Jesus. "Is there no end to their challenges?" Miriam wondered as a group of Sadducees pushed through the people once again to badger Jesus.

Unlike the Pharisees the Sadducees don't believe in resurrection. They were however, in alignment with the Pharisees in trying to outwit Jesus, dismiss him in front of the people, and erode his popularity and authority.

So they approached him and said, "Teacher," they said, "Moses told us that if a man dies without having children, his brother must marry the widow and raise up offspring for him. Now there were seven brothers among us. The first one married and died, and since he had no children, he left his wife to his brother. The same thing happened to the second and third brother, right on down to the seventh. Finally, the woman died. Now then, at the resurrection, whose wife will she be of the seven, since all of them were married to her?"

The Sadducees smiled smugly, as the Pharisees tittered behind their hands.

Jesus replied, "You are in error because you do not know the Scriptures or the power of God. At the resurrection people will neither marry nor be given in marriage; they will be like the angels in heaven. But about the resurrection of the dead—have you not read what God said to you, 'I am the God of Abraham, the God of Isaac, and the God of Jacob? He is not the God of the dead but of the living."

The robed men visually stiffened at Jesus' words, while the Pharisees, standing on the periphery of the group distanced themselves from the Sadducees by talking among themselves.

Tamar leaned against Miriam, "They've been insulted publicly! They don't believe in angels or the resurrection and Jesus made resurrection plain!

"But the key," said Jerome overhearing the women, "is that the Sadducees are overlooking the words that God said to Moses at the burning bush. Remember? God said, 'I *am*', the God of Abraham, the God of Isaac, and the God of Jacob.' Not 'I *was*'."

CHAPTER SIXTY-THREE

AFTER THE SADDUCEES DISSOLVED INTO the crowd, the friends turned their attention to a group of Pharisees quietly talking among themselves and smiling as if in triumph. One, a lawyer, who had been listening to Jesus and his responses to the Sadducees, moved away from the group and walked up to Jesus. Miriam wasn't sure if the question was sincere, or not.

"Teacher, which is the greatest commandment in the Law?"

Jesus replied: "'Love the Lord your God with all your heart and with all your soul and with all your mind.' This is the first and greatest commandment. And the second is like it: 'Love your neighbor as yourself.' All the Law and the Prophets hang on these two commandments."

The teacher of the law surprised Miriam with his response. "You are right Teacher . . . To love God with all your heart, understanding, and strength, and to love your neighbor as yourself, is more than burnt offerings and sacrifice."

Jesus nodded. "You are not far from the kingdom of God." The Pharisee, bowed his head humbled, and moved away from Jesus yet stood not too far from him, but away from his own peers.

Jesus posed a question to the crowd. "Why do the teachers of the law say that the Messiah is the son of David? David himself, speaking by the Holy Spirit, declared:

"'The Lord said to my Lord:

"Sit at my right hand

until I put your enemies

under your feet.'"

"David himself calls him 'Lord.' How then can he be his son?"

The Pharisees, still listening to Jesus and waiting for an opportunity to trap him with their own learning, remained mum and shifted uncomfortably in front of the people, because they couldn't answer Jesus' question and they were still smarting from the response of Jesus to one of their own who they hoped would show him up regarding the greatest commandment. The people listening, poked one another and chattered with knowing smiles, delighted with Jesus' ability to shut up the so-called experts.

A disciple sitting by Tamar and Miriam leaned toward them. "You see, David calls the Messiah his Lord, so how could he be David's son? Jesus uses David's psalm as his argument."

"We know the view of the religious leaders is that the Messiah would be the son, or of the line of David." Miriam placed her hands on her knees, eager for his response.

"Agreed, but it is not fully the truth. He is not David's *son*. Maybe by lineage, but Jesus, I believe is the Son of God. As he says."

"Both divine and human . . . " Tamar whispered.

As the Sadducees, scribes, and Pharisees huddled in groups on the edge of the throng, Jesus called to his listeners and said that while the Pharisees and Sadducees had authority, under Moses, they did not practice what they preached.

The religious leaders gaped in shock, stunned at Jesus' words. With extreme discipline, they held firm in their presence in front of the people only to be blasted again by Jesus who boldly spoke out against them in front of the ever-growing crowds.

"Watch out for the teachers of the law. They like to walk around in flowing robes and be greeted with respect in the marketplaces, and have the most important seats in the synagogues and the places of honor at banquets. They devour widows' houses and for a show make lengthy prayers. These men will be punished most severely."

Pointing to the groups of men he addressed them personally. "Woe to you, teachers of the law and Pharisees, you hypocrites! You shut the door of the kingdom of heaven in people's faces. You yourselves do not enter, nor will you let those enter who are trying to.

"Woe to you, teachers of the law and Pharisees, you hypocrites! You travel over land and sea to win a single convert, and when you have succeeded, you make them twice as much a child of hell as you are.

"Woe to you, blind guides! You say, 'If anyone swears by the temple, it means nothing; but anyone who swears by the gold of the temple is bound by that oath.' You blind fools! Which is greater: the gold, or the temple that makes the gold sacred? You also say, 'If anyone swears by the altar, it means nothing; but anyone who swears by the gift on the altar is bound by that oath.' You blind men! Which is greater: the gift, or the altar that makes the gift sacred? Therefore, anyone who swears by the altar swears by it and by everything on it. And anyone who swears by the temple swears by it and by the one who dwells in it. And anyone who swears by heaven swears by God's throne and by the one who sits on it.

"Woe to you, teachers of the law and Pharisees, you hypocrites! You give a tenth of your spices—mint, dill and cumin. But you have neglected the more important matters of the law—justice, mercy and faithfulness. You should have practiced the latter, without neglecting the former. You blind guides! You strain out a gnat but swallow a camel.

"Woe to you, teachers of the law and Pharisees, you hypocrites! You clean the outside of the cup and dish, but inside they are full of greed and self-indulgence. Blind Pharisee! First clean the inside of the cup and dish, and then the outside also will be clean.

"Woe to you, teachers of the law and Pharisees, you hypocrites! You are like whitewashed tombs, which look beautiful on the outside but on the inside are full of the bones of the dead and everything unclean. In the same way, on the outside you appear to people as righteous but on the inside you are full of hypocrisy and wickedness.

"Woe to you, teachers of the law and Pharisees, you hypocrites! You build tombs for the prophets and decorate the graves of the righteous. And you say, 'If we had lived in the days of our ancestors, we would not have taken part with them in shedding the blood of the prophets.' So you testify against yourselves that you are the descendants of those who murdered the prophets. Go ahead, then, and complete what your ancestors started!

"You snakes! You brood of vipers! How will you escape being condemned to hell? Therefore, I am sending you prophets and sages and teachers. Some of them you will kill and crucify; others you will flog in your synagogues and pursue from town to town. And so upon you will come all the righteous blood that has been shed on earth, from the blood of righteous Abel to the blood of Zechariah son of Berekiah, whom you murdered between the temple and the altar. Truly I tell you, all this will come on this generation."

Wide-eyed, mouth open, Miriam stole a glance at Jacob, who had furrowed his eyebrows and rubbed his mouth in shock as he watched the religious men, clearly affronted complaining loudly to one another about Jesus' remarks, but Jesus, ignoring them left, quickly.

CHAPTER SIXTY-FOUR

MIRIAM WAS WROUGHT, AS WAS Tamar. This was it. The leaders could never let this pass. Never. Shaken, the disciples and Miriam and her group hurried after Jesus who had something else to say to his own disciples who were still trying to process Jesus' character attack on the Jews. He cautioned them to serve with humility.

"But you are not to be called 'Rabbi,' for you have one Teacher, and you are all brothers. And do not call anyone on earth 'father,' for you have one Father, and he is in heaven. Nor are you to be called instructors, for you have one Instructor, the Messiah."

As Jesus and his followers entered the court of women where both men and women could gather and near the temple's treasury he sat down on a bench. Watching the people putting money into one of the thirteen the offering boxes, his eye caught a poor widow. She put two copper coins, about a penny, into the box. Jesus called his followers.

"Truly I tell you, this poor widow has put more into the treasury than all the others. They all gave out of their wealth; but she, out of her poverty, put in everything—all she had to live on."

Miriam said to Jacob. "There is a lesson here, but I can't get beyond the 'woes'."

Jacob responded in kind. "Neither can I. For him to accuse the teachers of the law like that in front of all those people is just . . . just . . . suicide!"

They left the temple grounds. As they were walking together, they overheard the disciples closest to Jesus saying how wonderful the buildings were and how impressed they were with the size of the stones used in the synagogue grounds and temple.

"Look, Teacher! How beautiful the buildings are! How big the stones are!"

Jesus said, "Do you see all these great buildings? Not one stone will be left on another. Every stone will be thrown down to the ground."

Tamar was so dumbfounded she walked into the back of Miriam who stopped along with Jacob and Jerome surprised to hear Jesus' words.

Jacob repeated, "There won't be one stone left on top of one another? They'll all be thrown down?" He looked to his friends who were shaking their heads in confusion.

"The temple destroyed?" mouthed Miriam. Tamar shrugged in distress.

She and the others followed Jesus to the edge of town and he asked Peter, James, John, and Andrew to come with him to the Mount of Olives, not far from Bethany.

Miriam's group, Jacob, Jerome, Timothy, Jonas, Caleb, along with Esther and Elizabeth and some of Tamar's friends, wanted to go along too, but Jesus made it clear, only his three disciples were going with him, so they sat outside the gates to mentally rest from Jesus' harsh words to the Pharisees and Sadducees.

Jerome asked, "Jesus must be wanting to talk to his apostles in private for a reason. I wonder if he's worried."

Jacob seemed defensive. "Why couldn't the others that are close to him go along?"

Miriam said softly, "Perhaps it's only information he wanted them to know. And I can assure you, Jesus is not worried."

Caleb spoke up. "Whatever is going on, he's got it under control and besides, those disciples are his inner circle."

The others were listening to Esther. "What are you talking about?" Miriam wanted to know.

.   Esther took a breath. "I was telling Elizabeth and Timothy, I've had the blessing of being healed from leprosy, so I know first-hand the reality of his miracles. We've also seen his other miracles and have heard his words. Jesus is a radical—not in a violent rebellious way, but he is counter-culture to our times. Look who his inner circle is: uneducated fishermen! He's not defying our Jewish leaders, but he is pointing out their hypocrisy. He wants us to recognize sin, but still love the sinners, contrary to the Pharisees' teaching. He's engaging all of us, not just the elite and that is so contrary to the hierarchy of our synagogue leaders!"

And so they rested with the group until Jesus came back and they all made their way to their dwellings at the close of the day. Jacob and Miriam leaned against a tree listening to their new and old friends talk about the teachers of the law. Many of the disciples had better insight as to what was going on politically because of the amount of time they spent with Jesus and the reaction of the synagogue leaders. Clearly, they were worried about the escalation of Jesus' remarks to the Pharisees.

Someone asked, "Where's Judas?"

"Judas Iscariot?" There were two Judas in Jesus' group of disciples.

"Don't know," came an answer. "Only Peter, James, John, and Andrew went with Jesus. The rest of us are here."

"Wonder where he went?"

"He holds the money so he's probably helping to provide some of the poor with food for the Passover meal."

Jacob took his wife's arm. "Come on, let's go. We need to help prepare for the Passover meal ourselves." Obediently, she followed him.

Walking along a road near the temple grounds, they saw Judas scurrying along the courtyard to one of the chief priest's palaces.

"That's odd. What's he doing there?" Jacob commented. Tomorrow evening the friends were celebrating the Passover feast and he and Miriam were helping with the arrangements.

They would learn later that when Jesus settled down with the four apostles on the slopes of the Mount of Olives he spoke of future events and end times and they would ponder his words and visualize the man of God speaking.

CHAPTER SIXTY-FIVE

THURSDAY NIGHT, JESUS AND HIS twelve apostles ate the Passover meal in a large upper room above a dwelling in Jerusalem. Tamar and some of her friends shared the meal in Bethany. Miriam, Jacob, Jerome, Esther, Caleb, and Jonas enjoyed their meal in Jerusalem near the edge of the city with the friends of Jerome. It was a good evening, although the specter of worry for Jesus hung over the guests but they argued that Jesus could protect himself if the Pharisees tried to arrest him and frankly, for what? Disrespecting them?

Jerome emphasized. "Jesus is Messiah, I'm sure of it, so if anything is going to happen, Jesus has it under control."

"We hope so," came the murmuring concern.

Miriam looked to Jacob who seemed far away. It had been a busy, emotionally draining week. Tonight, they could get some rest, enjoy Friday; Saturday was the Sabbath, then they could return home on Sunday. She missed her little boy and hoped that the end of this week would mark a new beginning for the believers of Jesus . . . if they could all just get through the Passover.

Shortly after she and Jacob went to bed, it seemed she had just drifted off to sleep when Jerome pounded on the door. "Get up! There's a mob on the way to Gethsemane to arrest Jesus!"

"Gethsemane? On the slope of Mount Olivet?"

"Yes, he's there now with Peter, James, and John, but I don't know for how long! Come, get dressed. Put a veil over your head," He ordered Miriam. "These people are crazy, and I don't know what they'll do seeing a woman out late."

"Stay, Miriam. I can't risk you getting hurt," pleaded Jacob.

"I must go."

As they hurriedly dressed, Miriam asked, "What about the others?"

"I'm leaving them here. I didn't wake them up. It's far too dangerous."

"Oh, but it's okay that we go along with you," Jacob retorted.

"Look, neither of you have to come. I just thought that Miriam would want to be there for Jesus."

"I do."

They went out into the night and raced out of the city towards Gethsemane catching up with a small mob of men representing the teachers of the law, elders, and chief priests. They carried torches, swords, and clubs.

Looking at the weapons, Miriam moaned. "Jesus and his men have no weapons! What are these people thinking? He's an innocent man!"

Jacob squeezed Miriam's arm hard. She cried out in surprise as he said hoarsely. "You keep your mouth shut! This is not the time or place to defend Jesus. We'll all be thrown into jail!"

Jerome didn't hear. He was far ahead. When they came to the garden, men were approaching Jesus and his disciples. Standing in the shadows, Jerome stood near bushes as Miriam and Jacob came up beside him. From where they were, they had a clear view of Jesus, Peter, James, and John.

"Oh, no!" whispered Jacob. "Is that Judas standing on the side of the mob?"

"Yes." Jerome was confused. "Why?"

"I saw him yesterday heading for the chief priests' apartments . . ."

Jerome shot him a look of incredulity.

"It is so. I saw him too," Miriam affirmed.

Just then, because it was so dark in the garden, Judas stepped forward from the mob and greeted Jesus with a kiss to identify him to his accusers. "Greetings Rabbi!"

Miriam was aghast. Her stomach flipped. How could he? Jesus said something to Judas she couldn't hear because of the noise everyone was making, but the guards leaned into Jesus as he stretched out his hands to be tied.

At that moment, Peter brandished a sword, a shrill cry ran out in the cold night. A man clutched the side of his face and screamed. Peter cut off the ear of a guard. In the torch light, Miriam could see a dark, oily smear on the side of the man's face.

"Put your sword back in its place," Jesus said to him, "for all who draw the sword will die by the sword. Do you think I cannot call on my Father, and he will at once put at my disposal more than twelve legions of angels? But how then would the Scriptures be fulfilled that say it must happen in this way?"

The man, named Malchus, pushed his hand to the side of his face howling in shock and pain. Jesus reached out, moving the man's hand, gently touching the ragged wound. Miraculously, the ear was back in place, but because of the darkness, confusion, and forceful arrest the miracle was lost on most of the mob.

Miriam staggered back and leaned against her husband. Quietly speaking, he held her hand. "What is his offense? He's only been teaching in the temple for a week and out in the open at that!"

Jesus affirmed Jacob's remark. To his accusers he spoke evenly, "Every day I was with you in the temple courts, and you did not lay a hand on me. But this is your hour--when darkness reigns."

The guards, only on a mission to capture Jesus and not listen to reason, seized him roughly pushing him towards the road. Miriam, Jacob, and Jerome hid behind bushes. Jesus' disciples ran away through the brush as did Peter, but Miriam spotted him chasing after the arresting party at a distance. A young man, whom the guards tried to seize by grabbing his tunic, ran away naked past Miriam, breathing hard.

Someone in the dark shouted to the departing guards, "Where are you taking him?"

"To Annas and Caiaphas the high priests. All the leaders and council are there."

Miriam put her hands over her mouth and shrank back into the darkness along with Jacob and Jerome.

In custody, Jesus meekly went along with his captors as Miriam, Jerome, and Jacob, like Peter, followed at a distance. It was critical to get the news to Tamar and the others in Bethany, but she couldn't go. She turned to Jerome. "Please, Jerome. You must get to Bethany to let the others know what happened."

Jerome was torn. He didn't want to desert Jesus, but there was nothing they could do. He was in no way able to run away. So he agreed. "I will and when we come back, we will try to find you and

Jacob." While he was so close to Bethany, now was the time to get the word out to the rest of the disciples.

Miriam looked up at her husband. "We must stay near Jesus, Jacob. I can't walk away."

CHAPTER SIXTY-SIX

JACOB WAS UNCERTAIN WATCHING JEROME disappear to Bethany. He worried for all their safety, especially, Miriam's, but he too felt the compelling need to see this through. Although he had his questions about Jesus' claims, there was no need to arrest him. If the Pharisees had problems with Jesus, they could have had a peaceful meeting with him. Not this, not arresting him in the dead of night with swords and clubs! This was just too over the top.

He took Miriam by the shoulders, gently. "Miriam? I'm sorry I was rough with you and told you to shut up. I was afraid. I, too am committed to know what is going to happen." With immense relief, Miriam leaned against Jacob's chest and wept.

They followed Jesus, the guards, and officers of the chief priests, as the teachers of the law, and the elders caught up to the procession. With open violence, they shoved, mocked, and hit Jesus as they propelled him along the road. Shortly, they arrived at the high priest's Annas' palace.

Time went by. "What's going on in there?" Miriam pulled her veil close around her head and chin.

"I'm sure the council is there with the high priest, Annas, and maybe even Caiaphas. If Caiaphas isn't there, then they'll bring Jesus before him too," A man from the shadows whispered. A short while later, still being pushed along, they spied Jesus, in custody, leaving Annas' house. Up ahead they saw Peter and another man, possibly a disciple, following quietly and quickly.

Those huddling in the cover of trees and brush, along with Miriam and Jacob left the cover of the trees and hurried after the two men. Soon enough, they discovered they were taking Jesus to Caiaphas' palace, and not the usual meeting place of the Sanhedrin. It was still dark, so they didn't see Jesus' bloodied and battered face or his robe splattered with blood and his wrists scraped raw and bruised.

As the night progressed into the early hours, several more people were now aware Jesus had been arrested. When the arresting party reached Caiaphas' palace some of the people huddling at a discreet distance from the palace gates said that the Sanhedrin—they didn't know how many— had assembled inside.

"Not all of them," someone said from the cluster of people watching.

"This is clearly a secret move on the leader's part, but they still need enough for a quorum in condemning Jesus," a sympathizer of Jesus lamented.

Miriam, Jacob, and other supporters gathered together in the protection of the dark trees lining an outside wall of the palace, watching. Suddenly, Peter and another man went up to the gate.

"What's going on?" Someone asked. "Is that Peter?" They saw the man said something to the gatekeeper and he let the two men in.

"Yes, that's Peter!" Jacob whispered. "But I can't tell who the other man is."

"Whoever he is, he knows the servants, and otherwise they never would have let them in."

Minutes went by without any apparent action. It was a brisk spring morning a couple of hours before dawn and at this hour the servants had a fire going in the courtyard for warmth. Miriam, Jacob, and the others crept closer to get a better look but could only hear could murmurs coming from the yard.

A rooster crowed once, then twice. "That's strange. There's still a few hours before dawn." Jacob looked up into the still darkened sky.

"It's probably the fire and the talk of the servants waiting outside that's roused the rooster," Miriam said absently.

CHAPTER SIXTY-SEVEN

JEROME, WILDLY LOOKING AROUND FOR his friends, came running up alone, clearly out of breath.

Miriam took hold of his sleeves. "Where is everyone?" She pulled at the fabric in dismay.

"I found a shepherd along the way and told him to make haste to Lazarus' house and tell them the news about Jesus." He panted leaning over with his hands on his knees trying to catch his breath. "I came as soon as I could because I knew they would eventually take him here."

One of the men in the shadows near Miriam stepped forward. "He's been before Annas, the high priest, now he's in front of Caiaphas, the other high priest, and the Sanhedrin who are up there with Caiaphas will surely question him too. They can recommend death—and I don't know for what possible reason—but only the Romans can condemn and kill him."

"So what you're saying is that he has to go before Pilate." Jacob interjected running a trembling hand through his hair.

"Yes," the man responded in discomfort. "Pontius Pilate, as the procurator and Roman governor of Judea has the absolute power over the Jews and is answerable to the emperor. He's here at Herod's palace for Passover Week because he wants to keep tight control over the city with all these pilgrims wandering around. When he's here, he hears trials only early in the morning at the Praetorium."

"Do you think there's a chance Pilate might acquit Jesus regardless what the Sanhedrin want?" Miriam asked hopefully.

He shrugged. "There're bad feelings between Pilate and the Jewish leaders. In fact, he has bad feelings for us all. Remember when Pilate refused to take down his standards of the Roman eagle when he came into the city? He knew that it would cause an uproar because of our prohibition of idolatry. He could have arrested or killed all of us, but even he knew that he couldn't do that. So, trust me. He hates us."

"I remember when he took money from the temple to build a new aqueduct and the people protested in the streets. His soldiers beat them unmercifully." Jerome heard the stories while traveling. It was nearly a massacre.

"And what about the time he killed some Galileens and mixed their blood with their sacrifices?" Miriam shuddered in revulsion.

"So, to answer your question, 'is there a chance he will let Jesus go?' I don't know. He hates the religious scruples, rules, and regulations of the Sanhedrin and all the other leaders. On the other hand, if the leaders come to him with blasphemy charge, there's no Roman law that recognizes that."

"They're going to come up with something more, like sedition." Jerome had been saying this for some time now—it was the only legal route the Jewish leaders could take and one that the Roman rulers would take note of. "But they still have to follow rules of the Sanhedrin and go through the formalities of a legal trial with the Jewish high court. They've covered themselves starting with Annas, Caiaphas, and the Sanhedrin."

Someone from the darkness spoke up. "I agree. The Romans care very little about anyone breaking Jewish religious laws unless the Jewish leaders accuse him of treason."

As the dawn broke, it wasn't so much that Jerome was physically tired, but emotionally drained. "That's why they arrested Jesus in the dead of night. To get him before Annas, then to Caiaphas and the Sanhedrin. That way, they could get him before Pilate in the morning, have him tried, and to their hopes, condemned . . . and it's all legal."

Stealing a glance at Jacob talking with the man who was near them, Jerome sensed a change in him. He was nearly wringing his hands in distress as he listened to the man explain what was likely to happen when Jesus came before Pilate. What was happening to Jesus was wrong, and he knew it. If this had been the old Jacob, he would have wanted to be home in bed and not standing out here in the cold and darkest hour waiting to see what was going to happen.

CHAPTER SIXTY-EIGHT

THE GATES SWUNG OPEN AND a formation of temple guards led Jesus, stumbling, away. Behind them, swept the priests, the elders, and the teachers of the law arrogantly hurling insults at him, condemning him for his blasphemous false claims of being God's son.

Those outside the gates of Caiaphas' palace listening to the Pharisees could see Jesus' end was near if Pilate didn't acquit him, which, knowing Pilate's hate for the Jews in general, was uncertain. Miriam, Jacob, and Jerome made haste to follow.

Grieving and filled with fear, the small group stole behind the procession as the city stirred in the dawn hours to a new excitement. People, seeing a bloody and beaten Jesus marched through the streets in the direction of Herod's palace and in the custody of the temple guards gathered and gossiped along the paths, at vendor's stalls, and on street corners.

As they neared Herod's palace, many people were milling around speculating on Jesus' fate before Pilate. Crying, and wiping her eyes with her sleeve, Miriam spotted Caleb at a vendor's stall close to the courtyard selling morning breads. He was talking animatedly with the vendor and she recognized the man as Caleb's former employer. She shouted his name. Jacob yelled out loudly and waved. Caleb, spying them, stopped his conversation and ran the short distance towards Miriam and Jacob coming to a halt in front of Miriam and Jacob with his hands on his hips.

"What is going on? Why didn't you come and get us when you heard that Jesus was about to be arrested?" he demanded looking between Miriam, Jacob, and Jerome. "This is crazy!"

"Where are the others?" Miriam asked. They too, would be distressed not to have been alerted of the imminent arrest.

"They're all are here too. Jerome's friend told us the news as he roused us from bed. He said that you three must have already gone out. We nearly went crazy walking the streets, looking for you! The Pharisees, the temple guards or even the Romans could have arrested you for being supporters of Jesus!"

He paused taking in a deep breath. "We've been asking people where they were taking Jesus. Most only knew that he was being brought before Pilate so we all came directly here. So why didn't you wake us up to go with you?"

Not getting an answer from either Miriam or Jacob who were now desperately looking through the crowds for the others, Caleb turned angrily to Jerome. "Why didn't you let us know?"

"It was my fault," Jerome admitted almost tearfully. "I feared for your safety—"

"But it was okay to drag Miriam and Jacob out in the middle of the night!" Caleb pointed to the couple scanning the groups of people hanging around the courtyard of the palace.

"Please. I'm sorry. There was nothing you could have done anyway, and as it was, we kept in the shadows for our own safety because, to your point, we would have been arrested too. Even his disciples took off—except Peter and some other fellow who inconspicuously followed behind the arresting officers. And truth is, there's not a thing any of us can do. Jesus has been arrested and has already been brought before the high priests, as well as the Sanhedrin. It was all planned and done in secret so they could bring Jesus before Pilate this morning." Jerome was beside himself with his own anger and grief.

Murderous excitement was building as the people grew more boisterous and rowdier.

"Caleb! Where are the others?" Miriam snapped at Esther's husband who stood there, lost. Just a boy he seemed today. Wet-eyed, runny-nose with tousled hair. He looked small and thin and young.

Caleb tilted his head over his shoulder, rubbing his eyes and said, "Stay here. Don't move. I'll go find them and bring them back." He ran.

"Miriam, I don't know what to say." Jacob's voice cracked. "I am so remorseful. I now see how much I misjudged Jesus. I, I was blinded by the so-called righteousness of the Pharisees because I believed in them. I didn't expect it would go this far. I had hoped that they would come to an agreeable discussion and end up supporting Jesus. I never dreamed this would happen! Miriam, one of his own disciples betrayed him. Judas! He identified Jesus in the dark for the guards by kissing him in greetings. Calling him rabbi!"

Jacob couldn't stop talking. "We saw him go to the high priest's house. He must have been telling them that Jesus liked to go to the Mount of Olives in the evening and that he often went to pray there in the garden of Gethsemane." He swallowed a sob. "How could I have been so misled?"

Pain and fear were infusing all who loved Jesus. The religious leaders were committing a monstrous act against an innocent man

from God because Jesus was drawing people away from the hypocrisy of the religious leaders. It amounted to pure jealousy, fear of losing their prominence, and their fragile equilibrium with the Roman
authorities.

"Miriam—remember at Caleb's wedding a man said he had been
with Jesus and he heard him say 'the Son of Man must suffer many
things and be rejected by the elders, the chief priests and the teachers
of the law, and that he must be killed and after three days rise again.'"

Miriam blinked at the recollection. "Yes, I do remember that." A
kernel of hope popped deep in her heart. They stared into each other's
eyes; Jesus predicted his death, but maybe there was something else?

Pressing through the crowd was Tamar, wailing loudly seeking
out Miriam. Her face was tear-stained, and her veil loose, hair falling around her face, they fell into each other's arms weeping. "How
could this happen?"

Caleb directed Esther, Elizabeth, and Timothy along with Jonas
to the waiting distraught, angry, and confused friends. They all
talked at once, letting out their fear and frustration.

Miriam couldn't come to grips with the enfolding events. "How
could Jesus enter Jerusalem to the adoration of masses proclaiming
him to be the Messiah with hosannas in the highest, then to be condemned and arrested?" The others could only shake their heads. It
was unbelievable. There were many answers; yet there were none
that made sense.

The friends stood outside Herod's palace in the courtyard, a distance from the entryway to the courtroom.

"Where are all the people who loved him, supported him, and believed in him? Where are the people he healed?" asked Esther nearly

in hysterics. Caleb put his arm around his wife's slender shaking shoulders.

'If they're like us, they're not saying anything. They're afraid of arrest or physical confrontation. We don't have the numbers of persuasion against this mob or the Pharisees and their people. We haven't any influence." Caleb held her close.

"His own disciples disappeared." Jacob wagged his head in dismay as he gazed at the people pressing for space hoping to get a good spot to see what was going to happen to Jesus. This was entertainment! "Where are they now?"

"I hope they're here, but they too, might be afraid. If Jesus is arrested, they could well land in jail too." Jerome looked for Peter, James, John, and the others, but by now the throng of people had grown and the rabble was threatening. Anyone for Jesus was keeping a low profile fearing a beating or stoning.

Pilate came out under the arch. It was difficult to hear him speak above the many voices egged on by the Pharisees, complaining about Jesus' rebellious ways.

"I can't hear what he's saying." Miriam stood on tiptoes to get a better look at the governor.

Jacob said, "He just asked the Jewish leaders, 'What charges are you bringing against this man?'"

Miriam strained to hear their response. The frowned in unison. "If this man were not doing evil, we would not have delivered him over to you."

They said other things that were lost in the noise. "What else are they saying?" Miriam leaned against her husband.

"They just said that Jesus was calling himself Christ, a king."

Many loud complaints filled the courtyard. "But he is!" Miriam whispered.

Jacob, his eyes glassy, simply said, "I know now."

She could only close her eyes. She wanted to shut out the anger of the crowd, the hatred of the Pharisees, the arrogance of Pilate. She had hoped that when Jacob came to the accept Jesus for who he said he was, they could both find joy, celebration, and completion in the moment. Now, although they were believers in Jesus the Christ, rather than experiencing joy, they would experience broken hearts and despair.

Pilate smirked. "Take him yourselves and judge him by your own law."

An officer standing near the group of friends sighed. "Pilate knows about Jesus' entry into Jerusalem last Sunday. He knows of his growing popularity, yet he knows that what Jesus has been doing has not been subversive. Jesus has only been teaching! Pilate is well aware of the egotistical jealousy the religious leaders have for him. He finds no fault with Jesus."

The officer shrugged. "So, he's not the instigator of the accusations and this growing fury." He swept his arm wide, taking in the throng. "It's the Jewish leaders. They are turning against one of their own. Jesus is a godly man."

"You know Jesus?" Caleb looked up in surprise at the Roman guard.

"Maybe," the man answered cautiously looking around and moved away.

CHAPTER SIXTY-NINE

JEROME SAID ALOUD, "THEY CAN judge him, and already have, but by Roman law, they can't kill him."

In hope Miriam asked, "Maybe Pilate will let him go, and he'll be spared?"

Jacob answered. "The leaders will never let Jesus slip out of their hands now. They've come too far." They turned their attention to the discussion under the arch between Pilate and the Jews.

The agitated crowd sullenly quieted down as Pilate called out. "I find no guilt in this man . . . "

But the Sanhedrin boldly interrupted, "He stirs up the people from Judea to Galilee! He is a menace and a traitor!" Pilate glared at the group then turned his heel and went back in his courtroom to confront Jesus again. The crowd erupted in howls.

Miriam and her friends huddled miserably together listening to those who would have him killed. Jesus supporters, frightened of the people swarming about, the Roman solidiers, and their own leaders whispered among themselves. "What will Pilate do to him?"

A man who overheard them answered, "He'll send him to Herod. Jesus is a Galilean and falls under Herod's jurisdiction and Herod happens to be here in Jerusalem. We can only guess what Herod might say. He has no sympathy for the Jews or alliance to God."

Pressing her knuckles against her mouth, Miriam looked back out at the crowd as it became more aggressive, shouting. "Send him to Herod! He killed John the Baptist, he'll surely kill this traitor, Jesus!"

Appalled, she held onto Jacob's robe when suddenly a battered and bloody Jesus came through the archway. The soldiers pushed him down the stairs where he went to one knee. They roughly hauled him up by the back of his robe and dragged him through the courtyard. Because of the intensity of the mob, who cheered and surged to follow, the soldiers tightly surrounded Jesus issuing threats of severe bodily harm to any who dared follow.

Falling back, the mob milled about in excitement and hate. Miriam looked silently and wide-eyed to Jacob. Touching her gently, he said. "We wait. They'll have to bring him back to Pilate for him to announce Jesus' fate to the crowd and our leaders."

When Jesus and his guards finally returned, he was more physically damaged than before. Blood smeared his face, his legs were striped with red welts, and his arms were bruised purple. Those who loved and supported him shrank back in grief and fear.

The crowd, eager to see Jesus' condition pushed and shoved screaming insults and threats. Miriam and her friends held firm in the midst of the chaos to wait for Pilate's pronouncement.

Time passed. Pilate stepped out again and called forth the chief priests and the rulers of the people. All strained to hear what he was saying. The crowd hushed to hear. "You brought me this man who you said was inciting the people into rebellion. I've questioned him and don't find any basis to the charges you claim and none that would warrant death. Even Herod has found no cause." The Jewish leaders grumbled angrily. The crowd complained. Pilate continued. "I'll punish him, then release him."

"No!" came loud demands from the crowd near hysteria. "Release Barabbas!"

Jerome shook his head in disbelief. "They're talking about the Roman act of clemency that acquits a prisoner from death. And they want the insurgent Barabbas let go!"

"But he was found guilty of treason!" Jacob gasped. "How can they let a true traitor, one who has even murdered, be let go?"

Miriam shrank back from the people who were shouting and arguing with one another and asked, "Do you think the Romans will release Jesus even though the people want Barabbas?"

"With this crowd?" Caleb ran a nervous hand along Esther's shoulders. "As long as the religious leaders are mingling throughout and inciting them to ask for Barabbas, Jesus hasn't a chance."

The synagogue leaders, elders, and others were working the crowd feverishly to ask for Barabbas. Men held up their fists demanding: "Release Barabbas! Release Barabbas!" and "Kill Jesus!". The frenzy had the Roman guards on high alert as they watched tense and ready.

An envoy from the frantic crowd came before Pilate who quickly asked, "Do you want me to release to you your king of the Jews?"

In unison they angrily responded, shouting, "He is not our king! If you release this man, you are no friend of Caesar!"

"Do not release Jesus! We want Barabbas!"

Greatly annoyed, but equally cautious, he demanded, "Then what do you want me to do with this so-called king of the Jews!"

The friends, unable to remain silent courageously yelled, "Release him! Release Jesus!"

Immediately, those around them drowned them out with their screams, threats, and shoving. "Do not release Jesus! He is not our king!" As they shook their fists a small group pushed toward them. Jacob and the men formed a tight circle around the women forcing the aggressors away who turned their attention to the archway where Pilate stood.

"Crucify him!" they shouted.

"Why? What crime has he committed?" asked Pilate still confronting the crowd.

There was no answer, only the shriek of, "Crucify him!"

Then Pilate brought Jesus out and sat done on the judgement seat at the Stone Pavement. In a frenzy, they cried all the louder, "Crucify him! Crucify him!"

Miriam, Esther, and Tamar screamed, "No!" But above the noise and chaos, no one heard them.

CHAPTER SEVENTY

MIRIAM AND FRIENDS WERE WAITING for him as he came out of the prison surrounded by his blood-spattered guards. As he stumbled out, their hearts slammed with shock at the utter brutality of his beating. So many people who loved Jesus, now wept openly in anger, disbelief, sorrow, and pain. They cried out to him as the slow procession passed.

The horrific scene also brought out the worst in others who were pleased with the grisly and satisfying entertainment. The Pharisees, Sadducees, elders, and high priests were greatly relieved. They had achieved exactly what they set out to do. So what they had endured a few years of challenge and trouble? Now, it was soon to be over, and the good news was that they would not miss the closing ceremonies of Passover and the Sabbath.

The weeping and jostling crowds closed in on the faltering Jesus. He could barely walk. He stumbled, staggered, and fell to his knees. He was unrecognizable. With puffy purple eyes nearly shut in his lopsided and swollen face, blood from his crown of thorns dripped into his ears, and over raw bleeding wounds on his cheeks and chin. Blood seeped through the back of his cloak and trickled down his arms, legs, and feet.

CHAPTER SEVENTY-ONE

JESUS COULD BARELY MOVE FORWARD. Without warning, the Roman guards lunged into the throng of people and pulled out a surprised and bewildered man, named Simon of Cyrene. Jesus grimaced in horrific pain as the soldiers unstrapped his cross, pulling more damaged skin off his shoulders. Dipping his head in agony, with blood pouring in his eyes from his crown of thorns, he could barely make out the man who was now made to carry his cross.

Voices, cries, and wailing of women filled the air. Their sorrow, like a cloak, covered all who loved and supported their beloved hoped-for messiah. Gathering strength, Jesus turned and said to them, "Daughters of Jerusalem, do not weep for me; weep for yourselves and for your children. For the time will come when you will say, 'Blessed are the childless women, the wombs that never bore and the breasts that never nursed!' Then they will say to the mountains, 'Fall on us!' and to the hills, 'Cover us!' For if people do these things when the tree is green, what will happen when it is dry?"

Miriam looked at Jerome who was wiping tears from his cheek with a sodden sleeve. "He's quoting from the prophet Hosea. He's warning about a future situation, worse than this one!"

Jacob hoarsely whispered, "What could be worse than this?"

As the procession trudged slowly along the road, the disciples moved closer to Jesus who was surrounded by Roman soldiers. Men and women were crying out, in a state of disbelief.

Tamar, moaned and pointed. "There's Jesus' mother Mary! Oh, how terrible for her! I can't imagine the pain that is searing her very soul!"

Two other men were led away with Jesus and they too, were condemned to die on their own crosses. The crowd, many in sympathy for Jesus, were overwhelmed with grief, but Jesus' legal and ruling detractors were satisfied. They were holding on to their positions, they were in control again, and the Roman government would leave them alone.

"Indeed", they smugly murmured among themselves, "A success story! We've averted a disaster. Of losing our authority over the people!"

Arriving at the execution site, they took off Jesus' placard, stripped him naked and with a rough rope, bound his wrists and his ankles to the cross. Then they got out thick, rusty, seven-inch long spikes and hammered his hands and feet to the wood. With each hammer thud, Jesus grimaced in pain and so many looked away unable to witness his agony. Before hoisting the cross upright with ropes, his executioners hammered the placard, "King of the Jews" above his head. Jesus, crowned in thorns, hung his head in increasing misery, thirst, and breathlessness.

On either side of him they hung the two criminals. Someone from the crowd offered Jesus a taste of wine mixed with gall, but he refused it.

Many, including the teachers of the law hurled insults and taunted him saying, "If you are the King of the Jews, save yourself!"

Even the chief priests ridiculed Jesus saying to one another, "He saved others; he cannot save himself. Let the Christ, the King of Israel, come down now from the cross that we may see and believe." They snickered, laughed and scoffed, competent in their superiority.

One of the elders said, "He trusts in God: let God deliver him now, if he desires him. For he said, 'I am the Son of God'"

Emboldened by the religious leader's sarcasm, the common people shouted and sneered, "Come down from the cross!" But many were horrified at the remarks of the Pharisees and priests and the people taunting their Lord. Many of Jesus' believers fell to their knees, silently crying and praying because under Roman law, mourning was forbidden for those executed. The scene was a dichotomy of hate and love.

One of the criminals who hung there hurled insults at him: "Aren't you the Messiah? Save yourself and us!"

But the other criminal rebuked him. "Don't you fear God," he said, "since you are under the same sentence? We are punished justly, for we are getting what our deeds deserve. But this man has done nothing wrong."

Then he said, "Jesus, remember me when you come into your kingdom."

Jesus answered him, "Truly I tell you, today you will be with me in paradise."

Miriam saw the guards were dividing his clothing as well as that of the others. Content with their spoil, they stood by the foot of the cross and guarded their Stonily they stared down the all the Jews taking in the smiling religious leaders and their factions and those mourning Jesus.

Jesus uttered, "Father forgive them for they know not what they do."

From about noon to three o'clock Miriam, and the others watched as Jesus suffered unbearable pain. Soon darkness descended. In the distance, Mary, the mother of Jesus, along with others held one another up and cried.

Jesus' devastated mother and a man crept closer to the cross. In a breathless voice Jesus looked at her and said, "Woman, behold your son!" Then painfully he raised his eyes to John and said, "Behold your mother."

The day continued to darken, causing the onlookers and the centurions to become uneasy and afraid. The air was deathly still.

Jesus spoke again, crying out in a loud voice "My God, my God, why have you forsaken me?"

Someone ran, filled a sponge with wine vinegar, put it on a staff, and offered it to Jesus to drink. "Now leave him alone. Let's see if Elijah comes to take him down," he said.

Many exchanged confused glances. Miriam thought she heard Jesus say, "It is finished."

Jesus, seeming to gather what little strength he had, cried out in a loud voice, "Father, into your hands I commit my spirit." He breathed his last.

CHAPTER SEVENTY-TWO

A TERRIBLE DEEP DARKNESS ENVELOPED the land, thunder clapped, and the earth shook. Many people stumbled to the ground in terror. It was so dark, the terrain so rocky and uneven, that people tripped and fell as they tried to get away from Golgotha.

The centurions clubbed the legs below his knee of the first man, who was barely breathing, and they did the same to the other criminal. Yet when they got to Jesus, they saw he was already dead, but a soldier thrust a spear in Jesus side anyway. Out gushed water and blood.

Miriam and Tamar went to their knees in heartache. Caleb held Esther in his arms. Jacob, Jerome, and the others held one another up. The bodies were still guarded by the soldiers. The darkness was lifting, and people were scattering. The only ones remaining were some men, Jesus' mother, and other women.

"Come," Jacob said softly. "There's no reason to stay. He's dead."

"But what will they do with his body?" Miriam wept. "I can't leave until we find out who will claim his body!"

"They throw crucified bodies into a common pit." Jacob bit his tongue to say this, but it was true.

Jerome crouched down. "Let's wait. We can't leave him here, hanging on the cross dead. Surely his inner group will come and get him."

"I think they are afraid," Esther said.

Tamar came up beside them and quietly agreed. "There's no one who will step forward, because they are afraid."

They weren't waiting long when Jacob pointed. A man was walking to the cross holding a bundle of linen and another man leading a donkey cart with a large parcel of spices used in burials. "I don't know who the man is that's carrying the linen, but look, the man with the cart is Nicodemus!"

Jerome looked through the dusk. "The other is Joseph of Arimathea . . . that's a surprise. He too is a member of the Sanhedrin. This is a bold act, for surely the religious leaders will know."

Tamar exclaimed. "He was a secret disciple of Jesus, but he, like Nicodemus was afraid of the Pharisees."

The small group now had withdrawn to the ridge because of the threatening stance of the soldiers. Others, who stayed, including Jesus' mother, her women friends, and the apostle John kept a distance too. They watched the two men awkwardly take Jesus down from the cross.

"Since Nicodemus and Joseph are members of the Sanhedrin, Pilate must have given them permission to take the body down and bury it," Jerome said in quiet surprise.

"They'll have to do it quickly. The burial has to be completed by sundown, before the Sabbath." Miriam heaved a deep sigh. It had finally come to this. "Where will they bury him?" Miriam realized that

Tamar knew both Nicodemus and Joseph because both men were secret disciples of Jesus.

"I've heard that Joseph has a new tomb, close to here. It's in a garden, and it's carved out of a rock." Tamar nodded so sadly. "I don't know exactly where it is, but I'm sure he's been taken there."

CHAPTER SEVENTY-THREE

"TAMAR, WHAT DID YOU FIND out?" Miriam took her by the arm and led her into a back room where Jacob, Esther, and the others were waiting impatiently for news. This was the Sabbath, and so kept themselves hidden from outsiders, particularly if any of the temple guards were looking to arrest any of Jesus' supporters.

"I found out exactly where the tomb is, but there's a Roman guard placed around it so no one can steal Jesus' body. They never expected so many people to lose their fear of them and openly say they believe in Jesus. They surely don't want people to think that he escaped from the grave!"

"How can anybody break into his tomb without being seen and stopped? It's senseless they should even think that someone would steal his body." Jacob turned his head so the others couldn't see the tears welling up in his eyes. Was it too late to believe?

"A Roman guard?" Caleb asked. "Who would be crazy enough to try something like that. They would be killed!"

Jerome nodded his head. "That's a four to sixteen-man unit with each man responsible for protecting six feet of ground and holding it. There's no way anyone could break through those men to get to the tomb!" Jerome was emphatic. "And at night? Four men are stationed in in back of the rest who are sleeping. Those four men are awake and alert in protecting or securing whatever they are tasked to do. Then, every four hours, another four are awakened and those who were on guard get to sleep, and so it goes until morning. If anyone tries to penetrate a full guard, they'll have to step over twelve sleeping warriors.

"Do you know what happens if a Roman guard deserts his post or falls asleep?" asked Timothy. "I'll tell you one way. They'll strip off his clothes and burn him alive in a fire fueled by his clothes."

The friends grew quiet. "The Roman guard is a disciplined military force with rigid standards. They would never break protocol," Jonas added.

"And," continued Tamar, "the Romans set a seal on the stone."

"How do they do that?" Esther asked.

"They put a rope across the stone and stick each end fast with sealing clay. That means that Jesus' body is under Roman protection beyond the guard and any tampering with the seal, will incur the wrath of the Roman empire."

"In other words, whoever tries to steal his body must get through the guards, roll the stone back which is no longer easily moved, and then break the seal in blatant defiance of the Roman governor." Miriam took a drink of water. Her mouth was so dry, and her head was pounding. The sorrow was overwhelming. It had been two days since Jesus was put to death.

The group sat back taking all of this in until Miriam broke the silence. "Recall when Jesus said he must go to Jerusalem and suffer many things at the hands of the elders, the chief priests and the teachers of the law, and that he must be killed and on the third day be raised to life? She waited for her friends to react.

The candle was lit. It was unthinkable. It couldn't happen. He'd never get out of the tomb alive!

Again, Miriam broke into their thoughts. "Where are the other disciples?"

Tamar shook her head and pursed her lips. "They're hiding. They're afraid they'll be arrested too. We woman are of inconsequence, so we can more easily move about the city, but the men don't dare. They'd be recognized. Having said that, I'm going back to the disciples to see what the next steps will be in the ministry. I'll be back to let you know what, if any plans are made. It's possible, everyone will go back to their homes, family, and work."

At the door she turned. "What are your plans?"

Miriam turned to Jacob. "We're planning on leaving tomorrow. There's nothing more to do. Jesus will be dead three days. I can't believe he was just with us!"

"And now gone. He was so much a part of our lives for so long . . ." Tamar quietly closed the door.

CHAPTER SEVENTY-FOUR

MIRIAM AWOKE TO A POUNDING on her door. Fully awake she felt Jacob heave off the pallet and grab his tunic. "Miriam, Jacob, get up!" It was Jerome, shouting. "Tamar is here! With extraordinary news!"

Jerome ran from the door before Jacob could open it up. They heard him hammering on the other bedroom doors down the hallway.

All the friends, Miriam, Jacob, Jerome, Timothy, Elizabeth, Caleb, Esther, and Jonas pulling on his tunic, crowded in the small middle room of Jerome's friend's house. His friend, tense with excitement put on a pot for warm goat's milk. Jerome had his arm around Tamar who was shaking, crying, and laughing.

Jacob whispered to Miriam, "Has she finally gone over the edge?"

Breaking from Jerome's arms, she threw her hands high. "He's alive!" She whirled around dancing, singing halleluiahs, and crying all at the same time.

"Whoa. What are you talking about?" Miriam gently put her hands on her shoulders to calm her down.

"Friends, I'm telling you Jesus is alive!"

The room erupted in questions everyone talking at once, while Tamar tried to speak above the confusion and explain. Finally, Jerome held up his hand. "Shhh. Let the woman speak."

Hand trembling, she took a proffered cup of milk and took a small sip, closing her eyes to calm herself. As everyone stared at her, she sat down, but popped up again.

Nearly dropping her cup, she began, "Very early this morning the women prepared the spices to put on Jesus' body because they couldn't do it on the Sabbath. Mary Magdalene and three other women collected the spices. They went to the tomb while it was still dark. I was sleeping. I was so weary with fatigue and overcome with sadness I slept like I was dead.

"They didn't want to wake me, because after many tormented hours I had finally fell asleep. So they left without me. On the way, they worried who would roll the stone away at that hour and were concerned the guards would never let them pass, but they went anyway.

"Later, they came running back, overjoyed yet frightened. They were shouting at all of us to wake up. Immediately I got up and started the fires, while everyone in the house was abuzz with questions and unbelief. Peter and the rest of the men insisted she repeat everything exactly as it happened.

"And?" Esther grabbed Caleb's hand and held it tight.

"When they got to the tomb, the guards were gone, and they saw that the stone was rolled away! Terrified that something happened to Jesus' body, they crept towards the opening."

"Oh," Miriam whispered faintly. She wasn't sure she could hear any more terrible news. Jerome rubbed his temples, and Jacob leaned anxiously forward.

Tamar place a hand over her heart. "They, they," she stammered. "They saw a young man sitting in the tomb dressed in dazzling white.

Overcome with fear they went to their knees. "He said to them, 'Don't be alarmed. You are looking for Jesus the Nazarene, who was crucified. He has risen! He is not here. See the place where they laid him. But go, tell his disciples and Peter, 'He is going ahead of you into Galilee. There you will see him, just as he told you.'

"There's more," Tamar nearly shouted. "In haste, they left, but on the way . . . " Tamar had to sit down.

"Take your time, Tamar," Miriam encouraged her.

With sparkling eyes, she looked up. Her face was aglow. "On the way, Jesus met them!"

Jerome shushed them as they celebrated. "What happened next Tamar?"

"'Greetings,' he said. They came to him, clasped his feet and worshiped him. Then Jesus said to them, 'Do not be afraid. Go and tell my brothers to go to Galilee; there they will see me.'"

Now they fell quiet, but Tamar had more to say. "No one in the house believed them except Peter and another disciple who went running out to the house to the tomb. When they got there, they found an empty tomb. Only the linens were left behind, including the face cloth folded up in a place by itself."

Miriam took their attention away from Tamar for a moment. "Remember when he said while he was still in Galilee that the Son of Man must be delivered into the hands of sinful men and be crucified and on the third day rise?"

"Yes," came the communal response.

"This is the third day."

They went silent for a long time.

Tamar bowed her head for a moment. Lifting her eyes to them she said, "And on the night of the Passover meal, while they were eating, Jesus took bread, and when he had given thanks, he broke it and gave it to his disciples, saying, 'Take it; this is my body.' Then he took a cup, and when he had given thanks, he gave it to them, and they all drank from it. 'This is my blood of the covenant, which is poured out for many,' he said to them. 'Truly I tell you, I will not drink again from the fruit of the vine until that day when I drink it new in the kingdom of God.'"

No one could utter a word. He *died* for them? Again, it was confusing, and they looked to one another for answers, but no one said a thing.

Tamar broke the baffled silence. "There's one other thing of—I don't know how to put it . . . "

"Just say it Tamar!"

She took a long drink of the now tepid tea and wiped her mouth. "Judas Iscariot?

"He's one of Jesus' twelve apostles. His inner circle." Jacob turned to Miriam. "Recall we saw him enter the courtyard to the high priest's palace?"

Tamar breathed out a hot shaking breath. "There was a reason he was there, Jacob. He was the one who betrayed Jesus in the garden of Gethsemane! With a kiss no less! He was paid thirty pieces of silver for his betrayal!"

"I would like to kill the scum!" Caleb shouted getting up.

Esther put her hand on his arm. "Don't talk like that."

"You don't have to worry. He went back to the chief priests and elders and told them he had sinned by betraying innocent blood. He threw the thirty pieces of silver they paid him into the temple."

"But what happened to him?" Caleb clenched a fist.

"He hung himself."

CHAPTER SEVENTY-FIVE

AFTER HEARING THE NEWS OF Jesus resurrection, and finding themselves in utter confusion—what did it mean? Even Jerome didn't have any explanations or answers, nor did Miriam. He's alive, but now what will happen? Jesus is going to Galilee? When? They packed up their belongings to make their way back to Capernaum. It was time to pray and gather introspection on all that they had seen and heard, but it was also time to get back to their everyday lives. Jerome had to get back to Ann, the children, and his goat business. Timothy, Jacob, and Jonas needed to get back to fishing.

The children of Elizabeth and Miriam had been without their mothers for over a week, and the households had to be managed. Esther and Caleb helped get their meager belongings together and loaded the donkey cart for the trip back. Esther would go back to helping Miriam with Joseph and the household while Caleb tended to the goats. But none of them would return to life the way it used to be. Everything had changed.

Nearing the gate of departure from Jerusalem, Tamar met them. "We'll be here for a while because the disciples are afraid of arrest. We will go to Galilee, when it's safe to leave the city. This news of Jesus is organic, a living thing, and will have some kind of impact on all us. We just not sure what, but we have faith and will look for him in

Galilee. If I come back to Capernaum, I will definitely see you." She kissed the women and gave Miriam an extra-long hug. "Pray we'll meet again. Pray for all our safety. Safe and blessed travels."

On the first day leaving the city, they came across a group of men walking who were talking about Jesus' empty grave. "What have you heard?" asked Jerome, overhearing their conversation.

"We heard the Roman guard went to the chief priests to tell them about an earthquake that rolled the stone away from Jesus' tomb, about an angel who had such power over them they became like dead men, falling to the ground and when they regained their senses, they saw the tomb was empty"

"If they had gone back to their Roman superiors and told them that story, they would have been put to death!" Jerome exclaimed.

"Certainly. That's why they went to the religious leaders who gave them money to lie and tell the people that his disciples came in the middle of the night and took his body."

"But, still, how will they explain to Pilate that they didn't stop the thieves? The Roman seal was broken!" Caleb threw up his hands.

One of the men scratched his beard and smiled. "The chief priests assured the guard that they would cover for them. I hope for their sakes, that's true. Because Pilate will surely kill them."

They walked for a few hours until they came to a small town to stay the remainder of the afternoon and night. They didn't put a full day of walking because they were deeply and emotionally drained. An inn was open to pilgrims, so while it was tight quarters, they all were able to stay in the same dwelling, sharing two rooms. Outside, they sat around a fire and as they were finishing their meals, a new guest arrived. He, too, was on his way to Capernaum.

"Are you coming back from Jerusalem?" Jerome asked the newcomer as he sat down with his evening meal.

"Yes." He dipped his bread in olive oil and took a bite. "So many unsettling events. I've heard conflicting stories of this man named Jesus. If you were in Jerusalem for the Passover, then you know who I'm talking about."

"We do. Like His apostles and disciples, we believe He's alive." Everyone around the fire nodded in agreement.

"I don't know. Rising from the dead? It's disturbing, but the evidence is compelling I have to admit."

Jerome and the man spent a few moments discussing Jesus, but tired from the long week's trials and the walk, they all went to bed with troubled, questioning hearts.

Miriam wasn't sure what to think. She believed he was alive, but where was He? When would He come back to His ministry in Galilee; would He come to Capernaum? Would He tell everyone how He rose from the dead to life again? Would He tell what it was like being dead? Would He prove to the religious leaders He truly was the Son of God?

Miriam wondered as Jacob lay on his back, if he was thinking the same things. Had he finally realized that he now believed for certain that Jesus was who He said He was? The Son of God? Was it too late for him to get to the kingdom of heaven?

Jerome, Jonas, Timothy, and Elizabeth all closed their eyes trying for sleep which eluded them until the deep, dark hours. A living Jesus was on their minds.

Miriam thought of Esther who believed that Jesus was alive again, but like everyone else she wondered to Miriam what would happen when the Pharisees discovered that there were people who believed that Jesus was alive. The leaders of the synagogues and temple could easily spread lies around His burial and refute His resurrection—yet what would the Pharisees do now that killing Him didn't work?

"They certainly can't kill him again!" Miriam said aloud.

The following morning, they departed, talking among themselves about what was going to happen now that Jesus was alive. There were many questions, few answers. They spent the night at a small inn after several hours walk. The next morning at breakfast a traveler joined them at the long table.

"Did you hear the news?" Sleepily he yawned wide, then ineffectively patted his messy hair in place.

In unison those at the table exclaimed, "Jesus is alive!"

"I am hearing that." The man helped himself to water and bread. "I met two men hurrying back from the village Emmaus, to the west of the city. Although I was heading north, we crossed at path roads. It was during the supper hour. They were ecstatic, beyond overjoyed. They were making their way back to Jesus' apostles in Jerusalem. They told me Jesus himself came up and walked along with them, but they were kept from recognizing him. He asked them what they were talking about.

"Surprised, one of them, named Cleopas, asked him, 'Are you the only one visiting Jerusalem who doesn't know the things that have happened there?' 'What things?' the stranger wanted to know.

"They explained to him what happened and about Jesus of Nazareth and how he was a prophet, teacher, and preacher telling all wonderful things about the kingdom of God.

"They told him, too, that the chief priests and rulers handed Jesus over to Pilate to be crucified and how disappointed they were because they thought that he was the messiah, the one who was going to free Israel form Rome." The man took a deep drink then continued with his story. "They also said that after Jesus was crucified some of the women disciples had gone to Jesus' tomb early in the morning but didn't find him! They said that they had seen a vision of angels, who said he was alive! Then some of their companions went to the tomb and found it just as the women had said, but they did not see Jesus."

The traveler helped himself to more bread before continuing. Miriam and friends were silent eagerly waiting to hear more.

He continued. "The stranger told them that they didn't understand all the prophets had been talking about. He asked them, 'Did not the Messiah have to suffer these things and then enter his glory?' Then the stranger proceeded to explain about what Moses and the prophets said concerning the coming Messiah.

"They soon came to a village and as the stranger was going to go on his way, they asked him to stay with them because it was late, and they hoped to hear more."

Miriam and friends were mesmerized by the story, exchanging glances with one another. Miriam wondered where this was leading.

The traveler leaned forward with a chunk of bread in his hand held high. "Then, as they were sitting at the table for supper, the stranger took bread, gave thanks, broke it, and gave it to them. Then their eyes were opened and they recognized him, Jesus! It was Jesus all along! And in a moment, he disappeared from their sight!"

Stunned, the listeners could only gape at their story teller. Jesus appearing then disappearing? It was all so amazing.

Before they could talk the fellow continued, "So, they got up and returned at once to Jerusalem. There they found the disciples and told them they saw Jesus themselves! What the women had said was true. And then the disciples said yes, it was true because the Lord also appeared to Simon!"

CHAPTER SEVENTY-SIX

"WHAT WAS THE SIGNIFICANCE OF breaking bread?" Esther wondered as she walked along side of Jerome.

He answered. "You remember when Jesus fed many thousands with just a few loaves of bread and fish. When he broke the bread, he gave thanks to his father God, in heaven and recall Tamar telling us he did the same thing at the Passover meal?"

"This is reminiscent of Jesus saying, 'I tell you, unless you eat the flesh of the Son of Man and drink his blood, you have no life in you.'" Hearing Jerome's words, Miriam gazed at Jacob.

"I do remember I found that hard to understand," Jacob acquiesced.

The man stood up to go. "I also heard that he appeared to one of his apostles, Simon Peter on the same day too!"

Miriam clapped her hands. "He appeared to two men traveling to Emmaus too!" There were so many affirmations of his rising from the dead!

"Will we see him again?" Miriam asked Jacob as they got up from the table to continue on their trip back home.

"I don't know. He told his disciples to meet him in Galilee, but we have no idea when since they are hiding in Jerusalem away from the authorities."

How could they stay connected to him? Miriam wondered if Jesus would travel to Jerusalem and confront the leaders of the synagogue, the chief priests, the elders, and the Sanhedrin. This could radically change the current forces at work now that their Messiah was alive. The rulers would be threatened all over again, but what could they do about it?

Interrupting her thoughts, Jacob asked cautiously of Jerome, "Will he now, in his power, overthrow the Romans?"

Jerome scratched his chin through his beard. "I don't know what can happen next. If I didn't have to go home to Ann and the business, I would turn around now and go back to Jerusalem with the disciples."

"But we don't know where he is!" Caleb threw up a hand. "He could be anywhere. First, he suddenly appeared to the women at the tomb, then appeared to the men who were on their way to Emmaus, then he appeared to Simon Peter. Then he said he'd meet them in Galilee. When?"

Miriam had to agree. "He has the power of spirits, Caleb. We don't know where he is right now, or where he's traveling, or where his kingdom is . . . we know it's heaven, but where is it? We can't go there. He can only come here."

The friends fell silent as they walked.

Several days later, exhausted both physically and mentally, they arrived home. Life continued for the women tending the children, preparing meals, and housework. Jacob, Timothy, and Jonas went fishing, and Jerome and Caleb tended to their goats.

During the following weeks, Miriam heard through Jerome and others that Jesus had appeared to many people, including nearly five hundred people in Galilee. How she prayed he would appear to them.

What were they to do without him? How could they continue their spiritual journey without his guidance?

They attended the synagogue on the Sabbaths and the hushed discussions were all about Jesus. The Pharisees and other teachers of the law never spoke of Jesus and the Jews were afraid to bring him up, but Miriam spoke openly in front of the women about her experiences in Jerusalem over the week of Passover.

They weren't the only ones who had been with Jesus throughout his ministry, death, and resurrection.

"Miriam!"

Miriam looked over her shoulder as Tamar came running toward her with a huge hug. "Tamar, You're here! I think and pray for you each day! So wonderful to see you! Please tell me the news!"

"I will, but let's get everyone at your house tonight."

That evening, after a rushed supper, Tamar held everyone's attention. "Miriam told me that you heard Jesus appeared to two disciples who were traveling to Emmaus and that he appeared to Simon Peter. Well, the same day he appeared to the disciples who locked themselves in their room in Jerusalem. Listen! They were behind locked closed doors out of fear for being arrested and trying to figure a way out of the city unnoticed from the temple guards who were on the lookout for them. While they were discussing their options Jesus appeared before them!"

"How did he get in?" Caleb demanded.

Tamar laughed. "He just *appeared* in the room!"

"What did he say?" Everyone asked at once.

"'Peace be with you.' Tamar put her hand to her mouth and giggled in utter joy. "After he said this, he showed them his hands and side. The disciples were overjoyed when they saw the Lord.

"Again Jesus said, 'Peace be with you! As the Father has sent me, I am sending you.' And with that he breathed on them and said, 'Receive the Holy Spirit.'"

"Sending you?" Jacob was bewildered.

"He's sending out the disciples to teach and preach his words of salvation," Tamar said.

"But 'Receive the Holy Spirit?' meaning the Spirit of God?" Jacob wanted clarity.

"Yes!" Tamar nearly shouted. "He also said that if they forgive sins of any, they will be forgiven, but if they don't forgive the sins of any, they will not be forgiven."

"They have the power to forgive sins?" This perplexed Miriam.

"No. God doesn't forgive sins because we do; rather the sins they forgive have already been forgiven because those are the people that believe in Jesus and in his teaching and have asked for forgiveness. This is the essence of salvation. And those who don't believe? Their sins simply aren't forgiven." She shot a look at Jacob.

Miriam put a protective hand on Jacob's arm. Tamar didn't yet know of Jacob's change of heart.

The rest were eager to hear more, and there were so many questions. Tamar tucked a loose strand of hair behind her ear. "One of the apostles, Thomas, wasn't with them when Jesus came, and when the others told us and Thomas about Jesus came to them, he didn't believe them!"

"How could he not believe after Mary Magdalene, the two traveling disciples, and eleven of his own close friends each stating with absolute certainty they saw and talked with Jesus?" Jacob asked pursing his lips. Tamar's eyes grew wide; Miriam subtly tilted her head with a smile. Tamar got it. Jacob believed!

"Continue, please!" Jerome was beside himself with delight.

"Thomas said, and I repeat, 'Unless I see in His hands the imprint of the nails, and put my finger into the place of the nails, and put my hand into His side, I will not believe.'

"Eight days later, we disciples and the core apostles still hadn't left Jerusalem. This time Thomas with the apostles. Jesus came, the doors having been shut, and stood in their midst and said, 'Peace be with you.' Then He said to Thomas, 'Reach here with your finger, and see My hands; and reach here your hand and put it into My side; and do not be unbelieving, but believing.' Thomas answered and said to Him, 'My Lord and my God!' Jesus said to him, 'Because you have seen Me, have you believed? Blessed are they who did not see, and yet believed.'"

This last statement made the friends think. How true. Because they heard and saw Jesus in his power, they believed that Jesus was the Son of God, but as time went on from these momentous events, blessed be those who never heard a word from Jesus' own lips and never saw his miracles with their own eyes, yet believed.

CHAPTER SEVENTY-SEVEN

"HOW LONG WILL YOU STAY in the area Tamar?" Miriam was concerned about how Tamar would exist now that life had changed so radically for her. She had sold everything she had to follow Jesus. Here and throughout Galilee or even in Judea, she would find it difficult without some kind of support.

"I'm staying in a home in Galilee, outside of Capernaum. I'm meeting with Simon Peter and a few of the others. I'm not sure they know what they are going to do either, but Jesus has assured them he will not leave them, and he would see them in Galilee. As far as I'm concerned, I am a disciple too, and I know he won't leave me either."

Jacob came in, nearly tripping over group of hens pecking around Tamar's feet. "You've come back!"

"Some of us have come back to Galilee to see if Jesus shows up and Simon Peter and six others have decided to go back fishing."

"Are they out now?" Jacob collected his gear, a skin of water, and an extra cloak he stuffed in his satchel as he readied to leave. He too, was going out tonight with Timothy and Jonas

"I suspect they are." Tamar answered his question. "Peter thought that they might as well fish while they wait."

Jacob paused. "I guess I was wrong about Jesus. I'm sorry I doubted him. If you see him, tell him I'm sorry, because I do believe in him now."

"Jacob, you can tell him yourself. You don't need me."

"Is he coming back?"

"Of course he is! I just don't know when."

Jacob screwed up his face.

After he hugged Miriam and left, Tamar asked Miriam about Jacob's change in attitude. "He's a different man," Miriam sighed happily. "He doesn't know how to talk about his belief in Jesus, but honestly, I too, am not sure how to proceed. I think of him often, but sometimes I just don't know what to say. Jacob, who doesn't confide in me, must feel the same way. How do we relate to the Son of God when we don't know when we'll see him again?"

"You will see him again. Whether now, or in heaven, if you believe in who he says he is and you follow his teaching, you'll see him again. I know you didn't hear all of his words, but even if you got "Love the Lord your God with all your heart and with all your soul and with all your strength and with all your mind'; and, 'Love your neighbor as yourself,'" then you have a solid foundation for his teaching. More will be revealed. I think in time we will be blessed with the Spirit of God as well."

"Spend the night and tomorrow you can go look for Simon Peter and the others. They'll be back in from fishing."

As they settled in for the night, with little Joseph in Tamar's arms, Miriam got up and went to her worktable. "What's wrong, Miriam?"

"Jacob forgot his meals. I hope they have extra to share on board."

"Tomorrow let's go down to the beach to see if the apostles and the others are around. Jacob should be in then too, and you can bring him some food. He'll be hungry after a night of fishing."

"He's always hungry," Miriam laughed.

The next morning, just after dawn, Miriam, Joseph, and Tamar made their way down to the area where the boats would be coming in from a night of fishing. Joseph walked for a bit, then was carried on Tamar's hip because Miriam was carrying Jacob's food over her shoulder along with a skin of water. Nearing the beach, they saw Jacob, Timothy, and Jonas helping another crew with an overflowing net.

When the women got closer to the shore, Jacob stopped what he was doing, and ran to Miriam, who laughed and said, "I wager he's after his breakfast!"

Jacob got to the women out of breath. "Jesus was here!" The women gaped at Jacob in surprise, then craned their necks looking for him by the nets the men were wrestling with on the damp shore.

"Where is he?" Tamar asked with excitement.

"We just brought our boat in and were really disappointed because we caught very little. Simon Peter and his crew caught nothing! There was a man standing on the beach who asked them if they had any fish and they said no, but then the man said, 'Cast the net on the right side of the boat, and you will find some.'

"I thought the man was crazy. How could he tell where the fish were by standing on the shore? Anyway, they did, and it was so full, they couldn't haul it all in, so we ran in to help. Mind you, it was in shallow water."

Jacob ran his hand through his wet hair. "Then one of the fishermen, John, I think it was, shouted, 'Its Jesus!' We hauled the net to shore and the man had a charcoal fire going with fish laid on it and bread, but he didn't look like the Jesus I remembered"

Miriam was speechless. Tamar bubbled with excitement.

Jacob continued babbling, almost. "I don't know how he knew where the fish would be but he told Simon Peter to get more fish from the net—they caught about 153 large ones—and though the net was full; it wasn't torn at all. Then the man said, 'Come and have breakfast!' But we still didn't recognize him as Jesus!"

"But John did?" Miriam finally found her voice.

"Yes, he did and then our eyes were opened." Jacob reached for a drink from the skin Miriam had over her shoulder.

"Where is Jesus now?"

"He's talking with Simon Peter." Tamar handed Joseph to Miriam and started ploughing through the sand and over the rocks to where the disciples were waiting. Jacob caught Miriam's sleeve. "He talked with me too . . . "

CHAPTER SEVENTY-EIGHT

THAT EVENING, SITTING AROUND THE fire, the friends gathered for a communal meal. This time, Jacob had actually seen Jesus unlike the others who only heard testimony from those who had seen him since his death.

"All authority has been given to him, he told us." Jacob was hesitant to speak about Jesus because he knew that his friends had known his doubts had run on for over a year. Turning his attention to Jerome he said, "We were hoping for a political messiah. Miriam was right. This isn't about earthly government. It's about kingdom of God. Here. Now. He wants us to tell everyone—not only Jew, but Gentile about the gospel, you know, his teaching."

"We need help there because we haven't heard all he had to say while he was with his apostles and disciples," Jerome said. "Only they have the whole story."

Because it was warm, they were all sitting at a distance from the outside cooking fire; the shadows were deep, so they were startled when Tamar appeared, greeting them before sitting down. "Friends, I'm leaving for Jerusalem with the disciples, but I'll be back."

"Can't you stay and tell us what is going on?" Miriam begged.

"I can't. I have to catch up with the disciples who are already on the road. I'll be back, I promise."

Miriam and Esther hugged Tamar. Elizabeth and Ann, who had been in the background for most of the time, hugged her too.

"Do you need anything?" Miriam asked, but before Tamar could say anything, Jerome hopped up and gave her a few coins, followed by the other men. Miriam said, "Wait," and disappeared for several minutes while Tamar sought out Joseph for a kiss and came back with a package of food.

More than a month later, Jerome had heard through his travels that Jesus appeared to his disciples in the area of Bethany, on the Mount of Olives. Jesus commanded that they make disciples in all nations baptizing them in the name of the Father and of the Son and of the Holy Spirit, teaching them to observe all that he had taught.

"After he finished speaking with them, they fell to their knees, worshipping him as he ascended into heaven!" Jerome pointed up, excited.

"Does that mean he's not coming back?" Esther asked with a mixture of sadness and concern.

"No, he said that he would be with us until the end of the age," Jerome answered solemnly.

"I don't understand." Esther said.

"I'm not sure either, but I think he'll be with us to the end of life as we and future generations know it."

"But if he's gone back to heaven, how will we learn all of his teaching? We've only heard a little bit." Miriam's second thought was Jesus' command of baptism. "How do we symbolize our death to sin and renewal of life through baptism if there is no one of authority to do it?"

Jacob asked, "Will the disciples come back here? Are they all still in Jerusalem?"

"Maybe Tamar will remember us and send someone back here to teach us---and baptize us," Caleb said hopefully.

"We've gone as far as we can . . . " Miriam worried.

"Not really," Jerome offered. "We know some of what Jesus taught, and we know he was walking on earth as man, but also as God. We believe in him, so we just continue to build a spiritual relationship with him. And as for us? We remain friends, meeting, and enjoying meals, and talking about what we've heard Jesus teach. And we encourage one another in our devotion to him."

"Tell us what's going on at the synagogues, Jerome, and with Jesus' disciples," begged Miriam so eager for word on the impact Jesus was having on the nation.

"The Pharisees, Sadducees, teachers of the law, the elders, the chief priests—all of them are losing their power with the rise of people accepting the truth about Jesus. The disciples themselves have been teaching and performing miracles in Jesus' name! Nearly three-thousand people came to Jesus fifteen days after Passover on the day of Pentecost. Three thousand people! Imagine."

Miriam was shocked in a powerful and uplifting way but was distressed when Jerome continued, "Stephen, one of the followers was preaching about Jesus as the Messiah and that only he—not the scribes or the leaders— were central to salvation and redemption. You know this is in direct conflict with our leaders teaching of the importance of the Law. His teaching enraged them. They said it was blasphemy. They stoned him to death.

"Persecution is being stepped up by a Pharisee name Saul," Jerome told them. "Not only did he witness Stephen being stoned, but he supported the death!"

The friends swallowed in fear and wretchedness. Stoning was a horrible way to die!

"Saul," Jerome went on, "fervently believes that keeping the Mosaic Law is the only way to usher in the Messianic Age and he's determined to ferret out those who were a threat to the Jewish leaders hoped for Messiah. He believes, with God on his side, that those Jews, now called Christians, need to be stopped from spreading the heresy of Jesus Messiah!"

Jacob opened his mouth to protest, but Jerome held up a hand. "It gets worse. He went to the high priest to ask for permission to track down believers and take them as prisoners!"

They were aghast. The men's first thought was for the safety of their families and they began talking at once. Jerome took control of the conversation. "Friends, listen. We are going to have to be very careful. This Saul will take us all to prison including children. We must lay low. We can certainly still meet and talk about Jesus' principles and teaching, but I caution you to be very careful who you speak to in the marketplace, women and who you talk to on the beach, men. We must pray to Jesus for guidance. We can't bury our belief; we must just be prudent who we share our hopes with."

Miriam held Joseph tighter as he slept innocently on her lap. Jacob place a protective arm around her and prayed for all their safety.

CHAPTER SEVENTY-NINE

JEROME MET JACOB AND TIMOTHY on the beach. "You've been gone awhile, Jerome. We missed you. I hope you have lots of news for us." Jacob dumped a basket of fish on a cutting table.

Timothy came over to greet him. "This is a surprise! Why do you have that sly goat Ziph with you? Haven't you been home yet?"

"No. I came directly here from my travels. There's trouble as we knew there would be. Our native born Jewish Christians are keeping a low profile in Jerusalem and aren't openly fellowshipping with each other in Jesus' name, but the Greek Jewish Christians—the Jews who believe in Jesus, are being driven out and dispersed throughout Judea and Samaria.

"The good news is that the Gospel of Jesus will be fortified beyond Jerusalem, but the bad news is . . . " Here he stopped. Jacob stopped filleting, Timothy stopped sorting, and Jonas nervously wiped him mouth.

Jerome grabbed Jacob's arms. "Miriam and Esther are being sought."

The men were stunned. "Why? For what? They're just women! Harmless!" Angry, he pulled away, throwing his knife down on the bellies of the dead fish.

"While we men have been talking and worshipping Jesus quietly with people who are like-minded, Miriam and Esther have been openly talking with the women in the synagogue about Jesus and the miracle of Esther's healing. The women in turn, have been telling their husbands, who have been telling the Pharisees!"

"What do we do now?" Jacob went white.

"Come, we must work this out." Timothy, Jacob, and Jonas followed him to Miriam and Esther.

Miriam was kneading bread and Esther was playing with Joseph when the men came into the yard. "Is everyone alright?"

"Come, sit, Miriam. Esther, bring Joseph to my mother, and come back quickly. We need to speak."

"Is Caleb alright?" Esther's lips quivered.

"Yes, yes. He's coming in with the flock. Jonas, get him to hurry." Jonas went after Caleb.

When all were gathered, Jerome explained the situation. Miriam was stunned. "Who is coming after Esther and me?"

"I'm not sure. It could be the Pharisee Saul, or it could be the Pharisees from our own synagogue. This is serious. They will arrest you both, put you in prison and who knows what will happen," Jerome answered. Miriam cried softly reaching for Jacob.

Esther sobbed loudly. "From imprisonment of the leper colony to the temple guard prison? This is all so wrong!"

Caleb came and threw his arms around Esther. "They are not taking you anywhere! I'll fight to the death!"

Jerome, with Ziph contentedly chewing his cud and standing by his side, held up a palm. "Stop, Caleb. We need to think this through. If they find Miriam and Esther, not only will they arrest them, but they could possibly arrest you and Jacob as husbands; who knows what their plans could be."

The group didn't know what to say until Miriam spoke up. "I have the answer. This is not easy, but Esther and I will go and—"

Before she could finish, Jacob jumped up. "No! Leave us? What about me? What about Joseph? Where will you go?"

"Listen, please. If they come looking for us, you tell them that we are in . . . in..the country of the Gerasenes."

"The Gerasenes? They are more Greek than Jew!" Jacob interrupted.

"They're Gentiles!" Caleb added in distress.

"But we can't just let you go into a country alone, two women," Jacob was overcome with desperation. "How you can you wander there alone?"

"Don't you see? If they come for us, and we are not here, they have no way to charge or arrest us—or you. Without us, they can't logically arrest any of you."

Jerome nodded. "Miriam has a point. The specific people the Pharisees wanted were Miriam and Esther for inciting the women of the synagogue. If they leave for a while, maybe this will blow over. They only have so many resources to track down Jewish Christians, and women at that. They have bigger fish to fry."

"We can take them across the Sea of Galilee, back to the little village by Hippus, in my boat. How long are you thinking?' Timothy turned to Miriam.

"About three weeks? Let us off where Jesus' freed the man with the demons and where the swine drowned themselves. It was a small inlet just down from the graveyard. Other boats collect there. We will look for the man who had the demon. Jesus told him to stay in his village. He's a man of God so he'll find protection for us."

"That's a long shot," Caleb said with worry. "You don't know if he's still alive."

"If he is, he'll be with his people who couldn't have been too far from the tombs he lived in. We'll find him. I know we will. And if we don't find him, we should find the people he witnessed to and they'll help us."

Jacob was lost. "This is insane. You have no idea what is going to happen. And what about Joseph?"

"Could Ann or Elizabeth care for him?" Jonas asked.

"No. I want him here with me," Jacob stressed. "My mother will care for him . . . and maybe once in a while Ann or Elizabeth could help?"

"In three weeks' time you can come back for us. We will be waiting for you. If it isn't safe to go back with you, bring us supplies and money."

"You don't know what is going to happen to you once we leave you there!" Caleb insisted again.

"Caleb, I don't know what to expect, but we have no other place where we can go that the Pharisees won't travel to in either Galilee or Judea. At least in the Gerasenes we'll be safe from the Jewish leaders.

Jerome pleaded with urgency. "Women. You've got to leave by to-morrow morning before it is too late."

CHAPTER EIGHTY

THE WOMEN WERE LEFT OFF in the shallows. It was late spring, the water was warm, and the day mild. Neither Jacob nor Caleb could control their emotions of seeing their women go off to a country where people might not accept them or offer them kindness.

"Don't think about it Jacob. This is the best we can do for all of us. If in three weeks, there's still trouble, we'll stay here. It will end sometime. Keep steadfast. I love you."

The women watched the men heave off, leaving them on a small, but busy beach. Many noticed, saw that they were Jews by the way that they dressed, and kept a wary eye on them. One man came up to them.

"Women!" He leered at them appreciating their good, healthy looks. "Why are you here? Looking for business?"

Miriam grabbed Esther tight to her side. "We are looking for the man that was freed of demons about two years ago."

"Are you sure you want him? I'm better and can pay much more. I'll even throw in some fish!" He stretched out his hand to slide his fingers down Esther's cheek.

Esther reacted like a mad child. She gibbered, drooled, and rolled her eyes. Hopping on one foot she gleefully went to the man, with her tongue poking out of the side of her mouth, grunting, and clawing the air. The man jumped back horrified. "Is she demon possessed?"

By now, men stopped working watching the unsettling scene and the few women buying fish stood like statues with their mouths agape as Esther acted out on the shore.

"She's not feeling well," Miriam held her arm not sure to laugh aloud or throw-up with fear. Insistent, she pointed at him and spoke loudly so all within earshot could hear. "Tell me, do you know the man I am talking about? The one who was demon possessed but now is not?"

Esther calmed down and meekly went close in to Miriam, hugging her and prattling, "Mamamamamama!" The man petrified of Esther, turned, tripped over a small rock, landed on his knees, got up, and ran up the beach.

Taking a deep breath, she smoothed Esther's hair and pulled her scarf back up over her head. "Good job," she whispered in her ear. "I think this will work."

As the two women disentangled themselves from each other, they each picked up their satchels and walked closely, side-by-side keeping an eye on the people staring at them in open curiosity and with no little fear. Leaving the beach, they found a road. Not sure which direction to go in, they stopped.

Behind them a woman called, "Wait!"

Miriam turned. An elderly, small woman hobbled toward them. Dressed as a widow, frail, but feisty, she hoarsely whispered, "I know who you're talking about. He isn't here. He's somewhere in the Decapolis, not sure what town. There are ten cities in the region and more villages."

The woman looked closely at the two women. Her eyes were milky and her sight poor. "You're Jews. I can't see very well . . . but you both look familiar to me. Come, let's share a meal. I don't have much, but I have shelter. Tell me your names. I'm Hannah."

Esther held up her satchel, "We can share too."

The woman, peered closely at Esther, bent over and began to cackle. Oh, what a mighty cackle. She laughed so hard she cried. "Oh, dear! This is so funny! And brilliant!" Miriam and Esther exchanged glances.

Walking beside Miriam, the woman, in between chuckles asked them many questions about where they came from. Miriam was cautious and mentioned a small village on the outskirts of Capernaum. The woman continued her questions about crops, flocks, and fishing. Miriam answered with a bit of color and before she could hold her tongue, she mentioned Ziph.

The woman stopped midway in the road. "Ziph! That beautiful goat! He's fathered half the flocks here! How do you know Ziph and his master, Jerome?"

Esther, not sure of trusting anyone yet, kept quiet. Miriam cautiously said, "Everyone knows Ziph and Jerome!"

Inside the woman's tidy home, she prepared a drink and served bread with a little olive oil. "Save your provisions. You are going to need them, because I don't know where the man is and he could be anywhere by now, but for starters try asking in the next town, about six miles from here, south."

After they settled by the table, she squinted. "Tell me, why are you really seeking this man?"

"He was demon possessed. Now he's not." Miriam wasn't sure what to say next.

"Yes, indeed he was. For some time too. Chains couldn't keep him from hurting himself, threatening others, and roaming the tombs. It was terrifying, yet tragically sad.

"Jesus expelled the demons from him. He wanted so badly to go with Jesus, but he was told no, to go back home and tell people what the Lord had done for him." Gently, she leaned back in pain.

"Are you all right?" Miriam reached for her in concern.

"Yes, yes. I'm just old. But your daughter, or young friend, is not demon possessed, is she? It was clever for her to portray herself as such." The old woman laughed again. "That will keep the men away from you." Esther squirmed but kept silent; Miriam bit her lip.

"You don't have to say anything to me, but if you are really looking for Jesus and not the man who had the demon, Jesus is not here. I'm told the Romans, at the instigation of the Jewish leaders crucified him. I'm also told that the grave kept him for only three days. He is risen." She closed her eyes and whispered, "Praise God."

Before Miriam could react, a man strode into the room. "Ah, my son, Theo. A fisherman. Meet my two new friends: Miriam and Esther."

"Are these the crazy ones from the beach?" The man stood back, not sure if he should get any closer.

"Yes, they needed refreshment and a little shelter from the sun."

"Mother, this is not wise. You could get hurt bringing in strangers! I must ask them to leave. The whole town is talking about the crazy woman!" He burst out laughing, then he sobered up. "Seriously, mother. Inviting strange people into the house can be unsafe, especially if one of them is crazy." He looked closely at Esther keeping quiet with her head down, she pulled her veil closer. He smiled.

"You're both Jews. Alone. Very unusual and even dangerous. Why are you here?" He asked flatly.

Miriam wanted to keep it simple. Certainly, she couldn't tell them they were escaping the Pharisees persecution for their belief in Jesus, the Christ. "We're from across the Sea of Galilee and are searching for the man that Jesus expelled the demons from."

"Why? He can't help you. Only the man Jesus can. He was the one who performed the miracle." Lost in thought he added, "We lost thousands of swine that day."

"We better be going." Miriam got up and grabbed their gear and Esther's hand, who still kept her head down and eyes lowered. "Thank you for your help. We'll continue searching."

Outside, the woman said, "I wouldn't go asking people in the town about the whereabouts of the man you're looking for. They haven't gotten over the loss of the herd of swine and they'll be argumentative, especially with women alone, without their men. Your question will bring up sour memories. They lost a great deal of income and food from the incident." She shot them a questioning glance. "Be careful."

Out of sight of the home, Miriam heaved a sigh, easing her stress. "Esther, that was brilliant pretending to be demon-possessed. That man ran like he was demon-possessed."

Esther wondered. "It worked but I hope we don't have to resort to that again."

"We need to find a safe place for the night. When we get to the next town, let me do the talking. Keep silent. We don't want to frighten, or make anyone feel uneasy."

"Miriam, we are in a country of mostly Gentiles. They think as little of us, as the Jews think of them. I think we should keep away from as many people as possible, particularly village gates or squares, but at the town wells, when we get water early in the morning, we can ask the women about that man. That way, we can avoid men."

She was right, of course. They had to be inconspicuous, and as women traveling alone, they had to be very careful. The plan was to be away for three weeks. Miriam wasn't sure how long they could stay on the run, as the days progressed and resources got low, but aside from water, she calculated they could last about two weeks, after that, they would have to augment their provisions by buying food with the money they had, or begging. Once the money ran out, they would have to beg.

They spent nights in the woods, or on the edges of pastures. Spring evenings could be cool, so they huddled together for warmth, not risking a fire. In the mornings before dawn, they would seek out the community well and ask about the man.

The women at the wells were sleepy. They weren't particularly interested in the newcomers who said hello, asked their question, filled their skins, and drifted off into the breaking morning.

For those who had heard of him, they said his nickname among the Gentiles was "Once-possessed" and a few villages were mentioned as to where he might be. This was helpful because their plan was to travel in a ten-mile radius so they could get back to the beach in three weeks and those villages mentioned fell within a few miles outside that range. Although they were frustrated by lack of solid information, they continued their journey from one town to another in prayerful hope.

CHAPTER EIGHTY-ONE

THE WOMEN, CONSERVING THEIR FOOD, gleaned in the fields where they could; there wasn't much available but early squash, beans, and leafy greens, but it was better than begging. Begging would open a door to community controversy. If they could withstand their fragile existence to make the deadline back to the beach, they would deal with their fate then.

That night, they found a copse at the edge of a large field. Lightening flashed through the sky and thunder rumbled in the distance. Branches waved in the sky as the wind picked up.

"On, no. Our first rain. Come, let's make a shelter with these leafy boughs," Miriam instructed, and the two women got to work as the first fat raindrops fell. "This is better than sleeping in the open, but it's cold." Esther squeezed close to Miriam for warmth.

Before they drifted off to a fitful, wet, and cold sleep, Miriam said, "I pray when we get back to the shore that Jacob will have a big bag of food and a skin of wine! I long for fresh bread and honey!"

"Don't talk," Esther sleepily admonished. "I'm so hungry I could eat these leaves!"

Shortly before sunrise, a strong hand grabbed the shoulder of a sleeping Miriam. Frightened, she instinctively threw out her hands to ward of the attacker, but he was too strong for her. At the same time, Esther yelped in pain and surprise. Another man had grabbed her.

Scrambling and kicking, the women scratched, punched, and kicked. One of the men fell back but soon stood upright and tackled Miriam. Esther stopped her struggle. The men were centurions.

Furious, they slapped the women in the face, and tied their hands together. Leading them out of the field, they spoke to them in Aramaic. "What are you whores doing in this field? Do you know who owns it?" They pushed them along the muddy road as the storm clouds continued to threaten.

"We're travelers, looking for a man who was once demon possessed, but now is not. We were unaware we were trespassing." Miriam was shaking.

"You hit an officer!" The man shouted at her.

"We didn't know who you were. It was dark; we were terrified of being killed!"

"Shut up woman!"

It was a short walk to an impressive strong hold. No one would have expected to find such an imposing structure in the backcountry. The officers roughly pulled and pushed the two frightened women along a well-maintained road, but going through iron gates, they walked a pitted cobblestone alley leading down to a darkened stone archway. Under the archway, they traversed a narrow, dank corridor that smelled of urine, human feces, and horse manure. It was impossible to avoid the reeking, smeared straw.

The biggest of the men unlocked a cell gate and shoved the women inside; both fell hard to their knees on onto cold stones strewn with filthy straw. There were no windows. The only light came in from the door. On the floor was damp, foul-smelling hay and an equally awful pallet covered in rat droppings.

Esther turned in horror to Miriam who struggled to get up. She bent and hugged her tightly. Thankfully, the officers didn't take their clothes for hidden inside were still the coins that their men had given them. All their other possessions, including food stuffs were left behind in their makeshift shelter, stashed under a pile of leaves.

Finding a clump of straw that wasn't overly filthy, Miriam sat on it, with her back to the weeping stone wall. "I'm so thirsty," Miriam whispered to Esther who didn't hear her.

She had finally fallen asleep with her head on Miriam's lap. The guards had dumped them hours ago and no one had returned. Struggling with thirst, Miriam couldn't sleep, so she dully stared at her surroundings, thinking about Jesus, his brief life, and his death. Her hope was in him risen. She believed that should she and Esther die in their circumstances, there was hope of eternal life. She could live with that.

The dungeon grew densely dark. Vermin were active, even boldly running across Esther's ankles who woke with a sharp scream. They held each other tightly, with knees drawn up and feet hidden.

A light bobbed against the walls. A rough scraping sound came from the grated door. "Here. Water. Bread. Eat, while you can." The light receded along with light footsteps muffled by the straw.

"Wait! Who can we speak to? This is a mistake!" Miriam shouted while Esther whimpered. Slowly Miriam got up and found a tin of water and a dish of something white with moving parts. She pushed the plate to the other side of the gated door and took a sip of water. It tasted like water and gave Esther a sip as well.

"Let's conserve this if this is all we are getting," Miriam advised. "The food we can't eat. It will sicken us."

"What are we going to do, Miriam?"

"Pray. Then pray some more."

Throughout the night, the women dozed on and off. Rats skittered, large insects scaled

the walls then dropped to the hay, only to scuttle up the walls again. Miriam pulled her head scarf around her head tightly feeling an occasional insect tap her head.

Horrified at first, she strengthened herself against the filth, vermin, and creeping insects. Pray. Pray. Pray. That's all they could do.

CHAPTER EIGHTY-TWO

THE MORNING CREPT IN COLD, grey, and quiet. There was little sound but constant dripping from somewhere in their cell. Miriam moved, waking Esther, who moaned in grief. Gently rousing her, Esther sat up and Miriam stiffly got up and relieved herself in a stinking corner. She moved to the gated door to peer out in the gloom. She couldn't see far, but there was light at the end of the hallway.

Turning, she said, "When the guards come back, we'll insist we see a judge!" She looked down at the metal plate she had shoved under the door during the night. It was filled with a white paste and squirming maggots. Even the rats didn't eat it.

Hours went by. No one came until late afternoon. A surly guard, not one of the arresting officers, pushed a tin cup of water under the grate. Seeing the plate of maggots, he laughed, said something in a language Miriam didn't understand, and turned to leave.

"Wait!" Miriam shouted. "You can't just leave us here. We've done nothing wrong but sleep on someone's property! We demand to see a judge. What are we accused of?" The man kept on walking.

"They're going to leave us here to die. I've heard many stories about how they get rid of people. They just leave them to starve to death or die of thirst in jails. They don't have to justify themselves, Miriam. It will take a miracle to get out of here!"

"A miracle. That's what we need." Miriam sat down and prayed. Esther joined her.

The evening had fallen hard in their cell. The darkness was suffocating, the rats were scratching and searching, and the cockroaches were scrabbling for human debris. Miriam paced, while Esther watched in hopelessness.

A light danced off the walls, coming closer. The guard, squinting in, said something unintelligible and slid a plate and cup of water under the grate. A second later, he grunted, the torch dropped from his hand and the fire caught the hay that was dry. A slim figure stomped out the sputtering fire, jangled keys, and slid open the lock. He didn't say a word to the women. Without question, they followed him out into the wet, black night. Though weak from lack of food and little water, their adrenaline kicked in and they ran for their lives, for what seemed like hours.

Slowing down, the man led them off the main road, down a path so narrow, they followed one by one directly behind him with Miriam holding the back of his shirt. No one spoke a word, only the sound of labored breathing and light footsteps filled the air as they made their way up a hill. Finally, a small clearing materialized. To the left where huge boulders. He led them around one, hugging it close. It was so densely dark, he guided himself with his hand gliding along the surface.

Beyond the other side of the enormous rock a weak light appeared from the depths of a cave. He ushered them in. Exhausted, weak, and frightened, they both collapsed on the stone floor. A woman crawled out of the depths and handed them each a small bowl of water. Parched with thirst and with the effort of running blindly, they greedily drained the contents.

"Please, my friends, go slow or you'll just spit it up."

"What's happening?" Miriam's hand trembled as she placed her empty bowl on the ground, and gladly accepting a piece of dried meat. Esther, wide-eyed and shaking kept quiet, chewing.

The man spoke first. "We've heard through our system that you've been traveling for weeks now looking for Once-possessed. Two women can't be traveling alone, without people taking notice, particularly when they are looking for a man that Jesus freed. Gossip is well and alive. Particularly when it starts with Hannah and Theo in the fishing village outside of Hippus."

"You know them?" Miriam was shocked.

"Yes, they are believers. The Way as some call it, is a new approach to God. We are spreading the word when possible, but we must be careful. We're in a mostly Gentile nation, so we are not at the mercy of the Pharisees or elders, but even though most of the cities throughout Decapolis are Greek in character, they're are the control of Rome."

The woman spoke up. "I'm surprised you've made it this long without trouble. God must be with you. I'm Ruth and this is my husband Enos. We've learned your names."

"God is with us," Miriam praised. "But how did you find us?"

"After we heard about your traveling from Hippus, we knew we had to keep a lookout for you. Traveling alone is dangerous." Miriam exchanged a look with Esther but kept quiet as the man continued.

"It was a good act. We like how you fooled the man on the shore who thought Esther was demon-possessed." He chuckled thinking back over the story. "That's a man to stay away from. Anyway, when

Theo said who you were looking for, his mother supposed that you were believers of Jesus escaping persecution in Capernaum. She concluded that you were seeking someone who believed in Jesus so you could find shelter. They haven't come this far yet in persecuting Christians."

"Yes, that was our plan because we had no idea who might be sympathetic to Jesus' followers and we were afraid to confide in Hannah and her son," Miriam admitted. "We got the information of our looming arrest from our friend Jerome . . . "

"Yes, we know Jerome! And Ziph!" The woman broke out into a smile, her eyes lit up, but then she dissolved into tears. "They were a bright light traveling through the country side. He always had news and Ziph was a character. They would visit us often . . . and then we had to leave . . . "

Her husband grabbed her hand. He nodded toward Miriam encouraging her to continue.

"Jerome said the Pharisees of our synagogue and possibly even the Pharisee Saul himself was coming to arrest us for speaking out in the women's section of the synagogue about our belief in Jesus. How could we not let them know about Jesus? He healed Esther!"

Esther spoke. "I had leprosy. He healed me without even touching me. He heard my prayers and look!" She held out her dirt-stained hands and wrists scraped raw from the ropes. "See how beautiful my skin is!" She beamed. The couple stared at Esther.

The husband, Enos said, "We too, follow Jesus, have heard him teach, and have seen for ourselves many of his miracles. I was a teacher of the law. When I came to believe, I tried to discuss my belief with the other teachers and leaders, but they would not listen.

Manically, and with such dramatic fanfare, they threw us out of the synagogue in front of the Pharisees, Sadducees, scribes, and chief priests. We were cut out Jewish society in a heartbeat. Ha! But it made it far easier to follow Jesus."

"And we did follow him to his cross and resurrection!" Ruth wiped her eyes with a tattered corner of her scarf and briefly smiled.

"We couldn't stay in Judea, and it would be a matter of time before they persecuted the believers in Galilee, particularly religious leaders who believed, so we escaped to the Decapolis. The majority of people in the ten larger cities here are Gentiles. For the most part, they don't care."

"But I want to go home to Judea to my children, family, and friends . . ." Ruth softly cried into her sleeve.

Enos ducked his head, rubbing his forehead. "It seems Saul is concentrating on Judea, then will be going to Galilee, or dispatching letters of intent to the synagogues so they too, can begin the persecution."

"But how did you know where to find us?" Miriam asked.

"Our network has been keeping track of you. When you were last seen, you were near the lands of a Roman governor who arrests anyone trespassing on his land. You were walking his roads, which are open to all, but not his lands. When you hadn't been seen for a day, we figured you were in his prison."

"We can't thank you enough for the risk you've taken." Miriam heaved a sigh.

"We are in this together. Our goal is to keep all the believers as safe as we can." Enos took a chunk of bread.

Worry took hold of Miriam. "Our husbands are sailing from Capernaum to Hippus in seven days' time. If it's safe, we go back with them. If not, then they will bring more provisions and money, and we'll have to stay."

"Let's get some sleep and talk more in the morning, but let us pray, first. Enos began.

CHAPTER EIGHTY-THREE

THE NEXT MORNING, OVER MEAGER portions of bread, but plenty of water, Enos, in between nibbles of bread to make it last longer, began. "When Jesus freed Once-possessed, he commanded him to go back to his home town and tell them all what the Lord had done for him. He did. He traveled and spoke of Jesus' mercies and healing. He spoke of other things too that the Spirit of God laid on his heart and his witness has influenced many, including Theo and Hannah. That was nearly two years ago. Since then, travelers have spread much of the Gospel of Jesus as has our mutual friend, Jerome.

"Naturally, the Jewish authorities tried and are trying to put an end to the truth, but the Gentiles are always open to another god. They worship many, so another isn't an affront to them . . . but what's even happening here, is that they are putting away their other gods and turning to the truth found in Jesus."

Ruth interjected. "We have a network here where we can safely meet, share supplies, fellowship, learn more, and understand, but we keep out of sight. This cave is one of a few we can use as hide-outs, if we need to hide."

The little group became pensive, then Enos spoke up. "We can get you back to your meeting point, but we'll have to keep low and out of harm's way in the event your captors come looking for you, which is likely if they have nothing else better to do. Once we get you to the boats, you'll know how safe it is for you to return to Capernaum."

"What about you?" Miriam asked.

"We are from Judea. Maybe your men will have word of what is going on there. We've even considered going to Samaria, but they hate Jews and we Jews are supposed to hate them as well. But we don't. They are made in God's image. We all are," Enos emphasized.

"I miss my family and friends," Ruth repeated with a sigh. "But we are so different now in how we think about God and salvation and the law."

"If we can't go back, and I don't see how we can since I was a religious leader, we'll stay here and send for our family members who are willing to come. Not all believe in Jesus."

"Who arrested us?" Esther wanted to know.

"A very wealthy man, a commander and proconsul of the territory owns much of the land around here. He has a small contingency of soldiers. They must have caught wind that two women were traveling their commander's roads and chatter has it that the women were Jews. He might have come to the conclusion that you, like many of us already here, are escaping prison from the Jewish leaders."

"But why would he care? The Romans hate the Jews too."

Enos tilted his head. "My point."

"Oh." Esther gazed out the mouth of the cave. The weather had cleared, and the sun was rising on a cool morning before the heat set in.

"There is a safe house we can get to by evening. I'm afraid we have little to eat, but it will sustain us."

"We have meager belongings back in the shelter, but we can't go there, but we have money!" She dipped in her hand into the secret pocket of her robe and pulled out a handful of coins, Roman coins. "We might have lost all our belongings and supplies, but now we can eat!"

Enos smiled, Ruth clapped her hands. "Even the locals will sell us food if we can pay for it with Roman currency!"

"We'll keep off the main roads and travel the secondary ones. We'll come across a vendor or two, but we must keep you two out of sight. They will be looking for you and a third person."

And they did. The group halted on the top of the hill that looked down on the road from the cave and there rode the same two soldiers who arrested the women riding on horseback toward town, leading a donkey with the jailer in the cart, beaten, and tied up. Miriam's heart thudded in fear. Esther held her hand tightly.

"They'll show him off as an example in the town square with threats to people who might think about coming to your aid. Let's get moving." Enos looked the two women over. "We've got to get you cleaned up." He wrinkled his nose. "They might not see you, but they can smell you." He wasn't being funny.

"At least they won't be mistaken for Jews," his wife stated, stashing the bowls in her satchel. "No respectable Jewess would be caught so . . ." She blushed. "I'm sorry. I didn't mean to insult you."

"No offense taken!" Miriam looked at her clothing stained with fetid straw from the prison.

They took paths and secondary roads and passed no one. Up at a crossroads was a vendor selling fruit. "We're nearing the outskirts of the village," Enos pointed out. "Let me get us some fruit, and the three of you hide here behind the bushes".

Miriam gave him a coin.

When he returned, he handed each on a handful of raisins and figs. Hungrily they devoured the treats.

"Enos, stay here out of sight. We'll be back shortly. I'm going to the seamstress house," his wife said.

"Stay hidden!" he ordered. "Come back shortly! Don't dawdle. We must get out of the commander's jurisdiction."

She led them surreptitiously along the sides of the road, to a small dwelling on the edge of a settlement. Miriam looked about tentatively. "Who lives here?"

"A friend of mine. You can bathe inside, and she'll have extra clothes for you. You will have to pay her, but I know she'll be fair. She's a seamstress and one of us."

Ruth knocked on the doorframe. "Come in!" Came a muffled response. Ruth stepped over the threshold into the one room dwelling with Miriam and Esther close behind. A woman, stood up from her sewing. She had been sitting close to window taking advantage of the bright morning light. With the sun shining on the side of her face, she turned slightly to greet her visitors standing in the shadow of the door.

Miriam, staring at the sunlit face, squeaked like a mouse, stumbled, then fell toward the woman who caught her. They squealed with indiscernible joy. Esther froze and a gasp escaped her lips and ran to the two embracing women. Ruth, in astonishment, stepped back, confused and surprised.

Tamar held Miriam, shrieking with happiness and incredulity. "What are you doing here? Ruth? What is this? How did you find them?" She laughed and cried at the same time, dragging them to sit on cushions and demanding the story.

Miriam, then Esther, and finally Ruth explained the events leading to them all being here. The surprise was beyond comprehension. "It's a Jesus wink!" Tamar laughed. "He brought us together. What would the chances be left to chance?"

"Please tell us how you came here!" Esther clasped her hands.

Tamar, jumped up to prepare a drink. "After Pentecost—you heard what happened there? We were in Jerusalem in a large private room. Suddenly, as we were all praying, the Holy Spirit descended on us: He came in like a wind, descending like a fire, instilling us with revelation and wisdom. It was amazing, astounding, incredible! Shortly after, the apostles went out and called to the multitudes that were visiting the city and converted many who confessed their sins, were baptized, and were also given the gift of the Holy Spirit! It was awesome!"

A flash came into Miriam's mind. All of them so wanted to be baptized and to continue in the faith. They needed the Holy Spirit too as well as leadership by those who were close to Jesus, so the teaching would be true and not grow from their own imaginations.

Tamar continued. "Later, Peter and John were arrested and brought before the council, but not before five thousand more believed! God was working wonders!"

Enos came barging in. "I didn't want to wait any longer . . . " He was thankful they had clothes on.

"Enos, I'm sorry for leaving you alone! Come, sit. Everyone knows everyone!" His wife quickly filled him in.

"So what happened to the two apostles?" Asked Miriam.

"The council let them go telling them to not to speak in Jesus' name. Well, that didn't last long. They continued even more boldly.

Converting many. Our fellowship grew. We were growing influential in Jerusalem; then the leaders dragged Stephen before the council and killed him."

She paused to wiped eyes. She cleared her throat. "After Stephen was stoned, the Pharisees stepped up the persecution of believers in earnest. They expelled the Hellenistic Jews from Jerusalem. Those who were native Jews, but turned to Jesus, took their chances and stayed in the countryside and small towns outside the city, not drawing attention to themselves.

"Some of us scattered, some stayed in Jerusalem, including Peter and John. Phillip went to Samaria to evangelize, and I, after fits and starts, came here. I didn't want to stay in Jerusalem, Judea holds heartache for me, and I was afraid to come back to Capernaum learning that Pharisees there were directed to clamp down on Christians. Then there was Saul."

CHAPTER EIGHTY-FOUR

"SAUL IS A BRILLIANT AND letter-of-the-law Pharisee. He's determined to eradicate the followers of Jesus whether man or woman. So many of us have dispersed from our home cities to find safety elsewhere," Tamar explained. "I had to leave. I traveled from Jerusalem to the southern end of the Sea of Galilee, paid passage to Hippus then moved from village to village until I settled here, where I met Enos and Ruth and others of like spirit."

Enos said, "The believers are growing, but we have to be careful and thoughtful. We are willing to evangelize when we can, but we keep in mind the beliefs of the Gentiles who have many gods, and the Romans who also worship many gods as well as their own emperor."

Tamar nodded. "We meet quietly, in homes to worship and study. Because I was a disciple of Jesus, I lead Jesus' teaching and recount his miracles." Miriam raised her eyebrows. A woman teaching?

Tamar caught the expression. "Even though I'm a woman, I'm the only one who can give firsthand information about Jesus' teaching. Enos can too, but I was with Jesus from almost beginning to end. Until we can find a disciple that can take over and teach the men and women all of Jesus' work, I'm it. Yes. I know my role would be outlawed by the Jewish religious leaders, but I must share what I know."

She pointed at Ruth's husband. "Enos, is the overall leader of the church as we call it now. There's so much more to say, but we must get you two cleaned up. We can talk more tonight. Please spend the night here and tomorrow we will all journey to Hippus."

After the women fell asleep, Enos nudged Ruth. "Let's go outside for a moment."

"Husband, is everything alright?" Ruth scrutinized her husband's face in the darkness.

"I'm concerned about the escape. While I was waiting for you and the women to come back, two of the commander's foot soldiers stomped by. This is the second set of soldiers we've seen, and we don't see them often on secondary roads. They stopped at the vendor's stall and I hustled there too to find out what they were asking. While I was buying fruit, they wanted to know if the vendor had seen two women with either a man or another woman. The soldiers made it clear that two female prisoners had escaped with the help of an accomplice who surprised the jailor, but the jailor didn't know whether a man or woman knocked him down and got the women out." Ruth's hand flew to her mouth.

"Don't worry. The vendor didn't see any women. Satisfied, the soldiers moved on, but they are making the rounds. We have to be very careful."

Before light, Tamar shook each woman's shoulder to wake up. Enos was already outside scouting for any unwanted activity. "It looks like it's clear," Tamar whispered.

"No one could see us come here, could they?" Miriam asked.

"Unlikely, the other homes are well beyond mine. I'm going with you," Tamar answered.

"But if you leave, won't that cause people to be concerned about where you are?" Ruth asked with worry in her voice. "We don't want them to go looking for you."

"If I leave for a period of time, they won't worry because they think I've gone to do a fitting or have gone to purchase fabric at the port." Tamar hauled her satchel off the floor.

"Without letting anyone know? Don't you think that's risky? You don't think people will question your whereabouts?" Miriam smoothed her shawl nervously.

Tamar held out her hands staring at Miriam. "I've got to go with you. Please don't leave me behind. If we find out it's safe to go back to Capernaum, I want to go back."

Enos said, "Hold hands and let's pray this thing through." They prayed.

Miriam was dressed in widow's clothing and Esther was in clothing neither typical of the Jews or Gentiles. All articles of clothing donated by Tamar.

They would now look different to the patrols should they be seen. They weren't in complete disguise, they couldn't change their faces or heights, but it was a good effort to alter descriptions.

They slipped through the early morning light and followed a well-worn path to get beyond the next village. Putting distance between themselves and the palace prison, they hoped that the commander would not pursue them. While the initial offense was minor, the escape could be major.

After a few hours, Tamar handed her travel pack to Enos and asked that they stop a while so she could to fill her skin. A narrow brook ran between the path and the dirt road. The party moved ahead to wait as she traversed down a slight slope towards the water.

As they waited for Tamar, they rested on the ground talking among themselves, when Enos suddenly shot up a hand for quiet. Clip-clopping of horses coming from the direction of the prison came closer. Enos stood to see. Behind the mounted soldiers, a patrol was guiding an empty donkey cart. Immediately and silently, he directed them to lay down in the brush, which barely covered them. Crouching in the bush, they didn't see the large hare that darted across the road. The soldiers' horses spooked. The same time the soldiers halted, calling to their horses, Tamar stood up in surprise. They saw her.

"Get her!" The leader hollered to the men on foot who took off after Tamar like lightening. Tamar, shocked, stood still. There was no way she could out run them. Crudely, they hauled her over the brook and dragged her to the mounted men.

"What are you doing out here alone?" The leader demanded, leering at her.

"I'm looking for wild figs."

"Where is your basket?"

"I, I put them in my shawl . . . "

"She leaves her head uncovered," one of the shoulders snickered.

"You don't have any figs. Maybe you should tell us the truth."

"I'm looking for figs. I know that your commander has lovely figs, but we can't go on his property, so I'm walking the hills. I haven't found any."

"Where do you live?"

"By the village Alph."

"That's a few hours from here. You've wandered quite a distance."

"I'm hungry," she said simply.

The leader barked and pointed with his spear. "Search the area!"

Enos stood up and hurried toward Tamar. The leader sat on his horse like a stone statue as Enos hastily made his way to Tamar.

"The truth is, we are here together, sir!"

The soldiers began to laugh but stopped abruptly as the leader held up his hand.

"Please, we're only meeting here. She's a widow . . . and I'm not."

The other soldier on horseback, said, "Let them go. They're not worth our while. If they were Jews they would be stoned. It's my experience they'll find themselves in worse trouble than being inconvenienced by us anyway."

Tamar and Enos stood close together as the patrol moved ahead. In the back of the donkey cart were Miriam and Esther's stinking garments.

Once they were out of earshot, Enos said, "You didn't get rid of their clothes?" He demanded of Tamar.

"No, I thought I could wash them and reuse them . . . I left them by my outdoor wash tub."

They watched the men leave and hustled back to Miriam, Esther, and Ruth. "They've got your clothes, so they know you've changed. They've seen Tamar and me. The only one that can't be recognized is you, Ruth. I've got to keep you safe. You need to go back home."

"No! I want to go with you!"

After nearly five hours of walking, they came to a small home in a clearing. "This is one of our safe houses. Wait here." Enos left them and cautiously went up to the door and tapped. The heavy wooden door swung open to reveal a wizened old man and a chicken, who hopped out and immediately pecked in the grass. Enos spoke briefly, then waved the women inside.

"Your clothing still might help you avoid the authorities." The old man shrugged and put water and bread before them. "Your only chance of getting away from this mess is to stay off any road or well-used path. I'll tell you where the next place you can go and it's about another five or more hours from here."

"Will we get to Hippus on time from there?" Miriam was worried. It was taking longer than she thought.

"It's hard to say. If you had wings, you'd make it in time, but now that people are looking for you? You can't take the main roads and that means it will be a circuitous route adding on quite a bit of time.

"As long as you are in the jurisdiction of Albunus—he's the pro-consul of the territory, the one who sent the officers to arrest you, and if he has the resources, he will track you down. Especially since you escaped and injured his jailer, who he probably had killed by now. He suffers no fools."

They talked through the evening. Miriam and Esther were distraught. If they missed Timothy's boat, it would be at another three weeks for their return. Their money would be gone, and they would have to rely on finding other Christians to help them for the duration.

Miriam stood. "Enos, if you will show us out of Albunus' territory, Esther and I will make our way to Hippus There is far too much risk for you, Ruth, and Tamar. Let us go on alone."

Tamar shook her head. "I told you, I'm going too! If I can be safe in Capernaum, I want to go home, and I'll take my chances. I can't go back to my house anyway. They found your clothes there, and unbeknownst to them, they met me on the road. If I go back home and they arrest me for aiding escapees, they'll recognize me from the road and question what I was really doing so far away from home. And Enos will be implicated. No. I'm not going back!"

Enos fiddled with a piece of crockery. "Tamar is right." He stroked his wife's face. "I've put you in jeopardy too."

"Let's leave the territory," his wife pleaded. "We can start over in Hippus, or go north to Bethany."

This was getting complicated, Miriam thought, but there was no way to dissuade her friends who risked their lives for hers and Esther's.

The old man said, "Accept the fact that you are going to miss your boat. You will not make it in time. That's a reality, so give me tomorrow so I can go to our friends and get some supplies from them. They'll be generous. Now, please bow your heads." He led them in prayer.

CHAPTER EIGHTY-FIVE

THEY FOLLOWED A CRUDELY DRAWN map made by a shepherd. It was the best the old man could get in short notice. He was also able to get satchels, skins, hard bread, dried fruits, and cheese. A few coins were added along with a small trowel for digging root vegetables, a hook, line, and sinker; a small knife and a flint.

Carefully he wrapped up several eggs, a flask of olive oil, and a small amount of flour. "Use this when the hard bread runs out, which won't take long. Where you're traveling I don't think you'll come across many vendors, so ration wisely. God speed."

The first two nights they spent in the woods. On the third day Miriam said to Enos, "I think we've passed out of Albunus' territory. Do you think we can take the main roads?"

"Miriam, we're not going to make the deadline. Why take the chance of getting caught? Accept we're still at risk, because he could have a political colleague who will take up his cause."

"We merely trespassed on his land!"

"And I knocked out the jailer and helped you escape! This is no light matter and if he did away with the jailer, we have to live with that and ask God for forgiveness . . . at least I do.

"So for now we stay on the deer runs and sheep paths, and sleep where we can. We have to search out food and water, but we have some tools. Once we get to the little settlement outside of Hippos, we'll will shelter with Theo and Hannah. If not, we at least have money for some kind of shelter, even if it's a boat shed. We can also buy some food."

Days and nights through the woods and paths finally brought them to the boundaries of Hippos. Rounding the city, they came to the small village by the Sea of Galilee. They had been creative with food, rationed accordingly, and always had plenty of water, but depending on roots and berries the last few days had left them weak. By this time, their food had run out. They needed shelter and nourishment.

While the women were camping in the woods, Enos went to Theo and Hannah's house near the shore.

A couple of hours passed before Enos came back to them. "Tonight, you'll be warm and dry. We can stay at least the night. Hannah is going to ask her son if we can stay longer. And here! I brought us breakfast. As soon as it gets dark, we can go to Hannah's so let's eat and rest."

Miriam's heart filled with gratitude. Oh, how she prayed that Hannah's son would let them stay until they could meet up with Jacob and Caleb who would be coming back for them . . . *When?* She was losing track of time, but was certain by now, Timothy's boat had already come and gone. Prayfully she ate. *Please God. Let them return!*

When darkness fell, Enos led the way to Hannah's holding his wife's hand as Miriam and Tamar walked behind, overjoyed to be sheltered. The many days out in the open had taken a toll on all of them physically, but spiritually, they increased in their knowledge of Jesus and his teaching. Tamar, Miriam was delighted to learn, was a skillful teacher. With her first-hand knowledge and spiritual insight, they all felt as if they had walked along with Jesus, too, while Enos had a wealth of Scriptural knowledge and prophesy. Miriam knew that their Lord was guiding and equipping them with hope through their friends.

Under the cover of dark, the small group huddled by the door as Enos knocked lightly, looking around. Hannah and Theo's house was on a small path off the main road the villagers took to the water. There was a mist in the air and the wind was slightly blowing; no one was around. The door creaked open, and even though it was nearly summer, the warmth of the hearth fire was a welcomed relief.

Miriam spoke up once they were settled. "Hannah, did any men on a boat come looking for us?" She pointed to herself and Esther.

Hannah nodded. "Yes, the men from Capernaum came. They asked for two women, Miriam and Esther. But they were told no one had seen them since they frightened one of the men on the shore. The men left, saying they would be back in three weeks should the women show up." She handed Miriam and the others water and cakes of raisins. Miriam's hand shook as she accepted the treat. Her mouth was dry and her heart sore.

"How long ago was that?" Esther asked.

"I don't know because I heard it second hand. Maybe a week?"

"If Theo is agreeable to allow us to stay with you until we can figure things out, we would be most grateful and careful. Our men should be back then in a couple of weeks." Esther shot a look at Miriam who bit at her lip.

Enos persisted. "Can the women stay until then?"

The old lady replied, "I will ask Theo when he comes back from fishing tomorrow morning. I'm sure we can work something out, but we must avoid town gossip. I think you're safe here, but let's be cautious. Come. I'll show you where you can sleep."

In the dawn of the following day, Theo came back from fishing. As Miriam was folding her bedding near an open window, she overheard Theo asking his mother, "How can we fit five more people in here without gossip?"

"Why can't we say they are friends from afar visiting?"

"Oh, sure. And when the townspeople find out we have that crazy woman here who they think is demon possessed what will happen then?"

"We can say she's cured." His mother smiled hopefully then leaned into him. "Please, son. They need help and soon they will be rescued by their families. It won't be for long. Please."

"Oh, mother. I need a wife to keep you in line!" He laughed and put his arms around her fragile shoulders. "But I am concerned. Our house is small, and people fear demon possession. They will be sure to remember the woman who acted frighteningly on the beach. We need to talk about this, but right now I'm hungry."

They slipped back into their home to find Miriam, Esther, and Ruth busy cleaning and putting away their bedding while Enos repaired a broken stool. Hannah clapped her hands in delight. "Finally, a repair man!" Her son shook his head.

"Hannah," Miriam quietly approached her. "We have nothing to give you, but we can at least help with the household chores." She looked expectantly at Theo who held up a string of fish.

"Not to worry. We will eat well this morning," he nodded. "In fact we eat well most mornings as long as the fish cooperate." He handed her the fish to prepare.

As they finished up eating, Theo carefully asked, "How are we going to overcome the fact that we have so many people in our house, and especially one who people will believe is possessed?"

"But we can say she is cured," his mother insisted.

"Theo's concerns are valid," Enos said looking at Hannah. "Some may not believe she is cured.

"I worry about the reaction in the village having a demon-possessed person in their midst. They never did get over the loss of their swine when Jesus allowed the demons from the possessed man to go into them. The swine drowned themselves," Theo explained

His mother maintained her defense. "Theo, we'll simply say that Esther is in her right mind and nothing more. We don't have to talk about demons or healing because that would be lying. She acted crazy, but so did King David when he was on the run from King Saul who was trying to kill him. Remember? He went to Achish, king of Gath. When the servants of Achish saw him, they said, 'Can this be David, the famous David? Is this the one they sing of at their dances? Saul kills by the thousand, David by the ten thousand!'

"When David realized that he had been recognized, he panicked, fearing the worst from Achish, king of Gath. So right there, while they were looking at him, he pretended to go crazy, pounding his head on the city gate and foaming at the mouth, spit dripping from his beard. Achish took one look at him and said to his servants, 'Can't you see he's crazy? Why did you let him in here? Don't you think

I have enough crazy people to put up with as it is without adding another? Get him out of here!'"

Miriam nodded at Esther. "The act saved his life and I'm sure Esther's act saved her and me from a great deal of harm too."

"Ok. Ok," Theo relented. "Let's just take it day by day. No reason to look for trouble."

"Good. Then it's settled. Let's move beyond the worry." His mother stood up to clear the bowls. Miriam nearly collapsed with gratitude. She and Esther were so close now to truly being able to go home. Yes, it was still possible there would be problems with the Jewish leaders, but she wanted and had to go home for her son Joseph and her husband. She was willing to take her chances. Miriam left the house and stood in the tiny shelter of the side garden that had a view of the sea. *When, God, will Jacob return?*

CHAPTER EIGHTY-SIX

AT SUPPER ONE EVENING ENOS addressed Theo. "We all can't continue to stay here. Your home is welcoming, but it's far too crowded and it's unfair to you and your mother that we are infringing on your hospitality. I might have been a teacher of the law and scribe, but I'm strong. I can work. Can I get on a fishing boat? If I can earn some money, Ruth and I can get a room somewhere." He turned to Ruth. "What do you think?"

"If we stay in the area, we at least know Theo and Hannah, and they know others of our belief and we can continue to worship." She thought for a moment. "We are just across the Sea of Galilee from Judea. Our family could visit, and we would be safe here from the Pharisees. I think you getting work here would be good."

"I can get you a job no problem." Theo nodded then sighed. "But that leaves the rest of you and this house is small."

"I can sew, Theo. If you get me some old sailcloth or sacks, I can sew us a tent. We could put in on the backside of your house, away from prying eyes. We'll only be here for a couple of more weeks anyway." Tamar clasped her hands in excitement.

"Son, that is a wonderful idea! Can you get the material?"

"I believe I can." He considered Tamar. "You sew? That's a sought after craft, especially by the fishermen. I'm sure you could find plenty of opportunity here and I will wager you could trade your skills with the fishermen that stop here for goods and fish."

In response, Tamar grinned. "If you can get me some supplies, I can start with the tent."

The tent went quickly with Miriam and Esther helping. Summer was upon them, and the nights were mild making their outside camping comfortable. Enos was hired on a boat and shortly thereafter, with communal monetary help, he and Ruth moved into a room outside the village.

Theo was attentive to the women, but he was a man that also cared deeply for his mother. Miriam noticed he was a man of humor and kindness. The little group fell into a routine: Theo off to fish, the women cooking and cleaning, and the continued meeting with believers who willingly shared their provisions. The food and drink would be enough to get them all through the next several days until the boat arrived to take them back, hopefully, to Capernaum. Theo always brought home fish, so they were never hungry.

Excitement for their husbands, friends, and homes were building with the women, but Miriam was noticing a change in Tamar. "Tamar. Is there something I should know about?"

"I don't think I want to go back."

"Why? You have a wonderful group of friends and have us as family now. You might even find a husband; create a life!"

"Miriam, for such a short time, I've made some wonderful friends here. I can have a livelihood here, sewing."

"You can sew back home!" Miriam didn't want to lose Tamar again.

They were interrupted by Hannah. "Tamar. Don't you think you should tell Miriam the real reason you don't want to go home?"

Before she could answer, Miriam gasped at the revelation. "It's Theo. Isn't it?"

Hannah sat down amidst the women. "Theo wants to marry Tamar."

Esther whooped, "Wonderful! I thought there was something going on between you two!"

"I'm usually so good in picking these things up, but I didn't," Miriam confessed. "I think it was because I was focusing on Jacob, Joseph, and home." The night before they expected their husbands and the others on Timothy's boat, Miriam could barely sleep, she was so excited. She missed her husband and little Joseph!

"Esther, are you awake?" Miriam whispered.

"Yes, I'm so restless! So eager to see Caleb and be home, safe, with friends and family. You know, Miriam? Maybe Caleb and I will be blessed like you and Jacob with a little one. I so want to go home to him!"

CHAPTER EIGHTY-SEVEN

TIMOTHY WATCHED THE SUNRISE ALONG with Jacob. "So far it looks like fair weather. No red sky." The waves gently slapped the hull of the moored boat, the wind to port.

Jacob and Caleb were bursting with desperate hope for their women. Even if the sky was red, they would have pushed Timothy and Jonas to make the voyage. Hastily they continued to secure the gear. Three weeks prior, they made the trip and met a group of men on the shore who had remembered the women but hadn't seen them for weeks. No one fitting their descriptions had been seen in the village, or city to their knowledge. Jacob and Caleb along with the others were heartsick. They feared for their wives lives, but Jerome prayed that they would be given strength and hope. They couldn't give up.

Now, three weeks later, as the sun rose, Jerome arrived with armfuls of provisions and set about loading the boat with the last minute items. "Ann baked several loaves of bread and raisin cakes and I brought two more skins of wine. This will be a time for celebration. Now that the Pharisees have backed off, including Saul, we can enjoy the break for as long as it lasts." But Jerome knew that the confrontation between the Jewish religious leaders and the Christians would continue. To what degree he didn't know.

Before the men pushed off from the shallows, Jerome led them in prayer for safe journey and waiting women. Then Jonas hoisted the sail. Catching the wind, the vessel leaned to starboard and the bow pushed through the slight chop.

Halfway to their destination, the smell of the air changed. "Do you smell that?" Jonas asked Timothy.

"I sure do. This is not a good smell."

"Smells like a storm coming in," Jacob sniffed. On the horizon, black, rolling billows appeared pummeling through the air as the clouds raced toward them. The seas turned from a slight chop, to moderate until the wind caught the waves and tossed them violently, swamping the boat with jarring swells. The wind howled and spray flew in all directions.

"Jacob! Jonas! Drop the sail!" Timothy screamed into the gale-force wind as he wrestled with the tiller. Jerome and Caleb grabbed the wet, slippery lines to the main sail but the wind was too strong to furl it as they hastened to drop it. The wind snapped the sail full and the starboard rail dipped under the water; they feared they would capsize. Mercifully, the wind dropped down dramatically, the boat righted itself, but the wind gusted again filling the sail viciously, tearing it in two helpless flapping shreds. The men ducked down to avoid their faces slashed by the whipping lines, strips of lacerating cloth, and the swing of the boom. The boat lurched, crashed up and down into the angry swells and as waves crashed over the port side the vessel listed dangerously to starboard. All aboard were praying.

CHAPTER EIGHTY-EIGHT

MIRIAM, WHO SLEPT LITTLE, WAS up at dawn and hurried down to the beach. Wrapping her scarf tight around her head and shoulders, she looked out into the storm and rain clouds in the distance. The sky was black, and the winds were picking up. She knew how the weather could change in a heartbeat at the center of the Sea of Galilee. Even large boats, with the most seasoned fishermen at their helms were in immediate danger.

Esther came up silently and stood beside her taking her hand. "This doesn't look good."

"No, it doesn't," breathed Miriam. Had all they come this far only to be lost by a storm?

They stayed all day on the beach joined by Tamar, waiting and watching. By suppertime, Hannah, knowing the ship would unlikely come in by now, came to them and brought them food. "I'll wait with you."

As the evening fell, Theo came. "Women, come back home. I'll stay here and wait. You need sleep."

Miriam nor Esther didn't want to leave, but Tamar insisted. "You won't be sleeping much tonight, but at least you will be dry." It had begun to rain.

All in the village were now aware that a boat was expected two days ago to pick up Theo's and Hannah's friends. On the third day the weather cleared and the men from the village went back to fishing, but everyone was mourning the lost men. All who knew the Sea of Galilee were convinced that the men had encountered the storm and their small boat just couldn't withstand the wind and waves.

Miriam didn't want to think how bad it could be. The women still waited, under canvas Theo had brought them to keep out of the rain. Miriam's anxiety was heightened. She needed to get home to her son Joseph! Could he now be fatherless?

"Maybe with the help of the believer's prayers, a miracle will happen," whispered Hannah and prayed.

Three days later, Theo, finishing up his supper with the women, swallowed hard. Awkwardly, he cleared his throat. "You can stay as long as you need to, but we all know how these storms can be. Unforgiving."

Miriam and Esther avoided each other's eyes. It was certainly too painful for Miriam to contemplate that they had come this far, only to have their husbands and friends meet disaster. No. It was unthinkable. She would pray. Pray hard.

Theo broke the mood. "I have news. I know this is a difficult time for both of you and I pray that the Lord can get you through this. I want you to know that you have blessed me more than you know . . . you brought Tamar to me. I would never had met her if it wasn't for you and Esther. So . . . we're getting married."

"We know, Theo. Do you think women living together don't know what's happening in the household?" Miriam smiled sadly.

Theo laughed cautiously. "I can't have any secrets." Both women rose to hug him, then Tamar and Hannah. At this point, all were crying and laughing at the same time. A bittersweet moment.

"God gives and takes away, but never our blessings," Tamar said softly. "Never our blessings."

A week passed. During the evenings, Tamar taught, along with Enos about Jesus and his Gospel. Many in the city caught word of a new teaching, some called it the Gospel, others, The Way. Slowly people began to show up at Hannah's and Theo's house to listen.

One evening, a strange little man came. Putting a hand on Miriam he said tilting his head toward Esther, "I heard you've lost your husbands. Miriam nodded.

He continued. "Let me recite to you a psalm:

"Some went out on the sea in ships; they were merchants on the mighty waters. They saw the works of the LORD, his wonderful deeds in the deep.

"For he spoke and stirred up a tempest that lifted high the waves. They mounted up to the heavens and went down to the depths; in their peril their courage melted away.

"They reeled and staggered like drunkards; they were at their wits' end. Then they cried out to the Lord in their trouble, and he brought them out of their distress.

"He stilled the storm to a whisper; the waves of the sea were hushed. They were glad when it grew calm, and he guided them to their desired haven.

"Let them give thanks to the Lord for his unfailing love and his wonderful deeds for mankind."

Tears filled their eyes. Esther turned away, pulling her veil to her eyes. Both women buried his words in their hearts. What could they say? Miriam went to comfort Esther

"I think it's time we go back, Esther. I'll take my chances. I need to be with my son, Joseph. If something has happened to Jacob, I can't leave the child alone, even though his grandparents are caring for him and providing him a home. I understand if you decide to stay, but you are welcome to come back and live with me and what's left of our family."

"Miriam, you know I'll go with you! After all we've been through? I could never leave you."

Theo and the rest understood, certainly Tamar. "It's possible we can still visit. You both have meant so much to me. Isn't it a wonder how we all became friends? Please, when you get back, seek out those who are of like mind in Jesus. Strengthen your relationship with the Lord and continue praying. He'll never leave you. You'll find strength and comfort in his promises, even through your loss."

Theo made arrangements to interview two captains who were willing to take passengers back to Capernaum. He wanted to ensure the women would be safe even though it was only a day trip under good conditions. Settling on a good boat, he told the women they could leave two days hence.

Miriam was eager to get home, heartbroken over Jacob and unsure how Ann and Elizabeth would be faring because not only Jacob and Caleb were lost, but Jerome, Timothy, and Jonas. They were gone too. It would be a sad reunion.

CHAPTER EIGHTY-NINE

"HOW CAN THIS BE?" JEROME saw a man in the distance throwing a net over the side of a boat. Another man was beside him.

"Do you see a boat over there or are my eyes playing tricks on me?" It was near dawn and the shipwrecked men had been on an island for they didn't know how long. Jerome twisted toward Jonas who was weak, shivering, but awake.

""I do see a boat! I do!" Jonas threw a handful of sand and small stones at Timothy and Caleb who woke up. "See there? A boat!"

"Jacob. Wake up." Caleb crawled over to where Jacob was lying curled up like a newborn. "There's a boat out here. We have rescue!"

Jerome waved weakly and stood up. The man on the boat dropped what he was doing and stood beside the other man pointing. Shortly a third man joined them and nearly as quickly the net was hauled in and the sail was tugged up.

The wind was brisk, the water choppy, and the boat made steady headway toward the beach. As they got closer, the men on the sand jumped up and down waving. Debris of wooden staves lined the shore along with other small bits of rubble.

As the vessel drew closer, the men hobbled slowly into the water, splashing, falling, but still waving. Now they could hear their hoarse cries.

Maneuvering the boat with oars closer into the shore, a man dropped over the side in chest deep water and laid out anchor. He pushed through the water to the men, who were half-walking, half-floundering toward him.

"We were wrecked in a storm!" Jerome's eyes were red and strained. "We've been here for days and days." He coughed, trying to take in air over his excitement. "We've run out of food. Thank God the water is fresh!"

The man grabbed Jerome and hoisted him up as the captain and the other mate hauled him over the rail. With effort, they pulled all the other four dazed, sunburned men aboard.

The mate gave them a portion of bread they ate in a state of stupor. Tentatively, one of the men asked, "Are one of you Miriam's husband?"

Jacob, unable to speak, raised a hand and collapsed on the deck.

The crew couldn't believe the men's rambling, barely coherent story. It was a true miracle they were found because there were no islands in the Sea of Galilee and the crew had been fishing here for years! The men took turns telling the story about the storm.

"When the boat broke up, we thought we lost Jonas. He's not a great swimmer. Neither is Caleb. But between Timothy and me, we were able to grab as much food as we could and hold on to floating planks while Jonas and Caleb held on to us. We dragged Jacob, who was semi-conscious from a hit to the head onto a piece of plank.

"We could only hold onto the floating planks and each other," Timothy added. "We drifted through the night, knowing that our only hope for survival was a fishing boat to see us in daylight, so we held on, prayed and sang to keep awake and not surrender to the cold and deep."

"It was still dark when my foot, then Timothy's foot struck something solid. It was the bottom!" Jerome looked over at Timothy, still wide-eyed with shock. "We couldn't believe it was that shallow. We began walking forward as the water level became more and more low. Just at dawn, we could make out an island in front of us! We couldn't believe it. There are no islands on this water!"

"We dragged ourselves and Jacob to shore then just we all collapsed from exhaustion. When we woke up it looked like we were on a sandbar." Jonas hands shook. "It was a miracle."

"Please, tell us about our wives," Caleb could barely speak.

"They're planning on leaving today for Capernaum. They believe you are lost because of the storm and Miriam, worrying about Joseph is planning on getting back to your village. Today."

"We've got to get back to them. Can we make it?" Jacob slurred his words. His lips were chapped and cracked.

"We'll try. If we don't, we might cross paths. If that doesn't happen spend the night with my mother, me and Tamar. You need rest and food."

Jacob nearly collapsed a second time. "Tamar?" He had no other words to say. He closed his eyes.

"She met Miriam and Esther on their way coming back here. She's to be my wife soon." He told them the story, but they were too tired to listen.

Suffering from their trials, Timothy, Jerome, and Jonas passed out on heaps of wet nets, while Jacob and Caleb tried to keep watch for any boat that could be carrying their wives. The effort was short lived. They too, succumbed to sleep.

Theo, along with the captain and mate, marveled at their survival. They knew this would be a story for the ages. Finding land in the middle of the Sea of Galilee! It was unheard of. Truly, this was a miracle.

As the vessel entered the small cove under sail, the sleeping men groggily got to their elbows and stared over the gunnels at the beach. Jacob and Caleb struggled to kneel.

"There!" shouted Theo. "There's the boat they're are leaving on. The crew is packing it up now." The rescued men had lost their energy. They could barely speak. All they could do was pray they could get to shore before their wives boarded.

Stacked along the floating dock that went out to the transport boat were wrapped bundles of goods and possessions waiting to be stowed. On the shoreline two small groups of people huddled, waiting patiently. Two figures stood in the foreground one beside the other. Behind them stood two others. Many other people were milling about, and fishermen were sitting on rocks or on the sand sorting their fish or mending their nets. The beach was bright now with early morning sun and work.

"That could be them. Miriam, Esther, Tamar, and my mother." Theo hopped to the bow of the boat and madly waved a dirty rag.

CHAPTER NINETY

HANNAH STEPPED BESIDE MIRIAM AND Esther. "That looks like the boat my son fishes on. Look, someone's on the bow waving."

Even the fishermen stopped what they were doing, pointed and talked excitedly with one another. This signaled a problem. The boat was too far out for anyone to wade to it, so a couple of men hauled a skiff across the rocky shore and put in. Miriam and the women ran down to the water as the captain of the transport boat hollered for all passengers to board.

"We can't board now!" Miriam took Esther's hand and waded ankle deep into the water. Shore birds flew in arcs up high watching the confusion below. "We don't know what is happening. If that is Theo's boat, he might be hurt, or . . . "

"Maybe they found a body." Esther covered her mouth.

A mate to the passenger vessel shouted a warning the boat was leaving. He waited for a few more minutes, then shrugged seeing two of his passengers not making any move to get to his vessel; they watched an incoming fishing boat in distress.

None of the women moved or even watched the boat leave. They could replace their meager belongings. The money for travel was lost. It didn't matter. They had to find out what was going on in Theo's boat, as did everyone else standing on the beach.

As the skiff came alongside the fishing boat, the wind died and the mainsail lifted. The boat languished in the water and the captain yelled ecstatically. "We found the ship-wrecked sailors!"

"They're alive?" The question was cautiously incredulous. The men in the skiff took in the ragged men in the cockpit.

"Yes, yes, but we've got to get them to shore!"

Theo threw a bowline to the skiff. His mate dropped the lifeless sail and the captain steadied the helm as the men in the smaller boat, straining at the oars, moved the larger vessel laden with men and fish, slowly through the glassy water.

Coming into the shallows and before grounding, they dropped anchor. Men rushed into the water to the anchored vessel. Carefully, they hoisted the still exhausted and weak men over the rail into the waiting arms of their rescuers who sloshed back to the beach with their human cargo.

By now, two donkeys with their carts were on the shore. Miriam and the others ran to greet the men, praying the men were theirs.

Miriam shouted, "Jacob!" Miriam darted through the crowds to touch his hand, stroke his face. The men moved quickly and put Jacob and Jerome on one cart, and Jonas and Caleb on another. Timothy was lain on a make-shift pallet that two fishermen carried.

Theo was right there with them, directing the effort. "Bring them to my house." Spotting Tamar, he pointed. "Tamar, quick, go. Prepare five pallets." She ran ahead. "Miriam, Esther get out of the way. Mother, take your time, but step aside."

The donkeys' strained with their loads over the sand and rocky shore. Miriam stumbled after Jacob's cart keeping her eyes on him, trying to keep out of the way, but only wanting to touch him. Once at the house, the rescuers carefully lifted them and carried them inside. Tamar was in the midst of preparing the last two pallets and directed they be laid on the floor until she finished.

A man from the village was already inside, with a damp cloth soaked in aloe. It was the little man who had recited the psalm. Gently, he looked them over as the women and Theo stood back, and the villagers stood outside.

"It's a miracle they found an island. The only island I've ever heard of was one that appeared decades ago during a severe drought. We haven't had a drought in years." From his kneeling position, the man spoke over his shoulders to his audience. "They never would have survived the storm, floating in the middle of the Sea for this long." Gently, he wiped their faces, hands, and feet. "Let them sleep. Give them water and small portions of food when they wake up."

Miriam bent down and kissed her sleeping husband, her heart bursting with gratitude. She got up to after the little man to thank him, but he had already disappeared into the crowd around the house.

They cared for the men during the remainder of the day and night. Even Theo didn't go fishing the next day. One by one, the men came around, took some water and a little bread. Thanking God for surviving, they were awestruck at the miracle of being alive.

"Miriam." Jacob lightly held her hand. "There's so much to tell you. It's safe . . . well safer than it was . . . the Pharisees still hate the Christians, but the Pharisee Saul, now called Paul converted! He's not tracking down the believers. He is one!"

"What?" Tamar dropped a bowl of water splashing an equally surprised Enos who came by with Ruth to help.

Enos, who had been a scribe and teacher of the law exclaimed, "He was the worst! Can this be true? He tracked down men and women believers like animals to imprison. He approved of Stephen's stoning!"

"It's true, he's now an apostle." Jacob told the story.

Miriam and Esther were elated. "We can go home now!" The room was filled with discussion and surprise.

"Saul? Now Paul—another miracle!" Miriam clapped her hands.

CHAPTER NINETY-ONE

A DAY LATER, THE MEN were well enough to go back to Capernaum. With no money, this was going to be difficult. Miriam looked at the few coins in the palm of her hand. "We were given money for passage by a group of believers and we forfeited it, except for these few coins. We can't ask again. The believers here can barely survive themselves. What will we do? We need to get home to Joseph!"

"Timothy and Jerome are anxious for their wives too. What're we going to do without money?" Esther looked to Caleb who didn't have an answer.

"We could offer to fish with some of these men. Earning enough wages, we can get passage." Timothy pointed to his men.

"It'll take some time. Most of the fishermen already have their crews," Theo stated, worried for all of them. They were in the process of putting up another tent in the back of the house for the men. There were now ten of them he was going to have to figure out how to feed.

Coming in from a day of fishing, he traded his wages for fish. They needed to eat and just about all the flour, oil, fruit, dried meat, and other provisions were now gone except for fish.

Swapping ideas about what to do, everyone in the house had overlooked that this evening was a Jesus' teaching and fellowship night.

Tamar spoke. "Tonight our meeting is here!"

Just as she said this, Enos and Ruth came in with a basket of fruit. "Come," Tamar crooked her finger at Miriam. "We must set up the back garden with a seating and eating area. Esther, start the fire for the fish."

"Do you see this?" Theo later asked Tamar. "More people than usual have showed up. Look at all this donated food and drink!"

"They're eager to see our rescued friends from Capernaum, hear the news about Saul and share the good news." Tamar placed a hand over her heart in thankfulness.

"They know, too that Theo is taking care of eleven people including himself," Hannah whispered. "See how generous they are!"

She went to help lay out bread, curds, cheese, honey, dried fruits, nuts, berries, and more. The men brought wood for the fire to cook the fish that they brought.

After the blessing and the meal, Jerome stood as spokesperson and began telling them about the threat of persecution of the women because of Saul's crusade against the Christians. Miriam and Esther were singled out because of their remarks about Jesus and the miracle of Esther's healing from leprosy.

The listeners were astonished. "Esther! You are beautiful."

He stunned his listeners again when he told them the details of Saul's conversion and that now he was called the Apostle Paul. "Think about this. Jesus spoke to him from heaven. 'Saul, why are you persecuting me?' Saul asked, 'Who are you Lord?' Jesus replied, 'I am Jesus.' Then Jesus told him to go into the Damascus and he would be told what to do. And Jesus struck Saul blind! Later, he was baptized and regained his sight!"

"How can this be?" The asked among themselves.

"Despite his zeal for thinking he was doing God's will by persecuting the Christians, he soon came to realize that he was terribly wrong. He personally was shown proof that Jesus, who died, is alive! He knows the Scriptures like the back of his hand. He came to understand Jesus' death on the cross fulfilled ancient prophesy. He now understood that Jesus' death was appeasement for man's sins and that his resurrection confirmed his messiahship."

The people, hearing vague stories, now had a clearer picture of Saul's conversion. Jerome concluded, "The Lord has appointed him to advance the Gospel to the Gentiles."

Now, the people were baffled. "To the Gentiles? This means that there are no differences between us!" They mulled this over for a while, realizing that it was logical. The kingdom of God was available to all creation.

"Tell us about the ship wreck," a man asked.

Jerome explained their plan of dropping off the women, then coming back for them in three weeks. "When we came back, and the women weren't there, we returned home anxious and troubled as you can imagine. However, we had a backup plan and that was to return in three weeks."

Timothy spoke up. "We set out, but midway a violent storm came upon us so suddenly we couldn't even drop the sail. It broke up the vessel, leaving us to float in rough waters, waiting to surely die."

"Until the miracle of an island appeared," Jonas added. "And we all know there are no islands, except in severe drought, in the Sea of Galilee."

"And then the miracle of the rescue by none other than our fellow believers," Jacob said hoarsely with great emotion. The miracle of the island brought the talk back to Jesus and his other miracles.

A man asked, "I have a question that has been bothering me. We know about his commission to us to spread his Gospel, but what about baptism?"

"Why can't we all be baptized?' Miriam asked. "The Sea of Galilee is minutes away!"

"But who will baptize us?" Someone asked.

"Any true believer has the authority to baptize: those who are godly men of Jesus the Christ," the old man said.

Miriam didn't realize he had been sitting in the now dark back garden. He was the man who cleaned the faces, hands, and feet of her husband and friends. All eyes turned to him as he slowly stood up.

"Tomorrow, at dawn, Jerome and I will baptize all of you. Miriam is right. Come down to the water." He conferred quietly with Jerome at length then left.

All the people were excited. "Finally, an open expression of our faith even in a Gentile country!" Enos hugged Ruth tightly.

"Who is that old man?" Miriam asked Hannah when the fellowship ended, and everyone left for the night. "He was here when the men were brought in from the boat, and he must have quietly slipped in tonight. I didn't see him until he stood up and spoke."

"His name is Simeon. He told me he's been with Jesus since the start of his ministry."

Tamar squinted her eyes, thinking. "I've never seen him."

"There are some people you might not have seen that were there with Jesus," Jerome responded gently as the friends gathered to clean up.

"I wonder what he means?" Jacob watched Jerome pick up cups and jugs. Tamar shrugged her shoulders.

Miriam motioned to her friends. "Just simply what he said. Just because we don't see doesn't mean we don't believe."

CHAPTER NINETY-TWO

THE BEACH WAS CROWDED IN the hour before dawn. Even more people showed up; they dotted the shoreline in ankle-deep water. The water was warm, and the day would prove to be bright and summer hot.

Jerome, with the old man Simeon by his side stood waist deep in water and addressed the crowd. "Some of you have walked with Jesus. Some of you have talked with Jesus. Some of you have even been healed by Jesus." He paused, glancing to Esther. "And some of you never saw, heard, or talked with him, yet you believe. Jesus says, 'Blessed are those who have not seen and yet have believed.'

"Sin is death. Confess your sins and turn from them. Receive eternal life. Purify your hearts." The crowd bowed their heads in prayer and confession.

After several minutes, Jerome spread his arms out wide. "Understand. Baptism does not save you. Salvation only comes through faith in Christ. In baptism, we are identifying with Jesus. We are turning from our old life of sin, into a new life with Jesus. As you are lowered into the water, you are aligning yourself with Jesus in the tomb. As you come up from the water, you are being raised like Jesus from the dead into a new life."

Simeon turned to Jerome and asked, "Is Jesus Christ your Lord and Savior?"

Jerome bowed his head and said, "Yes."

Before Simeon immersed him, he said, "I baptize you, Jerome in the name of the Father and of the Son and of the Holy Spirit. Buried with him in death and raised with him in new life." Gently he immersed him in water and raised him up. Simeon and Jerome proceeded to baptize all those gathered on the beach.

Short hours later, Miriam sat at the stern of the boat with Esther sleeping on her lap. Two of the believers, a fishermen and his mate offered to take them across the Sea of Galilee to their home. Caleb, Jonas, and Jerome idly talked. Jacob helped, fiddling with the lines as the captain manned the tiller. The wind was moderate, the swells were gentle, and they were making good time. The water was a dense, deep blue, accented occasionally by a white cap.

She breathed in the clean air. She was anxious to get home to Joseph, her home, her in-laws, and her friends. Ann and Elizabeth would be overwhelmed to see all of them home safely! Surely, they believed after all this time, their men had come to disaster. She wondered about their faith. Did it hold true for Elizabeth or did she lose it in despair? Would Ann turn to Jesus now that Jerome would be coming home after many weeks?

She was happy for Tamar. She found a man who was grounded in his faith, a mother-in-law she loved, and so importantly, a community of believers. Ha! And her friend had a very good business going as a seamstress. They had both come a long way since they first met in the river, those years ago.

Watching her own husband letting our line, seeing the sail fill, she knew that he too, had come a long way in his own walk of faith. God allows us choices, she realized. Some believe, some do not. One thing she was sure about, while she had been blessed seeing Jesus' miracles, she didn't need miracles to sustain her faith.

For more information about

S.A. Jewell
and

Of Friends and Followers
please visit:

www.teamofGod.org
www.SaraJewell.com
teamofGod@earthlink.net
www.facebook.com/sarasantosjewell
www.facebook.com/teamofGod

For more information about
AMBASSADOR INTERNATIONAL
please visit:

www.ambassador-international.com
@AmbassadorIntl
www.facebook.com/AmbassadorIntl

*If you enjoyed this book, please consider leaving us a review on
Amazon, Goodreads, or our website.*